Explosive

By Mark Young

Published by Funky Ink Press

Copyright © 2016 Mark Young

The right of Mark Young to be identified as the author of the Work has been asserted by him in accordance with the Copyright, Design and Patents Act 1988

All Rights Reserved

This book is a work of fiction and, except in the case of historical fact, any resemblance to actual persons, living or dead, is purely coincidental

ISBN 978-0-9955676-1-0

Prologue

June 2014 - Afghanistan

The village lay in the open desert to the west of the Helmand river. Not marked on any map, it was just a rag tag collection of primitive huts and lean-tos surrounded by a mud wall, and now it lay quietly sweltering in the mid afternoon sun, waves of heat drifting lazily up off the drab dun coloured rooftops into the cloudless sky.

Mullah Abdullah, the local Taliban commander, took a sip of tea and turned from studying the flat featureless desert to watch the four British soldiers as they moved amongst his Mujahadeen. Abdullah's leathery battle scared face, swathed in black tribal headgear, rarely showed much, but today, as a cry rose up from his assembled troops and swirled around the dusty compound, there was a crinkling around the eyes, an excitement.

There were perhaps seventy five of his men there today; battle hardened troops carrying assorted Kalashnikovs and RPG's, with cartridge belts bestrewn around their shoulders. The men smoked, chewed and spat as they watched the largest of the British soldiers, big Frankie Crawford, lift up two wooden boxes about the size of cat carriers, and place them carefully down into the base of the dry riverbed that ran through the compound. The riverbed was enclosed by high hard packed mud walls stronger than concrete, and the channel had been blocked off at both ends so that it created a kind of natural amphitheatre. The excitement and cries around the riverbed grew in volume and intensity, the crowd becoming more agitated as big Frankie leaned down to open the boxes.

Private Miles Franklyn, the youngest of the British quartet, looked up at

Corporal Mohsin Khan and grinned as the baying crowd grew more excited. 'How much you think Nicky's taken today, boss?' he asked, squinting into the sun.

They both looked over to watch Nicky Holloway who was at the long table down by the side of the dry riverbed where he had now been joined by Abdullah. Holloway was shouting and waving his hands at the crowd, flicking his fingers up and down in different combinations, the semaphore universal, understandable anywhere in the world where you had a race track. 'Smack or cash, man. Smack or cash?' Khan said absently as he pushed his helmet back on his head and wiped the sweat off his brow.

Then Big Frankie Crawford was straightening up and giving the thumbs up signal across the compound to Corporal Khan. 'Time to shoot'em up boss,' Franklyn said.

Khan nodded, rose and made his way down through the cheering Afghans to the dry riverbed where he opened a silver attaché case and took out a syringe and a small bottle. He carefully opened the bottle and then delicately drew a small amount of liquid into the syringe and gently held it up to the light, checking the level, all his movements measured and careful.

A village boy now stood next to one of the open boxes holding a monster sized rat which was making high pitched squeaking noises. As the boy turned the rat over you could see on its side a bare patch of lightly scarred skin with markings of an incision and stitching not long healed. By now the other rat was out of its box, held by another boy and both were then placed on the ground abreast of each other. Khan leant down and expertly injected both rats, and as he stood up they were released by their respective handlers. The crowd jostled and pushed, trying to get a closer look as the rats began to sluggishly move around the enclosed riverbed; at the same time Frankie slapped the button on what looked like a large chess timer clock that was prominently displayed on the table.

Three minutes thirty seven seconds later, as the injected Triacetone Triperoxide intermingled and detonated the Pentaerythritol tetranitrate which had been surgically implanted into the rats some five days earlier, the larger of the two rodents exploded sending blood, shit and tissue skywards in concentric circles of blast. The crowd erupted, screaming and throwing caps and canteens into the air. Nicky Holloway watched them for a moment and then surreptitiously began stowing the packages of heroin and cash from the bankers table into his rucksack. The remaining rat sniffed the air and then began to slowly gnaw away at his compatriot's decapitated head.

Chapter One

It was about eleven thirty in the morning when I finally got out of the Old Bailey. I pushed through the strengthened glass door, stepped out and began to walk down the famous street as I looked around for a taxi. Digging out a cigarette, I scanned the darkening sky – looked like rain, which figured, given the day I'd been having.

Watching the PCO guys drag my kiddie raper client down to the cells to start an eight year stretch hadn't exactly been fun, especially after I'd told him he was gonna get four, tops. And that hadn't been wild optimism either, just the only way I could think of to get the guy to open his wallet. Still, it had worked, and maybe later, when he'd calmed down a bit, I could waltz back in and wave an appeal on sentence around - tap him up for some more cash. That's if I could stand the thought of having to shake the guys hand again. Anyway, my guess, he was going to love prison. Rape in the showers, surrounded by guys with similar interests – I'd bet he was never going to want to get out.

I felt my cellphone vibrating against my leg and stopped to dig it out. No caller ID, but I took it anyway, punching the connection as I began to walk. The male voice that came through was quiet, with a hint of the Indian sub-continent.

'Mister Calver, my name is Khan,' he said. I had to struggle to hear above the traffic, so I stepped into a doorway to muffle the background roar. The quiet voice continued. 'You helped my son, Mohsin, a while back.'

I couldn't place the name. 'Give me a clue,' I said.

'He was a soldier. They were animals. Attacked him in a public house when all he wanted was a glass of water for his daughter.'

His words conjured a vague memory, and then the story was coming back, and then I had the outline; a young British soldier calling me months back after he'd been arrested for assault. He'd gone into a pub in uniform with a string of shiny medals pinned to his chest, a decorated Afghan veteran just asking for trouble, and three drunken locals had obliged. I remembered now because they'd come at him with a pool cue and he'd put all three down without sustaining a scratch. Predictably the bar staff had backed their guys, but after I'd done the two step with the prosecutor, she'd agreed to drop the assault charge, but then stuck all four with lesser public order offences to which my guy copped a plea, as eventually did the other three, although I'd heard they weren't happy about it. I vaguely remembered a pre-sentence report waffling on about combat trauma and suggesting probation involving treatment, so that's what he'd got, and that had been it; another satisfied customer and a very small legal aid payment for me.

'Yeah, I remember now. How's he doing?'

There was a pause, and then he said, 'not well, I'm afraid.'

I waited.

'They say,' he said and stopped again; sounded as if he was swallowing hard, then the dam seemed to burst and he blurted out the rest, 'they say he's killed Safia.' Then he said, more calmly, 'you must help him.'

Eventually I got the gist. Mohsin Khan had been arrested for the murder of his wife, Safia, and was being held by the police. Now, call me heartless, but my first thought was: good. Murder was big stuff, big fees, and boy did I need some of those right now. It could also be a reputation builder – if you won. Or – excuse the pun – a killer if you lost, but I didn't want to think about that right now, just the possibility of a semi high profile case and maybe a big fat fee at the end of it. I tried to recall what I knew about the man, Khan? Not much; all I remembered was a soft spoken, respectful guy who had talked to me about his two little girls with lots of pride and love, and that he hadn't wanted to talk about his job in a bomb disposal unit.

'Mr. Calver?' he prompted me.

'Where is he?'

'He's in custody at Liverpool Street Police station, and......and he's not thinking straight. He won't ask for help.'

'Listen,' I said, 'if he won't ask for me, I won't get in. Period. Has he been interviewed yet?' I asked hopefully.

The one thing the police love above all else, outside of framing people, is to get their hands on a nice, docile, compliant suspect who can be persuaded to forego the presence of a lawyer during questioning. That's because most cases don't get built by the cops, they get built by the suspects themselves, every time they open their mouths. They don't seem to get it that what they say in interview will almost certainly come back to bite them on the ass months down the line when their interview tape gets played back to a jury. Every innocent little untruth, white lie, confusion and misunderstanding will get twisted and amplified a thousand fold by a skilled prosecutor, who will then turn it around and stick it to them, but good. That's why they need to ask for a lawyer and why they should then keep their mouths shut – but they never do, unless they're pro's. It was an almost universal law of criminal practice that it was absolutely essential to get to your guy before he opened his mouth and stuck his foot in it.

'They say he's waived the right to a lawyer and they won't wait. Please help him, Mr Calver.' He paused, and then uttered the magic words: 'If it's your fees you're worried about, I'll cover them, generously. If you will come to the station now, I will make it worth your while.'

'How worth my while?'

'Shall we say ten thousand, as a fee and on account if you take the case forwards.'

I whistled under my breath. My kiddie raper client today had been a rare exception; private paying clients in criminal defence work, unless it was a white collar rap, were about as common as virgins in a brothel, so Khan was starting to look like a real prospect. I checked my watch. 'I'll be there in twenty minutes,' I said.

As I finished my call, as if on cue, a cab pulled up to disgorge two preening and posturing high class silks. I jumped for the door, just beating a Sky TV journalist who'd been waiting there for it. As I relaxed back in my seat I watched the woman give me the finger as the cab pulled away.

'Women nowadays, they have no respect,' my Sikh cabby opined gravely.

'You got that right, brother,' I said. 'You gotta check behind you – it's a jungle out there.'

'Survival of the fittest, right?'

'Right,' I said, putting my earpieces in and easing back to listen to my new audio book of Alice's Adventures in Wonderland. As Alice hurtled down the rabbit hole I felt the same way as we manoeuvred our way through London's mean streets, but instead of an empty marmalade jar, I dug out my hip flask and took a couple of stiff shots of high end Russian blue label vodka.

Chapter Two

All police stations look pretty much the same after a while and the one at Liverpool Street, or Bishopsgate, to give it its official title, was no different. Not too shabby on the outside; utilitarian and functional on the inside. No bustle, just a tired and bored looking desk officer on a phone; in the background the hum of air conditioning, phones, voices, computers and the banging of swing doors as people came and went. The Police are the one public service to have been seriously over resourced for at least the last forty years, although perhaps not so much recently; a combination of Maggie Thatcher's zeal and one of the strongest unions on the planet. Like the majority of defence lawyers, I pretty much hated them; every bad story you ever heard about them was true, and then some.

In the corner sipping a take out coffee was a smallish brown skinned man. The top of his head was bald but he had grey hair down the sides, and he was dressed in an expensive looking cashmere coat. When he saw me he came over with outstretched hand. 'Mr. Calver, good of you to come so quickly. I am Rashid Khan, Mohsin's father,' he said, the voice cultured, educated, and the smile warm.

I shook his hand as I looked around. 'What's happening, anything?' I asked.

'They said someone will be out to see me soon. I spoke before to a DI Stanton, but he wasn't very helpful.'

That figured. I'd run into Stanton myself a few times over the years and it had never been a pleasant experience. He was basically old school. A copper who didn't think the rules applied to him; kind of guy who if he thought he could get away with it would use his fists on a suspect. He was just about tolerated by his superiors but if they could have got rid of him easily, you can bet they would have, but then again, he got results.

I took a sip of my takeout coffee and looked up to see the swing door at the back crash open again as Stanton came through. He hadn't changed much; big, with a beer gut hanging over his belt, drinkers red face and tightly curled iron grey hair.

He ignored me. 'What can I do for you, Mr. Khan?' he asked.

'My son, Mohsin,' Khan said tentatively. 'Mr. Calver has—'

'You're son's been charged with murder, earlier this morning, and now he's being processed. He didn't want a lawyer,' Stanton said, flicking a tight smile in my direction. 'So unless there's anything else, gentlemen, I—'

'Our guy still breathing, is he, Stanton?' I asked, casually. Then, 'but never mind, let's take a look at the custody record, instead, shall we?'

The custody record was meant to be a strict record of everything that occurred during the time that a suspect was held, and any breaches of the code that covered the record could have consequences, for example, you could use a breach as grounds for trying to get something said in interview deemed inadmissible and excluded from trial. I would get a copy of the record anyway, but asking for it now was a way of needling Stanton, even though I knew the chances of finding anything amiss were pretty remote.

Stanton watched me, taking his time, then he grinned as if remembering something: 'Must be tough,' he said, voice quiet, turning slightly to exclude Mr Khan from his words. 'Your wife running out on you like that, Jonas. That's a hard thing for any man to deal with. Even worse,' he added, eyes locked on mine, 'I hear she left you for another lawyer. How about that?'

I kept my expression blank, easy smile locked in place, but I could feel a red blush creeping up my neck and I was powerless to stop the slight shake of my hands. Stanton continued to watch me, eating it up. I cast a glance at Khan, but he was out of it, still in shock at the enormity of what his son was facing.

'Spare us your insights, detective,' I finally managed. 'The custody record? Then we can talk bail and go see Mohsin.'

Stanton laughed. 'You know the rules, Calver. Prisoner gets a copy of the record, and if you want to see him, speak to the desk sergeant. As for bail — on a murder charge? Are you kidding me?'

I was about to go back at him but Khan, having woken up, grasped my arm firmly and pulled me away towards the desk. 'Leave it,' he said. 'Let's go see my son.'

As the cell door banged shut behind us, Mohsin Khan was sitting on the bunk bed, his head resting against the wall. He opened his eyes and looked up, no expression on his face. He seemed gaunter than I remembered, but he still had that shock of dark lustrous hair and those steady luminous eyes, but now he looked defeated, lost. I could see him vaguely trying to place me, and then as recognition spread across his face, he said, 'I don't need a lawyer.'

Great start I thought; I could already feel that big fee starting to slip away. Maybe a spell alone with his father might pull him around.

'Look, I'm going to leave you guys to talk while I go and find out what they've got - then we'll see if I can help.'

As I left the cell I didn't hold out much hope; the boy seemed apathetic, as if he'd already given up, so I needed to come up with something quick if I was going to turn things around. I went looking for a half way decent cop. Not as easy as you might think in a police station, but I got lucky. I found her bending over removing a coffee from a vending machine. She saw me as she straightened up.

'Hey, Calver. What's up?'

I had always got along well with DS Chandler, or as well as I ever got on with any member of the police. 'Hey, Rachel,' I said, selecting black coffee and punching the button. 'You working the Khan case?' I asked.

She eyed me up, on guard. 'Why? He one of yours?'

'Yep,' I lied, sipping my coffee – it wasn't bad. 'Tough gig, Rache. Partnering a dickhead like Stanton. I feel for you.'

'What do you want, Jonas?'

'Tell me what went down. You know he wont talk to me.'

She knew it was customary to speak to defence lawyers, give them an idea of what they had, so long as it didn't foul up an investigation, and since they'd charged him, that was no longer a risk. But she still had her partner to contend with and he'd never sanction giving me anything.

'He confessed, Jonas. What can I tell you?' she finally said.

'Come on, Rachel, confession's not enough on its own.'

She looked around and then gestured to an alcove off the corridor. 'Okay, Calver, but you didn't get it from me.'

I nodded as she collected her thoughts. 'We were working close by on something else when we got the call about 8.25p m and were there within five, ten minutes. Flat was in disarray and the wife, Safia was found lying in the hallway leading to the living room; multiple stab wounds, blood everywhere; we're waiting on whether any sexual assault took place. Blood stained knife from the kitchen was found in the drain outside; five will get you ten it's our murder weapon. Oh, and bloodstained clothing was found in the washing machine – we managed to turn it off before it completed the wash cycle.'

I thought about the washing machine. Didn't make sense. I looked at her, expecting more. 'What about time of death?'

'Between six and eight, until we can narrow it down. We picked Khan up at the Mosque about 9.15 pm. We even held him over night before questioning, because the FME said he was on something; booze, drugs, who knows what. He declined a lawyer and said he did it in interview. It's a slam dunk, Jonas. Case closed.'

It was pretty hard to argue with that, on what she'd told me. I sipped my coffee some more – still good. Rachel's phone beeped; she looked at it, sighed. 'My master calls. Gotta go, Jonas.'

I thanked her and made my way back to the cell, turning over in my mind what she'd told me and looking at it from every which way. Even if Khan wanted me to act, I could just feel the case slipping away to an almost certain guilty plea and no big money trial. I heard raised voices as I approached the cell but they stopped speaking as I came in.

Khan senior looked at me expectantly, coughed, and said, 'Mohsin has decided that he would like you to represent him, Mr. Calver.'

Mohsin looked less than enthusiastic, but I guess it was easier to go with the flow. Going through the motions of letting me act would comfort his father who was starting to look pretty frazzled.

I relaxed; looked like I'd bagged a live one after all, even if it did end in a guilty plea. 'Good,' I said to Mohsin, 'now, tell us what happened?'

He grimaced with a humourless smile. 'That's just it. I can't remember,' he said, looking from one to the other of us.

My first thought was: *not the old amnesia routine again*, but then, as I reflected, I thought, why shouldn't memory loss be a factor, especially with a combat veteran. I watched him carefully, trying to evaluate, but what did I know? He could be stark raving mad inside and I wouldn't know, but then again maybe it was just bullshit, a desperate excuse, or maybe what he'd done was so terrible he'd blocked it out. 'You better explain,' I said. 'You must remember something because Chandler says you confessed. What did you tell them?'

'I don't know, man,' he said slowly, a bewildered look on his face. 'They, they confused me, Jonas, and, and I couldn't remember. I get these blank spaces and when I couldn't tell them anything, I got frightened. They pressured me, man,' he said, his voice turning whiny and resentful, and he wouldn't look up and meet my eyes.

My guess was that he *was* confused, but he knew more than he was saying; nothing unusual in that with a client facing criminal charges – they always had something to hide. I checked my watch; they'd be taking him to court soon, so we were about out of time, but I was curious to see whether a bit more pressure might shake something loose. 'Okay, but can you remember *anything* about the day, anything at all?'

'It's fuzzy, Jonas, just little bits and pieces floating around,' he said.

'Okay, well tell us about the little bits floating around.'

He looked at me for a long moment, and again I could sense something bubbling away there just beneath the surface, something maybe like resentment.

He sighed, and said, 'all I remember from that day is Safia's sister, Rana, bringing Aisha back from school at about ten to five and saying she would stay and wait for Safia to get back from work, if I wanted to go out.'

He paused rubbing his face, looking tired. ' I know I left the flat, but I can't remember where I went. Next thing, its after nine and the police are coming into the Mosque and taking me,' he said.

I studied him, looking for deceit, but his eyes looked flat and empty. Maybe it was just stress and tiredness. 'Okay, Mohsin, that's enough for now,' I said as I checked my watch again. 'They gotta run you by the Magistrates in a few minutes and then to the Crown Court within 48 hours for bail, but we know from Stanton they're going to oppose it, they always do for murder—'

'But you will *try* to get him out, won't you?' Khan senior said.

It was time for a reality check. 'Mr Khan, let me be blunt. As far as the police, and by extension, the court, are concerned, your son has brutally stabbed his wife to death and admitted it. Now, I'm no magician, and even if I were, on those facts, we won't make bail.'

I could see my words hitting home, Khan seniors shoulders slumping, and that was good, but I did feel for him. I continued, 'but, we are going to *apply* for bail. That's because it will force the CPS, the Crown Prosecution Service, to give us details of the strength of the evidence against Mohsin, otherwise we'll have to wait weeks for disclosure. So don't go getting your hopes up, the application will fail, but, we'll get an early peak at what they've got, and that could turn out to be invaluable, or it could turn out to be nothing.'

Khan senior nodded grudgingly while Mohsin continued to look blankly at the cell wall, apparently unfazed by the prospect of prison, but then I guessed that if you'd spent your time defusing bombs, prison would seem like a walk in the park in comparison.

He nodded. 'Okay, Jonas, you're the boss.'

I said, 'one last thing. You'll have had a shrink when you were on probation before and I'll need to speak to him. What's his name?'

'It's a she actually. Doctor Rose Tremayne at the Nightingale Centre,' he said.

As he answered, he was absently rubbing his left hand which seemed to have a recent cut between the thumb and forefinger. When he noticed me looking at his hand he frowned, and then stopped rubbing, closing his eyes again and laying his head back against the cell wall in the same position it had been in when we arrived.

'Good,' I said, as I snapped my notebook shut, but I didn't feel good.

Chapter Three

I fired up my ancient desktop computer and then checked the practice client account online and there it was – ten grand, just cleared, from Khan senior. I toasted the screen with my highball and then transferred a couple of thousand to the office account to stop us breaching our overdraft limit, and then I scribbled a note to myself to issue a bill. It was about the only accounts rule I could remember from law school; you mustn't take money out of client account until you'd issued a bill for it.

I leaned back in my spring back chair and looked out of the office window across east London towards the gleaming spires of the city, the place where they really knew how to make a buck. I took another sip of watery scotch as my mind drifted back to the bail application. It had gone much as expected, culminating in an uncomplaining Mohsin Khan being shipped off to Belmarsh on remand, but I did get a couple of things.

To the CPS this was just another domestic London murder case – no big deal – but what that meant is that they didn't bother bringing out their big guns for the bail hearing. So what I got was a stressed out and harassed junior counsel, overloaded with too many case files, who was only too willing to listen to my bullshit if it would lighten her load.

We used the age old ploy of her leaving the file out whilst she trotted off to speak to another defence attorney. At this early stage so soon after charging, the file was stripped down and insubstantial, really just a skeleton, but one thing stood out: they had a witness, unnamed on the file, who could place Khan outside the flat at around five past eight that evening. And time of death was now firmed up to between 7 and 8 p m.

When my harassed opponent had returned, I'd used another tried and tested ploy; essentially monopolising her by asking a load of irrelevant questions which she had to search through her papers to answer, whilst a queue of frustrated defence lawyers had built up behind me. As she had started to fray at the edges, she'd let something else slip. They had motive as well; a statement from the sister in law that Safia had been having an affair, was just about to leave Mohsin, and was due to tell him the night she died.

With all that, the bail application really became a non-starter, so in the end we didn't even make the application, and Khan stayed banged up.

As I contemplated all this there was a knock on the door and Emma came in. She took in the highball glass, quick flash of disapproval, followed almost instantly by a smile. Emma was an ex-client – I'd put her violent boyfriend away for two years when I'd been a prosecutor – and now she essentially ran my practice; without her the whole thing would come down around my ears. She was secretary, receptionist, telephonist, cashier, PA, paralegal, gatekeeper and agony aunt all rolled into one. She said, 'Ali's been round again, threatening all sorts if he doesn't get the rent by Friday.'

'How much?'

'A grand.'

'Do him a cheque.'

'Don't joke about it, Jonas?' she said, not believing me, but then starting to smile again when she realised I was serious. 'So are we solvent again?'

'You bet,' I said with a brash smile.

She held my gaze, wanting to believe me, then she looked down at the crisp new Khan file lying open on my desk. 'Suppose you'll be wanting to speak to Pascal?' she said, unable to completely hide her disapproval.

'Come on, Emma. She has her good points.'

'Which are?'

I decided not to rise. Courtney Pascal was my part-time investigator, and she and Emma did not get along. I scrolled through my contacts until I reached Pascal's name, then I hit the call button.

In the North London Mosque prayers had just finished. Little cliques of shoeless men wandered about, some chatting, others making for the exits. The Imam, Khalid Muqtadir, dressed in drab, greeny brown robes walked amongst them. He was stocky with a rather striking face, and his pointed chin was covered by a short cropped black goatee. As he walked amongst his pious flock he would stop here and there for a quick word or a squeeze of the arm as he made his way towards the offices and private rooms at the back of the building.

Beside Muqtadir walked Maqsood Qadir. Qadir was lithe and fit, and though dressed in billowing white robes, he still exhibited the vestiges of a military bearing, a throw back to his time in the Saudi Arabian air force.

As the two men walked through the private corridors they discussed various mundane administrative matters. They passed out of the rear of the building through a small back door into a garden, a place of greenery and quietude. In the background could be heard the soft sound of cooing birds. Muqtadir turned to Qadir. 'This, this arrest, the other day,' he said distastefully, 'and the police in the Mosque. It is most troubling, Qadir?'

'There was no actual arrest on the premises, sir,' Qadir replied at once. 'A misunderstanding now resolved. Everything is as it should be.'

'I hope so,' Muqtadir said, watching his highly competent second in command, weighing the matter, and then nodding to himself. 'I must go,' he said abruptly. He held Qadir's gaze for a moment longer, then turned and quickly walked back up the path towards the building.

Qadir watched him leave, then turned to the large cage to his right and lifted the blanket covering it, and folded it back over the top. He took from the folds of his robe a small metal cylindrical object and a notebook sized piece of paper on which was written a message which he carefully checked, then rolled up and inserted into the metal cylinder. Then he reached into the cage and lifted out a large pigeon, slowly stroking and calming it, before attaching the cylinder to the pigeons leg. He smoothed the birds feathers and then kissed its breast before holding it aloft and gently pushing it into the sky. He watched as the bird took flight and turned south east towards its destination.

Satisfied, he then took out a cheap mobile phone and speed dialled a number. He held the cell to his ear and spoke rapidly in Arabic, his other hand never still, and as he spoke he smiled.

In GCHQ, many miles away, Qadir's call was monitored and translated, although the recipient remained unidentified. The call seemed like a soliloquy; a riff about some kind of April fools day anniversary, but then half way through, the speaker quoted six letters that didn't appear to make any recognisable name or acronym. The junior MI5 officer didn't think the call worth tagging for pushing further up the chain for analysis, so the transcript was logged and filed, although it was also passed on to other close allies under Intel sharing arrangements.

The bar was on the border between Hackney and the City and was already busy when I arrived; neon, poles, spotlights and dry ice hanging in the air. At first blush I thought it was some kind of Drag act strip joint, Pascal's idea of a joke, but maybe it was just the light. On closer examination the clientele looked like the usual bunch of after work city boozers interspersed with a few more exotic looking punters, all schmoozing around looking for a party. As I stood at the bar waiting for my drink, trying to see through the dim half light, I felt a tap on my shoulder. I turned to my left and a jolly looking beefy guy with a handle bar moustache, clad in leather, smiled, and gestured; seems he wanted to buy me a drink.

A number of retorts sprang to mind, but I canned them and politely declined. I sank my double in one whilst I continued to scan the crowd, fleetingly thinking that maybe the guy was one of Pascal's whack job friends, before remembering that she didn't have any - friends that is, but then there she was, about 3 metres away, leaning against a post, watching me.

She turned, without acknowledgement, and walked away to a quiet corner where there were tables and chairs. I followed, taking out a fifty and waving it around until a harassed waitress turned up and I ordered us another round of doubles, hers Tequila, mine Johnny Walker Black.

I hadn't seen her in a while, but she never seemed to change. Nearly thirty now but looking about seventeen, maybe not in a good way, and stick thin with a brush of orangey red hair. Sometimes, in the right light, she eerily reminded me of early David Bowie. I'd first met her around seven years before when I'd defended her on a murder charge. She'd killed her step-dad. I got it reduced to manslaughter, and even got the sentence down on appeal to six years and she was out in four. She was clever, but what really attracted me to her when I was looking around for an investigator, was the fact that she had been a spook before she went to prison. You'd have thought MI5 would have just loved such a great cover story; an agent with a genuine rap sheet, but no, they'd brutally cut her loose when she went down, and I knew that that betrayal, rather than losing her liberty, had been what really burned her, because she had felt that Five were her family.

When she'd come out, she wasn't exactly overrun with job offers, so I'd chucked a few things her way, testing her out, and she'd always come up with the goods. I knew she loved the work, what little I could give her, but it wasn't in her nature to show it, so we had slowly and fitfully built up a working relationship that seemed to work.

She turned her head to look around and the light caught the single diamond earring twinkling on her ear lobe; it was, she'd told me, the only thing she had left from her real father who had died when she was fifteen.

'So what's the deal with this place, Pascal?' I asked.

'Maybe I thought you could do with some romance, Calver,' she said, looking over at the bar. I followed her gaze; it was the guy with the handle bar moustache, sitting on a bar stool, legs splayed, watching me with a kind of dreamy look on his face.

I loosened my collar and drained my glass. It was time for business; I ordered us another round of doubles, settled back and told her Khan's story. She listened, like she always did, intently, without showing it; eyes clear, missing nothing.

'So what d'you want from me, Calver?' she said when I'd finished.

'The works. Run down witnesses – see if we can get anyone the police haven't spoken to yet – statements, background checks on everyone; and most important of all, check our guys story, what there is of it – for all I know its got more holes than a Swiss cheese.'

'Anything else?'

'Yeah, check his army record.'

I didn't tell her about Safia's alleged affair. Firstly because I didn't want her to think the case was hopeless and secondly because I liked to keep something back, so I could check on her, make sure she was earning her money.'

'Okay, Calver. Now let's talk about what I want,' she said, smiling thinly. 'See, I'm curious, so I'm asking myself, why are you suddenly waving fifty's around and buying doubles?'

'Yeah, and what's the answer?' I said, cursing under my breath.

'Guy's got money. So you can forget legal aid rates. You go private, I go private, and I want it up front.'

I already knew that I'd have to pay more on this one, but I needed to keep her in check or she'd clean me out. When it was legal aid she knew I couldn't pay much, but on a big private case everyone wanted a piece of the action; they all thought I had a blank cheque, and part of the game was to disabuse them of that. But fact is I needed her on this one, and she knew it.

I hammed it up a bit; looked down at my drink, took another shot, looked around, eyed up a beautiful androgynous looking blonde writhing around on a pole. Pascal watched me, motionless, waiting.

'Five hundred,' I said.

'Fuck you, Calver,' she said, rising to her feet.

'Okay, okay,' I said quickly. 'Seven fifty, to start with. You get me something good, we look at it again, step by step. Come on, Pascal. You know my practice is down the pan; I'm struggling, but if I play this right, we can both get something out of it.'

'Seven fifty now. I'll get to work and come back when I've used it up. Yes?'

'Fine,' I said, taking an envelope out of my pocket and passing it over.

She let it go that I had pre-gauged her price. She was hooked. She spirited the envelope away and looked at her phone screen. 'You got access to the crime scene, Calver. I mean like, right now?'

'Yeah. Police are done, and I just happen to have a key.'

'Let's go,' she said.

I checked my watch. 'What we going to see this time of night?'

'You'd be surprised. Trust me. Let's go.'

I looked at the bar. Moustache was still watching me, dreamy smile on his face. I finished my drink in a gulp and chucked some notes on the table. Pascal retrieved a tenner, and then we were on our way.

Across the capital, east of the city in Stepney, the tall man stood on the roof of the purpose built block of flats and carefully scanned the early evening sky. He had been coming now for a few days and would have to leave soon if nothing turned up, but then a slight fluttering sound, and then the pigeon was there, on the ledge, small metal canister firmly affixed to its leg.

He slowly approached, careful not to startle the bird. He gently stroked its flank before removing the canister and taking out the note. He read through the few words twice. It was a shortened transcript of Qadir's phone call although the seemingly random letters were different. It was the final message, the one he had been waiting for.

He smiled grimly, kissed the bird one last time, then slowly wrung its neck, dropping the small corpse onto the asphalted roof and then grinding his desert boot into it until all that was left was a smear of grey feathers and blood.

A short cab ride later we stood outside the block, across the street, looking up at the first floor walkway fronting the flat. In fact it was easy to see, bathed in light from street lamps and even the blue and white crime scene police tape across the doorway was visible from distance.

We approached and stooped under the tape, Pascal unlocked the door and we stepped inside. She flicked the switch and the hall light came on bright and clear, and then she was moving slowly down the hallway. I followed closely behind into the living room; smart, looked like IKEA furniture, large screen TV and plush carpets, but there was also the contents of desk drawers – mostly papers – strewn around the centre of the floor.

'Burglary gone wrong?' Pascal queried.

I shrugged. 'Chandler didn't say anything.'

Pascal nodded and moved on, examining everything as she went. I left her to it and went into the smaller of the two bedrooms. It was clearly the children's room, giant cartoon characters on the walls, fluffy animals and other assorted toys everywhere, but there was also a dark red blood stain smeared across one of the bedspreads. I shuddered and reached for my hip flask as Pascal entered the room; she held her hand out and I passed it over. I went over and pulled the blinds to look out on the street at the back of the flats. Pascal came and joined me and we both leant on the window sill and looked out, silent, each contemplating our own thoughts. She handed me the flask back and I took a long drag to steady my nerves; murder scenes did that to me.

We watched for a moment before Pascal pointed way down the back street towards the end of the cul-de-sac. I struggled to see what she was looking at, and then caught it, a camera lens reflecting off one of the street lights, high on a pole, seemingly focused on the street. I estimated it was a good hundred metres away but didn't seem to be directed our way. I made a mental note; maybe it would be important later on, although it was unlikely the police would have missed it.

We moved back into the main room and I went over and stooped down to study the dark red stains on the carpet leading into the hallway. It was where I believed Safia had been found; another visceral shiver and I was reaching for my hip flask again.

Pascal came back in carrying some papers and a framed photograph which she handed to me. 'Check it out,' she said.

It was three soldiers including Khan, in combat gear, crouched down in a posed portrait. They still looked young, fit and full of hope. I slipped the photograph out of its frame and put it in my folder – I'd bring it back after the trial, if there was one.

'You said he was arrested at the Mosque, right? Take a look at these,' she said, handing me some flimsy papers she had been holding. It was some cheap looking flyers from the North London Mosque, referring to upcoming sermons by a Dr. Khalid Muqtadir.

'So?'

'So you want me to visit, have a nose around?' she said, looking to jack up her fees some more.

Time to rein her in. 'Whoa there. Let's not get carried away here. We're investigating a murder, not Khan's religious beliefs.'

She looked at me, irritated. 'Okay, we're done here,' she said, 'but word of advice, Calver. You want this job done right, you, or your rich sugar daddy, are going to have to pay for it, yeah?' Having made her point, she turned and stalked off. I smiled and followed.

Chapter Four

I sat in the Queen Elizabeth pub just down the road from my office and dug into a full English breakfast. Pascal, sipping a bloody Mary, watched me slurping my way through the grease. The pub had a light sprinkling of morning alcoholics, breakfasters – mostly builder types – and guys studying form in their newspapers.

'So, we still got a case or what?' Pascal asked. She had dug up details of the affair between Safia and a Rashid Syed, a local taxi driver, so at least I knew she was doing something for her money. The affair was motive; that's what the prosecution would say anyway. Their witness, the victim's sister, would testify that Safia told her the night of the murder that she was going to tell Khan she was leaving him, then she ends up dead. The crown would be asking the jury to put two and two together, so we needed to find a way of making it add up to five.

I wiped my plate with a last piece of buttered toast, flicked it into my mouth and reached for my rum laced coffee. 'What'd lover boy say?'

'Shit scared. Got two small boys he's desperate not to lose and only admitted playing away when I threatened to talk to his wife. Adamant there was no way Safia was going to tell Khan. Neither of them could have stood the heat at the time.'

'You believe him?'

'Not sure. It's possible. Honestly? I don't know, but I got him to sign a statement in case.'

I sat and ruminated whilst I sipped my coffee. I looked out the window at the stalled traffic in the high street, glad I wasn't out there breathing in the fumes. I noticed Pascal had turned to the large TV screen over the bar to watch a breaking news story. Looked like an off duty soldier had been stabbed to death that morning, and not too far away, in Highbury, north London. The head of counter terrorism was being interviewed and was speculating that the killing was terror related. Pascal smiled as she listened.

'What?' I said

'You can bet they already know its terror related,' she said, eyes narrowing. 'Probably another cock up. Under surveillance, and then letting it run when they should have lifted him.'

'You were involved with that, before?' I asked, tentatively. I'd never asked her about her other life.

'Oh, yeah,' she said, a strange muted tone to her voice. She continued, 'I used to track them, you know. And I was pretty damn good at it. Forget your Oxbridge Arabic speakers; they see them coming a mile away. Best cover: freaky, nerdy, needy chick, desperate to convert to Islam. Worked every time,' she said, watching me.

Keeping it low key, I said, 'So you tracked, what, UK extremists, Jihadi's?'

'Hey, Calver, you never heard of the Official Secrets Act?'

'You started it.'

'Just brought back some memories, is all.'

While she was in such an expansive mood, I thought I'd dig a little, probe some more into the personal. 'I never asked you before, was prison bad?'

'Are you kidding me? How do you think it was?'

'Sorry.'

'But I could do gaol time standing on my head, and the worlds a better place without my stepfather in it,' she said, holding my gaze.

I said nothing, but I was surprised. I'd got murder down to manslaughter for her on the basis she'd had no intention to kill, and now I wasn't so sure. The nature of her trial meant that I'd never had to delve too deeply into what was in her head at the time, but what she'd just said was a little more definitive than what she'd told the jury during her trial.

She finished her drink and looked away, the spell broken. 'So, our big case is dead, then?' she said, quickly backpedalling away from any more personal revelations. In a way I was relieved; talk like that tended to make me nervous.

But I'd been thinking about the Khan case too. 'No, we're not dead yet. I need to put the affair to our boy, see how he reacts, and then I think I'll stop by and talk to his shrink, Dr. Tremayne. Then we'll meet up and chew it out.'

But first I had a call booked for 11am. The CPS had rung earlier and lined it up with Emma.

At precisely 11, the call came in. It was Sophie Ludlow, junior counsel for the prosecution, and she started off nice and cordial. 'I thought I'd just touch base with you as I'm about to send you over the unused material,' she said.

Although she was "junior" counsel, the term in fact referred to any barrister who was not a Queens Counsel, QC or "silk" in the parlance. In fact many junior counsel were very experienced lawyers and I knew Ludlow had been around a good few years. Unused material was generally all the evidence the CPS and the police had acquired during an investigation which was not going to be used against the defendant, but which might undermine their case or enhance ours, and they were under a legal obligation to disclose it to us. It could sometimes be a treasure trove of information for the defence and I was obviously anxious to see it, but there was no need for her to phone and tell me she was sending it over, so she obviously had something else on her mind.

'What's the hurry, Sophie?'

'No hurry, we're just getting terribly efficient, is all, and I knew you'd want to see it,' she said, laughing lightly, before adding, 'and you'll never guess who's leading us?'

As it was a murder trial the prosecution would be lead by a QC and Ludlow would do the donkey work as the junior. 'You're right. Who's leading you?'

I should have known by the slightly smug tone of her voice that I wasn't going to like what was coming.

'Richard Patterson,' she said, and waited.

Lord Richard Patterson QC was one of the leading barristers at the criminal bar; he also currently happened to be living with my ex-wife, Carmen; the one I still loved.

Curiouser and curiouser. It didn't take much serious reflection on my part to see that the CPS instructing Patterson was no coincidence. There were perhaps five or six other leading counsel at the criminal bar that they could have instructed; in fact there were two or three names that came up time and again on major murder prosecutions and Patterson's wasn't one of them, so he was no automatic choice for this case. No, this was done on purpose; they knew it would needle me and throw me off my stride.

Then I remembered DI Stanton's comments at the Police station, and it all started to make sense – he'd probably got the idea after talking to me, and run straight to the CPS to get Patterson pencilled in for the trial, but why was I so surprised? My marital travails were no secret in the tiny incestuous legal community within which I worked, and, after all, if I had been prosecuting I wouldn't have hesitated to use the same trick to put horns on my opponent.

When I said nothing, she pushed the knife in a bit further. 'Of course, you'll be instructing a leader as well, I take it?' she said and again waited expectantly. You see, I wasn't a Queens Counsel; I wasn't even a barrister, I was a solicitor with a higher courts advocacy certificate which allowed me to appear in the crown courts alongside my illustrious cousins from the bar, dealing with major crimes like rape and murder. It wasn't so long ago, only around twenty years in fact, that only barristers had had the right to argue these serious criminal cases in the crown courts. Humiliatingly, in those days the solicitor would often be seen sitting quietly behind the barrister, taking notes of the proceedings, or worse, carrying the barristers bags to and fro from court.

Although the change had happened years ago, remarkably, a residual resentful attitude toward solicitor advocates lingered on and remained strong in a small minority of barristers and judges; generally the older side of the profession, who remembered the closed shop and the good old days. In fact I was currently facing a complaint from a judge which I believed in no small part arose from just such prejudices.

Ludlow's faux solicitous comments were clearly designed to knock my confidence, no doubt in the hope that they could get one of their own installed to lead the defence, but that wasn't going to happen. 'Sorry to disappoint you, Sophie,' I said, 'but the day I need some simpering, inbred upper class dick to hold my hand in court is the day I'll give it all up.'

As I replaced the receiver, cutting off Ludlow's stunned silence, I looked up and there was Emma, standing at the door, watching me, anxiously. 'Problems?' she said.

'Guess who's leading the prosecution on Khan?' I said.

She watched me, her mind going through the gears. She knew all about Carmen. 'Not, Patterson?' she said, eyes widening, and I didn't need to say anything. 'Oh, Jonas, I'm so sorry,' she said. 'Look, why don't you pass on this one. We'll muddle through somehow – we always do.'

'Not this time, Emma. Anyway, maybe I need to move on,' I said, more to keep her spirits up, than reflect the way I felt. Bottom line, we needed the money.

The Nightingale centre was a small group of black grey brick buildings that looked like a 1960's primary school, but inside it was all brightness; clear white walls, large green plants; an airy space, humming with activity. I was nonchalantly waived on through for my appointment with Dr. Rose Tremayne, consultant psychiatrist to Mohsin Khan.

I entered a small cosy office where behind a desk sat a rather striking looking young woman chatting away on a desk phone. She looked up at me and gestured at the chair across from her as she carried on with her conversation. I sat down and surreptitiously studied her whilst pretending to look at the diploma's stuck up on the wall. She had chestnut hair pulled severely back into a ponytail, bright eyes, and one of the buttons on her blouse had come undone revealing a small silver crucifix hanging around her slender neck.

She finished her call and looked me over with a slightly frosty smile. 'If you're Calver, you've wasted your time unless you've brought along a signed consent form from Mohsin Khan.'

Great. A stickler for rules. Just what I needed this time in the morning. We sat looking at each other. 'I'm on my way to Belmarsh now. Thought you might like to help us out. Guess I was wrong,' I said getting up from the chair and turning to go.

She waited until I got to the door, and then said, 'you know the rules, Calver, so don't try and make me the guilty party here. All you had to do was exercise a bit of foresight and get a form signed. How hard is that, *and* have you any idea how hard they come down on breaches of patient confidentiality these days?'

She was right of course. It was entirely my fault, and now she was making me feel guilty. I turned back and smiled sheepishly, holding my hands out in supplication. 'You got me,' I said. 'You're absolutely right, and I'm sorry for wasting your time.'

She continued to watch me, stern expression, then she smiled, this time without the frost and said, 'You want some coffee? Only you look like you could use some.'

I fingered the rough stubble on my chin. I hated early morning starts and I guess it showed. 'You know what? I'd love an espresso.'

Five minutes later we sat in a small canteen drinking very good coffee and I was starting to wake up and feel human again. 'Okay, Doctor, I understand client confidentiality, I'm a lawyer, but maybe you can give me some general pointers.'

She thought for a moment, filtering and sorting what she could reveal without breaking any rules. She said, 'so Mohsin Khan's like any other soldier in a combat zone. Inevitably they get to see and experience traumatic episodes, and this he certainly did in Afghanistan. In general terms, such experiences can have psychological consequences in terms of a persons mental health, and of course the extent to which that happens can turn on lots of things; their life experiences, background and even genetics can influence that. As far as Mohsin is concerned my involvement with him previously was rather superficial, dictated by the minor nature of the offence he committed last time, and the amount of resources we could commit to him. I can't give you any detail without a signed authority but I can say that there was some treatment given and he responded well to it.'

I was beginning to like doctor Rose. As we made our way back to her office she chatted some more about psychology and combat stress. I retook my seat, and said, 'Thanks for taking the time doctor, and for being as open as you could. On another subject, how would you feel about being an expert witness for the defence, if we end up needing one?'

She leaned down, opened a desk drawer, pulled out some typed papers stapled together, and slid them across the desk to me. It was an expert witness retainer agreement. I flipped through it; bog standard and unremarkable, apart from the fee rate. I raised a quizzical eyebrow. 'That's a misprint, surely? Seven fifty a day. Even I'd get out of bed for that.'

'I doubt your rates are quite so modest, Mr. Calver,' she said, a little of that earlier frost making a comeback.

I smiled, letting her know I was kidding, although in reality I was laying down a marker in the hope of keeping experts fees down. Call me greedy but the more the experts got, the less I would get for legal fees, and Pascal's not insubstantial bills were already coming out of my end.

I put the draft agreement in my case and snapped it shut and stood up. 'Hypothetically, Doctor,' I said, 'could a man suffering from similar symptoms to those exhibited by Mohsin Khan, be capable of murdering his wife, and then not remember doing it?'

'Hypothetically, certainly,' she said without hesitation. 'But you're talking about amnesia here, and that's one hell of a big and complicated area. And also,' she said smiling, 'pretty easy to fake.' She looked away for a moment, thinking hard. 'Thing is, Mohsin could be a candidate. He's suffered both concussion from combat injuries, as well as witnessing traumatic incidents, either of which can cause amnesia.

'But to answer your question properly,' she added, 'I would have to examine him extensively, and of course then you'd have to pay my frighteningly high fees, wouldn't you?'

I laughed. I liked her style. 'Don't worry, I'll get your fees green-lighted, but then we'll want you to see him urgently, initially to see if you can help him try and start recovering lost memory.'

She smiled, 'yeah, and what happens if I help him recover his lost memory of killing her?'

I didn't want to go there, so I didn't answer. We shook hands and I left.

Chapter Five

Belmarsh looked as forbidding as usual; ugly and squat, like a crouching toad full of poison. I meandered my way through their tough security regime and then on to the legal rooms, looking around as I went. The morale of prison staff seemed to get lower every time I visited, and as for the prisoners I saw, zoned out didn't really get close. I guess even the prison governor knew that if the drugs didn't flow into the prison like a river, they'd have a real problem handling the inmates.

As Khan took his seat at the table he looked tired and haggard, with bags under his limpid eyes. He was listless as we went through greetings and pleasantries but I was hoping I could snap him out of it with the grenade I was just about to lob his way, but first things first. I told him how much I'd liked Rose Tremayne and I sketched out what we'd discussed and the need for him to sign authorities, which I slid across the table to him, and which he signed without comment.

Then I watched him, allowing the silence to stretch out. Most people will try and fill it with talk and he was no different. He flicked his eyes at me. 'So, Jonas,' he finally said, 'you got the hots for my shrink, or what?'

I didn't smile. I held his gaze, allowing the silence to come back in for a few beats. Then I said, 'is that like Safia had the hots for Rashid Syed?'

There was no immediate, discernible reaction; no explosion. Time stretched out and he intermittently held my gaze, looking around and then coming back to look in my eyes. Finally, he said, 'I have no idea what you're talking about, Jonas, but if this is some lawyer trick, to shock me, you'll have to think again.'

'Why no anger, Mohsin? Most guys told that their wife is playing away, tend to get a little heated. Why not you?'

'Did you?' he fired back, immediately looking down, frowning.

I kept my face expressionless, but inside it felt like I'd just had my legs cut away.

'I'm sorry, Jonas,' he said quickly, without meeting my eyes. 'That was uncalled for.'

'Forget it. We have evidence Safia was having an affair with a local taxi driver, Rashid Syed and she was leaving you and told you the night she died. We have to put that to you, because the prosecutor sure as hell will.'

'Bullshit,' he replied, animated at last. 'Safia loved me, and would never leave me. I know that, Jonas. It may not be enough for you, but that's the way it was.'

He looked away, and then turned back to me, and without meeting my eyes, he began to speak again. 'My memory's shot. It's like a dream; sometime I get technicolour big budget Hollywood, then I'll get black and white stream of consciousness shit, and I can't tell what's real and what's not. You know I'm scared I did do something, but I don't know what.'

This time he held my gaze. I packed my papers away thinking hard. I couldn't seem to get a handle on the guy. It was like trying to herd cats. Did we have a case or not? Search me, but tonight I was going to meet up with Pascal; see what she'd got, and then we'd see.

As I settled back in the taxi for the return leg I dug out my hip flask and took another shot. I never liked it when a client got personal with me, pierced the thick carapace of my professional shroud and got stuck into my insecurities. I mean why would Khan even know about the collapse of my marriage, but then again, why wouldn't he? Our split had been pretty public, played out in a court case, which would surely have caught his eye.

Before I could get too worked up about it, Emma was there, buzzing me up on the cell, sounding stern, which usually meant she was scared or upset.

'I've just had the SRA on the phone, second call today,' she said. 'They wouldn't tell me what it was about, but threatened all sorts if you don't get back to them straight away. I refused to give them your mobile number and they got very pissed off.'

I took another slug from my hipflask. The Solicitors Regulation Authority, or SRA, was the professions regulatory body. Staffed by lawyers who couldn't cut it in the real world, they were always on the look out to bring the good guys down. Trouble was they could take away your practicing certificate if you didn't play ball with them, so Emma was right to worry. If they did that we'd both be out of a job.

I knew what it was about; it was about the complaint I had pending against me from Lord Justice Michael Feldman, and it was pure bullshit. A disgruntled client, playing the system, using a spurious complaint to found an appeal, and Feldman had piggybacked his way onto it, so he could have a pop at me, because he didn't like me or the way I had spoken to him during the trial.

'It's nothing, Emma,' I told her dismissively. 'A misunderstanding which I will sort out. When they phone again, give them my mobile number, tell them you're not authorised to speak to them further, and then put the phone down. Yes?'

'Okay, Jonas,' she said, relief in her voice.

I tapped the phone off, looked out the window at the urban landscape flashing by, and thought about Eddie Tate, south London drug dealer, and now ex-client. I'd acted for him a few times over the years, but the last time it had been different, because he'd tried to stitch me up. English lawyers have a pithy term of art for what Eddie did in the trial; it's called throwing away your "shield", and it essentially occurs when a defendant alleges that the police are lying. Now, in my experience, the police lie almost as often as they breathe, so it's a problem that comes up regularly. The consequence of losing your "shield" is that it allows the prosecutor to call evidence of your previous convictions, which in the normal course of events, would remain hidden from a jury for obvious reasons. Now, with a guy like Eddie Tate, who had a rap sheet like a phone book, if he wants to start lobbing accusations at the police, even if they're true, the outcome is going to be disastrous; the jury gets to see his previous, and basically he's toast, and that's what happened in our case.

But then Tate lodged a complaint denying that he had ever instructed me to challenge the police evidence. On reflection it was clear the whole thing had been a set up. Tate realised he was going down for this one anyway, and his best way out was to sabotage the trial, then go to the court of appeal and cry technical defects, citing my incompetence as counsel, failure to follow his instructions in challenging the police evidence, and a host of other arcane defects. Although the Court of Appeal later chucked it out, recognising it for what it was – a familiar and well used ploy by desperate appellants – that didn't stop judge Feldman chewing me out in front of the jury at the end of the trial and making it clear he was referring me to the SRA and that he supported Tate's central allegation that I was incompetent. There was a lot of other stuff but that was gist of it.

Thing is, with a fair wind, I knew I could beat it, so I wasn't that worried, but a live SRA complaint was a headache, it put added stress on my practice, and worse of course, it scared Emma, and that was bad karma.

Pascal came in through the hallway leaving her crash helmet and gloves on the table and then walked on through into the living room. Sarah, her mother's carer, watching TV, looked up and smiled.

Pascal nodded towards the bedroom with raised eyebrow.

'Sleeping like a baby,' Sarah said. 'Had a bit of trouble earlier when she wouldn't take her meds, but she's fine now.'

Pascal thanked Sarah and said she could get off home, then she slipped into her mothers room. For a long time she stood in the darkness silently watching the slow rise and fall of the old lady's chest, lit only by the green LED from the bedside clock. Pascal wiped a tear away and then she was moving again, the moment gone.

She began a slow methodical sweep of the flat, checking various sensors as she moved from room to room, finally studying readouts on a laptop. Satisfied, she grabbed a bottle of beer from the fridge and sat down at a paper strewn desk in the corner to wait.

I'd had trouble finding Pascal's flat in St. Johns Wood, but now I was travelling up in the lift, wondering what to expect. I knew it was an old Rent Act protected tenancy of her mothers in a block where the developers had managed to buy up the freehold and every other flat apart from hers. They were pressuring to buy, but Pascal had refused to sell, and I'd bet the farm that that wasn't going to change anytime soon.

I knew her mother had severe dementia and required constant costly attention, and that Pascal had power of attorney, so the developers would have to negotiate with her, which must have come as quite a shock. They should have done their homework and found out they had their worst nightmare as a tenant. I smiled when I thought about that.

The door was open when I arrived so I walked through and found her in the living room sitting at a desk in the corner swigging from a bottle of beer. The room was chaotic, but with a kind of cosy charm; books and magazines everywhere, on tables, chairs, the couch, even over the floor, lying on top of richly coloured rugs and mats spread over the carpet. There were four old desk top computers and three open laptops, all apparently running programmes and a large wall mounted TV running SKY news with subtitles and the sound turned down, and in the background her sound system was pumping out awful, deafening, discordant thrash metal music.

She toasted me with her bottle and leant over and pressed her touch screen and the music went down drastically in volume and then segued into Van Morrison singing about being down on funky Broadway, when the cows come home.

'You want a beer, Calver, it's in the fridge.'

I moved to the couch and lifted some papers to make room to sit down. 'How about a real drink?'

She pointed to a rather beautiful armoire of rich dark wood to the side of the wall mounted TV. I opened it. Inside it was like a distillery, filled with bottles of every alcoholic drink you could imagine. I dug out the Glenfiddich and poured a generous measure into a large cut glass tumbler. I held it up to the light and looked at the colour, sniffed the pungent kickass fumes and then whacked a shot down the hatch.

Then I sat on the couch, content, and turned to Pascal. 'So, Khan. What have we got?'

She pressed her touch screen again; there was some clicking sounds on a low table covered in books and papers and then the unmistakeable sound of a fast printer. I could just make out the tray under the magazines, now starting to fill up with printed sheets.

'Okay,' she said, pebble glasses perched on the end of her nose. 'This, coming off now, is my initial report. Basically its statements from Rana Chaudhry the sister-in-law, Rashid Syed the taxi driver, couple of army buddies, and some guys from under the railway arches where I'm told Mohsin goes to drink sometimes. There's also a draft statement for Mohsin himself which I'm afraid is less than comprehensive; I guess we'll have to fill that one out as we go along. I've also included some summaries of conversations with various people who I didn't think it worth taking a formal statement from and you'll have to take a view on them, whether you want anything more.'

I opened my brief case and took out my Khan case file papers, now paginated in a full lever arch file, and placed it down on the coffee table. I finished my drink and went back for a refill; then I went over to the printer and fished out the papers, now about a good inch thick. Then I sat down again and began to read.

Virtually all successful trial work is based on preparation; you can't skimp on it or hide from it; it's grinding, unglamorous, basic, and utterly unforgiving if you try to wing it and then get caught in front of a jury with your pants down. So preparation is what we did. Or perhaps more accurately, what we did is we trawled through the papers far into the night, stress testing alibi's, working hypothetical's, gaming scenarios, bullshitting each other as well, back and forth, up and down, until finally we'd just about worked our way through it, and finished the Glenfiddich along the way.

Pascal sat on the floor, legs crossed, engrossed with something on her tablet. I sipped my Guinness; by now it didn't worry me that it came out of a can, I was past that. I was trying to make some order out of our deliberations, but getting nowhere.

'Tell me a bit more about this guy Nicky Holloway?' I said to Pascal.

Irritation crossed her face at the interruption; from her tablet screen I could see she was playing chess. She looked at me: 'He was one of the group of four in the original unit and they virtually all joined up together and served in Iraq and Afghanistan. Nicky stayed a private whilst Mohsin was promoted over time up to Corporal, but I don't think Holloway had any ambitions that way. When he got out he converted to Islam and he seems to be a bit of a train wreck; doper, gives out leaflets and generally harangues people on street corners, but seems quite harmless and Mohsin still see him sometimes,' she said, looking up and taking a few gulps of beer.

'What about the other two?' I asked

'Well Miles Franklyn is dead – came back a vegetable and they turned his life support off – and Frankie Crawford's still out in Afghanistan in a training role. Crawford was transferred out of Khan's unit in mid 2014, and there's been no contact since then, so I didn't bother too much with him – I don't think they were close. Funnily enough, soon after, Crawford was in an action and was put forward for a Victoria Cross for demonstrating bravery under fire.'

She made a move on screen and then looked up at me again. 'Why the interest? I didn't even get a statement from Holloway. Didn't think you'd want one, and anyway, when I tried to speak to him he told me to fuck off.'

I sipped canned black gold, mulling. 'I dunno, but I do love that gung ho boys own shit, and I'll tell you what – so do juries.'

'You're dreaming, Calver. How you gonna get that in? Relevance and all that?'

As I left the flat, going down in the lift, I smiled. I could feel the fat unopened envelope of cash in my inside pocket – she hadn't even asked for a top up.

I spent another virtually sleepless night tossing and turning, worrying about where we were going with Khan, but the Glenfiddich I'd had earlier eventually kicked in, knocking me out for 4 or 5 hours. In the morning I sat in the office with a hangover trying to work through the prosecution paperwork.

It wasn't long before I found another ticking time bomb secreted in the paperwork. Details of a caution Khan had received for domestic violence against Safia just three months before the murder. A caution isn't a conviction, but it does involve the perpetrator admitting the offence and accepting the caution in lieu of being prosecuted and having it on their record as a conviction. The prosecution would almost certainly get details of it in before the jury as corroborative evidence of guilt – it showed his predisposition to be violent to Safia. Basically the case had just got a whole lot worse.

I wondered about a plea deal, but I'd heard nothing from Sophie Ludlow. Not surprising really, given the evidence they had – why would they need a deal? And Khan senior had said a plea was not an option. And Mohsin? I didn't really have a clue what he thought, he seemed happy to blindly follow his father for now.

There was a knock on my door and Emma poked her head round and then came in smiling. 'I may have some good news,' she said, 'they've just announced the trial judge. Lord Justice Wilson.'

Judge Wilson was head of the South Eastern circuit. Murder trials always required a senior judge, and I would be happy with this guy. He was fair, dispassionate and pretty good with juries.

'Good,' I said, but I could tell something else was troubling her. 'What?'

'Don't take this the wrong way, Jonas, but I was here when you split with Carmen before, remember, and I don't want to go through that again. How are you going to cope with Patterson every day, knowing he's living with her?' she said, watching me, concern in her eyes. When I didn't respond, she added, 'and what's the deal with them now anyway?'

'I don't know, Emm. I try not to go there,' I said, but the trouble was, I did go there, regularly, a couple of times even standing outside their palatial home in Cheyne Walk , Chelsea, in a woolly hat, surreptitiously trying to catch a glimpse of her.

'I'm cool, Emm. It's been a while, and I'm moving on,' I lied.

She watched me, unconvinced, then nodded, turned and went back down stairs to reception. As usual Emma had nailed me; not surprising really, as she was the only other person who knew what had happened.

It had been really simple in the end. Carmen had provided an alibi for her ex-boyfriend. That alibi was that she had spent the night with him, and that was good enough to secure his acquittal on a murder charge. It was also good enough to destroy our marriage. I could still remember the question the prosecutor had put to her. He'd asked her why she had spent the night with the defendant rather than her new husband.

She never satisfactorily answered that question to the court or to me. She told me nothing happened; that was it; live with it, but I hadn't been able to. In the end, that uncertainty poisoned us. Eventually she'd hooked up with Patterson.

Although I didn't fight the divorce when it came, during the months that followed, I had plenty of time on my own to contemplate what I had lost – most of us only get one real chance to meet the one, and I'd blown it. So most of the time now I just felt hollow, and I drank to fill the void, and I soothed myself with fantasy tales of Alice and the White rabbit, and I immersed myself headlong in my craft.

Now the trial seemed like it was hurtling towards me like a runaway train, unstoppable, and I wasn't ready, but even worse, the spectre of facing Patterson, the man who now possessed the love of my life, turned my stomach to knots.

Chapter Six

The morning of the trial of the crown verses Mohsin Khan broke bright and clear, the famous frontage of the Old Bailey casting shadows across the street as I approached the entrance. Despite all my nerves and anguish, I was glad all the talking was over, and now I could get down to doing what made me who I was.

As I approached the robing room I briefly thought back to the visit to Belmarsh the day before. I had pulled no punches in detailing what we were up against, and had watched as the colour had drained from Khan seniors face, and even Mohsin had briefly looked apprehensive before reverting to his usual stoner look.

As I'd hoped, even after I'd painted that nightmare picture of what the prosecution had by way of evidence, the Khan's had still been adamant that they did not want me to talk to the CPS about a deal. He didn't do it, and so he would roll the dice and take his chances, and if the jury convicted him, he would take whatever punishment the court deemed fit. They had great faith in my abilities. And that had been that.

Well, I thought as I pushed through the door of the robing room, we were about to find out whether that faith was justified.

The robing room was empty, apart from Lord Richard Patterson QC. He stood at the mirror with his back to me, fastening his wing collar. He saw my reflection and a thin smile flickered for a second. 'Morning, Calver,' he said in a rich baritone. 'Ready for the fray old boy?'

I put my bag down and began to robe up whilst surreptitiously casting an appraising eye over Patterson. He was tall and athletic and I knew he'd been a very accomplished skier, even going to an Olympics thirty years or so ago. I figured he was about fifty now, in his prime as a lawyer, and obviously very fit, with thick blondish hair, and an almost Scandinavian look. I knew he'd been born to privilege, wealth and his hereditary title, but I was impressed by his legal career. Many men in similar circumstances wouldn't have taken the decision to follow such a difficult and demanding career and then gone on to make such a success of it, apparently by sheer hard work, and he was now recognised as being one of the leading lights at the criminal bar. Having said that, it was also clear that he was very much part of the cliquey legal establishment where, especially between judges and barristers, the relationships were based on favour and patronage, the lines were blurred and there was an almost incestuous flavour tainting their interactions. Almost universally outside such judges favour and patronage were the poor relation solicitor advocates like me.

I watched Patterson as he removed a particularly impressive white horse hair wig from a tin box, and then place it on his head and admire the results in the mirror. Until relatively recently wigs had been another bone of contention between solicitors and Barristers. Previously solicitors were not allowed to wear them in court and this had led to some complaints that this was unfair, it being argued that a jury might take the bareheaded solicitor advocate less seriously than his magnificently bewigged opponent, and the client might suffer as a result. So the rules had been changed and now I had the God given right to wear this ludicrous hairpiece, but I never did.

Patterson turned to me as I struggled with my stiff wing collar and the ridiculous bands (thin strips of linen) that hang down from the neck, and then he was there, in front of me, looking down and adjusting my collar. 'Let me help you there, Calver,' he said. 'I know they're tricky if you're not used to them.'

'I can manage, thank you,' I said, roughly pulling away, determined to try and stop him undermining my confidence.

'Okay, old man,' he said, eyes twinkling as he moved to the door, where he stopped. 'Oh, by the way,' he added, as if it was an afterthought. 'Carmen sends her regards.' He watched me for a moment, but I turned my back on him, perhaps a little too quickly, and then I heard the door slam.

As Patterson rose from his chair to make his opening speech I looked across at the jury; twelve watchful faces. They had that look that all new juries have; slightly excited, expectant, wondering exactly what they were in for. The good old days of throwing jurors off if you didn't like the look of them were long gone and now you could only get someone off for cause if you had a suspicion of bias; hard to show in a case like mine, so I was pretty much stuck with what we'd got, but then so were the prosecution. They looked okay, these upstanding folk; a sprinkling of white amongst the brown skins – probably good for us I figured, given Khan's heritage and ancestry – and an even six girls and six boys, all ready to rock and roll.

Patterson flicked some imaginary fluff from the sleeve of his black gown and then slipped his hands inside the lapels and held them loosely there. He started off by introducing himself and then went on to flesh out what the case was all about, his delivery conversational and simple, as if he were leaning over the garden fence having a friendly chat with a neighbour.

He continued, 'members of the jury this is essentially a very simple story that is as old as the hills. It's a story about jealousy and face. Mohsin Khan was a brave and proud man; a soldier who had fought valiantly in Iraq and Afghanistan, but when he finished his soldiering and came home to his wife, he found that the woman he had left behind had changed. She now wanted more, a better life, a life that increasingly Mohsin Khan knew, because of his inability to find work or fight his addiction to alcohol and drugs, he would never be able to provide for her.

'So when Safia told him she was leaving him and taking his two precious daughters to go and live with another man – a man whom he considered to be nothing more than a common taxi driver from civvy street – he determined to act

'Mohsin Khan could not and would not countenance losing his wife and children to such a man, so he killed Safia in a brutal knife attack, and then, in what you may consider to be another cowardly act, he feigned memory loss – amnesia – to try to sow confusion and cover his tracks, saying he could not remember anything that had happened that evening.'

Patterson paused then to allow the stark imagery evoked by his deftly sketched little story, to sink in with the jury, before moving on to detail some of the witnesses he would be calling and the evidence they would give. He gave a hint of the forensic evidence to come covering the wounds to Safia's body, an unexplained cut to Khan's left hand, the knife found in the drain and the blood staining on Khan's clothing discovered in the washing machine. He highlighted some of Rana's testimony to come covering Safia's alleged statement that she was going to tell Khan the evening she died that she was leaving him; and he alluded to a witness placing Khan outside the flat at 8.10, around the time of death, and finally, to hammer it all home, he referred to Khan's comments in the police interview which he would be asking the jury to accept as amounting to an admission to the killing.

It was a clever summation of his case. Most prosecutors invariably over egged the pudding, and then it came back to bite them in the ass when their witnesses didn't quite say what was promised, but Patterson seemed not to have done this, he'd been scrupulously fair, which I have to say, was starting to worry me, hinting as it did at supreme confidence.

Then, pausing again and looking around, the court completely silent, jurors rapt, he hit his peroration, and he had what all budding screen actors covet: presence: 'But rest assured, members of the jury, we will show you, with the help of these witnesses, and with this evidence, exactly what happened that fateful evening, and by the end of the crowns case you will be in no doubt that Mohsin Khan wilfully murdered his wife, and that you must bring in a just verdict of guilty and provide justice for Safia. Thank you.'

I almost leant back in my chair and began a slow hand clap. It was a standard by the numbers prosecutorial opening riff, honed to perfection over years of practice and repetition, nonetheless, damned effective – one look at the jury convinced me of that.

Then Patterson was off and running, calling his first witness, Rachel Morris who had made the original call to emergency services. She testified that she went to the flat at about 8.15 pm to see Safia about the Before School Club arrangements, something she regularly did. She'd never known Safia not to be in at that time. She'd tried her mobile without success and then looked through the letterbox and saw Safia's bloodstained leg extending around the hall door. She called emergency services at about 8 20 pm. I had no questions for this first witness.

Patterson then called Detective Sergeant Chandler as she was one of the first responders on the scene; he questioned her about the initial call out and she testified that she got this from CAD, or computer aided dispatch, at 8.27 pm, which in turn emanated from Rachel Morris' original call timed at 8.23 pm. Chandler and DI Stanton arrived on the scene at 8.35 pm, having been engaged on another enquiry close by in Shoreditch.

Patterson led Chandler on, detailing the state of the flat, the body and what they found, including the kitchen knife recovered from the drain outside and the clothing inside the washing machine, which was running when they arrived and which they had immediately switched off.

'And what did you find in the washing machine?' Patterson asked.

'A pair of jeans and a tee shirt.'

'Did you subsequently ascertain who the clothing belonged to and the nature of the staining?'

'Yes I did. Mr Khan confirmed the clothing was his, but denied putting it in the washing machine, or said he couldn't remember. Forensics confirmed that blood found inside one of the turn ups on the leg of the jeans – apparently this area had not yet become fully immersed in the wash – was that of Safia.'

I could have objected to these observations but I knew Khan had confirmed the clothing was his and that they would be calling expert evidence confirming the blood stains.

Patterson moved on imperiously: 'Did you subsequently run any tests on the washing machine to try to ascertain when it might have been switched on that night?'

'Yes I did?'

'And what did you discover?'

'My notes showed that we switched the washing machine off when we arrived on scene at 8.40 pm, and we recorded where the wash cycle had reached by that time. Then by re-setting the machine on the same cycle and re-starting it, we were able to calculate that it took approximately 50 minutes to reach the same point in the cycle to where we had switched the machine off.'

'And what were you able to deduce from this, if anything, DS Chandler?'

'That someone switched that washing machine on that night with those blood stained clothes inside, at approximately 7.50 pm.'

Deftly done; their hypothesis was clearly that the killer was still in the flat at ten to eight, busy doing his weekly wash. Patterson lined up the punch line. 'In your opinion, Detective sergeant Chandler, was there anyone other than the defendant in the flat at that time who could have put those bloodstained clothes in the wash?'

'No,' she said, looking directly at the jury.

I let it go even though I could have objected that there was no foundation for the question or her opinion, but making too many objections didn't go down well with juries – they often felt you were just stopping them from hearing important evidence – so I kept my mouth shut.

As Patterson was beginning to wind the witness down he changed direction again and asked, 'now we've just seen the footage of the flat when you arrived, with all the papers and contents of drawers strewn around the floor. What, if anything, in your opinion, detective sergeant, was the significance of this?'

'I have to say it looked like a possible burglary, perhaps gone wrong.' She said, 'but then after I got over the shock of the body and looked more closely, I felt it looked like a set up; the contents of drawers appeared to have been carried to the middle of the room and tipped in an almost neat pile that looked undisturbed; it just had the look of being staged; it wasn't real chaos.'

Patterson then turned the witness over to me for cross examination. I rose briskly, nodding to the jury with a brief, 'good morning,' before turning back to the witness. Although I liked Chandler, she was a professional and would expect no quarter from me. She nodded to me warily.

'It wasn't real chaos,' I said slowly, repeating her last words. 'I think that's what you said, DS Chandler? That seems an odd phrase for an experienced police officer to use. What does it mean?'

'I felt the scene looked staged, set up to look like chaos by the perpetrator.'

Time to run a little interference. 'And did Mr Patterson tell you to use those particular words?' I asked, slipping the question in quick and fast.

'*Really*, my lord,' he said, rising to his feet.

Judge Wilson held his hand up stopping both of us, 'Mister Calver, let's keep things civil, shall we; I don't want endless holdups because of your improper questioning of witnesses. Clear?'

'Absolutely, my Lord,' I said, keeping my facial expression neutral, watching the jury. As a defence lawyer you constantly had to fight against the tendency of jurors to almost equate the prosecutor with the judge, leading them to give far too much weight to evidence produced by the prosecution and worse, treating it as being, the "truth". My question was a small attempt to redress that imbalance by suggesting to the jury that perhaps the prosecutor wasn't above underhand tactics like improperly coaching a witness. Any little edge that got me closer to reasonable doubt was worth a punt.

'Let's talk about the clothing in the washing machine,' I said. 'You testified that the blood stains were found in the turn-up of the jeans, yes?'

'That's right.'

'Are you able to tell the jury the age of those blood stains, detective sergeant?'

Chandler was powerless to stop her eyes flicking in Patterson's direction, as she attempted to get a handle on where I was going with the question.

'No. I don't believe forensics are capable of answering that question.'

'The turn-ups on these jeans were done after they were purchased, yes. In order to shorten the length for the wearer?'

'I believe so, yes.'

'So, for example, if Safia had sewed these turn-ups herself it's possible, isn't it, that she could have pricked her finger and left the blood stain when this was done, yes?'

'We don't think so,' she answered.

I could tell the jury were becoming frustrated by her flat refusal to agree any of my propositions, however reasonable – all good for us.

'Now, you ascertained that the Levi jeans and tee shirt belonged to the defendant, yes?'

'The defendant confirmed they were his, yes?'

'And you were satisfied with that?' I asked, my expression slightly perplexed.

She sensed something was coming, unsure now. 'I don't understand the question.'

'Did you ask the defendant whether anyone else in the family ever wore these garments?'

She could see it now, but it was too late to backtrack; if in doubt, keep it short. 'No.'

'So you didn't ask him whether Safia maybe sometimes liked to chill in his baggy jeans and tee shirt when she was hanging out at home?' I asked. Chandler's eyes flashed, but she kept her cool, her expression almost instantly reverting back to bland neutrality. What she didn't know of course was that I had no idea whether Safia ever wore Mohsin's clothes or not, but neither did the jury. Even if she did wear his clothes on occasion, this didn't really undermine the prosecution case, but it did muddy the waters, and that's exactly what I wanted; reasonable doubt.

'Sergeant?' I prompted her.

'No, I didn't ask that.'

'Now, time of death was between 7 and 8 pm, yes?'

'Yes.'

'So you cannot categorically discount the possibility that Safia quite innocently loaded the jeans and tee shirt into the wash and switched the machine on at 7.50 pm, and was *then* killed, before eight?'

'That's highly unlikely – to get in and kill in that manner would take more than ten minutes.'

I moved on again quickly, jabbing, bobbing and weaving, trying to keep her off balance. 'Your case, if I understand it correctly, is that Mr Khan murdered his wife and then set the scene up to make it look like a burglary gone wrong, yes?'

'We believe the evidence is overwhelming that Mr Khan killed his wife, yes,' she said, adroitly avoiding the second part of the question.

'Now, ignoring for a minute the fact that that there is quite possibly a completely innocent explanation for the presence of Safia's blood in the turn-ups, if Mr Khan had wanted to cover his tracks, why ever would he leave his own blood stained clothing in the washing machine?' I asked, incredulity spreading across my face. 'He would know the clothing would be found by the police, possibly before it had gone through a wash cycle, and with today's forensic tools, he would know, chances are they'd likely discover and identify the blood stains?'

The prosecution would have spotted this anomaly, I knew. They would have hypothesised and gamed it a hundred times, but I wanted to know how they were going to explain it.

'We don't know. He would have no reason to believe the body would be discovered so quickly. The machine was set for its longest, extended wash and he no doubt thought if it had gone right through there would be no trace of the blood stains left. Or he panicked; perhaps someone came to the door, the phone rang; any number of things could have spooked him. Or he just wasn't thinking straight.'

'Or,' I said, meaningfully, turning to the jury, 'someone else committed this murder and tried to make it look like the defendant.'

There was movement and a murmur from the jury box until the Judge fixed them with a stern glare. Chandler remained deadpan, showing her experience; the slightest change in demeanour could affect a jury.

'We don't think so. As I've said, the evidence of your client's guilt is overwhelming.'

But now it was out there and the jury would know where I was coming from. Reasonable doubt was the Holy Grail; it was going to be a slow build but at least I'd laid my first block in the foundation of Khan's defence, and now all I had to do was find something good to lay on top of it.

Chapter Seven

As DI Richard Stanton swaggered across the courtroom to the witness box I watched him carefully, primarily because I knew I'd have to cross examine him soon and I needed to get a handle on what made him tick, but also because he just kinda interested me. He moved with the kind of balletic poise that a lot of large men seemed to have, and despite the ill fitting brown suit that barely covered his expansive gut, the guy just oozed self confidence. He was the kind of cop you definitely would not want to get pulled over by on a dark night.

I knew many police officers disliked giving evidence in court – not Stanton, he loved it; a born exhibitionist with an inflated ego, nothing pleased him more than crushing uppity defence lawyers, and then blowing away the rubble.

He studiously ignored me as Patterson took him through his introductory evidence, quickly establishing his long investigative experience, commendations and background, before going on to cover his arrival at the crime scene. Much of this merely followed the testimony given by DS Chandler. Patterson then moved him on to describe Khan's demeanour when he was located at the Mosque the night of the murder.

'We finally tracked him down to the offices at the back of the Mosque,' Stanton said.

'What happened?'

'Well when we found him, he was on his hands and knees trying to hide behind a desk. When we pulled him out he was shaking, scared and appeared to be on something; drugs or alcohol.'

'What did you do?'

'We didn't want a scene at the Mosque. The officials there were clearly hostile and wanted us off the premises, so I told him we had orders to escort him to the police station as there'd been an incident. He didn't express surprise or ask any questions, he just got his coat. In the car we tried to engage in some small talk but he remained silent.'

'Did you arrest him?'

'No. He voluntarily accompanied us to the station, and when we arrived, because of his general state, I took him to the vulnerable victim's suite, got him a coffee, sat him down and told him what we'd found at the flat.'

I felt a tap on my shoulder as Pascal slipped into the chair beside me at the defence table. I'd been concentrating so hard on Stanton's evidence I'd blocked out everything else. I held my hand up to her so I could hear the exchange.

'What was his reaction?'

'At first, nothing. He looked dazed and out of it, so I repeated that we'd found the body of a young woman at the flat, and that she'd been stabbed to death. Then he did react; dropped his coffee and stood up and started to get agitated, pacing up and down, and muttering to himself, asking where his daughters were. It was then that I decided to let the FME have a look at him, so I told the constable to keep an eye on him and went to get the Doc.'

'Mr Patterson,' Judge Wilson interrupted, looking up at the clock on the wall with a rather odd expression on his face, almost as if he were in pain, 'as it's now nearly twenty past twelve, I wonder if this might be an appropriate time to stop for lunch.'

It seemed very early to me for a lunch break, and I could tell Patterson was as surprised as I was, but he hid his annoyance at having to break off mid stride, and said, 'certainly my Lord.'

As Judge Wilson adjourned until 2pm, I turned to Pascal who was looking up at the gallery; I followed her sightline and noticed two casually dressed but unobtrusive looking men, moving amongst the usual courtroom junkies, making their way towards the exit. I raised a quizzical eyebrow at Pascal.

'Spooks,' she said.

I started to grin but then realised she was serious. 'Come on,' I said. 'You can buy me lunch – and a drink.'

I sipped my Guinness slowly and then wiped the white foam moustache off the top of my lip. Pascal was doing something with a croissant and spraying crumbs all over the table. The pub was busy, mostly people from the court having lunch; in the background the sound of clinking glasses, cutlery on plates, the swirl of conversation and the intermittent beeping and ringing of cell phones.

'Could have been anybody,' I said.

She just looked at me. I took another pull on the black gold. 'Okay, what possible interest could MI5 have in my murder trial?'

'How about: he's a Muslim with Pakistani heritage; ex military, now involved in a murder. How's that for starters?'

'Okay, humour me. You get one look at a couple of anonymous looking guys, and you just know it's them – that's bullshit. How can you know?'

'You'd never understand, Calver, you're a fucking lawyer.' She gave up with the croissant, dropped it onto her plate and finished her Gin and Tonic. 'I was trained - pretty well as it happens,' she continued. 'It's called observational analysis – that's watching people, Jonas – watching and interpreting. Those guys were both trained in counter surveillance techniques; sitting back corner; nothing behind, whole courtroom splayed out before them, and that stillness, almost preternatural, like stone. I could give you a whole host of other tells but it wouldn't mean squat to you.'

She was obviously convinced, but I wasn't, not by a long shot, but she was far too smart for me to ignore her, especially on a subject she knew a hell of a lot more about than I did. I finished the last drops of Guinness. 'This is a domestic, Pascal, not some terrorist hit. But, okay, say I buy it, for a second; why would they come to the trial – two of them - when they can just get a transcript or send the office boy to take a note?'

She paused. 'Now *that's* a question,' she said, subtly driving me towards her favoured option – more billable time on the case.

I watched her as she feigned disinterest, slowly sipping the dregs of her second G & T. We were going nowhere with the case – didn't really have anything remotely resembling what you might call a defence; at present all I was doing on my cross was fire fighting - so anything she could discover that might give us an edge, get us an inch closer to reasonable doubt, was worth taking a punt on, but I still had to watch the pennies.

'Okay, Pascal, see what you can dig up, but go easy - couple of hours ought to do it; make a few phone calls.'

'Fuck you, Calver. If you think it's that easy, you do it,' she said as she stood up, shoving the table against me and moving out into the aisle.

I grabbed her hand. 'Three fifty fixed fee, that's it – if you come up with something, and you better come up with something.' I held her gaze; she shook my hand off and stalked off. I smiled; she'd do it for that and I'd just got another transfer into the client account from Khan's dad; a fifteen thousand advance on trial costs. Problem was, she might get nothing we could use, even if it was MI5 who were sniffing around my trial, and I was far from convinced it was.

When I got back to court I was told by the usher that the judge wanted to see me in chambers, so I grabbed my case and made my way over. A soft knock on the door and I was ushered inside where I found Patterson and, to my surprise, Judge Michael Feldman, my current nemesis and complainant to the SRA.

For a brief moment I was stopped in my tracks as I tried to process the scene. What the hell was going on?

Feldman was a strange looking man with unusual and unfashionable sideburns running widely down his cheeks, like a guy out of a Dickens novel. He reminded me now, all kitted out in his red judges robes, of an upper class toff out fox hunting. As a lawyer or a judge, I just didn't rate him; one of those guys who'd got there by playing the angles and sucking up to whoever was flavour of the month at the time. What got me was not so much the fact that he was a total dick – you soon got used to that with the judiciary - but the fact that he was just not very bright – he could generally only discern the faintest glimmerings of a legal argument if it were spoon fed to him in a form that a very young child might understand.

Now here they sat, Patterson the patrician prosecutor, and Feldman my bogyman judge, cosily sipping coffee, regarding me as if I were the butler come to freshen up their drinks. They had probably fagged for each other at Rugby or Eton, when they weren't being rogered by their house master, I thought wryly.

Feldman was first to break cover. 'Good, Calver,' he said. 'Take a seat. We have a problem—'

'Whoa there.' I said. 'Where's Judge Wilson? Are we on the record here? What's going on?'

'I'm afraid Judge Wilson's gone AWOL, old boy,' Patterson said. 'Been taken to hospital with a suspected stroke, so we have a problem, which is why we're here.'

'I don't get it,' I said, winging it, as my knowledge of the procedure to be followed in such a case was sketchy, at best. 'Surely the court should simply discharge the jury and set up a new trial. What's the problem?'

'D'you know what kind of a backlog we've got in the courts here, Calver?' asked Feldman. 'Months before you'll get a re-start.'

I looked at them as my mind began to whir into action, running the odds, as Feldman carried on talking, and in the background the spectre of my fifteen grand trial advance having to be handed back to Khan senior for the time being, hovered.

'……and as I have been in court, in my role as observer for the judicial studies board in preparing their report, and have watched the witnesses give evidence, I am in a perfect position to take over from Judge Wilson. I have also had the benefit of reading through his trial notes. I know it's unusual for a murder trial where a jury has been empanelled and witnesses heard, but I am ready and able to take over now, subject of course to the agreement of all parties.'

And there we had it; even in my imperfect understanding of the legal niceties I understood that in order to proceed in the way suggested they would require our consent. They both sat looking at me, waiting. The first question running through me head, after my fifteen grand advance, was, what was in it for Feldman. I knew what was in it for Patterson; he wanted to get on with the trial, and now he would have a much more favourable Judge, something that should never be underestimated. But what about Feldman? Maybe it was something as simple as Patterson being owed a favour by him, and calling it in.

To stall for time while I pondered it, I threw out a spoiler to see what reaction I'd get. 'I could argue the fact that as you're supporting a complaint against me for incompetent counsel, amongst other things, you should recuse yourself from any proceedings in which I'm involved, until the complaint is resolved,' I said, looking at Feldman. It was a fair point, although to be honest, I didn't really give a toss about the complaint, although I knew Emma worried about it and how it might affect the practice.

Feldman didn't actually squirm, although it looked like a fair approximation of it, but then Patterson was in there, to the rescue. 'Nice little earners, these big private paying cases, eh, Calver,' he said slowly, with a knowing look and a glance at Feldman. 'I imagine a large fee for a trial like this, with most upfront - I understand the defendant's father runs a large chilled food firm, so he's certainly got deep pockets – comes in handy to a little practice like yours,' he said. 'And if we're not going to trial for a few months now, won't you have to hand it all back, pro tem, old boy?' he said, with a tight little smile, and then as if as an afterthought, 'I mean, mustn't fall foul of all those pesky solicitors' accounts rules, and then there's the money laundering provisions as well, and what with that complaint still floating around in the background unresolved; tricky times, eh, Calver?'

Feldman just sat there watching me. My financial woes were clearly no secret. They knew they had me, and they wouldn't even have to withdraw the complaint. But then I thought, what did I have to lose anyway? My case was hopeless, and why would it be any better months down the line than it was now; best to get on with it, and I was pretty sure that I could handle Feldman in the meantime, but, fact is, as always, I needed the money.

I looked at both of them, and said, 'I'll talk to my client.'

Chapter Eight

I simply told Khan we were getting a new judge and left it at that. I think the way he was, the less I troubled him with stuff like that, the better, and so after a brief explanation to the jury, we were back in play, but this time under the baleful gaze of Lord Justice Michael Feldman.

Pascal's phantom MI5 agents had disappeared from the gallery and Stanton was back in the witness box as Patterson continued his questioning.

'You referred to the FME, or Forensic Medical Examiner, earlier. What did he find?'

'He found Khan was significantly affected by alcohol and Marijuana, and had admitted to doubling up on his medication, so he suggested we wait to question him until the morning – let him sleep it off.'

'What did you do?'

'We put him to bed in the holding cell and then in the morning I set up the interview; cautioned Khan again; asked him if he wanted a solicitor present for the interview. He declined legal advice so we went ahead.'

The prosecutor continued, 'inspector Stanton, the jury will shortly be going to view the video of your interview of the defendant. At the conclusion of that interview, did you charge the defendant with the murder of the victim?'

'Yes I did.'

'Why did you charge him?'

'Because we and the CPS felt the evidence against the defendant was overwhelming.'

Patterson then addressed Feldman: 'My Lord, with your leave we now propose to play the video of the police interview with the defendant.'

Feldman nodded and explained to the jury what was to happen and asked for the lights in the courtroom to be dimmed.

As the picture materialized on the screen we saw Mohsin Khan sitting the other side of the desk against the backdrop of a white wall. The camera angle was from above looking down and Stanton and Chandler could be seen in the foreground, this side of the desk. There was a date, time and counter tag along the bottom of the screen and the audio and image were clear.

Khan looked disoriented to me, as if unaware of his surroundings. He sat hunched forward, arms crossed on the surface of the table, eyes staring downward.

Chandler confirmed that the interview was being filmed and recorded, repeated the caution and got Khan to confirm that he had declined access to a Solicitor. The interview commenced with each party identifying themselves and then continued for some time with simple questions covering name, age, occupation and similar uncontentious stuff. Chandler asked the questions in a simple and friendly way and Khan's answers for the most part were monosyllabic.

Chandler then moved on to questioning Khan about his activities during the day of the murder; he stumbled and stuttered with his answers and there were long silences, but essentially, with slightly more detail, he gave the same story and timeline he had given me when I'd first questioned him at the police station. He remembered pushing his youngest daughter back home in the push chair, in the rain. Then Rana had arrived and he'd gone out again at about 5.50 pm. Then there was a blank, where he couldn't remember anything, until the police arrived at the Mosque at around 9.15 pm.

It was then that we first heard Stanton's voice on the audio track; you couldn't quite see his face as he had moved slightly out of shot. Up until then Chandler had been doing a good job; the questioning was straightforward and simple and she seemed to have got something of a rapport going with Khan despite his hesitant and garbled answers. 'Over three hours, Mohsin. Ten to six to nine fifteen. Where d'you go?' Stanton asked.

Khan looked up for the first time; until then he had been looking down at the desk as he spoke. When answering Chandler's questions he seemed to have been in a trance, his answers an unthinking reflex, but Stanton's tone and manner seemed to break him out of the spell. 'I want to see my family, man; where are they,' he said, now looking around wildly.

'Safia's gone, Mohsin, and we need to find out what happened, so where d'you go?' Stanton asked again.

He looked down at the desk again. 'I don't know where I went, man. It's like a black hole – gone. I know I went out, but I don't know where,' he said wistfully

'I think you went back to the flat, Mohsin. Why d'you go back? You have an argument, unfinished business, maybe? Is that why you went back?' Stanton asked, his questions short and punchy, tone impatient.

'Like I told you, I can't remember,' he said, and then more loudly, 'I want to see my children.'

'We can talk about that when we've finished here,' Chandler said, smoothly taking over from Stanton and immediately drawing the tension down. 'The doctor has told us that that cut on your left hand was made in the last twenty four hours. Can you tell us how you got it?

He looked down at the red welt on his hand, looking genuinely surprised to me, as if seeing it for the first time, and then he said, haltingly, 'I really don't know.'

Chandler, ignoring his reply, pushed some transparent plastic wrapped clothing across the desk. 'We found these jeans and tee shirt in the washing machine when we arrived at the flat. Can you identify them?'

Khan looked confused. He looked at the clothing and then up again, more animated now. 'What is this? The jeans and tee shirt are mine. So what? My clothes get washed every week.'

'But these got blood stains on them, Mohsin,' Stanton said. 'You must have come back. Then, you couldn't go back out on the street again, cause you're covered in blood, so you chuck 'em in the wash, yeah?'

Khan looked across the desk, from Chandler to Stanton, realisation of where their questioning was leading, slowly crawling across his face. He looked down at his hands on the desk. 'I want to see my, my....' He couldn't seem to finish the sentence. He leant back in the chair and looked up, blinking, tears starting to run down his face. I looked over at the jury in the half light; they were spellbound. The court was absolutely silent.

A hand came across the table; I guessed it was Chandler's. She grasped Khan's wrist on the table. 'Why don't you tell us what happened, Mohsin? Then it will all go away; you can see your family; see your girls.'

It was beautifully done by Chandler; just the right amount of empathy mingling with an implied promise of absolution; an ending of the torment, and then he could be with his family again.

He nodded. 'Yes, yes.'

'You went back to the flat, Mohsin?' Chandler said softly.

'I went back to the flat...' Khan repeated, dreamily. He looked gone to me; out to lunch, completely unaware of what he was saying.

'You killed her didn't you, Mohsin?' This time it was Stanton, pushing again.

Then, like a tag team, it was Chandler, softer tone. 'But you didn't mean to; it got out of hand. It happens, and with your military record the court will understand. Get it off your chest, Mohsin, End it now.'

'Come on, Mohsin,' Stanton said, conciliatory for the first time; cajoling. 'You made a mistake, and everyone makes mistakes. You lost it and you killed her, didn't you? Let it all come out, man.'

Khan looked broken. He was quietly sobbing. A white handkerchief was passed across the desk to him and he carefully wiped his eyes and nose. 'I must have,' he whispered, as if trying the words out, the tape only just catching it. Then firmer: 'I must have done it.' He stared across the desk, but his eyes looked empty and lifeless.

Then Stanton's business like bark, 'Interview terminated at...'

There was a rustling and movement in the court as the lights came up with the finishing of the tape. The jury were looking at Khan, but I couldn't read them. He was looking down at his hands again, lost in his own world.

Feldman then adjourned court until next morning at 10.30 am, when I would have to start my cross.

Chapter Nine

Khan walked slowly along the landing on the way back to his cell, head down, eyes watchful. As a suspected wife killer he was pretty low down on the gaol house pecking order and was fair game for any prisoner looking for an easy target. There'd been some hostile looks and comments and some pushing and shoving whenever he mingled with other prisoners, so he had tried to avoid being out of his cell as much as possible.

On the previous evening, coming back to his cell, he'd been pushed up against the wall. A big bald east Londoner, who he'd seen around watching him, had stood in front of him, pushed his face right up close, and spat, 'fuckin' Paki, walking around here bold as brass. You want to—'

But then the guy was stopped mid sentence as a tall brown skinned man had appeared behind him, slung an arm around the guys neck and pulled him back, saying, 'hey, brother, let it go, this not your business.'

The bald guy had immediately backed away with a look suggesting fear and deference. 'No problem,' he'd mumbled, before he and his two sidekicks had scuttled away without a backward glance.

Khan had started to thank the tall brown skinned man but he had merely nodded and walked off without a word. Now as the Belmarsh babble of early evening sound rose up around Khan, he turned and entered his cell, and there waiting for him was the tall brown skinned man from the night before.

He nodded to Khan and greeted him, 'Salam Alaykum.

Khan nodded back. 'Alaykum Salam.

He studied Khan for a moment, and then said, 'sit, brother. My name is Amir and I have a message from your friends outside.'

'What friends?' Khan asked, mystified. 'Who you talkin' about?'

The man didn't seem perturbed by Khan's reaction, and continued, patiently. 'A while ago you were asked to help us with a project, but there were obstacles and maybe the time wasn't right,' he said, studying Khan, searching for signs of acknowledgement, but Khan's face remained blank.

Amir continued; 'your friends believe you are now ready to help us, but time is slipping away and the urgency rises.'

Khan continued to look confused. 'Look friend, I'm grateful for your help the other day. As for the other stuff, I have no idea what you're talking about – really. Maybe you got the wrong guy.'

Amir looked less friendly. 'You're the right guy – you know anyone else in here on remand for the murder of Safia Khan?' he said, dropping the flowery formal speech making and sliding back onto the street: 'and check it out, that little run-in last night; that'll just be the start of it. I can keep the Kafir away, Inshallah, but you will have to show you're with us, or you're against us. You can't sit on the fence in here bro,' he said, holding Khan's gaze until he dropped his eyes. 'Sleep on it and we'll speak again soon.' He touched his fist against Khan's and then he was gone.

Khan sat for a long time staring into space.

Courtney Pascal knocked the Jack back, enjoying the slightly cloying sweet bourbon as it slipped down her throat. The man sitting the other side of the table watched her, his expression blank. He was what you might call nondescript; bland and unnoticeable; this was his gift. His clothing was an amalgam of dour browns and beiges; a tweed jacket, woollen shirt with corduroy trousers. If you had to guess, you would probably say he worked for the council, perhaps as housing officer or similar; in fact he was a retired MI5 officer and one of his last jobs had been to train Pascal.

They were in the small and intimate bar of a Knightsbridge hotel, it was gone eleven and Pascal had had to pull some serious favours just to get the guy there.

'Naughty, naughty, Courtney,' he admonished her with a waving finger. 'Old Bailey security's notoriously tight. They don't allow *anything* in, least of all camera phones. So how did you get the pictures?' he asked, looking down at Pascal's smart phone in his hand.

Pascal gave a rare smile. 'D'you recognise them?'

He looked again at the images of the two men, scrolling back and forth between the pictures.

'Come on, Christoff,' she urged, 'you don't work for them anymore.'

His look was troubled as he continued to slowly scroll the images, then he stood up abruptly, leaving the phone on the table. 'Look, I'll make some calls,' he said and went to leave, but then stopped and turned back. 'I think you should leave this alone, Courtney,' he said cryptically. He stood for a moment watching her, then turned and walked away.

Pascal watched him depart, lightly tapping the phone against her teeth, lost in thought. Everything she knew about Christoff screamed Zen like calm, so what the hell was this; what had spooked him? He'd seemed skittish right from the off when he'd arrived fifteen minutes late. Pascal ran the conversation in her head again like a film, stopping at various points, re-running it, analysing every nuance, facial expression and voice inflection, but nothing stood out. Maybe he was just being overprotective, worrying that she might get hurt nosing around what sounded like an MI5 operation, when she was no longer part of it.

As she pondered all this she casually looked over at the curvy redhead behind the bar who'd been watching her since she had arrived. Pascal inclined her head slightly and the woman smiled and then swayed her way over, attracting admiring glances from a couple of Arab businessmen sitting at a nearby table. She placed a napkin down on the table, followed by a tall wine glass into which she poured some chilled white, then she smiled again and swayed her way back to the bar. Pascal looked down through the bottom of the glass at the number written on the napkin, her eyes hooded. She reached for her phone and began texting; a moment later the redhead smiled languidly and reached for her phone as it began to buzz with an incoming message.

I sipped my late night scotch as I lay stretched out on the couch listening to my audio book. Alice's bedraggled band of animals and birds were sat on the riverbank discussing how to get dry, and the Dodo had just suggested a Caucus-race. It seemed remarkably similar to some of what I'd witnessed at the Old Bailey that day, but the prose soothed me; the absurdity and the humour took me out of the real world, and with a bit of booze thrown in, I was gone – flying, but then I was being hauled back to reality by my door buzzer, bursting into life. I checked my watch – 11.40 pm. Who the fuck would buzz me up at this time? I checked the entry CCTV. A large man in Islamic dress stood in the porch; I'd never seen him before. I pressed the audio buzzer: 'Yeah, what?'

The man looked up at the camera, unconcerned, relaxed. 'My name is Maqsood Qadir and I have important information that could help you with your defence of Mohsin Khan,' he said. His voice was quiet but strong with authority.

I really didn't feel like it, but I knew I'd feel guilty if I didn't bite and find out what he was selling, but at the same time you had to watch out for all the crazies out there; the people who crawled out of the wood work whenever there was a murder case going on.

'What's wrong with office hour's pal, and how d'you find my address?' I asked, stalling whilst I tried to clear my head of the alcohol.

'If you want to help your client, Mr Calver, you'll see me.'

The fact that he looked completely unconcerned as to whether I saw him or not, clinched it. I hesitated briefly, then pressed the release button. 'Come on up, friend.'

I led him through to the living room, gestured to the couch and offered him a drink, both of which he declined. He stood looking around the room and then at me. There was nothing in his expression, but I could still detect a faint air of disapproval.

'Okay Mister Qadir, it's late and I'm tired, so make it snappy. What is it you think you can help me with?'

'I come from the Mosque frequented by Mohsin Khan. He is a devout man with many friends there; friends who would like to help him.'

Maybe I had got the wrong end of the stick here. 'Well, why didn't you say so,' I said. 'If you guys are clubbing together to make some sort of contribution to our fighting fund, that's very commendable.' I knew most Mosque's had a sprinkling of fabulously wealthy benefactors, and if I could tap into some of that, things might very well be looking up.

A slight smile flickered on the man's thin lips. 'I think, perhaps, you misunderstand, Mister Calver. Whilst we might have been willing to do something in that area, surely it doesn't arise? Our information is that Mr Khan's father is paying your fees, something we understand he is more than capable of covering.'

'You're very well informed,' I said, wondering just where the hell the guy was getting his information. Anyway, now he had my attention. I freshened up my scotch and turned back to him.

He couldn't quite hide his displeasure as he took in my refilled glass, but he obviously had more on his mind than my degenerate drinking habits. He turned to stand at the balcony windows and looked out over the rooftops of east London and started to speak with his back to me. 'Mister Calver, there are two areas where we may be able to help you. Firstly bail.'

I broke in, 'Sorry but that's done and dusted. Brutal murder plus overwhelming evidence of guilt equals no bail. Unless there's a change of circumstances, we've got no chance.'

'What if I told you we could provide up to a million sterling for security or a bond, or whatever you lawyers call it.'

I whistled, my mind whirring through the possibilities. 'Maybe, maybe,' I murmured slowly. 'It might be worth a punt.' They must want him out bad. Why? I could think about that later, but for now I felt a glimmer of excitement. A bail application, if successful, would work for us with the jury and would also poke a fiercely burning stick in Patterson's eye; and I did need to get the guy mad - then he'd start making mistakes – and this would be a very good way to start.

'Let me run it overnight; then I'll talk to you,' I said.

'Fine. Secondly, I'm assuming you might be interested in any information we could give you about a Mr Rashid Syed?'

I whistled again, but this time silently. Syed was the taxi driver, alleged lover of Khan's wife, Safia. Pascal had been digging for dirt on the guy, but she'd got zilch so far. I had wanted to set him up with the jury as the patsy; the real murderer, but without information, I'd been going nowhere with it, so this could be a nice little break for us.

But then my caution started to catch up with my excitement and I started to get a slightly uneasy feeling about the guy standing in front of me; perhaps I should haul back a step and look at this. I very much doubted that Qadir's motives were entirely altruistic; they had to be running an angle here.

He had been watching me and clearly picked up on my back step. 'I can see, Mister Calver, that you have many questions about all this, but can you afford to - what do you people say - look the gift horse in the mouth, especially when time is becoming so critical?'

He smiled expansively, knowing he'd got me. 'Look, I can answer your questions when we have more time. As you say, it is late and you have the fat detective, Stanton, to cross examine tomorrow.'

I raised my eyebrows. They *had* been keeping close tabs on the trial.

He smiled again. 'Rashid Syed used to be a regular at prayer until quite recently; the falling off in his righteousness may have coincided with his extra marital relations with Safia Khan. We have a file on Syed; it can be made available to you in your defence of our brother Mohsin Khan.'

So there it was. A beautifully wrapped birthday present, dropped in my lap, but nothing in this world is free – especially information. I was sure there would be a price to pay somewhere down the line, but right now I had a client to defend and I had no intention of looking this particular gift horse in the mouth. I made the usual noises about having to speak to my client, which I would do in the morning at court. Qadir refused to leave me a phone number and said they would be in contact again soon, and then he left.

For a long time I sat sipping my scotch, turning it all over in my mind until I eventually passed out on the couch, again.

Chapter Ten

As I sat in my chair at the defence table the courtroom was quiet, having just re-convened. Stanton stood in the witness box, relaxed and unconcerned, smiling confidently as he awaited my first question.

Cross examining experienced police officers was often difficult. They were trained in how to give evidence and over time developed sophisticated techniques to obfuscate and break up questioning. They often took long pauses and answered slowly, trying to spot traps and corners to avoid, and questioning them often turned into something of a cat and mouse game. Stanton's arrogance and ego could be turned against him if I played it right, but I would have to be careful.

I stood up slowly and turned towards Stanton and began my cross examination. There was no point jumping in and hitting him head on so I started with some fairly innocuous questions designed to clarify the take down at the Mosque. I put it to Stanton that Khan had lost his cellphone and that was why he was discovered on his hands and knees at the Mosque, because he was looking for it, not because he was trying to hide. Stanton didn't accept this.

Then I moved on. 'You testified that on the car journey from the Mosque to the station, the defendant remained silent. You specifically said, he asked no questions. Is that true?'

Stanton paused, as if thinking back, but in reality his well developed antenna was picking up on a possible trap, and he needed the pause to gather his thoughts.

'I believe so. I took a number of calls on my mobile during the journey so I wasn't exactly concentrating on the defendant the whole time.'

Clever answer: always leave yourself room to manoeuvre and never be definitive.

'Well either he remained silent, or he didn't remain silent. Which is it, Inspector?'

Stanton maintained his relaxed posture but I could see a slight colouring starting to appear in his face. 'I don't recall the defendant saying anything during the journey.'

'So you don't recall him asking you if he could borrow your phone so he could call his wife, in case she was worried. You don't recall that?' I asked, zeroing in and holding Stanton's gaze.

'No. I don't recall that.'

'Let's move on to the interview.'

'Please do,' he said mockingly.

'During the interview you put it to the defendant that: "You killed Safia, didn't you?" And he replies in terms: I must have…. I must have done it.'

'That's right.'

'Now the defendant had already told you, more than once, that he had no recollection of anything – where he was, what he was doing, who he was with – during the period beginning when he left the house at around 5.50 pm and ending when you arrived at the Mosque at around 9.15 pm. Yes?'

'That's what he said.'

'And when you interviewed Mohsin Khan, it was the morning after he'd ingested a significant amount of alcohol, Marijuana and anti depressant drugs?'

'Yes, although the levels may be disputed.'

'Lets not beat about the bush, Detective; he'd had a shed load of mind altering substances. Yes?'

Stanton shrugged so I moved on, keeping the pressure on. 'He'd just been told his wife had been stabbed to death in the most brutal fashion, and we shall be calling expert evidence to show that at this time, Mohsin Khan was suffering from Post Traumatic Stress Disorder. Now, Detective Inspector, given all of that, are you, as the prosecutor implied in his opening speech, seriously trying to suggest to this jury that Mohsin Khan's words: "I must have done it", represent an unequivocal confession to murder.

It was a risky question, but I felt that given the build up and Stanton's unreasonable replies to my earlier questions he might just be clever enough to know that flatly denying the reasonableness of my proposition might damage his credibility with the jury.

'I guess it's a matter for the jury,' he finally replied. He was still breaking clever; too experienced to fall into the trap of denying what was clearly reasonable.

'Isn't it true, Detective Stanton, that what we have here in the interview is a psychologically vulnerable, stressed out individual, answering clever questioning by experienced police officers, without the protection of a lawyer. He had no idea where he was or what he was doing when it's alleged his wife was killed. Indeed it might be said he doesn't even know where he is during the interview. This is a man who's spent his entire adult life deferring to authority and taking orders and now he's being told by authority – the police - that he killed his wife. Is it any wonder that when such a man is pressured and consistently told by those in authority that he must have done something, in a moment of stress or panic, he will just agree to it. We know he wanted to see his family, his children – he asked three times during the interview – so he knew if he agreed to what you were asking, he'd get what he wanted.'

Stanton smiled. 'What's your question?'

I smiled. 'If that's the only response you've got, Detective Inspector, I'm happy to leave it for the jury.' Before he could respond, I was moving again. 'Apart from Mohsin Khan, did you question anyone else as a possible suspect?'

'No, we didn't.'

I looked down at my papers; it was a little courtroom device designed to increase the pressure on a witness, to suggest I had got something and was about to spring a surprise. 'Did you question a Rashid Syed?'

'Yes, we did.'

'Tell us about Mr Syed,' I asked.

Stanton paused again, thinking, then, 'after we'd charged the defendant we received information that Safia Khan may have been having an affair with Rashid Syed, so of course we interviewed him.'

'In fact, Inspector, on the prosecutions case, Syed is motive, isn't he? The man – the common taxi driver from civvy street mentioned by Mr Patterson in his opening – who caused all this. He's the man Safia was going to leave the defendant for, yes?'

'Yes,' Stanton finally answered.

'And Rashid Syed confirmed the affair?'

For the first time, Stanton looked mildly uncomfortable although I couldn't think why as it was part of their case that Safia was having the affair. It was possibly because they didn't like Syed as a witness and weren't going to call him.

'Yes.'

'Inspector, in terms, what did he tell you?'

Stanton paused again, thinking, but trying not to show it, his glance flickering to Patterson, who so far had been very quiet. This might be a cause for comfort, but if he wasn't objecting, it usually meant that I wasn't hurting him. But he remained seated, unconcerned, satisfied his Pit Bull could handle me.

'He confirmed the affair and said they wanted to be together,' Stanton replied, still keeping it short.'

I looked over at the jury; they seemed to have forgotten me, which was good; they were absolutely focused on Stanton. It was time to start making use of the sparse memory recovery stuff that was beginning to filter through to me from doctor Rose Tremayne's intense therapy sessions with Khan.

'Did you also know,' I said looking over at the jury meaningfully, signifying something was about to come out, 'that far from Safia being about to leave the defendant, in fact, they'd patched things up. They were going to try again, and that just a day before the murder, they'd agreed that she was going to tell Rashid Syed the affair was over, that her children came first, and that she was going to stay with her husband?'

Stanton couldn't quite hide his surprise which flashed on his face before his rigid self control re-exerted itself and the familiar sphinx like mien dropped back in place. 'We have absolutely no evidence of that,' he said.

'Well you can't ask Safia, can you, and Syed will definitely not be confirming it - Why?' I asked, pausing and turning to the jury again, 'because if he admits he knew this – that she was breaking it off and going back to Mohsin - it gives him a cast iron motive for murder.'

'We have no evidence she broke it off and— '

'*If,*' I jumped in before Stanton could finish, 'and I'll put it as a hypothetical, given your stance. If, she had broken it off as I suggest, would you have considered it appropriate to question Syed as a possible suspect?'

Stanton had no real option other than to concede the point or lose all credibility with the jury, but he wouldn't concede it easily. 'It's a hypothetical, and if it'll help you; yes he'd be a suspect if she'd broken it off, but we have no evidence she did, so it don't arise,' he finished with a smile.

I tried to match it with a smile of my own, and said, 'one final question, detective. Did you search Rashid Syed's home?'

The question came out of left field, clearly catching Stanton unawares although you would have to have been watching him very carefully to see it. He swept his gaze over Patterson, who had lifted his head from his papers for the first time, but it was a simple yes or no answer, with little scope for prevarication.

'No, we didn't search Syed's house. There was no reason to.'

'Thank you, detective. I have no further questions,' I said, and sat down. I'd really achieved nothing other than fire fighting, chipping little bits of the prosecutions case away and raising the spectre of Syed as the jealous murderer, but even with those small pluses, any analysis would show that my final few questions would not stand much scrutiny. It was clear that motive was no big deal for the prosecution; they hadn't even known about the affair when they'd charged Khan; they'd rely on the forensics of blood stained knife and clothing, his presence at the scene, his famous last words "I must have done it", and probably the double edged sword of his mental state, and they didn't really need much else. And anyway, was it likely Syed would murder the woman he apparently loved if there was any possibility that he could win her back? Why give up after just one day, and kill her? Or maybe the affair was just a bit of fun and who's going to kill over that? But then what did the jury know; they could only speculate and that was the point; you had to plant the seeds, and then try to direct their thoughts in a certain direction.

My negative view on the effect of my cross examination was validated by the fact that Patterson barely bothered to re-examine Stanton, asking a few minor questions to clarify and re-emphasise certain points. Re-examination was a tool used for trying to repair damage that may have been done in cross examination, and the fact that Patterson saw fit to do so little really said it all. Soon after, Feldman adjourned for lunch.

I stood leaning against the wall of Mohsin's holding cell, underneath the courtroom. He sat on the bench looking up at me, waiting for me to speak, looking tired but untroubled.

'Tell me about the Mosque and Maqsood Qadir?' I said.

He looked puzzled. 'What's to tell? I prayed at the Mosque with my family, and Qadir is some kind of assistant to the Imam there. Why? How do you know Qadir?'

'Well he seems to know you pretty well and is apparently avidly following your trial, along with the rest of the Mosque. He visited me at home last night; seemed very concerned about your welfare.'

'Man, I've suddenly got all these friends.'

'What d'you mean?'

'Nothing,' he said, looking evasive. 'What did he want?'

'Seems they want you out the joint, Mohsin, and prepared to put up a cool million to see it happen,' I said, carefully watching his face.

No reaction, apart from a smile. 'Jonas. I don't really care whether I get out or not. Right now, bein' in here – at least it keeps me off the booze and out the bookies, right?'

'Wrong. If I get you out, it's sending a message to the jury. It's saying this mans innocent. It'll help; maybe it's not quantifiable, but its there, and you can't afford to ignore that.'

'So what they want for their million?'

'I don't know, but there's more. They're prepared to give me information on Rashid Syed; apparently they have a file.' Again I watched him carefully; alert for any reaction, but there was none.

'What you want me to say, Jonas?'

'I want you to be straight with me. I want you to tell me what this is all about. I can't defend you blind.'

He shrugged. 'I can't help you, man. Just do your best, yeah?'

'Fine,' I said, snapping my file shut. 'I'll tell them you're up for it, and we'll see where we go.'

He knew I was pissed, but didn't seem able to tell me anything, and why the hell didn't he seem worried about getting out? He hadn't seen his two young daughters for an age, and although they were being well looked after by the grandparents, you'd think he'd want to get out just for that. As I mulled it over, I was looking down at the prosecution witness list in my hand. 'By the way,' I said absently. 'D'you know an Eddie Nelson? Prosecution are apparently going to call him.'

He looked puzzled again, although this time it looked genuine. 'Never heard of him.'

'Good enough,' I said. Then I told him we'd set up the bail application and see what they'd got on Syed. He nodded and I made my way back upstairs.

In the end the afternoon session was cut short when Feldman was called away to deal with an urgent application in another case, but before he adjourned I confirmed that I would be making a bail application when we next convened, and Feldman listed it, without comment, for 9.30 next morning, to be dealt with before the jury arrived.

Chapter Eleven

As I got out of the taxi outside Khan's flat, I had on dark clothing and a hoody and seemed to blend right in. It was about 8.30 in the evening and still light. I leant against the wall across the street from the block and watched. I had no real plan, I just wanted to get a feel for the place, and it wasn't just geography, I wanted to zero in and feel the street craic. I'd often done it before in other big trials – visited the crime scene informally after all the chatter had died down – and tried to draw in something from the scene. And it did, on some level seem to help me, giving me a better feel for the story.

I'd studied the scene before when I'd come with Pascal, but now I had more time to soak it up and absorb the feel of the place. For a while I just relaxed back against the wall and watched the people in the street and those passing by on the balcony walkways outside the front doors of the flats.

'You looking for Crystal, man?'

I turned to look at the black kid, all of fourteen, sitting astride a mountain bike, observing me through a scarf wrapped around most of his face. Jesus, they were getting younger.

'You not a cop, are you?' he added.

'Well if I am, you're just about fucked, aren't you, junior.'

'How's that?'

I smiled. 'No, I'm not a cop. I'm the lawyer representing the guy lived over there.' I pointed. 'Killed his wife, they say.'

'Like, I could be hot shot lawyer, you think?'

I looked him over, or what I could see of him, which wasn't much. 'Why not. Give it a few years, bit of hard work, bit of studying, who knows, but I'll tell you this, it's a lot harder than drug dealing, and it sure as hell pays less.'

'What wheels you got? Beamer, Porsche, Audi?'

I took a card out of my wallet and held it out to him. 'You want a paralegal job sometime, kid. So you can try it out. Give me a call.'

He just looked at me; then slowly held his hand out and took the card. It wasn't pure altruism on my part; it was a good bet he'd have plenty of friends who might just need the services of a defence Attorney at some time. Emma would have been proud of me. 'Incidentally, kid,' I said, remembering why I was there. 'I'm told there are some railway arches round here where the street drinkers congregate; any ideas?'

'What you want with those guys?'

'Information,' I said, holding out a twenty, which quickly disappeared. He gave me brief directions and I moved off.

It was starting to get darker now and the streets were thinning out. I heard their murmurings some way off before I saw them, then glimpsed the flickering light of a fire in a sawn off water butt that they were grouped around. I walked up to them; five guys and a woman passing a bottle of cheap cider between them, some smoking. They knew I wasn't of their group and they avoided my eyes as the fire crackled away in the bin, smoke slowly rising.

I pulled the three quarter size bottle of Vodka from my jacket and cracked the lid off; all eyes focused on the bottle and for a second, time stood still for them. Then the murmur rose to a hubbub and they began to meet my eyes, their own intermittently slipping back down to the bottle.

'Which one of you's Nicky Holloway?' I asked. 'I want us all to have a nice drink together.'

It turned out he wasn't there, but they did direct me on to a nearby Khat house; I left them happy with the bottle. Khat, the Somalis favourite green chewing weed, had recently been made a class C drug, so possession was an offence, but I'd heard they'd gone underground, if you knew where to look, and I knew just the person to get me in.

She answered on the first ring and agreed to meet me in the pub I was in, in half an hour. Forty minutes later I was stood outside with Pascal and a Somali friend of hers, Abdul. He listened to me, and then made a call; he gestured to us to follow whilst he jabbered away in what I assumed was the Somali tongue. We came to a house secured with iron grills over the windows and padlocks, obviously empty and secured; we passed down an alley at the side into the back garden. There we met another tall thin black man with the high cheekbones of North East Africa; a brief discussion ensued in the same language and then we were being guided down some back stairs into the basement.

It was flickering twilight down there and grungy; mattresses around the large floor area with people on them, some smoking pipes and some chewing. Pascal spoke quietly to one of the men. Money changed hands; she offered me some green leaves; I declined but she popped some in her mouth and then whispered to me, 'that's Holloway over there,' pointing to a medium sized wiry shape lying on a mattress in the corner. His eyes were closed but I didn't think he was sleeping.

'Maybe I better have some of that,' I said. She handed me a small bunch, eyebrow raise quizzically, and I moved over, tentatively nibbling at the leaves in my mouth. I sat down on an empty mattress next to Holloway. I sensed he was immediately aware of my presence but his eyes remained closed. I looked him over; I knew he was early thirties, but he looked considerably older than that. You could discern what had once been a muscular physique but he now looked as if he was wasting away. He was wearing black skinny jeans that looked baggy on his legs, and brown desert boots.

'You want something, mate?' he said, voice querulous and reedy; eyes still closed.

'How d'you do that?' I asked.

He stayed silent for a beat, then asked, 'what are you, journo? Old bill? Government?'

'Lawyer,' I said, watching him.

'Well,' he exhaled slowly, 'to quote Shakespeare, let's—

'Kill all the lawyers. Yeah, I've heard it. Look I'm acting for—

'I'm not interested,' he said. He got slowly to his feet, then looked down at me as if memorizing my face, then turned and walked away. I watched his back receding across the floor towards the staircase, but then I saw the momentary flash of another face, over by the doorway, as someone lit a cigarette, and it was a face I recognised. It was my late night visitor and recent benefactor, Maqsood Qadir. He peeled off from the group he was with and followed Holloway up the stairs.

South of the river in a small subterranean office deep within Thames House, headquarters of MI5, a small group sat around a table drinking mostly take out coffee. They had just arrived for the briefing and some were still bitching about the early hour, others were fiddling with their mobile devices.

The people around the table were all involved to varying degrees with counter terrorism, specifically Islamist counter terrorism. Essentially their job was to identify persons of interest operating in the UK and then decide on their possible threat level. Individuals identified and deemed of sufficient threat or interest would then be monitored, and at all times the critical decision, constantly held under review, remained: should they intervene, and if so, when. Lift the suspects too soon and maybe lose the chance to pick up further Intel, or let them run and face the risk of having them commit some outrage later on. Getting that decision wrong could be catastrophic, not only for the public, but also for the intelligence officer concerned.

The group all looked up as John Condon, head of the unit, entered the room; mobiles were put on mute, heads raised, eyes focused. The early part of the meeting was taken up with status reports on ongoing surveillance operations, but then after twenty minutes or so Condon turned to Averill Lammy, a cool blonde agent of twenty nine on secondment from the FBI, and said, 'I hear there's been some movement on Qadir and the other K A. What's his name, Holloway?'

'That's right, boss,' she said in her Texas drawl, now slightly anglicized after two years in London. 'In fact, we were just about to pull the plug on them – no further action – until we got the latest flash. As you probably know, we considered Holloway to be basically a harmless junkie who does some low level dealing, hands out leaflets outside the Mosque and harangues the crowd a bit at Hyde Park Corner. The only reason we took an interest in him was because of his military background and his regular attendances at the North London Mosque where he crossed paths with Qadir, but there never seemed to be any other connection or interaction between them, until last night.'

'So what d'you get?' Condon asked.

'They were both clocked at an underground Khat house in East London last night, and that's not all. Mohsin Khan's lawyer, Jonas Calver was there as well, with his ex five sidekick, Courtney Pascal.'

'So, Courtney's back on the plot, eh?' Condon said, a certain relish in his voice accompanied by a wintry smile and a narrowing of the eyes. It seemed as if he was about to say more on the subject, but instead, he turned back to Lammy, and said, 'so what's the story on Khan then? I know you looked at him as a known associate of Holloway's.'

'That's right, boss,' Lammy said. 'Khan's a clean-cut guy, but had some problems, like a lot of them do, when he came out the army, but he's no Islamist, and we soon lost interest; seemed Holloway was just a drinking buddy. Anyway, when Khan was charged with his wife's murder, it flagged up again and we had another look, sent a couple of guys down to check out the beginning of the trial, but looks like it's being played out as a classic *crime passionnel*; she's having an affair, so he whacks her.'

'But you don't think so?'

'I don't know, boss. We know Khan was approached by the Brothers in Belmarsh, but that's not unusual of itself; he's a Muslim, Pakistani heritage, but I don't know. You tie it all together and there might just be something going on there.'

Condon, with getting on for forty years counter-terrorism experience had seen it all, from the Provisional's in Northern Ireland and on the mainland, through 9/11, and especially 7/7, which had left a scar on the security services, making them desperate to avoid a repeat of that experience. More recently the fall out from the killing of Lee Rigby by two disaffected Islamists on the streets of London was still reverberating.

Condon studied Lammy's face as she calmly waited for his response. He'd been impressed by her ever since she arrived two years earlier on an exchange deal with the FBI, to learn about MI5's techniques for identifying and monitoring home grown Islamists. She was meant to go home after 12 months but had asked to stay on and her bosses had agreed, and now she was one of his most trusted people.

'What do you suggest?' he asked.

'I think continued surveillance of Holloway and Qadir is a must, but the problem we have is that Khan's on remand in Belmarsh. If there's a link, or something going on, we're not going to see it, or pick up anything, unless Khan's back on the street. Now, I did check and Calver is to reapply for bail later this morning, although consensus is he won't get it, unless he can pull some rabbits out of the hat.'

'Couldn't we just have a word with the judge or the prosecutor, boss?' piped up the youngest member of the team, and then immediately fell silent when he saw the looks on some of his co-workers faces; he lowered his head and took to carefully studying his tablet.

'Bobby, you ever hear of the separation of powers?' one of them said, but Condon was smiling wolfishly. He looked over at Lammy and said, 'let's take a run at it people – see what happens.'

Chapter Twelve

What most people don't know about bail is that there's actually a presumption that it should be granted - in all cases - but you'd never guess that if you were a regular visitor to our courts. The one thing our criminal justice system is very good at is banging people up, even before they've been convicted, despite the fact that our prisons are already overflowing with folks who shouldn't be there – like the weak, the poor, the vulnerable and the mentally afflicted; and let's not forget the innocent.

Now, although we have this presumption that you should be granted bail, it's pretty easy for a prosecutor to rebut it, and Patterson was going all out to do just that. It was 9.30 a.m. in Feldman's court; no jury yet; they wouldn't be here for another half hour. Meantime Patterson and I were going at it hammer and tongs, even though I was still tired from my late night at the Khat house and couldn't stop yawning.

Patterson had set out the reasons why bail should not be granted, essentially saying there was a great risk that Khan would just abscond – maybe even fly off to relatives in Pakistan – and then not turn up at court for the rest of the trial. This was especially likely as the evidence against him was so strong and he was facing the near certainty of a life behind bars. This was Patterson's strongest point but he also suggested Khan might also interfere with witnesses or even commit further offences whilst out on bail; far safer just to keep him inside.

I expected Feldman to be against me from the off, but he seemed strangely muted, simply listening for the most part without interruption; maybe he'd had a bad night like me.

To counter the argument that Khan would abscond we offered to surrender his passport, to agree that he would reside with his father and that he would report daily to his local police station so they could keep track of him. Then I played my ace card and produced Mr Ali, a prominent member of the community and Qadir's mate from the Mosque, and he provided evidence of his wealth by way of bank statements and confirmed his willingness to offer significant security to ensure Khan's attendance at court.

I was less than optimistic about our chances even with Qadir's mate, so after making my submissions I zoned out and went back to scribbling notes for my coming cross examination of Rana. I was only half listening as Feldman prattled on in the background making great play of weighing the scales of justice and considering everything he's just heard, and then I had to shake myself as he starts to give his decision, and it sounds like he's going to grant it.

Patterson looked shell-shocked. I watched as Feldman ran through the various bail conditions he was to impose, most of which I had offered, but he added one, that Khan must wear an ankle tag, and he only asked for £100,000 security from Mr Ali.

I looked over at Khan in the dock, brooding and completely unmoved, and then up at his father, beaming away in the gallery – at least he was happy. For once it felt good to sit at the defence table. Then as the jury were taking their seats Feldman turned to them and explained that there had been an unexpected development requiring his immediate presence elsewhere and he must therefore adjourn until the next morning at 10 am.

I explained to Khan that there'd be a bit of a delay whilst they processed his release and sorted his electronic tag, but then I wanted to meet up with him, late afternoon or evening for a session. Then I phoned Pascal and lined her up.

Later we sat around the large conference table at the side of my office, Mohsin, Pascal and I.

Pascal looked at Mohsin and said, 'you ever run into the security services at any time, Mohsin?'

I looked up to catch his reaction. As usual, there wasn't one; the guy was either the most tightly controlled person I'd ever met, or the most spaced out, and it was beginning to burn me.

'Mohsin,' I said, 'I'm getting pretty fucking tired of getting the run around or the dumb idiot routine every time you get asked a question. Time to start talking old buddy, less you really do want to get banged up for life and never see your kids again.'

He looked down at his hands on the table, and then took a sip of coffee. 'I don't think you believe what I say, Jonas, so what's the point?'

'Hey, just humour us,' Pascal said.

'Yeah, just humour us,' I echoed her.

He rubbed his hand over the stubble on his chin and took another sip of his coffee. 'A young guy and a woman, a yank I think, as it happens, spoke to me few months ago.'

Watching Pascal, she looked like a Pointer dog who'd just sighted a pheasant in the undergrowth; head up, eyes lasered in on Mohsin's face.

'And?' I said

'I don't know. They didn't say anything definitive, just kinda danced around me, and hinted like maybe they were interested in me working for them, but I think that was just a front. They seemed more interested in Nicky.'

'Nicky Holloway? Did they identify themselves, show you any ID? What did they wanta know about Holloway?' Pascal asked quick fire.

'Jesus, man! What the fuck has any of this got to do with my trial?'

I was tempted to ask the same question, but I kept my mouth shut, intrigued to see where Pascal was going with it.

'Maybe something, maybe nothing,' she replied. 'I'm betting there's a watch on Holloway, and now we know there s a link with Qadir, and they sent a couple of their boys down at the start of the trial – something's going on.'

'That maybe so,' I said, 'but unless I can use it in our defence, I'm not interested.'

'Yeah. Me neither,' Mohsin said, 'and something else you may want to know: Nicky's a smackhead – nasty little habit he picked up in Helmand.'

I turned to Pascal. 'Courtney?' I said.

She stared out of the window for a moment. 'My contact can't get anything but says this sounds like a standard screening where maybe something flagged up, so they've upped it a notch. This stuff's going on all the time; they can't afford another 7/7, so they're having to look at every little thing, and I hear ninety percent of them come to nothing.'

'Good enough,' I said, dismissing MI5 from my thoughts. 'But what about this Qadir character, Mohsin?'

It was like watching a door slam shut; a look of discomfort or even resentment, it was hard to tell, spreading slowly across his face, and I knew before he opened his mouth he was going to lie, or his memory had gone again and he would just make it up. 'I don't know, man,' he said. 'I've told you, he's at the Mosque and they always help out when a brother's in trouble. That's all it is,' he said, but he wouldn't meet my eyes.

'So providing this file on Syed,' I said, holding it up and flicking through the few sheets of paper, 'is just helping you out, yeah? Come on, Mohsin, they provide this and talk about sticking up a million bail money, and its just helping?'

I focused on his face, waiting for him to look up and meet my eyes, but he wouldn't; he remained looking down at the table, so I waited. Then, no doubt to try and divert me, he said, 'so what's in the file, Jonas?'

It was obvious he wasn't going to talk about Qadir, and maybe it didn't matter. Maybe it was just some private thing unrelated to the murder, so maybe best to move along. 'As it happens, not very much,' I said. 'It seems to be a few badly typed up notes from someone who can't spell, of what Syed allegedly said to various people around the time of the murder. Don't know why they bothered, it's no use to me,' I said, skimming the papers across the desk to Pascal who immediately picked them up and started leafing through them.

'Look, I better be going,' Mohsin said, looking at his watch. 'If I want to be there to put my two girls to bed.'

'Okay, you get off old buddy,' I said, slapping him on the back and leading him to the door. Then I held him back a moment, remembering to ask him, 'yeah, look we just talked about Nicky Holloway, and you know I did reach out to him – not long ago – but he was pretty hostile.'

Mohsin laughed, and said, 'that's Nicky all right.'

'Well look, Mohsin, we may need Nicky as a witness. Can you get him to meet with us, Courtney and me, so we can talk?'

Again, his face took on that closed up look, hovering between resentment and suspicion. He said, 'Jonas, he's a fucking smackhead, how's that gonna help us?'

It had been a long day and I was getting tired of his whining bullshit and prevarication. 'Reality check time,' I said. 'At the moment the prosecution are this close,' I said, holding up my finger and thumb, just about touching, 'from satisfying the jury that you killed Safia, so I am going to have to come up with something pretty damn special to counter that, and part of that will be trying to explain to the jury why your memory is so bad, and why you said some of the things you said – like you must have done it. I don't have time to go through it all right now, but one way of doing that will be to look closely at PTSD, amnesia and your state of mind generally, so we're going to need chapter and verse about what happened in Afghanistan, and not just from you, and that's where Nicky boy comes in; you getting me?'

He looked at me for a long moment, debating whether to push it, but I guess my expression made his mind up. He nodded sheepishly. 'I'll see what I can do, Jonas.'

'Good enough.' We'd covered everything I wanted for now, so I told him to make sure he was at court next day bright and early.

After he'd gone, I said to Pascal, 'Eddie Nelson?'

'Eddie Nelson,' she repeated slowly. 'I need to do a bit more, but he looks like a jailhouse snitch, and, he's featured in a couple of old trials where Stanton was the investigating officer.'

I smiled. 'Now that I can use.'

'Meters running, Calver,' she reminded me.

'Hey, you come up with stuff like this, don't worry about it.' I said, feeling generous.

Chapter Thirteen

Patterson stood at the prosecutor's desk and I could tell he was loving it, because Rana was a great witness; short, sharp and pithy; she stayed on point and the jury were lapping her up.

Now Patterson moved up a gear. 'Now, I want to take you back to the night of the murder, Ms Chaudhry,' he said. Maybe I imagined it, but it seemed as if the jury leaned a little further forward in their seats, anxious not to miss anything.

'Safia told you something important that night about her relationship with the defendant; what was it?'

I could have got up and objected that the question was leading and it called for hearsay, but I stayed seated, mouth shut.

'She told me when she got back after Mohsin had gone out, that she was finally going to tell him, that night, when he got back, that she wanted a divorce, and she wanted him to leave.'

'And why had she chosen that particular night to tell him?'

'I don't know. I think she'd just had enough. She said she was going to do things step by step; get him out the house first and get him used to that, then divorce. I just didn't think it would work, but I supported and loved my sister, so I encouraged her; told her it was the right thing to do, and I'm convinced she did tell him that night; she seemed so pumped up to do it.'

'Did you see the defendant again that evening?'

'No. I left soon after with all the children for their sleepover at mine, and that's the last time I ever saw my sister alive.'

'Thank you, Ms Chaudhry. You've been most helpful,' Patterson said. I guess it couldn't really have gone any better for him, short of the witness saying she saw Mohsin Khan plunge the knife into Safia's chest. 'I have no more questions,' he added, 'but please wait there; Mr. Calver may possibly have something to ask you,' he finished condescendingly, with a slight nod to the jury, as if to say, get ready for amateur night.

I remained sitting at the desk for a beat, then I was on my feet again, ready to go. The witness watched me apprehensively; her CPS minders would have exhaustively prepared her for cross examination, without of course coaching her, as that would be improper, right? But even so, most people, especially non professional witnesses, even if they had been coached, dreaded this part of the trial process and wanted to get it over with as quickly as possible. And for the advocate, coming straight after the examination in chief with no time to reflect, it was often a split second decision what approach you took with a witness. Go aggressive and turn her defiant and hostile, or go subtle and friendly and maybe wheedle something out. I chose the latter, smiled to disarm her and said, 'you don't mind if I call you Rana, do you?'

A look of suspicion flickered on her face and she looked over at Patterson for succour, but he had his head down and was busy writing away. 'Of course not. No, I don't mind at all,' she said, relaxing slightly.

'Good. Now, you testified earlier about an incident that gave rise to Mr. Khan being cautioned, when he arrived back late for a family Sunday lunch, and you were there with Safia and all the children waiting for him,' I said, looking down and checking my notes. I had to be very careful dealing with this topic, the domestic violence caution Khan had received a few months before the murder and which Patterson had just made great play of when taking Rana's evidence in chief.

I looked at the jury as I re-read her testimony to her. 'And you said, and I'll read it out verbatim, "I don't know what set him off, but he got in a frenzy and grabbed the roasting tray from off the table in front of Safia and threw it against the wall. What got me was that the roasting dish was sizzling hot from the oven, and he didn't even seem to feel it when he picked it up – it must have burnt his hands like hell"'

'Yes,' she answered, not sure where I was going.

'"I don't know what set him off", you said; so there doesn't appear to have been any obvious trigger for the outburst.'

'That's right,' she came right back at me. 'He came in; he was mumbling something I didn't understand and he wouldn't sit down. Then when Safia began carving the meat, he lost it.'

I let the words sink in; courtroom silent as I ranged my eye along the jury box.

'Did you know that the defendant suffered a very serious knife injury in Afghanistan? Indeed we shall be calling expert evidence to show he now suffers from Post Traumatic Stress Disorder as a result of that and other such incidents' I said.

'My lord, really,' Patterson, blustering, was on his feet again, paying me back; trying to disrupt the flow and distract the jury.

'I quite agree, Mr. Patterson,' Feldman said, nodding enthusiastically, despite the fact that the prosecutor had not even articulated an objection. 'Mr. Calver, kindly restrict yourself to asking questions that are relevant to the issues in this trial,' he said sharply, sideburns beetling; his head of steam was now building up nicely and I knew it wouldn't be long before we faced off.

'My lord, the questions I am asking are relevant, and this will become clear *if* the prosecution will stop making these spurious objections,' I said, barely managing to put a cap on my anger, and reminding myself that I must stay focused and not get emotional.

'I take it, Mr. Calver, that PTSD is going to feature somewhere in your defence?' Feldman said.

'Amongst other things, yes my lord, very much so,'

Rana was now getting well versed in the ways of the court and didn't wait to be given the go ahead by Feldman. 'Yes. I knew he was stabbed out there and it was pretty bad.'

Feldman let it go this time.

'Rana, given the seriousness of that knife injury and the fact that the defendant had been diagnosed with PTSD, do you not think that Safia's use of the carving knife might have set the defendant off?'

My strategy here was desperate and dangerous, even suicidal. It wouldn't be a very big jump for the jury to think, well maybe that's what happened the night of the murder; Safia innocently picks up a knife, and he loses it, game over. But we had to give the jury some explanation as to why Khan was cautioned, for what the police were exaggeratedly calling "domestic violence", especially as there didn't appear to be any other incidents where it was alleged he had raised his hand against Safia. It was a high risk strategy, but I was playing a long game and I didn't think we had much to lose, so I was betting the farm.

Rana obviously hadn't thought about it before, but now she did, cocking her head to one side. 'I suppose,' she allowed, reluctantly, 'now you come to mention it, that, yes,' 'it could have brought that incident on.' She paused, then, 'but so what, he still killed her.'

You always tried to prepare for the unexpected when you embarked on a cross examination, and when you got that kind of sting in the tail show stopper answer, it was essential not to show any kind of emotion or surprise at the answer, so I kept my face completely impassive and moved smoothly on.

'Now you testified that on the night Safia died, earlier, she'd told you she was going to tell Mohsin that very night that she wanted a divorce and for him to leave the house. You said you encouraged her and that you were convinced she would tell him, because she was so,' I looked own at my notes for the quote, '"pumped up", you said, yes?'

'That's right,' said Rana, keeping it nice and short now we were getting into uncharted waters.

'I put it to you, Rana, that you're mistaken. Far from Safia leaving Mohsin Khan, they were in fact going to try again, and that is what she was pumped up about.'

I know it sounded desperate, as if perhaps we had just cobbled it together to fit the facts, but it was based on instructions from Mohsin, via Rose Tremayne.

'That's not true,' she replied, looking over at Mohsin in the dock, her look withering. Then she turned back to me, and said, defiantly, 'I am certain my little sister did tell him that night she was finished with him.'

It was all down hill from thereon in. I tried to shake her, but she was implacable, so after a few more questions I let it go. Thing is, it was my job to "put" my clients case to the witnesses, however fantastic it sounded and that was what I was doing here with these questions. But it wasn't working, probably because all the extrinsic evidence pointed the other way, that their marriage was over, she was having an affair and wanted out, big time, and I think that's what the jury believed.

They sat in the coffee shop in Dalston, east London, Mohsin Khan drinking a tiny bitter espresso, and Nicky Holloway a heavily sugared latte. Nicky looked hyper and was sweating profusely even though it was not cold in the café. He was dressed in a long fawn coloured robe, almost like a dress, with a short grey kind of tunic top over it and a white and black checkered wraparound style turban headdress.

'No way,' Nicky said.

'Look,' Khan said, 'my brief says they *need* to speak to you.'

'Fuck for? What do I know? I mean, I know you didn't kill her an all, but I wasn't there. What can I tell them?' he said.

'It's not about that. It's about what happened in Afghanistan,' Mohsin said. Their eyes met and locked for a second, then Nicky looked away sharply, hyper again, eyes flashing around the little café, alighting here and there, but never stopping for long.

'You got any shit, man?' Nicky asked, scratching his forearm and looking about wildly, still avoiding Mohsin's eyes. 'cause I'm hurting real bad,' he wheedled.

Pascal had anticipated that Nicky would probably want something for his trouble so she had supplied Khan with a small amount of heroin. He looked about and lowered his voice. 'I might be able to get you something, Nicky, but, you gotta help me out too,' he said.

Holloway, immediately brighter, said, 'yeah, yeah, yeah, no problem, man,' a lightening volte face.

'Long as you understand, you get a snifter now, and then a proper fix when you meet and talk with them, yeah?' Khan said, opening a small tin and showing Holloway the tip of a foil wrap showing under the tobacco.

Holloway smiled dreamily and licked his lips, but then a shadow seemed to cross his face as if he had remembered something he'd rather forget. He looked up and met Khan's eyes for the first time and said, 'man, has that Qadir spoken to you about the wedding, only he's on my back 24/7; don't give me no peace.'

At the mention of the wedding, Khan seemed to stiffen, jolted by half remembered scenes flickering in his mind of Qadir talking to him menacingly, but as he tried to freeze and focus the images they drifted away, and then they were gone, his mind blank again. As he came out of it, he forced a smile, calming himself, looking around the café and sipping his espresso as his screaming nerves subsided.

Nicky watched him with alarm; he was edgy as well, and if he didn't get a fix soon he'd start climbing the walls. 'Hey, chill, man; Qadir can wait; just gimme that shit, yeah?'

'Yeah,' Mohsin said absently, checking his watch; he needed to be at the Nightingale centre in less than an hour..

Pascal sat in the white builders van parked across the street and watched the two men as they sat in the café drinking their coffee. They looked edgy and uncomfortable, especially Holloway whose body language screamed junkie, even from across the street. Pascal looked down at the small block of pure Turkish Brown heroin on the floor of the car, then she looked up and let her eyes roam slowly around the esplanade of small shops and businesses, noticing for the first time another car, further up the street, a beat up old black Jaguar with two occupants, a youngish male, and a female with long blonde hair, both drinking take out coffee.

That it was a stakeout was blindingly obvious; and it looked like the two in the car were the MI5 officers Khan had described as having approached him a few months back. After the meeting Pascal had called Christoph and asked him to run a check and he had identified the blonde as probably being an Averill Lammy on two years secondment from the FBI. As Pascal watched, the male occupant got out of the car and hailed a cab, leaving the female inside.

Pascal turned back to the café and idly watched Khan and Holloway as her mind wandered, returning as it so often did these days to her unjust and unceremonious ejection from the security services. Fact is she'd never really got over being pushed out, and it still rankled. Now she swiveled her eyes back to the beat up Jag and the blonde inside and her hackles rose. Years of resentment at her treatment by five, much of it nurtured during her time in prison, now welled up, becoming magnified and then concentrated down upon the girl in the Jag, and it didn't help that Christoph had said Lammy was one of Condon's favorites. Pascal gripped the steering wheel until her knuckles turned white, the pent up rage boiling up inside her as she watched the girl in the Jag, and then suddenly, without thinking, she was out of the van and marching towards the black car.

Without pausing she wrenched the door open and climbed into the passenger seat. 'Must be amateur night, Lammy,' she said. 'You're sticking out so bad even a junkie like Holloway's going to make you, and if he doesn't, maybe I'll just pop over and have a quiet word.'

'Oh I don't think you want to do that, Courtney,' Lammy said calmly, without even turning to look at her, her eyes remaining trained through a small pair of binoculars, on the café window and the two men inside. 'Then you'd have to tell them you've been watching as well.'

Lammy still hadn't moved a muscle, calmly sitting there, now raising her takeout coffee to her lips for a sip. This girl was no greenhorn, and she knew Pascal's name. They sat in silence, Pascal starting to feel embarrassed at blundering in like a rookie and then lashing out because she was pissed off – and without having any clear idea what she wanted from the confrontation. She needed to get a grip, fast.

'So you're Courtney Pascal?' Lammy finally said, lowering the binoculars and turning to look at her for the first time. 'John speaks very highly of you,' she added, in a way that suggested she might not exactly share that assessment.

Pascal studied her. The girl was certainly pretty, her best feature being her clear grey eyes, icy and knowing but with a, probably artificial, hint of warmth. The use of Condon's first name was intriguing, probably something going on there. Pascal continued to watch her, turning her gaze into a frank appraisal. Then she said, 'you know, Lammy, you're kinda cute - for a G man.'

The ice maiden regarded her with an amused look. 'Hey, Courtney, let's stop playing around shall we.'

They sat regarding each other; seemed like checkmate. Then Pascal said, 'I agree, let's cut the crap. How about you tell me why you're watching my client?'

'Who says we are?'

'So you're watching Nicky then?'

'I'm just having a quiet coffee, Courtney. How 'bout you?'

Silence descended again, Pascal aware Lammy was using it, playing games. The silence lengthened.

'How's Christoph?' Lammy finally asked. 'I know those old retired guys like to stay plugged in with their contacts, like they're still part of the game,' she said, cutting some more ground from under Pascal.

'My guess, Lammy, you're just a grunt, stuck out on low level ops no one else wants, shadowing whack jobs like Holloway.'

'And what would you give just to be a grunt, eh, Courtney? How's it feel to be on the outside with your nose pressed up against the window, desperate to get back in?'

In less than five minutes the girl had managed to identify Pascal's weak spot, and then drive a nail through it. Wounded, Pascal sat back and told herself not to rise, concentrate on getting something, but it was hard, the girl was way ahead of her.

Lammy glanced at her. 'Wow, have you got it bad,' she said, without a hint of sympathy in her voice. She seemed to be mulling over something, and then she said, 'look you were in the game, and from what I've heard you did okay, so, okay, maybe we can help each other out a little bit,' she said, taking a chance on using her initiative and hoping Condon wouldn't blow a fuse, if she told him, which she'd think about later. She continued, 'you know enough to know that we were always going to be interested in someone like Holloway. He's a classic unbalanced radicalized veteran, so who knows what he's going to do – and that's the point. We can't afford another 7/7 or Lee Rigsby so we have to watch anyone who gives the slightest cause for concern.'

'So who you looking at?' Pascal said, watching Lammy, fighting against the unaccustomed feeling of gratitude to the girl for letting her in, and talking straight to her, if she was talking straight to her.

'That's classified,' she said, 'but, it won't hurt to state the obvious, that Khan's an associate of Holloway's, so when the murder happened, we had a look. We also thought he might have potential to help us out on the odd thing here and there.'

'And?'

'Courtney, I'm going out on a limb here, so I need something back, if I'm going to talk to you,' she said, raising the binoculars again and sweeping the café window. 'You know, I had a look at a few files when this blew up; yours of course, but I also looked at what we've got on Jonas Calver as well. Some interesting stuff about his ex-wife and that trial she was involved in.'

The words hung in the air between them. And what the hell was she hinting at by name checking Calver? What the hell was that all about? Pascal didn't know much about Calver's personal life, but she did know he'd been cut off at the knees by the breakdown of his marriage and she knew it somehow turned on his ex-wife's alibi given in a murder trial, but this was getting too close to Calver's personal stuff. Maybe she should just stick to the mission she was being paid for, digging up leads for the defence on the murder charge. 'What do you want to know,' Pascal finally said.

'We think Khan's just an old army buddy of Holloway's, but we'll be watching what's thrown up in the trial, but what d'you know about the Mosque guy, Maqsood Qadir?'

'Who?' she answered.

'Come on, Courtney, stop playing games, or get out the car.'

'Okay. To be honest, we don't know. He's not a witness, but he is hanging around the periphery and has offered help for Khan, which isn't unreasonable given Khan's link to the Mosque. I believe he's ex Saudi air force; looks clean, but I'm sure you know a hell of a lot more about him than I do.'

Lammy slowly nodded her head, then said, 'so tell me, Courtney, did your man do it or not?' She watched Pascal, and then added, 'say, maybe we can help you with that as well.'

Pascal knew she was being played, but so what; she could handle that. The main thing was that Lammy viewed her as a viable source of Intel and it looked like she was prepared to do deals. So Pascal would keep the channels open, reserving judgment on the girl until she knew more. Gut feeling; she didn't like her, but then she didn't like most people.

'You gonna tell Condon about this?' she asked.

'About what?' Lammy said, poker face. 'Here's my number,' she added, handing Pascal her card. 'Maybe we can help each other out; you hear anything, get in touch and maybe we can trade. If it's good, maybe I can put in a word and get you back on the team.'

Now she was showing her inexperience, over playing her hand, Pascal thought, as she took the card and climbed out of the car. She leaned back in, 'say hello to *John* for me,' she said, holding Lammy's eye, before adding in an exaggerated American accent, 'and you take care now,' as she slammed the car door.

Chapter Fourteen

Maqsood Qadir slipped into the Halal butchers shop in East Ham and quickly turned sharply to the left so that he was no longer visible from the street. When the man behind the counter recognised his visitor he quickly straightened up with a show of deference. Qadir removed his rather striking mauve coloured jacket, turning it inside out, and putting it back on so that it was now a drab brown colour. He then pulled a woollen bobble hat down on his head and moved through a door at the back of the shop, having been inside for less than 30 seconds, and then he was getting into a taxi and closing the door as the vehicle moved off.

Sometime later he sat in the back of a black limousine as it pulled to a halt outside the Nightingale centre. If his information was correct, Mohsin Khan should just be finishing a session with Doctor Tremayne. A few minutes later Khan emerged and Qadir barked a short guttural command in Arabic to the burly man sitting in the front passenger seat. The man watched Khan as he approached the car; when he was alongside, the man climbed out and taking Khan's arm, guided him into the back of the car all in one smooth movement. Khan didn't initially resist until he recognised Qadir, but by then it was too late as the big car was moving away from the curb.

Another peremptory order from Qadir and a Perspex screen slowly rose leaving the two men cocooned in the soundproofed rear of the car. Neither man spoke for a while.

Finally Qadir said, 'so, my friend. How have you been?'

Khan was looking out of the window, watching urban south London as the big car made its way towards the river. His hands were clasped tightly together in his lap, fingernails cutting into his palm. He said, 'what do you want, Qadir?'

'We are told, my friend, that you have problems with your memory. As you are an honourable man, I will give you the benefit of the doubt and not assume that this is just some cynical ploy for use in your murder trial. So I will help you – with your memory,' Qadir said, his look knowing and calculating. He paused for a beat, looking intently into Khan's eyes, and then said, 'I will remind you: the wedding.'

The jolt coming again was sudden and immediate, Khan stiffening at the mention of the word, jumbled memories coursing through his mind; Qadir in a workshop, angry and shouting at him. It started to fade out but then for a second, Khan saw a glimpse of it; he shuddered.

Qadir continued to watch him, then said, 'you must answer the call. There is no more time.'

Khan was silent for a beat, his look bewildered, nerves jangling, then slowly subsiding. Then he murmured, 'did you kill Safia?'

Qadir laughed softly, shaking his head as if exasperated at the words of a recalcitrant child. 'Come, my friend. Why would we kill Safia and get you sent to prison for life? You are no good to us there, where you can do nothing for us.'

Khan turned back to stare out if window, seeing nothing, his mind in turmoil. 'I don't know,' he said.

'No, my friend, I think deep down inside you're very scared that you did kill her, and you're looking for someone else to blame.'

Khan remained motionless, a picture of misery; he said nothing, so Qadir continued, 'you know I am your friend so I will say this. For a long time I have held at bay our more fanatical brethren but, if it is your final decision not to carry out the work asked of you, I may no longer be able to restrain them. Perhaps,' Qadir said, his voice becoming silky, 'you should concentrate on the living, your two young daughters, rather than the dead.'

Khan didn't respond immediately; he seemed to shrug, and then turned from the window to face Qadir again. His voice when he spoke was calm but resigned. 'If you touch my children, Qadir, I will bring the whole world down on you and your friends.'

He turned back to the window, looking out, feeling powerless and lost. A moment later he murmured, 'but for now, I don't seem to have a choice.'

Qadir smiled and clapped his hands. 'It is the right decision, Inshallah,' he said, picking up a cheap disposable cellphone, pressing a speed dial number and raising it to his ear.

Khan leaned his head back on the plush interior leather seat and closed his eyes; inside his nerves were screaming.

With his goatee and wispy moustache, pockmarked cheeks and small black feral eyes, Eddie Nelson really did look like a rat. He had been in the witness box for around ten minutes and Patterson had just finished running through his back story for the jury; honest john used car dealer doing his civic duty, but I wasn't buying it – he looked like a small time con to me.

'And what time was that?' Patterson asked.

'Must have been about five past eight, right chief,' he answered, smiling at the jury.

A slight curling of Patterson's lip told me he wasn't enjoying this witness. 'And why were you there?'

'Punter saw the motor on the web page. Said he might buy if I run it over, so I did. Wouldn't do it as a rule, but money's tight right now, yeah? So I get over there and he tries to chip me,' Nelson said, his face a picture of incredulity at the unfairness of it all.

'What happened when you arrived there?'

'Well, after I'd parked up, I couldn't find the house,' he said, chuckling away. 'So I asked this Pak—.' He stopped mid sentence with a sheepish look, realising what he was about to say; started again. 'So I asked this geezer, coming out of the flats for directions, and he said it was around the back.'

'And who was that person who gave you the directions?'

'Like I told you, it was Mr. Khan, sitting right over there,' he said pointing at Mohsin.

'Thank you Mr. Nelson. I have no more questions for you,' Patterson said.

As Nelson made to walk out of the witness box, Feldman woke up. 'Mr. Nelson. If you would wait there please. Mr. Calver may have some question for you.'

Some in the jury giggled. Nelson stopped in his tracks, looking sheepish again and said, "oops", before stepping back into the witness box.

I had a problem; Khan didn't know whether he had been there or not at the time Nelson said he was, but when in doubt, attack, and this time Pascal had given me some ammunition.

I stood and pretended to study a single sheet of paper in my hand. I looked over at Nelson who seemed relaxed, but I could detect a faint tick in his lower lip. I said, 'tell me, Mr. Nelson, have you ever given evidence in a criminal trial before?'

Nelson licked his lips and looked around. 'Now you got me, chief,' he said, smiling again. 'Memory like a sieve.'

'Well, perhaps I can help you. Seven years ago you testified for the prosecution in the trial of Joey Miller for armed robbery. Remember now?'

'Could be, yeah. Sounds about right.'

'What happened?'

'He was convicted,' he said with satisfaction.

'He was indeed, but what happened after that?'

'He was banged up.'

'And after that?'

'How should I know,' he said, a slight edge coming into his voice.

'Well, let me remind you. His conviction was quashed by the court of appeal, and you know what they said?' I asked, pausing for dramatic effect. 'They said your evidence was wholly unreliable and that the police should investigate whether offences of perjury or perverting the course of justice had been committed.'

'I told the truth then, and I'm telling the truth now,' he said, but the ready smile had gone.

'Tell me something else, Mr. Nelson. Who was the investigating officer in that case. I'm sure you can remember that.'

I saw him glance quickly up at the gallery; I followed his gaze and there was Dick Stanton.

'I think it was Inspector Stanton,' he said.

'That's right, the same Richard Stanton who is investigating officer in this case. Coincidence or what?'

I heard Patterson start to rise next to me, and quickly pre-empted him. 'I'm sorry my Lord, I withdraw that.' Feldman looked at me over his glasses but stayed silent.

I banged on a bit more in the same vein with Nelson, asking how Khan was dressed, exactly what he'd said, and a few other points, just hoping the jury would get a fix on the guy and realise what was going on. Trouble was; maybe Nelson was telling the truth, so all I could do was try and discredit him and hope it would colour the whole prosecution case, but then again, maybe I was just reinforcing Nelson's evidence and his placing of Khan at the scene.

And this time Patterson chose to re-examine. 'Mr. Nelson, a couple of quick questions to clear up any doubts. You heard my friend Mr. Calver helpfully reading from the judgement of the court of appeal. Have you ever been prosecuted for perjury or perverting the course of justice.'

'No I have not,' Nelson said, indignantly.

'You testified that you saw the defendant, Mohsin Khan, just outside the flats where he lives at between five and ten past eight on the night of the murder.'

'Yes.'

'Is that the truth?'

'Yes it is, so help me God.'

I looked around the courtroom and felt like I was slowly drowning. What should have developed into a devastating cross examination, given the ammunition I had, had meandered around ineffectually and then dismally petered out in the dampest of squibs. Then Patterson had deftly re-emphasised the essential point in his re-examination, that Nelson had seen Khan just outside the flat just after the time of the murder, and that's what the jury would remember when they came to deliberate. That is, unless I could pull my finger out and start hitting the target. Maybe I'd have better luck with the forensics.

Patterson was bringing the prosecution home now, finishing his tail end witnesses. He took the Home Office pathologist through his long list of qualifications. Doctor Manfred Kohler certainly looked the part, a tall thin man with a look of prodigious cerebral intellect.

Patterson deftly teed Kohler up, taking him through the steps taken preparatory to his examination of the body and then onto the detail of his findings.

'And what, in your opinion, doctor, was the cause of death?'

'Multiple stab wounds,' he answered crisply. 'In fact it was not possible to isolate exactly which stab wound caused the death, as at least three of them could independently have been enough to end her life.'

Patterson looked up at Feldman. 'My lord we have some photographs here,' he said, handing them to the court usher, 'which we would like the jury to see as exhibit MK12.'

I started to rise to object, as the prosecution had never disclosed the photo's to us. Most likely cock-up rather than conspiracy, and Patterson's look of surprise seemed to bare that out. He passed a set over to me, and waited as I flicked through them. They were horrifically graphic, but there was no way I could have kept them out, even if I'd wanted to. I nodded my assent. As the jury passed them around I heard gasps as civvy street collided with a horror movie.

'Doctor, could you give us a simple overview of how death occurred in this case,' Patterson asked.

It was pretty obvious that Safia had died from stab wounds, so there was nothing much to this evidence as far as I was concerned, but from Patterson's side it obviously gave them the opportunity to inflame the jury with the photograph's and the grisly cause of death. Kohler essentially said she'd died from a range of wounds to the neck, head, abdomen, arms, chest and legs and that some of the stabs or blows had damaged the bone, requiring the use of considerable force. One of the chest wounds was 14cm deep and had punctured the left lung causing it to collapse. Another had severed a vein and artery in the right kidney causing catastrophic bleeding.

'And what about time of death, doctor?'

Kohler rambled on about the various tests carried out relating to body temperature and food found in the stomach, but essentially he said that he believed that the attack and death occurred between 7 and 8 pm.

'Doctor, tell us about the knife found in the drain outside the flat?' Patterson asked.

Kohler told the jury that the knife had obviously come from the empty slot in the knife block in the kitchen. It was a short carving knife with a 15 cm long one sided blade, tapering to a point. Tests identified small amounts of blood from both the defendant and the deceased on the blade and handle.

'And are you able to match the knife with the wounds?'

Kohler frowned. 'All I can say is that this knife,' he said holding it up for the jury to see again, 'could certainly have made those wounds.'

Patterson studied his notes. 'We now come to the clothing found in the washing machine. Tell us about the traces of blood you found.'

Kohler too looked down at his notes for a moment and then told the jury that the jeans and tee shirt could have been drenched in blood but they would never know, as when they got to the clothing in the wash, it was saturated with water and washing powder, but, they had found a small trace of Safia's blood in the turn up on the left leg of the jeans.

'And finally, doctor, you examined the small cut found on the defendant's hand when he was arrested. What can you tell us about that?' Patterson asked.

'All I can say about that is that it was a small cut across the palm of the left hand between finger and thumb. In terms of age it could certainly have been made at the time of death and by the knife found in the drain, but it is impossible to say more than that or whether the wound was a defensive wound, self-inflicted or just an accident.'

'Thank you doctor; if you would wait there please,' Patterson said, concluding the examination in chief of his final witness.

Feldman looked at me expectantly as I remained seated at the defence table. 'Mr. Calver, cross examination?'

I rose to my feet. 'Thank you, my Lord,' I said, turning to face the pathologist. 'Doctor Kohler,' I said, studying his pathology report, 'did you find anything inside the stab wounds themselves, that is, within the flesh or bone in the body that, how can I put it,' I said watching the jury as their ears pricked up, 'shouldn't have been there?'

'Yes, we found a very small piece of metal, perhaps 3 millimetres squared, lodged in one of the left side ribs,' he answered, and I heard a slight undercurrent of murmuring from the jury box.

What I loved about most home office pathologists was that they weren't just prosecution whores; they usually told it like it was, and didn't give a toss about any agenda that the prosecutor might have; I was hoping that Kohler was of that school. 'Did you ascertain where this small piece of metal might have come from?' I asked him.

'Unfortunately we were unable to do that.'

'Could it, for example,' I said, looking over at the jury, again, 'have come from the carving knife found in the drain?'

'It didn't. We carried out a minute examination of the knife and there are no breakages or parts missing, and more importantly, the metal does not match.'

'I'll come back to that point in a moment, doctor, if I may, but turning to the size of entry wounds, there are various measurements in your report, yes?'

'That's correct.'

'Now, the carving knife has a blade width where it meets the handle – that's where it's widest – of just 1 centimetre, yes?'

'Yes.'

'Looking at your admirable report, doctor, it seems to me that many of the entry wounds measure far wider than 1 cm. How can that be?'

'Well, it could be because of movement of the blade in the wound, either because the victim was twisting and turning to evade the blade, or because the perpetrator twisted or moved the blade in the wound,' he answered, keeping his eyes down on his report.

'Forgive me, doctor, but if that were the case, would not the wounds be more ragged; these wounds were by and large, clean.'

'You would tend to expect that, yes,' he said.

'Actually, doctor, given the presence of that small piece of metal lodged in the rib, and the fact that the majority of these entry wounds are far wider than the width of the carving knife, isn't it far more likely that in fact these wounds were made by a completely different knife?'

'I can't answer that with any degree of precision,' he said after a slight pause.

'Off hand, doctor, can you think of any other way, that that small piece of metal could have ended up in that wound, other than from the tip of a knife breaking off when it got stuck in the rib?'

Kohler remained mute, looking down at his report.

'Doctor?' I prompted him.

'I can't exclude it,' he finally said.

Well hallelujah! I thought, but it didn't get me very far. Maybe Khan just used two knives and took the other one away with him. Even so it was progress of a sort and maybe got me a little closer to reasonable doubt.

'Finally, doctor, the slight wound to Mr Khan's hand is consistent with it being caused accidentally, yes?'

'Yes, along with a number of other possibilities.'

'Thank you, doctor.'

Patterson was on his feet. 'That concludes the case for the prosecution, my lord.'

I sat there as the stress ebbed out of me, feeling like a wrung out dish cloth. I vaguely pondered our options. Asking the judge to dismiss the charge on the basis that the prosecution hadn't made out a *prima facie* case was plainly hopeless, so I guessed I would have to sit down with the team and try and come up with something like a strategy.

It was only just gone noon but as it was Friday and I wasn't near ready to start the defence case I was hoping Feldman was going to adjourn, and thankfully he did, directing us all to reconvene Monday morning at 10 am sharp for the start of the defence case.

I was already due to meet Pascal for lunch later, so I texted her to get there half an hour early. With the crown resting, I felt like splashing out a little of Khan senior's money on some decent nosh.

Chapter Fifteen

Corvino's was a hidden gem tucked away about two minutes walk from the court. Select and expensive, it was somewhere to go if you wanted a bit of exclusivity and privacy. Needless to say I rarely ventured there unless a client was paying, an event about as rare as a meteor strike, but today, with the crown resting, I fancied it.

Inside it felt like twilight; low lights and large plants casting flickering shadows across the coloured mosaics on the walls. I was led by a harassed looking Italian waiter to a table towards the rear of the seating area. The restaurant was busy and there was the quiet hum of wealth and lively conversation combining with the clink of glasses and the waft of good Italian food seeping out of the kitchen.

I studied the menu.

'Jesus, Calver, where d'you find this place?' Pascal said, as she slid into the seat opposite. As the waiter hovered I ordered a double Scotch on the rocks for me and a Margarita for Pascal, and to save him coming back, I ordered straightaway a bottle of Mouton Cadet and the veal for me and Pascal went for Lasagna.

'Christ, Courtney, I take you to one of the best Italian restaurants in London, and you order a fucking Lasagna,' I said, slowly shaking my head. 'Maybe we should have just gone to Pizza Express.'

We shot the breeze awhile as we waited for the grub and I ordered us another round. I was just telling a rather bad joke, trying to engage her; when I looked to check how it was going down, expecting to see at least a smile, she was looking past me, over my shoulder, towards the entrance, with a rather strange kind of strained expression on her face. She said slowly, 'of all the gin joints in all the towns....,' and let the unfinished sentence hang there.

I quickly looked around and there was James Patterson being led to a table about half way down the room, and behind him was Carmen.

What can I say? The world stood still. My heart stopped. Maybe all those things. And she looked great, pure class in a smart blue tailored suit. Patterson stiffened when he saw me, and then quickly recovering, nodded uncomfortably. Then Carmen spotted me, and for a second I thought it was joy on her face, just for a second, but maybe I was deluding myself. Then whatever I'd seen was gone, replaced by the mask she showed to the world, and then there was a brief, tight smile and a nod in my direction. Then she whispered a comment to Patterson and they both laughed; maybe it was a little forced, and maybe it was for my benefit.

'D'you want to go, Jonas?' Pascal asked.

'No way,' I said as our food arrived and the wine was uncorked and poured. We started to eat and I struggled to make some light conversation, but I couldn't concentrate and all the time I wanted to turn around and look or go over.

'Look. She's here now, so deal with it, or let's leave,' Pascal said. Then she frowned and said. 'Look, Calver, you can tell me to fuck off if you like, but sometimes it helps to talk, so why don't you? I followed the trial at the time and I know she kept the guy out of prison with an alibi, but what was it all about. She's the love of your life, and you split; something doesn't add up.'

Apart from Emma, I'd never really discussed what had happened with anyone, least of all Pascal, who had never shown the slightest interest in my personal life, but maybe it would help to talk, I'd tried everything else. I finished my veal up and took a shot of wine.

'Jonny White, druggie ex, and father of Carmen's daughter, Tyra,' I said as I swirled the red wine around the bowl of my glass, sniffed it and took another shot. 'I don't think there's much doubt that he murdered the Turkish drug dealer. Carmen provided him with an alibi. He couldn't have killed the guy, because he was two hundred miles away tucked up in bed with her. And she was unshakeable; I mean rock solid – I know, I was at the trial and watched – and she didn't give an inch when the prosecution laid into her on their cross.'

'I don't understand,' Pascal said. 'If, as you so clearly believe, he was killing the Turk two hundred miles away, then he wasn't sleeping with your wife. What's your problem? You may be clever, Calver, but you really don't get the simple stuff. Carmen's motive is her daughter, and you should know there's nothing a mother won't do to protect her child. However much of a scumbag he is, for her daughters sake, she would not want the guy in prison for life, if she could avoid it – think about it, Calver.'

'Guess what? I have thought about it, and I don't buy it. I've never believed what she told me, not a hundred percent,' I said, pausing, unable to quite keep from choking up, then continuing, quietly, 'she betrayed me, Courtney. She ripped my fucking heart out, and stomped all over it. Snorting coke, when she'd promised she'd never touch it again, and—' I stopped, trying to grab a breath, getting worked up again, 'and, screwing that slime ball dealer who's almost certainly a murderer as well, and now look at her. Shacked up with that fucking reptile, knowing that I'll keep bumping into him – even having to go up against him – for the rest of my career.' I stopped, played out, becoming maudlin as the wine lethally mixed in with the scotch. Then the red mist was coming down and I was off again, but this time it was physical and I was on my feet, turning and walking, weaving slightly, to their table. I could hear Pascal's, *don't*, Calver,' ringing in my ears, but it was too late to stop now, I was at their table, and they were both looking up at me, surprised.

And then, as I looked down at her, all the rage was gone and all the memories and longings welled up and overwhelmed me, leaving me speechless.

'Jonas,' she nodded up at me, self-contained, showing nothing but a faint half smile. 'It's good to see you. Tyra's been asking after you, how are you?'

'How is he, she asks,' Patterson said, jovially, trying to keep things on an even keel. 'He's been giving me hell all week, and she asks how he is. Why he's fine, aren't you Calver, my boy.'

'I ain't your fucking boy, Patterson; that would be Feldman,' I said, turning back to Carmen.

She took a deliberate sip of her spring water and looked down at the table. 'I think you should go, Jonas. You're drunk.' Then she turned to Patterson and took his hand in both hers, and said, 'and we should be going too darling. Get the bill, I'm going to freshen up,' she said, ignoring me, rising and walking away.

As Patterson watched her go, a smug look of proprietorship on his face, he said, without looking up at me, 'I can't wait for you to put your witnesses on, Calver, because I'm going to bury you, and when I'm done, we'll get you disbarred as well.' Then he looked up at me, face devoid of expression, and said, 'and I don't want you bothering Carmen again – she finds it very distressing. Oh I've seen you, Calver, hanging around outside the house in Cheyne Walk. Happens again, I'll be seeking a stalker injunction, and you'll be talking to the police.'

Even with the alcohol I'd had, I could feel the hot flush of shame running up my neck. I said nothing, as I had nothing left to say. I walked back to our table. Pascal had gone, but she'd left a yellow post-it note stuck to my brief case. It read: "you're a fucking asshole Calver, but I understand. I'm going to do some digging." Do some digging? What the hell was she talking about? My alcohol addled brain tried to process what had just happened. I gave up and chucked some notes on the table and left.

Saturday morning I sat in the Queen Elizabeth and finished up another full English breakfast, smacking my lips as I wiped greasy egg yolk off the plate with the last of my buttered toast. Pascal watched, flicking her eyes between me and the TV screen up behind the bar. I worked the small Tabasco bottle, jerking a couple of dollops into my Bloody Mary and then took a long hard pull, my first of the day.

We didn't talk about Corvino's.

'I'm thinking of calling Syed, our taxi driver lover boy, and I don't want to subpoena him – he needs to come voluntarily as our witness,' I said, eyeing up Melissa, our beautiful black barmaid, as she carried a plate stacked full of bacon rolls over to a table of construction workers.

'Jesus, Calver, haven't you had enough grease for one morning,' Pascal said, watching the guys as they fell on the bacon rolls. She turned back to me, and said, 'what makes you think lover boy's going to come to court for us? You've practically accused him of carrying out the murder. Why's he going to want to help Khan?'

'That's where you come in, my friend,' I said. 'I want you to go and persuade him. Lie, if you have to, but get him to court. I'll decide whether to call him when he's there, but just get him there, okay'

'Thanks, Calver. Sounds like a real easy one. So why don't you do it?'

'Hey, you wanta earn some extra money or not? You know the score. I can't talk to witnesses,' I said.

She was about to argue some more when a young woman approached us.

'So this is where you run your law practice is it, Mr. Calver?' Dr. Rose Tremayne said, her face appearing as she slowly unwound a long scarf. She looked around, slipping off an expensive looking leather jacket with a load of zips and tassels, and then slid into the seat opposite.

'Only on Saturday mornings, Doctor,' I lied. 'Thanks for coming.' I introduced her to Pascal who went to the bar and got her a coffee, and then said she'd go and see Syed, but would need a cash top up before Monday, so I took out my wallet and peeled off a couple of fifties.

'Thanks for the *expenses*, Calver,' she said, nodding to Rose Tremayne and then making her way out.

Rose raised an amused eyebrow. 'Wow! Glad she's on our side.'

'Yeah. Well, sometimes I wonder about that,' I said, only half joking.

'Look, as I said on the phone, I don't have much time, so what is it you need to know?' she said, serious now. She'd only agreed to drop in as she was driving down to see her mother.

I said, 'the prosecution rested Friday, so come Monday morning, I have to put on the defence case. Before too long we'll have to decide whether to call

Mohsin to give evidence, but right now I have to finalise our strategy for the rest of the trial, and for that I need to hear from you about where you are with Khan and his treatment. Two questions: are you getting anywhere with unlocking his memories and is he actually capable of giving evidence, because to have any chance of winning, I'm guessing he'll probably have to, although the final call on that will be his.'

'Whew,' she said looking at her watch again. 'Well, he is starting to recover memory. You know that from the stuff he gave you about him and Safia reconciling and trying again.'

'Yeah,' I said slowly, wondering just how much of that had been reality and how much convenient wishful thinking on Khan's part, but I kept silent.

Rose continued, 'but it is slow, but, the more he remembers, the quicker it seems to come, but of course, times the one thing we don't have. I think he will be fit to give evidence, but I need more time with him. Now, I really have to go,' she said getting up and putting her jacket back on. 'As to what he might say in the witness box……….' she said as an afterthought

My thoughts entirely, but all I said was, 'thanks for stopping by, Rose. If you could maybe double up on the treatment and see what we get, that would be good.'

'I'll be happy to. He's a good man,' she said, and then added after a loaded pause, 'I think.'

I waved her off, feeling better because I knew she was solid, someone we could rely on and most important of all, I knew the jury would like her.

Chapter Sixteen

Pascal stood in the waiting room of Star Taxis and looked around the shabby interior. Through an open hatchway she could see a large woman wearing an earpiece and mike, vigorously directing cabs for pick up. The woman turned to Pascal and asked, 'where you going, love?'

Pascal gave her an address in central London and said she wanted to spring a little surprise on an old friend; could she get Rashid Syed to do the run, but not tell him who the fare was.

The woman smiled conspiratorially, scrutinising Pascal, eyeing up the heavy dark clothing, thick black and white Goth makeup and orange hair. 'Why don't you come through here, dear; let me have a look at you,' she said.

As Pascal came through the woman confirmed something on her head piece and said, 'Rash's on his way – five, ten minutes.'

Pascal nodded and came through, smiling tentatively as she looked around the pokey paper strewn office. She took a seat next to the woman who was now taking another call on her head set. Spread over the table were work sheets, rota's and driver call out sheets that the woman was working on as she fielded calls; a folder containing completed sheets also lay open there. Whilst the woman watched another punter come into the waiting room and took another call, Pascal casually leafed through a few pages until she found the date of the murder, her eyes intently traversing the pages which showed in columns: driver, timed call-out, pick-up and destination, all initialled by the drivers.

As a particularly loud crackle of static came through the headpiece and while the dispatchers head was still turned away, Pascal suddenly ripped the sheet out of the folder, flicking some pages over to cover the loss, and spirited the stolen sheet under her jacket, just as the woman turned back to face her.

There was faint look of suspicion on the woman's face, as if she was aware that something had just happened, but she couldn't quite work out what it was. Then more noise through her headpiece distracted her again and she gestured towards the door, 'Rash is outside sweetheart; nice to have met you,' she said.

Pascal scrambled into the front seat of the car, keeping her head turned away, mumbling the destination as she squirmed around fastening her seatbelt. The cab moved off slowly into traffic and then Syed turned to get a look at her.

'You!' he said, anger and maybe a bit of panic in his voice. 'Look, I've told you all I know. Now I want you to leave me alone.'

'Hey, Rash. Cool down baby. I just want to talk. I've found a way for you to get back in good with Mina, and maybe even get a shot at holding onto your two boys.'

His look was guarded and suspicious but the reference to his two sons had grabbed his attention, as she'd known it would. Pascal studied him; he looked tired and stressed, unshaven with dark rings under the eyes, and even his shock of pitch black heavily gelled hair, drooped disappointingly.

'Rashid, you don't look so good. You sleeping on the couch, yeah? Listen, we can help you turn things around. My boss, Jonas Calver wants to call you for the defence. It's your chance to set the record straight, to put your side. If anything's going to get Mina back on side, it'll be that.'

'I don't know man,' he said slowly, turning it over in his head. 'In the paper, man, that Calver, lawyer guy, he saying *I* done it. Me! What the fuck's that all about?'

'Rash, that's just lawyer talk. He has to say that, but now he wants you to get on the stand and tell everyone, especially Mina, what happened. You weren't going to leave Mina. This was just a bit of fun. It got out of hand and you deeply regret it,' she said, slowly piling it on.

But now Rashid could see it, and he was slowly nodding his head, a small hopeful smile creeping onto his face. 'That's right,' he said, nodding some more. 'That's right. Mina will see that, won't she?'

'Of course she will, Rash. All you have to do is be there Monday morning at 9.45 at the Old Bailey.'

His smile faded a bit and he stopped nodding as the thought of appearing in court hit home. 'I don't know, man. I'm not so sure. What if he twists things around?'

'He wont,' she said, impatiently. Then she slowed down again remembering that she had to persuade, not bully or she wouldn't be able to pull him around. 'Look do you want to lose your two sons? You don't patch things up with her right now, it'll happen, and you know it. Mina's no traditional Muslim housewife, she'll divorce you, and we all know what will happen to the kids if that happens. How bad d'you want your kids, Rash?'

That clinched it, as she'd known it would. 'Okay, okay. I'll be there.'

'You won't regret it, Rash,' she said, wondering how true that was likely to be. 'You can drop me here,' she added, handing him a twenty as she stepped out near Tower Hill tube station.

As Mohsin Khan leant forward a drop of sweat slowly rolled down his forehead and then sheared off, splashing onto the work surface below. He blinked and then wiped the old tennis wristband across his eyes. He was seated on a high stool and on the workbench in front of him was a miniature cylindrical vice in which was held a small plastic circular looking object. Khan drew in a long breath through the white nose and mouth guard covering the lower half of his face and pulled the small magnifying goggles down from his forehead over his eyes, then he leant forward again and made a tiny adjustment to the device with a small pointed instrument like a screw driver. Then he leaned back, sighed and pushed the goggles back up again and glanced over at the computer screen at the side and the three D image that was slowly spinning around on the screen; it seemed just about identical to what was held in the vice.

Khan put the pointed instrument down, pulled the goggles off and got up and stretched. His muscles ached; he'd been working straight through for around three hours and he was just about played out. He looked around the little work room with its wall racks of tools, the couple of desks with computer screen and the long work bench, then his eyes flicked over the large 2.5 litre container of nitric acid on the work bench and then further up, just under the extractor fan, the large partially covered container of battery acid. He moved over and looked into the liquid, checking on the water evaporation, and nodded to himself, satisfied at progress. Then he looked out of the little window into the rose bushes and lawned area outside. Hard to believe it was just a shed in someone's garden he was standing in.

It had been a long day. It had started when Qadir's man had picked him up and then taken him on a hair-raising and tortuous car journey the obvious intent of which was to foil anyone who might have wanted to try and follow them. At one stage the big man driving the car had executed a complete turn across two lanes of traffic amid much frantic hooting and screaming of obscenities. Then on to a small terraced house where his ankle tag had somehow been neutralised or subverted, as the nerdy guy had called it, something that took all of five minutes. Apparently it would indicate he was where he should be for the next six hours before reverting to real time.

Then it was on to the garden shed in the grounds of an old ramshackle house in Stoke Newington. The property was in the process of being converted into flats and the shed wouldn't be due for demolition until the second stage of building work, not due for another eight months or so, and until then it would remain fenced off from the builders and the work site. If you wanted somewhere quiet, cut off from prying eyes, you would be hard put to think of a better place.

Khan checked his watch, grimaced and pulled his face mask off. The big man would be here soon to take him back.

Sunday had been draining, prepping up the defence case most of the day and then long phone calls with Khan senior, Rose Tremayne, and then fielding calls from Pascal about Syed, who she'd spoken to, and Nicky Holloway, who she was going to speak to. And then I'd had to wrestle with what to do about Syed, our taxi driver lover boy who Pascal had assured me would be at court first thing, when I'd finally have to decide; should I call him or not?

The problem I had was that the prosecution had not called Syed as a witness, but I still wanted to cross examine the hell out of him, but the rules of evidence said you can't cross examine your own witness. But if I got him on the stand as our witness, even though objectively he had nothing positive to say about our case and it was maybe dubious ethically and high risk, there were a couple of tricks we could try, to engineer a situation where the court would have to allow me to cross examine him. In the end I figured things were going so badly we really had nothing to lose, so let's throw the dice and call the guy.

But now standing in court Monday morning with a decidedly ill at ease Rashid Syed sitting before me in the witness box, I wasn't so sure. I started off with a few innocuous questions to try and relax him, but I wasn't helped by Mohsin sitting in the dock and glowering at the witness, the most animated I had seen him for a long time. So I cut to the chase. 'What was your relationship with Safia Khan, Mr. Syed?' I asked him.

He looked up at Feldman, nervous, body language shot to hell, 'your honour—I, I'm not sure about this now.'

Mild consternation on Feldman's face as he considered the witness and weighed up what was going on here whilst I leaned back against my chair, relaxed. 'Well I'm afraid, Mr Syed, that now you're here, you must answer the questions put to you.'

Syed looked down for a moment, and then swallowed quickly before reluctantly nodding.

'Mr. Syed?' I prodded him.

'We—we were good friends, that's all,' he said, hesitantly.

I looked down at my papers. 'Well, it was a bit more than that wasn't it, Mr. Syed?' I asked smoothly, but Patterson was already on his feet.

'My Lord, it might be worth reminding my friend that *he* called Mr Syed, and he should accept the answers he's given, rather than trying to cross examine his own witness when he doesn't quite get the answer he's looking for.'

'Quite so, Mr. Patterson,' Feldman replied, then turning to me, added, 'if you don't understand the basic rules of evidence, Mr. Calver, perhaps you shouldn't be practising in my court? You must accept the answers given by your witness. Now proceed.'

'Fine,' I nodded mildly, before turning back to Syed. 'Mr. Syed, perhaps you can tell the jury how many times you had sexual intercourse with Safia?' I asked.

I heard the expected rustle of his court gown as Patterson catapulted himself skyward, but this time, my witness was having none of it, much as I'd hoped. 'Your honour that's not right, what he's saying. It wasn't like that. Look, I don't want to answer no more questions,' Syed said.

And then Patterson was blustering as well, 'my Lord, again, my friend attempts to lead his own witness.'

I had remained standing throughout this little squall, and now I said, 'my Lord, given that the witness is declining to answer defence questions or is answering in a way which is inconsistent with a previous statement given to the defence, I would like to make an application in the absence of the jury.'

I had had an inkling that this might happen and Syed had played into my hands. If your own witness refuses to answer your questions or says things inconsistent with what they had said before you can ask the court to declare the witness as "hostile", and then you can cross examine.

Feldman was predictably all over me as the door closed behind the jury but it was mainly bluster, as what I was doing was within the rules. In the end, Patterson looking ahead and clearly seeing that what I was doing was unlikely to damage his case much, gave Feldman a way out.

'Judge, I agree with you,' Patterson said, 'but I have to say for the crown that we're essentially neutral on this witness; we chose not to call him, given the strength of the other evidence. Frankly, if Calver wants to go down this road, let him, and if you were to take the view his behaviour is improper in any way, then no doubt you would take the necessary action, at the end of the trial.'

Feldman nodded, weighing things. He snapped his notebook shut and said, 'we will proceed on the basis set out by the crown. Call the jury back in.'

As the jury were taking their seats I skipped over to the witness box and whispered to Syed out of the corner of my mouth, 'behave and answer a few quick questions and I'll have you outta here.'

Then we were back up and running again. 'Now, Mr Syed,' I said, 'you made a statement to my assistant, Ms Pascal sometime ago, and in that statement, you said, and I quote, "I loved her. I loved Safia more than life itself. Still do". Now that's a little more definitive than, "it was a fling", don't you think?'

I handed copies of the statement to the usher for Patterson, Feldman and Syed. It had been taken by Pascal from Syed weeks ago when she had first questioned him.

Syed looked down at the statement, obviously confused. 'I don't remember this; I was upset, yeah,' he said, a thin edge of resentment creeping into his voice.

'Okay, well perhaps you can help me with this,' I said, 'isn't it true that your wife Mina had left you and taken your two sons and gone to her mothers, when she found out about the affair?'

'No, no....' he started to reply but I came back in fast.

'and then when you heard Safia was going back to Mohsin Khan for a reconciliation, you were angry weren't you? You didn't want to lose your two sons did you?'

Patterson was still idly scanning the statement he'd just been handed. I turned back and faced the jury. 'Where were you on the night of the murder at ten to eight?' I asked Syed. The question was grossly improper on a number of grounds, but I figured Patterson and Feldman would just assume there was something about it in the statement they had just been handed and which they were avidly reading, allowing me to raise it — there wasn't.

'I don't know man,' he said after a moment, clearly puzzled and slightly unsettled at the turn my questions had taken.

I glanced over at Patterson; he was reading and down to the last page.

'Perhaps I can refresh your memory', I said, holding up copies of the taxi log Pascal had provided me with, and passing it to the usher for distribution.

'Your taxi log for that evening shows you had a pick up from an address three doors down from Safia's flat, timed at ten to eight, the time of the murd—,'

The end of my question was lost, engulfed in the cacophony of sound erupting around the court from the jury, the public gallery and Patterson. Feldman looked like a general who had just lost control of his troops. I sat down to let things settle, thinking maybe we'd just edged a little closer to the Holy Grail of reasonable doubt. Time would tell. I looked up and winked at Mohsin, and he actually smiled.

Chapter Seventeen

Pascal stood outside the squat in Bethnal Green, East London and waited. The house looked like a fortress; the door had heavy duty boarding riveted on, and Pascal knew from experience that there would be furniture piled up on the other side, blocking entry to all, especially any bailiffs who might come along and attempt to evict the occupants.

She'd called earlier and left a message for Holloway on the number given to her by Mohsin Khan. She banged again noisily on the door whilst she looked around the garbage strewn front garden. Noise from above; she looked up as a small window was opened and the face of Nicky Holloway appeared, blowsy with sleep, uncomprehending.

'Nicky,' she shouted up, 'Pascal, remember? We need to talk, so shake a leg.'

He watched her for a moment, and then it was like a light bulb going on as his addled brain registered that there might be some smack in the offing. 'Come down the side, there's a broken window, but you'll have to climb through,' he said, voice croaky, but you could hear the urgency; a man full of craving.

Pascal scrambled through the window and picked her way up the darkened staircase over various obstacles towards the light splaying out from an open door on the landing above.

Inside she was surprised at how clean and Spartan the room looked; a single spring bed with just a blanket over it, a table on which there was a milk carton, an ashtray full of cigarette butts, some drug paraphernalia – burnt foil, spoon and hypodermic needles – and an old-fashioned portable TV spewing out the ubiquitous Jeremy Kyle show. Then another smaller table set up against the wall in the corner on which sat a large open book, which Pascal guessed was the Koran, as well as a photograph in a frame and a small plastic style wallet.

Holloway stood rubbing his hands and looking at her expectantly. Pascal, determined to draw things out, tee the guy up so he would be begging to talk, didn't speak. She moved over to the smaller table and opened the wallet; it held a selection of sharp knives or, perhaps more properly, scalpels. She looked up at Holloway, 'what, you a surgeon now, Nicky boy?'

'Medic,' he said impatiently, anxious to get on to the important stuff. 'Royal Army Medical Corps attached to the Battalion. Just like to keep my hand in, like. Look, man, can you give me something?' He paused rubbing his hands over his face. 'You want me to talk. I'll talk, but you gotta give me something, yeah?'

Pascal studied him for a moment. He looked down at his feet, and moved his weight from one foot to the other. Pascal took out a fake mobile phone, opened it and broke off a small piece of heroin. Holloway watched her every move, eyes brightening, tongue running along his dry lips. 'Oh, man, what d'you expect me to do with that?' he asked.

'I need you to talk, Nicky, not trip out and give me a load of junkie bullshit. Talk the talk, you'll get a nice chunk, and, Nicky, this shit is pure, so watch it.'

That seemed to mollify him; he quickly grabbed the chunk of horse and moved to the table where he set about cooking up a fix with a lighter, spoon and hypo. As he tightened a belt around his arm and looked for an undamaged vein, Pascal picked up the framed photograph; it looked like the same photo Calver had taken from the crime scene.

She walked over to the bed where he was now lying, head back against the wall, eyes closed. 'Happy days, eh, Nicky,' she said, handing him the photograph. 'Who's the other guy?'

He slowly opened his eyes, looking serene now, face calm and relaxed as the poison coursed through his veins. He smiled as he remembered back.

'That's Milesy – Miles Franklyn – my dead brother in arms. God rest his soul.'

Pascal picked up the milk carton, wishing she had something a bit stronger, sniffed it tentatively and then took a couple of gulps, pondering. With a junkie you had to be careful, give him just enough to keep him on an even keel and get your story, but not too much so that you push him over the edge. Although Holloway was now slightly junked up she still needed to relax him, get him comfortable so he would talk freely. She said, 'so, Nicky, you boys were tight out there I guess?'

'Oh yeah,' he said slowly, beauteous smile spreading across his face, part heroin, part warm memories. 'There were four of us originally. Big Frankie Crawford's not in the picture, as he was moved out of the unit towards the end. We were like the Beatles, man, the fab four, only with guns instead of guitars.'

'There were good times I know, Nicky, but some bad shit as well. Mohsin got stabbed out there, and you saved him, right?'

A shadow crossed his face and the smile slipped; his eyes still shut, he said, 'we saved him alright. Me, Milesy and Frankie. Fuckin Taliban, but we sorted them.'

'I bet you did, Nicky. Tell me what happened,' Pascal said, pushing again.

'Hey, read the report,' he said, 'and how about another hit, man?' voice tetchy again.

'What report?' Pascal said. There was no record of a report that she was aware of.

He waived his hand vaguely, 'There was a board enquiry, man, I'm sure; look at the papers, yeah. We went in and Mohsin was hanging back on the radio; he got nabbed by the guy with the knife and I shot him.'

Pascal absently took out the mobile case and extracted another small lump of heroin, and then idly bounced it up and down in her hand as Holloway watched, licking his lips and rubbing his hands.

'What happened to you four at the end, Nicky? Fill me in on that, and this is yours.'

He eyed the small ball of heroin in Pascal's hand, still bouncing up and down. 'There's no mystery. Frankie, I lost touch with when he was moved out.

We was never great mates. I think he's still out there. But Milesy. Milesy was shot by a sniper, brought back a vegetable and his mum switched off the life support.'

'Did Milesy ever regain consciousness after he got back?'

'He was gone, man,' he replied wistfully, 'and he never came back.'

'Pascal tossed the small lump of heroin to Holloway.

After another two hours of rather tortuous questioning, Pascal had very little to show for it. She wrapped things up by reminding him to make sure he kept his phone on as he would get a call from Calver's office telling him when to be at court – meaning drug free – ready to give evidence. When he started to complain, she confirmed he would get a small snifter before starting his evidence, and a major fix at the close of play, which seemed to placate him.

As I entered judges chambers Patterson and Feldman were already there, deep in conversation. What worried me though was that they looked calm and relaxed; that didn't make sense, not after the little show I'd just put on.

As I took my seat Feldman, smiling pleasantly, said, 'you know, Calver, I might have been willing to overlook you breaching a few procedural or evidential rules, but using those taxi logs – no, not in my court. What you pulled today won't stand.'

I was confused. I said, 'and just what did I *pull* today?'

'Well we can start with handling stolen goods,' Patterson said, 'and then take your pick: conspiracy, perverting the course of justice.'

'Whoa there,' I said, mystified, but I could feel a small chill starting to spread through my gut. 'Just what the hell are you talking about?'

Feldman, now running the show, said, 'as I'm sure you're well aware, Calver, the Taxi logs you so memorably waived around in front of the jury, were in fact stolen, this very weekend as it happens. Furthermore, the crown inform me that the police already have a prime suspect based on information received from the taxi firm.' He looked down at his notes. ' A miss Courtney

Pascal apparently, who I understand is currently in your employ as an outside clerk?'

I felt icy fingers of fear closing round my stomach, then blinding rage. Rage at Pascal for not telling me about something so fundamental – that she'd nicked the logs – something that could wreck our whole case, end my career, and send her back to prison.

I took a few deep breaths trying to steady myself, trying not to let it overwhelm me. In situations like this, when I'm at a complete loss and everything is turning to shit, I usually come out firing scattergun, just hoping for a hit. 'If there's any allegation of criminal behaviour against me, or those associated with me, I categorically deny it,' I said with as much bluster as I could manage, desperately hoping that Pascal wouldn't be picked up by the police before I could get to her.

I continued, 'and until you have compelling evidence, rather than dodgy ID hearsay, you have no choice but to proceed on the basis that my production of this evidence was bone fide. If you will allow me to, I can quickly get Syed to verify the taxi logs as being legitimate, irrespective of how they came to be here. Indeed, under English law, even if the logs were stolen, it does not automatically mean they are inadmissible.'

Feldman looked taken aback by my last assertion, but Patterson didn't, and now he leaned forward in his chair, and said, 'judge, that's actually right. Just because the logs are stolen doesn't mean you have to exclude them. However I would ask you to use your discretion under s.78 Police and Criminal Evidence Act 1984 and exclude them anyway, because their admission as evidence, given their dodgy provenance, would likely endanger trial fairness.'

'Judge I—' I began

'Thank you, Mr. Patterson. I quite agree,' Feldman said, ignoring me. 'That is exactly what we shall do. You may have thought, Mr. Calver,' he said, turning to face me, 'that its too late to change what you've done, but you're wrong. I will be directing the jury to ignore Syed's evidence in it's entirety and he will now be discharged.

'And if it turns out that you, or any of your associates had any hand in the theft of this evidence, not only will I see to it that charges are brought, I will also make sure that you are struck off the Solicitors Roll and that you never practice again in our courts. D'you hear me,' he said, sideburns jostling madly up and down as he tried to maintain some semblance of calm.

'Now, unless there's anything else, gentlemen, we shall go back in to court and you, Mr. Calver, will call your next witness,' he said, slamming his desk diary closed for emphasis.

I exhaled slowly as the pent up tension dissipated. The fact is, whatever Feldman did, it was out there now and the jury had seen me flourish the taxi logs and wave them around my head and they were unlikely to forget it, whatever Feldman said. But that was small comfort when set against the catastrophe that would engulf us if the police could prove Pascal took the logs and she was acting under my orders; that didn't bear thinking about. Meantime I needed to leave them with a bit of bluster and remind them we were still in the game, even if we weren't..

'Two points, judge,' I said. 'I disagree with your ruling, especially as you have refused to let me speak on the issue, and if I take the view at the end of this trial that it has prejudiced my client in any way whatsoever, I will not hesitate to use it as grounds for appeal.'

Feldman regarded me balefully. What did he care about an appeal, he'd got what he wanted; a way of slapping me down again, courtesy of Patterson, who I had no doubt had provided him with all the ammunition, and pushed it with the police. It was also beginning to dawn on me that the crown obviously knew Syed had been near the flat on the night of the murder and that's why they hadn't called him, but what could I do about that now? It was almost as if they'd suckered me into the little performance I had just given with the taxi logs so they could neutralise the offending evidence and then have Feldman exclude it as he had just done.

'Call your next witness, Mr. Calver,' Feldman finally said, rising from his seat.

'Eh, Judge. That was my second point,' I said. 'My next witness is Nicholas Holloway and we wont be able to get him here today. I had anticipated Syed would take the rest of the day what with cross examination.'

Feldman was clearly steaming, but probably knew it was time to cool off. 'Court will be adjourned until 10 am Wednesday morning. I'm afraid we won't be sitting tomorrow, as I've been called away again.

Chapter Eighteen

Mohsin Khan, knees creaking, stood up slowly and looked around. Prayers had just finished and the Mosque seemed strangely quiet. He made his way towards the exit, his mind, after a long dark period of apathy, now tentatively beginning to engage with the outside world again, and in particular with the trial and Calver's seemingly disastrous start to the defence case. Not only that, his father now worried that they had made the wrong choice with Calver, because he didn't really seem to know what the hell he was doing, and the judge obviously had no confidence in him, constantly sniping and cutting him down to size in front of the jury. And the thing was, maybe the judge was right. His father had spoken to contacts in the community and they had given him the name of a good Asian Queen's Counsel who could perhaps be persuaded to take over from Calver.

Khan rubbed his face; fuck it. All he really wanted to do was have a nice long spliff or a couple of shots of vodka and just forget about it all, but then the other thoughts that had begun to trouble him recently began to crowd in. What about his daughters? What kind of a life would they have if he wasn't around to protect them. For the first time he was starting to get a real feeling that he had to beat the rap, to get out and be there for them.

'How are you, my friend?'

The words came out of the blue, snapping him back from his thoughts. Maqsood Qadir had come up unnoticed, and now stood in front of him with that maddening smile on his face.

Qadir put a proprietorial arm around Khan and led him towards an alcove, saying, 'is it ready?'

Khan shrugged. 'I just have to pack and close it – maybe an hour's work.'

'Good. Schedules moved up. I need you to finish now, clean up the site and give the package to my driver and he will drop you back – he's waiting outside for you now,' he said, gesturing with his hand towards the back entrance.

Khan stood his ground, just watching the guy. He was getting tired of being ordered around by this fucking camel jockey, but then the thoughts of his daughters surfaced again. Qadir just watched him, seeing the realisation spread across his face; then that fucking maddening smile again. Khan turned on his heel and walked away towards the back exit trying to be as casual as possible but inside he was steaming with anger and resentment.

When Khan arrived at the garden shed in Stoke Newington he was glad it was quiet after another hair raising journey.

Now he sat on his high stool at the work bench and began slowly and painstakingly to finish packing the white substance he had mixed earlier into the small device held in the vice. It was hot and dangerous work and the sweat dripped down his face into his mouth mask and his goggles became steamed up so that he had to keep wiping them as he worked away. Eventually his work was done and he clipped firmly into place the smooth rubbery cover with plastic type rim. Then he leaned back and admired his handy-work. It looked the part, and he was proud of his workmanship, but then his faced turned grim as he remembered just what he had created. But he had no choice. He sighed, then ripped the face mask off and pushed the goggles up onto his head. He better clear up and get going; he wouldn't be coming back here if he had any say in the matter.

He carefully removed the plastic style box from the vice and packed it into a silver attaché case that had been specially designed with foam shaped interior moulded so the device fit snugly into it, essential to keep the item stable in transit; then he clipped the case shut and locked it. He spent the next hour laboriously cleaning up the shed, all the surfaces, the packaging and all the chemicals, placing all the detritus into plastic bags for dumping in the bins on the street at the front. Then he took a last look around before quietly slipping out and padlocking the shed door.

Across the street Pascal watched Mohsin Khan emerge from the gap in the huge hedge fronting the heavily scaffolded building, and then carefully and furtively look around before climbing into the large black car with the mud obscured number plates. The car moved smoothly off into traffic as the door closed.

He sure as hell didn't have that silver attaché case when he'd gone in; something was going down, she thought. No point in following them as they would almost certainly be going back to base. She decided to stay and have a nose around. She hadn't followed Khan in before because the waiting driver would have seen her. Now she raised herself up from her prone position lying across the front seats of her beat up old Golf GTi and got out and slowly stretched. She'd been lying there for over an hour after the frenetic careering chase across London.

After scrambling around for twenty minutes on what was effectively a building site she almost missed the shed, but then caught a glimpse of it through its screen of covering trees. The padlock took her around twenty seconds to unlock with a hairpin, and then she was in.

She flicked the light switch and then leaned back against the door for at least five minutes, unmoving, just looking, acclimatising and feeling. The place looked very clean and ordered. She went to work, examining every inch of the place. A pretty good clean up job had been done, but Pascal knew that there was always a trace. However good and clever you were, there was always a trace.

It took her over an hour and when she'd finished she sat in her car for a long time, thinking. Then she took Lammy's card from her wallet and made the call.

'Hey, Courtney, I've been waiting,' Lammy said, picking up instantly. She was cool; no surprise in her voice, almost as if she really had been waiting for the call. Pascal so wanted to dent that smug tone.

'Let me guess, Lammy. Your sitting on your but wondering just how you're going to explain to *John*, how you and your boys lost Khan?'

There was silence, then Pascal twisted the knife. 'Hard to miss a big black car like that....' she said, and left it hanging.

'Okay, Courtney, you've had your fun, but you better tell me what you've got. Did you tail him from the Mosque?'

'Maybe,' she replied, slowly, playfully.

'Courtney, d'you really want to go up on a charge of withholding evidence,' she said, no longer friendly, an unpleasant edge to her voice.

'Hey, yank, this is my country. You want to fuck with me, you'll have to find me first, and given the fact that you couldn't even track that big black car across London, I don't give much for your chances,' Pascal said.

Silence; then Lammy said, 'Okay, okay, Courtney, calm down. Look, you're right, my ass is on the line and I'm on the clock, so help me. Did you see where he went?'

'Two things; not over the phone, and you don't tell Condon. We meet, now. We talk. That's it. Maybe we trade, maybe we don't. Come to my flat; I can be sure we're not being surveilled that way, and Averill—'

'Yeah.'

'Come alone and forget the wire; don't try and be cute.'

'Courtney, maybe you should try being a little more trusting' she said.

Pascal terminated the connection. Hell would freeze over before that happened.

An hour later they sat in Pascal's chaotic living room, Lammy cradling a large Scotch, Pascal supping from a bottle of Bud.

Lammy seemed skittish. She said, 'so you tailed him, Courtney?'

'You bet I did.'

'So. Where'd he go?'

'Not so fast. I want something in return.'

'Look, maybe he went down the drug store for a coke. If you have something, I need to know what it is; then maybe we can trade.'

'How about a bomb factory,' Pascal said, holding Lammy's gaze.

Lammy looked away, and said, 'you're kidding me?'

'Do I look like I'm kidding you?'

'What do you want, Courtney?'

'That's better,' Pascal said, taking another long drag on her bottle, emptying it in the process, and tossing it in the waste bin with a crash. Then she went and mixed herself a scotch and walked over and topped up Lammy's drink. She said as she screwed the cap back onto the bottle, 'there was an incident in Helmand, about three months before the brigade pulled out, when Khan was seriously injured in a knife attack. Holloway seems to think there was an enquiry, but I can't find any trace. I want to know what happened.'

'That's it?' Lammy said.

'No, that's not it. I want to know now, before I talk to you. Also you mentioned Calver's wife. I want to know what you have on that as well.'

'You don't want much do you, Courtney?'

'This is bullshit, Lammy. This stuff I want, it's nothing, so stop pissing me about. Anyway, there's another condition.'

'Which is?'

'If I talk to you, it doesn't leave this room.'

Lammy laughed suddenly, crazily, and said, 'are you out of your fucking mind, Courtney? A bomb factory, and I don't tell my boss—'

'And just who is your boss?' Pascal interrupted. 'Let me guess, probably CIA, via the Feds.'

'That's bullshit,' she answered too quickly, her face subtly reddening. 'Condon's got operational control, you know that. I can't keep something like this under my hat; *I* could even end up on a charge.'

'I understand that, but I'm not asking you to keep it under your hat forever.

You – and okay, me as well – have a chance to possibly break something big here. You report this, everyone gets picked up right now. They can't afford to let something like this run, and you know it. They go in now, they'll get nothing. I've seen it happen too many times.'

Lammy sipped her drink, saying nothing, watching Pascal and thinking. 'What do you suggest?' she finally asked. Then she added, 'you know, Courtney, I know what this about; you want back in, and you think this could do it for you.'

'Me and you, Lammy. Work together couple of days. See where it takes us. Shit hits the fan, I'll testify you didn't know, and I didn't tell you.'

'Tell me what you got now; if its what you say it is, we'll do it your way, but, if I get even the slightest hint of something imminent, that there's danger right now, I'm calling it in.'

Pascal held her gaze for a long moment, then slowly nodded, and said, 'I trailed him to a property in east London; big house undergoing extensive renovation, but hidden away in the back is a garden shed, but inside it's like NASA, but now stripped and wiped clean.'

Pascal walked over to her bag and gingerly felt around inside before removing a small see through evidence bag which she then carried over and carefully placed on the coffee table in front of Lammy. 'I think that that tiny piece of crystal I found on the work bench is Pentaerythritol tetranitrate.'

'Jesus,' Lammy exhaled. 'PETN. Carlos the Jackal used it in 1983 to bomb the Cultural centre in Berlin. Then that underpants guy on the Northwest Airlines flight to Detroit tried it. What was his name?'

'Abdulmutallab,' said Pascal. 'And Richard Reid, as well as a whole load of others.'

'What makes you think it's PETN?'

'Outside in the bins I found empty containers for Nitric acid and battery acid. My guess, he distilled sulfuric acid from the battery shit, and then mixed it up with the Nitro.'

'What about a detonator?' Lammy said.

'Don't know, but that's why I don't think they're quite ready. They've got the bomb – Khan left with an attaché case – but I think the detonator will come next and will depend on the target.'

'Jesus, Courtney, you can't know that. What if you're wrong?'

'I'm not. You know the deal. Take it or leave it,' Pascal said.

Lammy stood up and stretched and walked around the room studying some of the pictures and the computer screens. She said, 'okay, we've got a deal, reviewable minute by minute. Let's talk about what you want first. I had another look at all the papers we have on Khan, including the military stuff, before I came over, as I knew you'd be asking for something. The Helmand shit is easy; there was an enquiry of sorts but it doesn't seem to have ever reported and the guy heading it up has left the force. His name is Peter Kendricks, living in,' she looked down at her tablet screen, 'Colchester,' she said, and reeled off the address. Suggest you start there. On Calver, I'll have to come back to you. That one's not so easy. You'll have to trust me. I'm trusting you.'

'Good enough— for now,' Pascal said.

She freshened up Lammy's drink and took a seat across from her. They eyed each other up, warily, seemingly each fascinated by the other. As the silence stretched out, Lammy was the first to succumb to her curiosity.

'So what was SO14 like? I hear you were seconded for a while. D'you get to meet Queen?'

Pascal actually smiled. 'Are you kidding me? The Royalty Protection squad is the most mind numbingly boring job I've ever done. I think Condon sent me there as punishment, cause I wouldn't put out for him,' she said, then added, 'just kidding – about the last bit.

'It was like being imprisoned in a stately home for three months, and the only excitement was when some poor mentally unbalanced refugee from our wonderful care in the community system broke in and pissed on one of the Corgi's.'

Lammy laughed, a little stiffly, as she still couldn't quite tell whether Pascal was being serious or whether it was another example of the, to her, unfathomable British sense of humour.

'And I hear you're pretty good at Judo too,' Lammy said

'You have been doing your homework, but how about you?' Pascal asked, never eager to talk about herself.

'Me? I'm just a good old fashioned Texan gal,' she said, and that was about as much as Pascal was able to get out of her.

They talked for a few more minutes, and then Lammy was standing at the door ready to leave. Pascal leaned up and kissed her quickly on the lips and then leaned back watching her.

'Courtney, are you putting me on, or what?' Lammy said, laughing. 'It's unnerving.'

Pascal leaned in slowly as if for another kiss, but Lammy leaned away, and said, 'whoa there, honey. Look, I do like you, but not that way.'

'You sure?' Pascal said. There was a moment as their eyes held where Pascal was sure the ice maiden was weakening, something softened in her eyes, but then it had gone. But Pascal knew she'd unsettled her, which of course was the whole point of the exercise. Lammy leaned in and gave Pascal a chaste kiss on the cheek and then she left.

Chapter Nineteen

It was mid afternoon when Pascal climbed out of her beat up old Golf and finished off the takeout coffee she'd bought earlier, chucking the empty container back in the car with all the other crap, before slamming the door. She looked around at the grubby old block of flats fronting the car park, horrible old sixties red brick and white wood, dingy and depressing.

On the phone Kendricks had sounded puzzled and then intrigued, and he hadn't needed much of a push to invite her down to Colchester, but first she'd had to deal with Calver's bullshit about the taxi logs. She'd finally taken his call late the previous evening and he was in a rage by then, ranting about how if she was going to steal the logs, why didn't she tell him? She thought the answer to that was pretty obvious, but had kept her mouth shut which only seemed to increase his rage. So then she'd had to listen to an extended self pitying riff about how she was ruining his career, and their case – the court had chucked out all the evidence – and the police were looking for her, and if they caught up with her she'd be going back to gaol, and maybe its only what she deserved, but this time he'd probably be joining her. She'd told him to calm down, and that she was sorting it, but he wouldn't let it go, so eventually she'd thought, fuck him, and hung up.

In the end she was glad to get out of London and away from Calver and now she was anxious to get on and talk to Kendricks. She'd mugged up all she could find out about him, which wasn't much, and made a few phone calls as she'd driven down. He was 41, unmarried, and had been a Major in the Royal Military Police, or Red caps, with 4 Brigade, 156 Provost Company.

Now she sat in his sparsely furnished living room sipping a heavily sugared coffee and looking around trying to get a handle on the guy. Kendricks was slim, with a lined and sun bleached face, short cropped salt and pepper hair and thick black glasses, more like an English teacher than a soldier, she thought. She noticed when he took his glasses off to slowly clean them with a small silk cloth, that his eyes seemed very bright; he also seemed a little jumpy.

Pascal expanded on what she'd told him over the phone; she was an investigator for Mohsin Khan's defence team and that they were looking for information about what had happened to him in Afghanistan.

'I'm not entirely clear, miss Pascal,' Kendricks said, 'why any of that could possibly be relevant to a UK murder charge, or any possible defence he might have.'

'Well, part of our defence is going to involve PTSD and in order to bolster that we need to know what happened to him in Afghanistan. We know that there was a serious stabbing incident out there, and that's what I was hoping to talk to you about.'

Kendricks remained impassive, watching her, so she went on, 'because I understand you investigated it, but I'm confused, because there's no record of any report ever having been issued by you.'

Kendricks got up and walked over to the wide windows. He pulled aside a rather dank looking curtain to reveal overgrown communal gardens with some large plastic coloured toys strewn about amongst the washing lines and refuse bins. Kendricks looked out for a moment and then turned back into the room and said, 'you know, I loved the service and always will, but I loved something else more.'

Pascal watched him. 'Drugs?'

He walked back to the couch and now she could see, with the curtain open and some sunlight streaming in, the jerky hyper movements. 'You know how many soldiers are dishonourably discharged for drugs these days? It's a fucking epidemic, but they keep it quiet. I was lucky; I had a good record and a nice guy for a boss, so they hushed up my random test and let me ship out, but Christ, I do miss it. Look at what I've got now,' he said, gesturing around the room.

He sat down and took a tobacco tin from his pocket and began rolling a joint. 'You don't mind, do you?' he said, with a sad smile. 'Got to get my jollies somehow, eh?'

'Oh, don't mind me,' she said. It looked like high end skunk, very powerful; hopefully it might loosen his lips. 'Tell me about the knifing, major,' she said, using his military title, hoping it might work to open him up.

'Hey, fuck the Official Secrets Act, right?' he said, drawing deeply on the joint and laughing, a bit crazily. 'Not much to tell really. Khan's little group had been on a sortie into the badlands, part community trust building bullshit and part recon. One of the Snatch Land Rovers was hit by an IED; one guy dead, the other likely to lose his legs. The injured were medivaced out by helicopter. As Khan's group made their way back they came under sniper fire around a small settlement of a few mud huts, so they stopped and returned fire, and that's when the shit hit the fan.'

'What happened?'

Kendricks seemed in his element now, his current problems forgotten, eyes shining. 'You have to remember, these guys were pumped up, adrenaline coming out their ears; they were pissed because of the casualties and then to get fired on like that created a, forgive the cliché, perfect storm. Up to this point everything I've told you is verifiable and not in doubt. They couldn't identify where the shooter had been and by the time they had firmed up he was long gone. As in all these type of conflicts the civilians get fucked; they're caught between a rock and a hard place. The Taliban killed without hesitation anyone who they caught helping us out.'

Kendricks stood up again, the talking making him restless. He went out to the kitchen and Pascal heard the fridge opening. He came back with two cans of polish beer, cracked one open for himself and put the other one down in front of her, gesturing with his head for her to take it. It looked like extra strength beer, and hell, she needed a drink, so she cracked hers open, toasted Kendricks and took a long drag, as he continued.

'Khan was on the radio outside while Frankie Crawford, Nicky Holloway and Miles Franklyn all went into one of the larger huts. They say when they got inside there was a man with his wife and daughter and there was a stand-off. Then Khan appears in the doorway with a knife held to his neck by the adult son.'

Kendricks sighed, took another puff on his spliff, put it down and swigged from his can of beer. 'Up to this point,' he continued, 'I buy their story. Then all hell breaks loose when one of them opens up, probably Nicky. Khan goes down unconscious with a serious neck wound and then there's an explosion, and the Afghan family all end up dead.'

Just then Pascal's mobile began to play a loud Megadeth thrash metal track. She looked apologetically at Kendricks as she checked the caller; it was Calver. He would have to wait. She clicked the phone off and chucked it back in her bag.

'Fucking mobiles,' Kendrick opined. 'Only use mine for my dealer, otherwise it stays off,' Kendrick said.

'So what happened, Major?'

'The only thing we know for sure is that the family ended up dead. Holloway, Franklyn and Crawford all said it was a bomb factory, that the girl asked to go to the toilet and then she made a grab for something hidden under a pile of clothing on the bed, and the mother ran towards them screaming so they opened up and they say the girl must have detonated a suicide vest that was under the bed covers. They say they were firing through an arched doorway and that's why they were protected from the blast.'

'But you don't buy it, do you, major?'

'I don't know. It could be true, but anyway, is what happened after Khan lost consciousness of any interest to you. It won't help your case, will it?'

'Tell me anyway.'

'I think the explosive force of the blast was much too big for a suicide vest, and it was military grade ordnance, although it could have been stolen. There was very little left for us to examine afterwards, just minor body parts.'

'Why no report then, major?'

'It's complicated, but how about politics and a very ambitious Brigadier,' he said.

'Explain?'

He sighed and took another long drag on his spliff. 'I got nowhere with the investigation. Khan was unconscious and couldn't tell me anything and the other three essentially stonewalled me, and hey, maybe they were telling the truth, but the real problem was that I uncovered something else during the investigation. Something the brass really didn't want out there.'

Pascal was now completely engrossed. 'Which was?' she said.

'Heroin dealing, believe it or not. We got a tip and searched a C-130 Hercules just before it took off for UK and found around two million pounds worth of smack. We narrowed it down to two four man units, one of which was Khan's, but we couldn't prove anything, not to a criminal burden of proof level anyway, but I know it was them. Brass wanted to split the unit up immediately and started by moving Crawford straightaway to another unit, but I always thought it should have been Holloway – I figured him for the prime mover. Franklyn was due to go as well, but, anyway, about two months later, before I was ready to formally report on my findings on the death of the Afghan family, Frankie Crawford is cited for valour with his new unit; mentioned in dispatches for singlehandedly storming a Taliban hideout of six guys with RPG's and AK47's.

'When he was put up for the VC, the whole show was shitcanned; the Afghan death and the drug thing. Soon as the Brigadier got a whiff of medals we were shut down so fast it made my ears pop. They didn't want anything detracting from or besmirching the regiment's good name what with all this positive coverage they were getting. They said there was nothing justifying the convening of a board or enquiry, and about a month later I had my mysterious random drug test, and here I am.'

They both sat for a while, not speaking, Kendricks looking intensely sad as he puffed away on his second spliff. 'You know,' he said after a while, 'that Miles Franklyn was a good kid. I always thought he wanted to tell me something, but he never got around to it. Just before they were due to move him out the unit a sniper got him with a headshot; didn't kill him. He went into a coma on the chopper evac, and then back in the UK, every mothers worst nightmare, having to turn the life support off because there was no hope. Funny thing is,' Kendricks said, looking up and meeting Pascal's eyes, 'they never found any trace of the Taliban there, or the sniper.'

As Pascal was leaving, Kendricks handed her a large brown envelope containing his notes from the Afghan killing investigation. He said he would say she'd stolen it if there was any blowback, but if it would help Khan, she was welcome to it. As she drove back to London down the A12 she thought about what he had told her and the culmination of it all in that war ravaged land thousands of miles away. Maybe she should look up Miles Franklyn's family, see if they knew anything, but then her phone was thrashing again; Calver bugging her with another call. She seriously debated shunting him to voicemail again, but then remembered she was running low on cash so alienating him unnecessarily wasn't a smart move. It was no improvement on his last call – where the hell was she, blah, blah, blah? What was she doing? Then a first – he apologised for his call the previous evening about the taxi logs and asked if she wouldn't mind stopping off at his on her way home, so they could catch up.

Pascal looked tired and drawn when she finally turned up. I tried to stay upbeat and civil but fact is I was seething about her giving me the run around about the taxi logs, not speaking to me, or taking my calls, endlessly flipping me to voicemail. And, plain fact is, I was scared of what blowback we might get from the logs and generally worried about how shit everything seemed to be going. Then I'd had Khan senior on the phone, polite but distant, hinting that maybe I wasn't quite up to the job and he was considering bringing in a heavyweight big hitter QC to take over. I would stay on the team, but Rahman Singh would lead us. What did I think? I didn't answer that directly, but I think he probably got the gist. And the day before I'd rather foolishly asked Emma to phone him to ask for another big tranche of funds, rather than calling myself, and I don't think that had done me any favours. Worse still, there was no sign of the money.

So neither of us was particularly happy when she finally took a seat on my couch and I set a large Irish coffee down on the table in front of her.

We engaged in some monosyllabic pleasantries and she handed over an envelope containing some notes from someone called Kendricks to look at that might help with PTSD angle. Then, as the silence lengthened, I took a deep breath and cut straight to the chase: 'Why the hell didn't you tell me you stole the taxi logs, Pascal? I mean—'

'Because you didn't need to know,' she said forcefully, as if she had been waiting ready to fire it back as soon as I asked. She got up restlessly and went over to get the whiskey bottle. I could tell she was angry, just managing to keep it in check, but then she was turning on me, brandishing the bottle: 'You know what, Calver? I used to think you had some cojones, but I was wrong. You're just another chickenshit lawyer who runs for cover soon as the police start making empty threats – and they are empty. Bottom line, they can't prove a damn thing.'

We glared at each other, neither willing to give an inch. I finished my scotch and contemplated my empty glass. It was pointless having a slanging match with her, so let's look for positives. 'You said they can't prove it,' I said, holding out my tumbler to her for a refill. 'Explain?'

She tilted the bottle and splashed a shot into my tumbler and then lifted the bottle to her lips and took a small sip. She said, 'I voluntarily attended Hackney police station this morning for interview under caution. They showed me some interesting CCTV of a rather attractive Goth girl with orange hair sitting in the taxi waiting room. I denied it was me. All they have, Calver, is Syed's word, which ain't worth shit, and the taxi operator's not talking. The logs were anonymously delivered to your office in an unmarked, sealed envelope. I've checked with my contact at the Met and they don't have shit, that's why they had to bail me to come back in a months time whilst they carry on investigating. You know the score, Calver. They'll NFA this, soon as the trial's over.'

I moved to the balcony to look out over the rooftops as I processed Pascal's comments. It was another demonstration of just how brave and resourceful she was; she hadn't even spoken to me, a lawyer, before going into the lions den for interview where it looks like she'd faced them down, without even breaking sweat.

' What if you're wrong?' I asked.

'You still don't get it do you, Calver? They've never had enough to charge me, they've just used the threat of it to box you into a corner, neutralise Syed as the patsy, and then get all the evidence chucked out. Have to say, pretty smart moves'

I sat down heavily as I picked my way through her logic; it looked sound to me. My first feeling was relief for my own skin, and then I started thinking about the case; we'd have to think of some way of resurrecting Syed as our killer, but we did still have him in there, because Rana had given evidence about him, so Patterson and Feldman wouldn't be able to completely excise him from the case.

I knew I'd have to sit down, take some time crunching trial strategies to deal with it but we were both getting very tired now so time to move on; I asked Pascal about Holloway.

'He's a fucking junkie, Calver. What can I tell you? Just to stand him in the witness box we're – correction, I – am going to have to feed him smack 24/7, whilst surrounded by an army of coppers. And how the hell is it going to help, calling a guy like that? Prosecution'll tag him as a registered addict within about five seconds and then Patterson will have a field day. Why don't you think about a deal, Calver, because you're going to lose otherwise.'

It was all delivered in a calm understated way, making her logic all the more powerful. 'You know daddy Khan wants to bring in a leader, to run things; how about that?' I said, draining my glass and getting up for another. 'Maybe I'll get to carry his bags.'

Pascal said nothing, her silence damning. She looked pretty whacked to me. She stood up, getting ready to go, and said, 'I'll email over Holloway's statement when I get home. And how about some cash, Calver? I've done a lot of work on this and now I'm running low.'

I'd been hoping she wasn't going to ask. She saw my expression; her eyes narrowed. 'You better be kidding me, Calver,' she said. 'I've been busting my balls for you for days and now I need paying, like now.' She glared at me and she wasn't going to leave without some money or a fight, but I didn't have any cash left.'

'You're gonna have to give me a few days, Courtney, to get the cash. I'm expecting some in from Khan right now,' I lied.

She went to the sideboard and mixed herself another scotch, then emptied it, straight up. I said, 'just a few days, Pascal, that's all I'm asking.' Then I made the mistake of adding, 'you owe me, you know.'

'I owe you?' she said quietly, the suppressed anger of earlier starting to subtly flare again, fuelled by alcohol. 'I owe you for what, exactly?'

I had had a really long day; the taxi log fiasco had scared the hell out of me, the trial was taking over my life and I'd had a skinful as well. All I'd asked for was a few days, and she couldn't even give me that. 'You'd be serving life if it wasn't for me, and you know it. Tell me Pascal, whatever did happen to your brother's baseball bat? I always wondered about that.' I knew I'd gone too far, but I couldn't stop – drink does that to you sometimes. She just watched me, open mouthed, loathing in her eyes.

'What did forensics say?' I ploughed on, goading her. 'Oh, that's right, the injuries were unlikely to have been caused by him hitting his head on the stone floor, it was more consistent with blows from a blunt instrument. They never did find it, did they?'

She didn't say a word. White faced and stricken, she turned and walked away without stopping. I called out, 'wait, Courtney. Look, I…' and then I heard the outer door slam shut behind her. I stood motionless for a moment and then I picked up the whiskey bottle and hurled it against the wall. I listened to the crashing glass, then watched as the damp patch spread and darkened. I felt like crying.

Chapter Twenty

Court was about to reconvene and already my day was going to hell. So far I had no witness – Holloway hadn't turned up – and no statement. Pascal had failed to email it over as she'd promised – no doubt on purpose. So now *if* Holloway turned up, I'd have to take his evidence blind without having a clue what he was going to say. Thanks a bunch, Courtney, I thought as I listened to her phone switch to voicemail again.

And then as I loitered outside the courtroom hoping Holloway might turn up early so I could grab a quick chat before we went in, I got Khan senior instead, marching towards me accompanied by a tall distinguished looking guy.

'Ah, Mr Calver, I was hoping I might catch you – you've been so difficult to contact recently,' he said, with a pained expression. Then gesturing to the tall man at his side, he added, 'this is Rahman Singh, Q C. I've asked if he might be able to help us, given how badly we seem to be doing. He'll be watching from the gallery this morning, and then we'll talk.'

Singh's smile was mocking as he thrust his hand out, but just then, over his shoulder, I spied Nicky Holloway furtively edging into view. I turned to Khan, ignoring the man's hand. 'Sorry, I can't talk now, my witness has just arrived, and we're about to start, but get this' I said. 'This is my trial, and I run it, and your not my client.'

As I turned and walked away, over my shoulder I heard Khan say, 'yes, but who pays your fees, Mr Calver?'

I ignored him. I didn't have time for his bullshit right now. I had about five minutes to find out what Holloway was likely to say, before we'd have to go into court, and my witness was not looking good.

He was unshaven and shabbily dressed in old black jeans, combat boots, grey tracksuit top overlaid by a scruffy looking blue jacket, and his eyes were all over the place, furtively darting here and there, the one constant being that he wouldn't meet mine. He began wheedling almost at once. 'Where's Courtney, man? I'm not good. I need something or I'm out of here. D'you hear me,' he said, voice rising.

By now I'd just about had it. The corridor was busy with barristers, CPS and sundry others attending court, but I didn't care anymore. I grabbed Holloway by the lapels of his jacket and slammed him back against the wall. 'Listen to me, junkie, and listen good,' I said, pushing my face up tight with his. 'I've had a very bad day so far, and we've barely started. Don't make it worse.'

He finally met my eyes, and I saw the bravado instantly fade, replaced by, what? Looked like fear and a craving for something that would make it all go away. He stuttered, 'sorry, sorry, man, but I *need* something.'

Despite everything, I did feel for him, as I'd been there myself with alcohol many times, but right now I just needed to get him into the witness box, and then start praying. Meantime a few white lies might smooth the way. 'Listen, buddy, Pascal's late because she's getting you some stuff. Good stuff,' I smirked, punching his shoulder. 'She's on the way. Had to go the extra mile to get the pure shit. Believe me, it'll be worth the wait,' I said, smoothing down his jacket.

He wanted to believe me. 'Smack?' he said.

'Fuckin' A, buddy,' I winked. 'Nicky, you do your stuff for me today, lay it on, how bad it was for Mohsin, with the stabbing and all – you come out, you get a lump of Turkish brown big as your head – you'll be tripping for a month,' I said, leading him towards the door of the court.

Pascal drew up outside the smart Spanish style bungalow in the Surrey heartlands; her verdict: select, expensive and gentrified. She got out the car and made her way up the garden path to the bright white front door. As she pressed the buzzer she looked back at her beat up old Golf; it looked seriously out of place.

A moment later the door was opened by a rather kind looking woman, mid sixties with short greying blonde hair. She smiled and said, 'you must be Courtney,' and then led her into a large living room, all white and pale colours, the room widening out into an open conservatory through which she could be seen the lush green garden outside.

'Would you like some fresh coffee, dear? Only I've been watching for you and it should be ready now,' she said, gesturing for Pascal to take a seat on the comfortable looking couch. A few minutes later she brought two mugs through and put one down in front of Pascal and said, 'how is Mohsin? We always thought he was such a nice boy, and Miles really loved him.'

Pascal was studying a large framed photograph she'd picked up off the mantelpiece; it depicted a handsome young man in dress uniform, smiling confidently at the camera. 'Mohsin's fine. And thank you so much for seeing me, Mrs Franklyn. Is this Miles?' she asked, tapping the photograph.

'Yes. He took it himself, with some type of time lapse camera. He was very into that; wanted to be a photographer when he got out,' she said, looking out at the garden again, and then down at her hands. Pascal could see her fighting to hold back her grief.

Pascal felt guilty about making her revisit such painful memories. 'If you'd like me to come back another time, Mrs Franklyn, I'd be glad—'

'No,' she said firmly. 'You ask your questions. Miles would have wanted to help his friend.'

So Pascal gently explained how the defence team wanted to get as much information as they could about what had happened in Afghanistan because some of more traumatic incidents may have contributed to Mohsin's PTSD and this was likely to form an important part of his defence. The problem they had was that Mohsin's memory was so bad that they were having to try to get the evidence from anyone else who had been out there with him.

It turned out however that apparently Miles had talked little about what happened out there. 'He just never spoke about the bad things,' she said. 'All I have from his time there is a box of stuff up in the loft, the army gave back to me when he was discharged into the care of the hospital,' she added.

Later she'd insisted Pascal climb up into the loft and bring the box down so they could both have a look, but when they got it down there didn't seem to be anything there of interest. Pascal could see a combat helmet, belts and pack and some old papers, and other bits and pieces. Mrs Franklyn said, 'why don't you take it with you, and then you can look through it at your leisure, when you have more time.'

Pascal began to shake her head, 'that's not necessary, Mrs Franklyn, really I—

'Please, Courtney,' she said. 'I want to help, and I know Miles would as well. Just take it, have a look and drop it back when you can, yes? If there's nothing there, there's no harm done, but if there is something there that might help Mohsin, well, at least some good will have come out of all this……this dreadful time.'

She looked so distraught that Pascal took the box and placed it in the boot of her car. Then Mrs Franklyn spontaneously hugged Pascal before she could pull away. She stood rigid and unbending, even as she saw the hurt in Mrs. Franklyn's eyes, but she didn't now how to unbend and relax into the warm embrace. As Pascal pulled away from the curb she watched through her rear view mirror the sad and forlorn figure of Mrs Franklyn as she turned and slowly walked back up the path to her house.

I could tell the jury were getting bored, because I was as well; it was like pulling teeth. After each simple question, mostly to do with his early experiences with his three compatriots in Afghanistan, Holloway would pause – it seemed like forever but was usually about ten seconds – and then embark on some long, convoluted and incredibly boring reminiscence about brewing up tea, or fixing the engine of a jeep.

In one way this was good because it allowed me, as I took his evidence, to read through the Kendricks papers Pascal had handed me before she decided to drop me in the shit. I had the paperwork spread out on my disk and was alternating between asking a question of Holloway, and then looking down and reading, occasionally turning a page on the desk as Holloway stutteringly went through his answers.

But now Holloway was starting to get hyper, to get close to cold turkey territory, so if I was going to get anything out of him, I better do it soon, or face meltdown. I moved him smoothly up to the Afghan knifing incident which we'd touched on in Rana's evidence and which had been fleshed out in the Kendricks papers I had just finished reading. I asked Holloway to tell the jury what happened.

There was an immediate change in the atmosphere in the court and movement in the jury box – at last, maybe they were finally going to hear something interesting. Some sat up straighter, and papers rustled as Patterson closed his notebooks and looked up, fixing his stony glare on my witness.

'Oh man, that was bad,' Holloway said, finally showing some emotion. 'We'd been on a patrol, two men down, one dead, the other cut in half, losing his legs from an IED. As medic I tried to help him, but the blood…..everywhere, man' he said, his eyes haunted as if he were reliving the incident. 'And God, the screaming. Don't think I'll ever forget it. Even after I'd jacked him full of Morphine, he was still screaming, begging for me to kill him.'

He paused, looking at the jury for the first time, and it was strange, like alchemy, a kind of frisson; the jury totally absorbed in the words of this hopelessly broken down junkie, holding them spellbound with his simple story.

'Milesy called up the chopper for medivac, and they were there inside five minutes, so we got him out, and you know what,' he said smiling incongruously, 'he survived. He's in a fucking wheel chair, but he survived.' Then he looked up at Feldman, and said, 'sorry judge.'

Feldman, for once catching the moment, said, 'that's quite alright Mr Holloway. Do go on.'

'Well, we carried on in the snatch Land rovers, just the four of us left as they'd taken the others out in the second helicopter and then we came under fire near a small settlement – just a few scattered mud huts. I was all for going on but Big Frankie wanted to stop and check it out and Corporal Khan,' he said looking over at Mohsin, who sat watching, showing no emotion, 'agreed, so we stopped. Sheltered up behind a wall, and then fanned out, seeing if we could scope out the shooter.'

He paused again, as if tired from speaking. I poured a glass of water and took it over to him without comment from Feldman. He sipped and then continued. 'Mohsin was on the radio outside while we three; me, Milesy and big Frankie went inside the main hut. By now it was clear the shooter was long gone. There was an Afghan man and his wife and daughter there, very frightened. Frankie asked them some questions with some sign language about the shooter but they said they didn't know nothing, but the girl seemed jumpy, suspicious, kept looking towards the bedroom and fidgeting, so we kept our weapons trained on them. Then there was sound of a scuffle outside and Mohsin appeared in the doorway with a man holding a knife to his neck. Mohsin was in a bad way, moaning and bleeding heavily from stab wounds to the chest. Then all hell broke loose. I think Mohsin must have moved because the knifeman was distracted for a second and showed his body, so I took the shot and as he fell away, Mohsin got cut bad. Same time the girl ran for the bedroom, and must have detonated a bomb hidden there as there was a huge explosion, killing the family.'

He paused again. All very exciting, and what he'd said seemed to follow Kendricks' investigation notes with more detail, but of course the only value of this testimony was how this traumatic incident might have affected Khan psychologically.

'How did this incident affect Corporal Khan do you think?' I asked, aware that the question was improper, but rightly guessing that Patterson wouldn't bother to object.

Holloway thought for a moment, and looked briefly over at Khan, before saying, 'I don't think he was ever the same again after that. I mean, who would be? He'd been stabbed twice in the chest and once in the back, not life threatening but deep and very painful, as well as a deep slash across the neck that was about 2 millimetres away from his Carotid artery, and if they'd cut that, he would have died there, I've no doubt about that.

'And I know he was quite a long time in recovery but I don't think the army gave him anything like long enough – they never do. Oh I know he had the counselling bit but that's all bullshit – he still had the nightmares.'

'Thank you, Mr Holloway,' I said, studying him carefully. He was now looking decidedly ropey – emotionally drained from re-living traumatic experiences and the effects of heroin withdrawal – and I didn't think I could risk trying to get anything more out of him now, not if Patterson was going to cross examine him. I looked down at my notes weighing it. Sometimes it was better to quit while you were ahead, especially with an unstable junkie – time to pull him out.

I thanked Holloway and said I had no further questions, and then offered him to Patterson for cross examination. He declined, something I'd been half expecting but not daring to hope for, but I knew why. Patterson didn't really need to challenge Holloway's evidence because it only went to explain Khan's confusion, memory loss or amnesia, and his suggestibility in the police interview; it didn't affect the central issue of whether he killed Safia or not.

Looking up at the clock I couldn't quite believe it was almost four in the afternoon. Feldman then obligingly adjourned until the next morning and I made a mad rush for the exit, desperate to avoid a painful confrontation with Holloway when he found out that there wasn't going to be any smack.

Chapter Twenty One

Lammy padded across the thick pile carpet, her skin glistening, while Condon lay on the bed breathing heavily, just a sheet draped across his sweating torso. She mixed a couple of strong Martini's and carried them back to the bed. In the background a large wall mounted TV showed the BBC news channel reporting on the upcoming visit of the US president who would be stopping off in London for a couple of days on his way back from the G8 meeting.

'Mmmm,' Lammy purred. 'I hear you already got the advance team crawling all over you?'

Condon tried his drink, nodded, and said, 'you know they've asked for you?'

She leant forward and kissed him on the lips. 'And what did you tell them?'

He frowned and looked away. 'What's happening on the oppo, Av?' he asked. 'Only you seem to have suddenly gone quiet on me.'

'You saying that was quiet earlier?' she said, running her hand down under the sheet.

He put his hand on hers, stopping its movement. 'Hey, Av, this is good, but I need to know what's happening?' he said, eyes cold.

She shook his hand off and got up and grabbed a bath robe, wrapping it tightly around herself and tying the belt. She walked over towards the curtains along one wall and peeped out, looking down over Hyde Park, giving herself a chance to compose herself and come up with a response that Condon would swallow.

She thought about Pascal, the deal, how much she could trust her, and whether she was ever likely to get anything out of it. It had been a couple of days and she'd heard nothing. With the US crowd streaming in, and POTUS, she'd probably never get a better chance to make her mark and really shine, but things needed to start moving real sharp or she'd miss her chance. On the other hand, if she gave the slightest hint to Condon about what she'd got so far— which might be nothing; couple of amateur whack jobs playing around with homemade bombs — she'd be instantly sidelined and others would grab the glory. As well as that, she knew that if she let anything meaningful slip now, Condon's innate caution would mean the operation would almost certainly be terminated and any chance of finding out what the hell was going on, would be lost. But if she kept her mouth shut too long, and something happened, there would be no pity or forgiveness, she would be out, even worse than Pascal, and she could even end up in a federal prison if she got it wrong. Fucking high stakes she thought and smiled; she loved to play the odds, and at present they were way on her side, but the small window of opportunity for action on her part was fast closing. She needed to move, get a grip on Pascal, lock her down, and try and keep Condon onside at the same time.

'When we lost Khan, John, I took it bad. I was embarrassed,' she said, turning back from the window. 'I wanted to do something to make it right.'

'What did you do, Averill?' he said, agitated, getting up off the bed and pulling the damp sheet around his shoulders. He moved over to the air conditioner unit, banging his hand on it as he tried to turn the heat back up.

'I spoke to Pascal and—'

'I don't believe you,' he said, incredulous, just keeping a lid on his anger. 'We have a chain of command structure here you know and you should fucking well try using it occasionally. You better tell me what happened, and it better be good or you're history. And Av?'

'Boss.'

'Everything, yes?'

Lammy nodded slowly as she hastily marshaled all the facts in her head, then gave him a highly edited version of what had happened, with her various interactions with Pascal condensed into a single one in the car outside the café when they had both been watching Khan and Holloway. 'She said she was onto something, that she followed Khan from the Mosque when we lost him. She wants to trade though, so I gave her some old info about the army investigation into Khan's knifing in Afghanistan – its old stuff and not even classified, so we lose nothing - as a taster, to show we're genuine.'

'And,' he said, looking at her expectantly. 'What did you get?'

'She wants something more. I said I'd check it out and get back to her. Boss, you need to understa—'

'No, Av. *You* need to understand,' he interrupted her. 'This department is not run for your benefit. If you're looking to hitch a ride back to Washington, using my section for your own personal aggrandizement, forget it,' he said, glaring at her. He walked over to the mini bar and took a bottle of beer out and cracked the cap off, and then sipping from it, he said, 'and you don't know what you're getting into with her. You think Courtney Pascal is some kind of fucking girl guide who just got off the boat. You know she killed her stepfather don't you – in cold blood as far as I'm concerned - and she just about walked away from it, with the help of that shyster lawyer, Calver. She's dangerous.'

'Boss, we have to play the angles. The key to Courtney is she's desperate to get back into five, and we can use that.' Lammy walked over to him and put her hands on his shoulders, and looking up into his eyes, she said, 'trust me. Let me run with it.'

'What does she want?' he finally asked.

Lammy silently exhaled. It looked like she might just have ridden out the storm, but she still had work to do on Condon.

'Essentially, she wants back into five, so that's down to you. I'd promise her whatever she wants,' Lammy said. 'But more immediately she wants some old stuff about Calver's junkie ex-wife.'

'What's that?'

'D'you remember the PKK scare, some time ago? We got Intel about them contacting a local London Turkish drugs gang about arms, and there was a visit by the Turkish prime minister coming up, so we had to take it seriously. Turns out it was total bullshit, but it did allow us to access the files of the Organised crime command at the National Agency because at the time they were running a long term under cover operation on this Turkish drugs gang. Anyway this Jonny White character was charged with murdering one of these Turkish drug guys, a low level bottom feeder kind of guy, and Jonny's alibi was that he spent the night with Calver's wife at the time of the killing.'

'You're kidding me?' Condon said, sipping his beer and enjoying the view of Lammy's firm breasts jutting out erotically from her diaphanous bathrobe.

'No, I'm not. And the alibi stood up so this White character walked. Anyway, one of the under cover guys has got phone footage of White with the drug guy about ten minutes before he was murdered.'

'So why wasn't it given to the murder squad?'

'I quote,' she said looking down at her phone screen: '"we were never going to jeopardise one of our biggest under cover operations of the last ten years over the killing of some druggy kebab seller." Three months after White's acquittal they sprung the trap and netted the main man and his top three lieutenants; jailed for 30 years apiece; kudos and promotions all round.'

Lammy leaned over and took the bottle from Condon and took a sip. 'So what do you want to do about Pascal, boss?' she said as she pulled loose the belt around her waist. As the bathrobe swung open Condon leaned down and began to nuzzle her breasts.

'Let's reel her in,' he said absently. 'Give her the stuff on Calver's wife, but I want something in return. Set up a meet. I want her tied up so tight, she so much as farts, I want to know about it. I want her tracked and bugged, so if she runs,' he said, lifting his head and looking dreamily at Lammy, 'we run with her.'

I flicked my phone off as I slammed my way out of the robing room. Emma was pissed; Holloway had turned up at the office as she was closing up and she'd had to threaten to call the police to get rid of him. He'd been screaming about how I'd stitched him up and how he was going to call the law society and get me de-frocked, as he'd called it. I'd laughed but Emma hadn't found it funny, so I'd had to work hard to calm her down and get her back on side. So all in all I was glad to get back into court and get away from all the crap in the office, but then the court usher was approaching me and telling me it looked like they were going to have to adjourn yet again, probably all day, because the judge had been delayed and wasn't sure when he would arrive, if at all.

Great, I thought. At this rate, with adjournments almost every day, I was beginning to wonder if we would ever finish the case. It looked like the whole under resourced criminal justice system was finally cracking up and grinding to a halt.

As I pondered this Mohsin Khan appeared, so I told him about the likely adjournment, and then said, hopefully, 'no dad today then, Mohsin?'

'Oh he'll be here, Jonas. He wants to talk to you, man' he said, looking at me meaningfully.

'Good,' I nodded. 'He needs to be told how far ahead of the game we are. I mean, d'you really want to jump ship now?'

He shrugged and, give him his due, did manage to look a tad shamefaced. 'Jonas, he's paying, man. He's gotta have a say.' 'What d'you say, Mohsin?'

He smiled. 'I think you're doing better, Jonas, better than before, but that isn't difficult. But Pop's guy, Singh. He don't. He says you're playing out of your league; you've lost the judge and jury. Without him taking over, we lose and I get twenty five years.'

'You know something, Mohsin?' I said, leaning back against the wall, crossing my arms and looking down at my shoes. 'I checked your boy out. Know what I found? He's done three murder cases, but get this, he's never done a murder *trial*. All three were pleaded out, only one of which he got reduced to manslaughter. The other two were straight guilty pleas to murder. And one of those was prepared for trial by another attorney before your boy took it over and pleaded it out. I spoke to that attorney last night, and he said he still couldn't believe it was pleaded out. He thinks Singh is too close to a lot of the CPS prosecutors.'

'Yeah, could just be sour grapes, Jonas. Singh took the case off him. What's he gonna say?'

'Have it your way,' I said, pushing myself up off the wall, totally pissed off but trying hard not to show it. 'But there's a couple of other things you might like to know about your boy. He comes from Pump Court Chambers which just happens to be the same chambers used by James Patterson, and Judge Michael Feldman, before he was elevated to the bench. And who did I see late yesterday afternoon having a coffee together across the road? Yeah, that's right,' I said, nodding my head. 'James Patterson and Rahman Singh. And if that isn't enough to scare you shitless, d'you wanta know what Singh's real specialism is, apart from bending over, holding his ankles and taking it in the ass from the prosecution? Yeah, that's right,' I said, looking him in the eye. 'White collar fraud.'

As I turned and walked away towards the court door, he called after me,

'Hey, Jonas.'

I stopped and turned.

'He's not my "boy", okay,' he said, smiling again. Two smiles in one day; that had to be some kind of record. Maybe something good was going on in Khan's life that I didn't know about.

'I hear what you're saying,' he continued, still smiling. 'I'll talk to dad. Sometimes he tends to listen to the wrong people too much. You know, people from the old country.'

I let out a silent, relieved sigh, and then smiled as I spotted Rose Tremayne approaching. As I walked forward to meet her and tell her about the adjournment, I offered up a silent little prayer that Khan's father wouldn't ask Singh about having coffee with Patterson, and find out it wasn't exactly true.

Pascal sat in her kitchen sipping coffee and listening to a Megadeth track on low volume. Out on the table in front of her she had sorted into piles the contents of the box she had retrieved from Mrs Franklyn.

There wasn't much there; uniform, couple of belts, helmet, various old rap CD's and some army papers. Although Pascal was not remotely sentimental, these sad remnants didn't seem much to show for a young life that, according to Franklyn's mother, had showed such promise.

She went through the CD's; looked like urban rap kinda shit that she hated. She picked up the helmet and wondered why the army hadn't taken it back; no doubt an oversight what with the catastrophic injury and the transfer back to a UK civilian hospital. Pascal had been in the old Territorial Army, now called the Army Reserve, for three months before prison, and she recognised the helmet as the Combat Assault Mk7 version. It still had the distinctive desert pattern DPM material covering it and retained a light patina of Afghan dust.

She idly placed the helmet on her head; it was much too large. As she leaned back in her chair with the helmet still perched on the back of her head, her smart phone began to vibrate on the table. She looked over and checked the caller: Lammy. She smiled.

'Whassup Lammy? You missing me?'

Pause, then: 'good morning, Courtney.' Cool and precise; no banter.

Sounded like Lammy wasn't alone? Pascal was immediately on her guard. She waited.

'I'd like to set up a meet, when it's convenient for you.'

As Pascal listened to Lammy's disembodied voice coming through the phone, she happened to look up and her eyes were met with the overhanging front of the helmet, forgotten, but still on her head. Her eyes were immediately drawn to a small hole that appeared to have been drilled through the front of the helmet, which she hadn't noticed before as the DPM material covering it acted as camouflage so it could not be seen from the outside.

'Courtney?' Lammy jogged her.

She leaned forward so that her front chair legs met the floor with a crack, and the helmet slipped down over her eyes again, momentarily enveloping her in darkness. She dug back in memory to her conversation with Mrs Franklyn. What was it she'd said? Pascal focused, Lammy's voice forgotten. She was pretty sure Mrs Franklyn had said Miles had wanted to be a photographer and that in the past he had used some type of time lapse camera.

'Courtney, are you still there?'

'Sorry, I was just checking my diary,' Pascal finally said. 'When's good for you?'

They agreed to meet at Lammy's Islington flat that evening, but Pascal's mind was elsewhere, racing with possibilities.

Chapter Twenty Two

In the end it didn't take long to reach a decision. We sat round my kitchen table eating disgusting cardboard tasting Pizza I'd ordered in, and sipping weak foamy beer from the corner shop across the road. Rose and Mohsin had obviously spent the day together after the earlier surprise adjournment, and it showed; Mohsin surprisingly pumped up and doing most of the talking whilst Rose sat and watched.

'I want to give evidence, Jonas. Rose says I'm ready,' he said, eyeing me up, expecting an argument, although I'm not sure why.

'Okay,' I said slowly, drawing the word out, stalling for time. 'But tell me this; when I ask you, in front of the jury: what happened between the hours of seven and eight on the night of the murder, what exactly are you going to say?'

He looked quickly at Rose who remained silent, watching him.

'Look, I've been thinking – lots. Before I just didn't care, but now I do. I can't go to prison. I was selfish. I wasn't thinking about my kids at all, just wallowing in self pity. I need to be out, Jonas, for my kids. I think I need to tell my story to the jury, even if it is full of holes. If I don't step up to the plate, tell the jury……' he said, kind of running out of steam and letting his words tail off.

'And say what?' I said, keeping the pressure on, although actually I was delighted that he now seemed to give a shit about the future.

Rose delicately chewed a mouthful of cheese and tomato dripping cardboard and tried to look as if she was enjoying it. 'He has been making progress,' she said, a slight smile glimmering. 'I don't want to exaggerate it, but he is starting to open up, to remember.'

'To remember what?' I asked pointedly, and my tone must have given me away, as her face fell, the slight smile freezing on her lips. I watched as the wheels turned and she got the first hint that maybe it wasn't exactly the truth that I was looking for here. Welcome to the trial process, I thought grimly. I laughed, but it sounded forced. 'Sorry, Rose. I'm just a little stressed at the moment. What is it that he's remembered?'

'Oh nothing really definite yet,' she said, 'but I'm sure it will come, and the more work we do, the more he seems to open up.'

Great, I thought. Just as I call him, he remembers everything, just in time to confess. She obviously read my expression, and said, 'did I do something wrong here?'

'Not at all, Rose,' I calmed her, 'but just tell me we've still got an argument on amnesia and PTSD.'

'Absolutely,' she said, wiping her hand across her mouth, taking a long sip of the foamy beer, and burping.

'So what are you saying here,' I said, looking from one to other, subtly trying to get to the nub. 'We take a chance; put him in the witness box, when even he doesn't seem to know what he's going to say?'

'Yes,' she said emphatically. 'Only way we're going to find out the truth.'

'Yeah, that's right,' Mohsin echoed her. 'Look, Jonas, you're just going to have to trust me. Just ask your questions; what will be, will be.'

I looked from one to the other again, trying to damp down the unbidden rage that was starting to rise in me at their total lack of understanding. God, what the fuck had the truth got to do with anything? You'd have thought they might have learnt something from hanging out with me over the last few months. My job was to get an acquittal, not discover the truth, whatever that was.

But then, fact is, Khan was right; it was axiomatic that a jury always preferred to hear direct from a defendant, and felt shortchanged if they didn't. Here the worry wasn't in calling a defendant who had a terrible record that would come out if he gave evidence; the worry here was calling someone who didn't actually have a clue what they were going to say when they were asked the critical questions. Suicide or what? And as to what Patterson might do to him in cross examination, I didn't want to go there. End of the day though, it was always the clients decision, and my job was simply to advise.

'It's your life, Mohsin, but I want you to be under no illusions about the risk you're running here; we get it wrong, they'll throw away the key.'

I watched him carefully as my words hit home, but he seemed strangely disconnected, as if he was acting, or playing a part, whilst something more important engaged another part of his mind.

I collected up the detritus of our Pizza and beers and binned them. 'Okay folks, let's sleep on it and be ready to go again in the morning.'

Pascal had been through all the items from Miles Franklyn's army box again and there was nothing there. She moved through the flat, her mind whirring away. Then she went and sat with her sleeping mother, holding the old lady's gnarled and liver spotted hand as she pondered. It looked like there could have been some kind of headcam in the helmet, although she was guessing, but if you added together what Franklyn's mother had said about Miles' love of photography with the hole in the helmet and some slight scrape marks around it suggesting something had been affixed there, it all added up.

She knew army regulations were pretty strict; no unauthorised modifications to helmets were allowed and there were periodical inspections to check the position, so he would have had to film covertly. So where was the headcam, if there was one, and where was the film, if any survived. The army? Mrs Franklyn? Or maybe hidden somewhere.

Pascal reached for her phone and called Mrs Franklyn. She had no answers, but was intrigued that there might be some remaining pictures of her son somewhere; she promised to wrack her brains and call back if she thought of anything.

Pascal went to the fridge and grabbed herself a bottle of imported high strength Filipino Red Horse beer, uncapped it, and took a slug. She'd found over time that the high alcohol beer tended to help her thought processes rather than hinder them; or maybe she was just deluded – anyway, she liked the taste. She went to the grandfather clock standing in the corner of her living room, opened the front panel and reached through to the small wall safe hidden behind where she keyed in the combination, opened the door and removed a sizeable chunk of Turkish heroin. Maybe it was time for another chat with Nicky Holloway. She grabbed her leather jacket and crash helmet, kissed Sarah, who'd just arrived back from the shop, and left the flat.

It was the same routine again when she arrived at the squat; banging, shouting; scrambling through the window and up the stairs, but this time, when she got to his room, he really did look the worse for wear. Shaking, sweating and wild eyed; perfect for what she had in mind.

Then more of the same routine; begging, pleading and whining, but also this time bitter recriminations about the stitch up that she and Calver had perpetrated on him, and why should he trust her when they'd promised him smack before and then tricked him. She flashed the heroin which immediately focused his attention and quietened him down.

'Tell me about the camera, Nicky. Milesy's headcam?'

It was the first time she had seen anything register with Holloway, but it was instant; his eyes changed subtly, went flat and blank, and he quickly looked away. But at the same time he just could not quite blank out the craving, which is what she'd banked on. He licked his lips, eyes flicking back and forth between the heroin and Pascal's face. 'Talk to me Nicky,' she said. 'Nod and you get a taster now, then we talk, then you get a big chunk, including what you're owed by Calver, yes?'

'But I'm already owed it,' he whined.

Pascal just sat there watching him, waiting.

'There's nothing to tell,' he finally said, scratching his forearms, 'but you ask your questions and see where we go, but, please, man, you gotta give me a hit now, or I ain't gonna make it.'

She nodded and tossed him a small chunk. Same routine, then after injecting between his toes he lay back, resting his head against the wall, eyes slow and dreamy.

'Milesy liked photography. So what? He had a little digital camera and he took some snaps around the base to send home and upload for mates. Lots of guys did it. Anyway those camera's are all obsolete now, man – everyone's got one of those fucking smart phones — except me,' he said with a laugh.

'Not good enough, Nickyboy, not if you want a real spike in the vein,' she said, juggling the remaining heroin from hand to hand and watching him. 'Tell me about the headcam?'

'What fucking headcam? I don't know what you're talking about. I've told you all I know.'

They went back and forth for a while, but he wouldn't budge, even with a couple of grams of smack bouncing up and down in front of him, which tended to suggest to Pascal that he was telling the truth, but there was something there. She knew she'd seen something in his eyes when she'd first mentioned the camera, but perhaps it was just fear that maybe there was something out there on him that might come back to screw him. But she wasn't going to get anymore out of him now. She broke off a sizable chunk of smack, mindful not give him enough to OD on, and chucked it at him. 'Better late than never, eh, Nicky? Don't leave town. I may need to speak to you again,' she said, as she picked up her helmet.

As she left the squat her phone burst into life with another Megadeth classic; it was Joan Franklyn, excited; her friend had reminded her that Miles had brought back an old laptop computer from Afghanistan and they'd given it to her young niece, Sophie. It had been checked over at the time and nothing had been found so they'd given it to the twelve year old for her school work. Would Courtney like her to get it back. She could have look at it as soon as the next day if she wished to?

Pascal kept cool and thanked Joan, and said yes she would very much like to have a look. Then for the first time that day, she began to think seriously about the meeting lined up for that night at Lammy's flat.

I looked up at Feldman. 'Call the defendant, Mohsin Khan,' I said loud and clear.

Khan, sitting in the dock, looked startled as my words registered, as if he somehow hadn't been expecting them even though we had agreed I would call him straightaway. He squared his shoulders and then marched across the courtroom to the witness box.

I hadn't realised he was going to wear his uniform, but now I was glad he had. He looked highly impressive, the medals on his chest glinting and sparkling in the artificial light in the courtroom, his face steely with determination. He sat and removed his cap and gloves and then sat ramrod straight as he waited for my first question.

Patterson studied him keenly as did the jury, perhaps intuiting that we were now getting down to the nub of the whole trial.

I treated taking this kind of evidence like icing a rather elaborate cake, laying layer after layer of icing on until we had the perfect finish. We started with background and history, building it up slowly, trying always to give the jury a real insight into exactly who the defendant was; his fears, dreams, hopes, essentially the man behind the mask.

So I started with where he was born, where he grew up; his early schooling, adolescence, onto sixth form, then university where he did chemistry and electrical engineering. Joining up, meeting Safia and the birth of the two daughters. All uncontentious stuff which I drew out of him lightly, trying to get him to have a conversation with the jury with as little input from me as possible.

It seemed to be working and I felt the jury were warming to Khan. After an hour or so of this gentle questioning, we were starting to approach the first contentious areas.

'Now we've heard some details from Nicky Holloway about your experiences in Afghanistan, and in particular when you were stabbed, and I'd like you to flesh those out for the jury, if you will. We heard that when you stopped at this little settlement, initially you stayed outside on the radio as

Milesy, Holloway and Crawford went inside one of the huts. What happened then?' I asked.

I really had no idea what Khan was going to tell us, if anything, and part of my strategy earlier in getting Nicky to give us the detail was to act as a memory booster – a reminder – for Khan. I'd also called Nicky for the detail, just in case Khan was now going to come up blank on the incident, and have nothing to tell us, so I was interested, and anxious, to hear what he was going to say.

'I guess I was out there about five minutes before I followed the guys into the hut,' he said

'What happened?'

Khan's voice was quieter now, slightly hoarse, and he spoke haltingly, as if groping for the memories as he went along. 'As I went through the first room I could hear voices, but then, as if from nowhere, I was attacked,' he said, a faint air of surprise and indignation in his voice. 'I felt blows, thought I was being punched, but later found out they were actually stab wounds, in my back, shoulder and neck. The guy was very strong; I was staggering, bleeding, didn't know where I was. He put me in a kind of headlock, arm around my neck with a huge knife held to my throat. It had a thick blade, very heavy duty with a green serpent motif on the handle, and that image has always stuck in my mind, endlessly coming back in nightmares,' he said, voice hushed with anguish.

After a moment, he continued. 'I've never seen a knife like it, before or since,' he said, talking faster now as if he were back in that mud hut, the courtroom and jury forgotten. 'I could feel blood dripping down my neck from the knife, and then the guy kind of frogmarched me towards the doorway which was covered by hanging beads, and he manoeuvred me through and stopped on the threshold, holding me there.'

Khan paused again, clearly now very weary and the strain of testifying about such frightening experiences was starting to take its toll, his face looked drained and washed out. He sipped some more water.

'In the next room Milesy, Holloway and Frankie were talking to the householder who was there with his wife and teenage daughter, and the guys had their guns trained on them, and obviously as I was forced into the room they were taken by surprise, and for a second everything just seemed to stop.

'This is the bit,' he said, faltering again and swallowing. 'This is the bit I can't forget; that I have nightmares about. Its like its frozen in my mind. That huge knife I can see out of the corner of my eye, feeling the tip deep in my neck, blood running down and the reflection from the table lamp glinting off the blade, up into my face.'

He paused for a long time then, and I was just about to prompt him when he continued. 'What happened next is very hazy and I have no reason to doubt what Nicky told you. I think the guy holding me must have slightly loosened his grip and so I pushed violently against him; Nicky saw what was happening and loosed off a round which hit my attacker and as he fell he dug the knife in, and that's when I passed out.'

I nodded. 'What happened next?'

Khan's eyes were closed now as he spoke, and there was a hesitancy in his voice as he attempted to articulate the images that his mind was processing. 'Well when I tuned back in again, I don't know how much later, it was much quieter. Nicky Holloway must have attended to my wounds, because they'd been dressed, and I don't remember him doing that, and I reckon he must have given me a shot of morphine as well because I wasn't in any pain. My last memory is being moved, or lifted and carried out, then there was a huge explosion, and when I woke up again I was in the field hospital.'

As I watched Khan, his face was difficult to describe; his expression was one of surprise and confusion, almost as if the testimony he had just given was as much of a surprise to him as it was to the rest of us, and maybe that was true. But then I wondered whether any of it actually mattered. All we were seeking to show here was that he had been traumatised by the stabbing, and frankly, what happened after that with strange explosions wouldn't change a thing.

Feldman then adjourned for a break. I was reasonably pleased with how things had gone, but I guessed the jury were starting to find my line of questioning frustrating and confusing, as much of what we were hearing about seemed to have little or no connection to whether or not Khan killed Safia. But

I still needed to pursue what had happened in Afghanistan, because it just *might* become critical later.

Pascal watched the squat from about seventy metres away at a junction. She cursed herself for having come on the Bike. It was basically a trials job made roadworthy by a sparring partner from the dojo, and it was noisy and distinctive; a bitch if she was going to have to follow Holloway.

She quickly decided to take a chance, and try and grab a taxi, if as she expected, Nicky was going to be on the move shortly. She chained the bike up opposite a small Halal butchers shop and went inside and asked the young guy, whilst flashing a couple of twenties under his nose, if he wouldn't mind watching the bike a couple of hours and holding onto her helmet until she got back. His face broke into a wide smile as he took the helmet and made a grab for both twenties, only getting one. 'You get this when I get back and the bike's still here,' she said waiving the other twenty over her shoulder as she left the shop.

Not a moment too soon because as she left the shop Holloway was already climbing into a cab. She desperately looked around and then saw another one up the road, dropping off around a hundred metres away. She began to run, waving her hands and shouting whilst trying to keep an eye on Holloway's cab which had just about disappeared.

Her target cabbie must have seen her in his mirror as he stopped and let her on board where she collapsed in a heap, telling him to proceed along the road where she could just still see Holloway some way ahead.

After five minutes she relaxed. They followed for some way. It seemed like Nicky was taking a gentle trip down the London tourist trail. As they came down Bayswater road, Pascal's surprised conclusion, based upon concentrated observation for fifteen minutes, was that there was patently no one else tailing Holloway. So what had happened to Lammy's boys she wondered. Maybe she'd find out at the meet that evening.

Pascal's black cab swung around Marble Arch, past Speakers Corner and down Park Lane, where Holloway stopped and got out of his taxi. Pascal came to a halt as well and watched thinking perhaps he was going into Hyde Park, but no, he turned the other way and began walking. Pascal paid off her driver and jumped out, name checking the road he'd gone into which was Upper Brook Street, so he was walking up towards Claridge's, the world famous hotel. She didn't think a junkie like Holloway was likely to have any business there, but maybe he'd surprise her.

Up ahead he turned right into the next street, and then it hit her where he was going; Grosvenor Square, home to the USA's largest embassy in Western Europe.

Chapter Twenty Three

I knew I needed to cut to the chase soon or I'd completely lose the jury, but I still had to nail down Khan's testimony about the killing of his friend, private Miles Franklyn, and the domestic violence caution, because these aspects might prove critical later in the trial.

'Now, I understand you witnessed the shooting of a close colleague by a sniper; tell us about that.'

Khan nodded. 'Yeah, that was Milesy, the baby of the group,' he said, a pained and sorrowful look drawing down over his face. 'He was just nineteen years old, and I felt especially protective of him. I still feel intensely guilty about what happened.

'I was leading a small team of six on a sortie and had just called a water stop. It was real quiet, rough scrub country, and the nearest settlement was around a mile away. I'd told Milesy, in fact I'd told them all, repeatedly, to be careful, not to expose themselves to incoming fire, to stay alert and watchful, but that day he must have been off the beat. I learned later he'd had an argument on Skype with his girlfriend the previous evening, and he may have been distracted.

'Anyway, when I saw him standing up straight without his helmet on I shouted to him to get down.' Khan paused there, his eyes haunted, unseeing, as the horror newsreel began to play out in his head.

'I'll never forget it, long as I live, because I was actually looking right at his face from about two metres away when he was hit, and it was a head shot with a snipers high velocity round. You know your mind,' he said, and then his voice dried up and he swallowed, trying to keep his composure, then continuing, falteringly, 'your mind just, you can't process what you're seeing, because basically there's this pink spray where his head had been, and he's dropping where he stood and then you hear the crack of the rifle report,' he said.

There was complete silence in the courtroom as Khan's words were absorbed. He stopped for a moment and had a sip of water and then, in a calmer tone, continued. 'The round didn't kill him, remarkably, or not then anyway. We think he was just turning when hit, so his head was at an angle, and the shell cracked off the back of his skull, without going through. Nicky Holloway did what he could before the chopper got there, but with a catastrophic injury like that, it was pretty hopeless. Milesy went into a coma and never came out. They got him back to the UK and eventually turned his life support off, as there was no hope.'

As he finished re-telling his story I looked over at the jury. At the moment they were on our side, no doubt about it. Compassion and pity for Khan was flowing freely and I needed to try and keep it that way.

Then I got him to explain to the jury in simple terms how he felt about the killing of his young friend. He eloquently talked of the grief, soul searching and guilt and how it had weighed on him, never really going away, the burden seeming to get heavier with each tour, building and building until the pressure got so bad he thought he might be having some type of breakdown, which maybe he had.

I looked up at the clock; three thirty and hopefully just enough time to get my last piece in and come in fresh in the morning. 'Now, you've heard from your sister in law, Rana about this Sunday lunch incident for which you received the caution. I'd like you to tell the jury, in your own words, what happened.'

'Well it's like Rana said. Safia was carving the roast and….I don't know. I guess the light must have caught the blade of the carving knife as I remember that; it comes back to me sometimes in dreams, that glint from the blade setting me off. So when that happened with Safia carving, I just freaked. Natural inclination was to run, to cause mayhem.

'I didn't attack her, or anything like that. There was a tussle is all. They were just trying to calm me down. Again, I don't remember throwing the tray against the wall, but I have no reason to doubt Rana's word about that. In the end I just accepted the caution to make it all go away.'

I didn't think there was anymore to be got from him on these background issues, and the jury were showing distinct signs of boredom and frustration, and I really needed to watch that. But I was pleased we'd now got these essential, but perhaps rather peripheral elements out of the way. Next session I could promise would be a hell of a lot more interesting – I hoped – as we would finally, maybe, get to see what he had to say about the day of the murder.

'Thank you, Mr Khan,' I said turning to look up at the clock and then Feldman. 'My lord, as I've finished this section of evidence, and given the time, I wonder if now might be a good time to adjourn, so we can come in with a fresh topic tomorrow morning?'

Feldman juggled some papers on his desk and closed his notebook. 'Yes, fine, Mr Calver, we'll adjourn until ten tomorrow morning, but I do hope we'll make a little more progress then than we have today,' he said, rising and moving off before I had a chance to respond.

As I got out I jabbed speed dial for Pascal. The call went straight to voice mail.

Pascal sipped from a bottle of Budweiser as she looked around Lammy's sumptuous north London flat, and tried to put a price tag on it. Islington was traditionally the stamping ground of London's wannabe Glitterati and Politico's, so a couple a mill would probably do it.

Lammy, dressed in a sweat stained tracksuit and no make up, caught Pascal's appraising look. 'No, Courtney, it's not mine,' she said, and then with a laugh, 'don't ask.'

Pascal scanned the living room; she couldn't work out whether the huge painting on the wall opposite her was an original Pollock or not; maybe it was. Then she dug her smart phone out and checked the screen. It had a special App that Christoff had designed, and now she held the phone out and slowly scanned the room. She was disappointed but not surprised. Lammy just watched her, saying nothing.

'Got something I need to show you,' Pascal said. 'Down in the car. Leave your phone here. Come on.'

Lammy shrugged then followed.

When they were sat in Pascal's Golf, she said, 'do I need to search you for a wire?'

' No. Look, it wasn't my idea, but I had to tell Condon something – don't worry, I didn't give him the real skinny – but he insisted on wiring up the flat.' She shrugged. 'You know the score, Courtney.'

Pascal watched her, held her eyes, then nodded. 'Good. How long we got?'

'Twenty minutes, maybe.'

'You got the stuff I asked for,' Pascal said

'You first, Courtney.'

'Why have you pulled surveillance on Holloway?'

'Have we?' Lammy said, looking startled.

'Nicky went for a scenic walkabout — around Grosvenor Square, would you believe,' Pascal said, eyebrow raised.

'Don't kid around, Courtney, we haven't got much time.'

'I'm not kidding. He was scoping out your embassy.'

Lammy watched her, evaluating; seeing, after a moment, seriousness. 'Jesus. You know POTUS is flying in.'

'Yeah I do, but let's not get ahead of ourselves. I've got a theory.'

'Which is?'

'Isn't it just a bit too obvious,' Pascal said. 'I mean we're talking about the most heavily protected man on the planet. How do you even get close.'

'That may be so, but I'm not in a position to play fast and loose with my president's life.'

'Very admirable, Lammy, but not very constructive.'

'Fuck you, Courtney. Its gotta be checked out. What d'you expect me to do?'

'Okay, I understand, Averill, but try this for size. I'd lay odds your security guys at the embassy will already have him on CCTV, as he walks past the entrance, twice. They'll tag it suspicious without any help from us, believe me. That's why I'm not convinced, yet.'

'And what if you're wrong?' Lammy said, but she was already crunching the angles, seeing how she could turn it to her advantage.

'I guess this could be a real career maker for you, Lammy – you play your cards right,' Pascal said, veering away, as if the thought had just occurred to her. 'You really want to pass up a once in a lifetime chance by handing this on to honest John Condon, mister cautious? Or worse, you're national security guys, who I guess will shortly be all over you.'

'Look Courtney, forget about me for a second, Condon will be here any minute. If you think there's a way we can keep this to ourselves pro tem *without* endangering POTUS, and pull something off, tell me now, otherwise I'm done here.'

Pascal was past trying to read her, and their time was up. 'I'm assuming you've picked up nothing, no chatter, Intel anything like that?' Pascal asked, knowing the answer.

Lammy shook her head.

'Well I think we're left with pulling either Holloway or Qadir, and sweating them, and when I say pulling them, I mean unofficially,' Pascal said.

'You mean we break the law, Courtney?'

'Or.'

'Or what?' Lammy said, frustration turning to anger.

'Or you flutter your eyelashes at Condon when he gets here, and make him think its his idea to lift – I'd go for Qadir myself – one of them and see what you can shake loose.'

'And then what, we try and play it from the inside?'

Pascal just looked at her, and then said, 'now, what about Calver's wife?'

After the bust up with Calver, Pascal was ambivalent about getting this stuff, but she'd asked for it and didn't now want to lose face with Lammy by letting her off the hook. So Lammy laid it out for her quick and terse, and made it clear the phone footage would not be released until they'd concluded their business, which suited Pascal.

Lammy got out the car and made her way back in as Pascal drove off.

Ten minutes later Condon sat looking pensive, sipping a scotch. He glanced over at Lammy who was watching him, expecting a diatribe about the trip down to the car, but it never came.

'Because you two mysteriously disappeared just when things were starting to get interesting, I've no idea what was said, so you better tell me,' he said, and it was clear he wasn't in the mood for bullshit.

Lammy had been thinking hard ever since Pascal had mentioned Holloway and the embassy, and she knew there was no more time. She had to call it now and make a decision. Condon had told her to give Pascal the info on Calver's wife, so he would expect her to have got something in return, so it was a question of what she told him now.

In the end she suppressed the intel about the embassy and repackaged some of the earlier information, simply telling Condon that Pascal had tailed Khan to the garden shed in Stoke Newington, but suggested all she found there was the empty containers for Nitric acid and battery acid which they believed was for manufacturing PETN for a bomb.

'Yeah, and he could also be using fertilizer in his garden or selling used cars, both of which might explain the presence of nitric and battery acid,' Condon said, before adding, 'but I agree, we need to check it out. Let's get a forensic team down there right away.'

'Boss, irrespective of what they might find, why don't we just pick Qadir up and talk to him. He's never been spoken to before. We could get him in under the prevention of terrorism legislation and sweat him or, maybe better, just get him in for an informal chat. Dress it up as another drive to combat radicalization. We're looking for important members of the Muslim community to help us out. Would he like to help?'

'Why not just pick up Khan. That's why we wanted him back on the street?'

She knew he was just thinking out loud, and stress testing her Qadir scenario. 'Khan's already subject to strict bail conditions although I grant you, they're not particularly effective. But he's in court all day, so he's not going anywhere for the time being, and I reckon the trial's almost over after which he'll go straight to jail. Holloway's a junkie and you know what it's like trying to get anything meaningful out of them. Boss,' she said again, looking at him and starting the slow burn sexy smile, 'there's no downside to talking to Qadir, especially if we dress it up in the way I suggest. I'm sure helping the government will appeal to his ego and vanity, and he just might let something slip.'

Condon put his arms around her and began to nuzzle her neck. 'Okay Averill,' he said,' but why not start softly, softly,' he added, nibbling her ear. 'Don't bring him in, you go out and visit – you can use your formidable feminine charms on him,' he whispered.

She giggled, grabbed his hand and led him towards the bedroom.

Chapter Twenty Four

Pascal sat in the coffee bar with Christoph. He looked at the bubble wrapped laptop on the table and sighed. 'I'll see what I can do. But I imagine you've been over it yourself and haven't found anything,' he said.

'Yeah, I looked, but you know some tricks I don't,' she replied. She'd picked it up early that morning from Joan Franklyn, but couldn't find anything on the hard drive. Christoph had been a code breaker and decrypt analyst, and if there was anything there, he'd find it.

He placed the laptop in his case and said he'd have a look and phone her back later. As he left, Pascal's phone began dancing on the table, Megadeth pouring out of the speakerphone. It was Lammy who told her two things; firstly Condon had green lighted speaking to Qadir, and she was going to arrange to bump into him, and secondly their forensic team had just called in to report that the Stoke Newington shed had burned to the ground the previous evening and there was just smouldering ash and embers left.

Pascal argued that she should accompany Lammy to see Qadir, but Lammy wouldn't budge. Pascal hung up in a rage and then sat sipping coffee and thinking. Then she got up and left.

I sat at the defence table, dog tired after another sleepless night, a kaleidoscope of worry assailing me from all sides. And there was still no word from Pascal – she seemed to have dropped off the face of the earth.

I looked around the courtroom then over at Khan already in the witness box, looking remarkably relaxed, given what was likely to be coming his way. Then as Rose Tremayne slipped into the chair beside me, it was "all stand" as Feldman scrabbled in from the side and into his seat where he moved energetically about until he found his favoured position. He looked over and greeted the jury before nodding to me; I sat for a moment and then rose to my feet.

Before jumping in I just needed to try and neutralise the prosecutions case on motive, so I said, 'now we've heard allegations floating around that Safia was having an affair and indeed, was about to leave you. Was that true?'

Khan looked down for a moment as he collected his thoughts, and then said, emphatically: 'No. Like any marriage we had our share of ups and downs. Safia had been unhappy, but who doesn't get down sometimes. We had our spats; sometimes she wouldn't let me see her phone or facebook but we were over that. In fact we were, if you like, starting again. We even talked about having a special meal to celebrate the new beginning but nothing had been arranged at that time.'

Good; he was sticking to script, but now we needed to move on so I started slowly, leading him through his recollections of what happened in the early part of the day of the murder. As we went along it was clear that his memory had firmed up as his answers were crisp and clear, but he began to slow up as we got closer and closer to the time of the murder. He confirmed that he was at home looking after Aminah when Rana turned up with her kids and Aisha from School at about 4.50 pm, which fitted in with Rana's earlier testimony.

'What happened next?

'I talked to Aisha about what she had been doing at school that day for a bit. You know, kidding around with her and Aminah.'

'What was Rana doing?'

'I think she was on the desk top computer with her kids, looking at facebook.'

'Then what happened?'

'After a while I think Rana realised I was getting a bit restless. I'd run out of drink and ciggies, but felt it would be rude to leave. So she said she would wait for Safia, who would be due back from work in about twenty minutes, if I wanted to pop out. I didn't need much persuasion, so I left about ten to six.'

'And where were you going?'

'When I left I was just going to pop into the corner shop, but when I came out I didn't fancy going straight back home so I thought I'd go down the arches, have a natter, and maybe a few ciders.'

This was all new stuff as far as I was concerned. 'Tell the jury about "the arches". Where and what are they?' I asked him

'They're just the railway arches down the end of the road, underneath the east London line going into Liverpool Street. I'd go down there for the craic. I'll be honest with you,' he said, looking over at the jury, 'they weren't the most salubrious bunch; street drinkers and junkies mostly, but I felt.....I dunno, safe with them, maybe, and there were a couple of veterans who often showed up and I enjoyed hanging out with them.'

To head off Patterson's possible cross, I asked, 'how is it you're now able to remember this, when you couldn't before, when you were questioned by the police?' It was a question I was no doubt going to have to ask a number of times before we were through.

Khan looked flustered for a second, a fleeting look of anger crossing his face at what he probably thought was a hostile question coming from his own lawyer, but then he looked over at Rose Tremayne and she nodded imperceptibly. He said, 'with help from doctor Tremayne over a number of sessions, which allowed me to go back and try and recover lost or missing memories.'

I wished he would try and follow my advice to keep his answers short and simple. 'We don't need detail, Mohsin, just tell us how long you were down the arches and what happened next?'

He rubbed his face and then closed his eyes in concentration. 'I was there for a while. I'd bought a couple of those big three litre bottles of cider from the shop. You know, the strong seven and a half per cent jobs that just about blow your head off, you drink enough of it.'

There was some muffled laughter from the jury which stopped abruptly when Feldman looked over at them sternly. Khan continued, eyes still closed. 'I shared the bottles around the guys, and they had some vodka and some big spliffs, and we had a little party,' he said, a small sad smile on his face as he relived the memory.

'How long?'

'I was there at least an hour, probably more, but you know how it is, in that kind of state, you just don't follow time.'

'Have a guess.'

'I reckon hour and half; maybe a bit more.'

'Then what did you do?'

'I went back to the flat to see Safia,' he said, a puzzled expression on his face, almost as if the words had popped out without his knowledge.

I looked down at my papers, trying to cover my shock, and for a moment the court was completely silent as if no one had heard him right, but then the noise rose and spread through the jury and gallery as the full import of his words sank in. I just stood there desperately trying to think of a question that wouldn't get us into any more trouble.

The squat looked as scummy as ever but this time it was clearly under surveillance. Pascal couldn't quite believe how obvious the black box van looked, but then she doubted that Holloway would notice, even if it had the words MI5 emblazoned on the side. She parked her bike around the corner in front of the Halal butchers again, but this time she was completely obscured from view by the corner of the building jutting out, which she could peek around, and watch the street, the squat and the van.

After around ninety minutes of an engrossing online chess game that seemed to have reached a stalemate, she was just about to call it a day when things started to move quickly. She heard the soft throaty growl of the BMW bike before she saw it, then it was gliding into view, coming to a stop at the curb in front of the squat. It was a beautiful bike – looked like an F800. The guy astride it was covered in leathers and helmet, so impossible to identify. The number plates were covered in crud and completely indecipherable. A few seconds later Holloway emerged carrying what looked like the silver attaché case Pascal had seen Khan take away from the shed. The biker handed him a helmet, he climbed on and they were away as Pascal cracked her bike into life. She noticed with a smile that the surveillance van was facing the wrong way and was going to find it impossible to turn quickly and follow.

Pascal kept well back and at times it was hard because the biker was very adept and fast, weaving in and out of traffic, but the very weight of traffic acted to hide her somewhat distinctive trials bike. They got onto Mile End road and soon after the BMW turned off into side streets. Pascal was starting to worry she would be spotted as the traffic was much sparser but then the bike turned abruptly into a drive and went straight into an open garage, the door coming down automatically as soon as the bike passed the threshold. She sat for a moment at the road junction as she deliberated what to do. She couldn't really sit watching in a quiet residential street like this, sticking out like a sore thumb and it was unlikely she could approach the house and see inside without being seen. She made a mental note of the address and then sped away.

Inside the garage the two men removed their helmets and silently made their way through a side door into the house. The larger man stooped slightly as he walked, whilst Holloway, already sweating and hyper, his eyes darting around manically, walked behind. Inside the living room was cool minimalist, all hardwood floors, cream colours, with no pictures or ornaments.

'I could do with a wee hit, Frankie,' Holloway said, trying to keep a light tone in his voice.

Frankie Crawford scrutinised the smaller man, gauging his state of readiness for the job to come. 'I need you straight for this one, Nicky, but do it right and I'll take care of you. Just like before, yeah?' he said.

Holloway nodded quickly, always slightly wary of the big man and his moods, anxious not to provoke the guy. Now he surreptitiously studied Frankie, trying to satisfy himself the big man would be good for the drugs, when the job was done.

Crawford had been super fit as a soldier, but now, especially after the last Afghan tour, he was not such an intimidating figure. He had a chronic ache in his shoulder that was just about continuous, even with tranquilisers, which seemed to last about half an hour before the pain resumed and fanned out, making him want to scream. His eyes, when not suffused with pain or meds, looked dead and empty as if he had seen too much on the battlefield, which he had, in spades, everything you could imagine. But he still retained some of his bearing, and his face was clear and lean, topped off with short grey blonde hair.

He led Holloway into a utility, gym room, bare apart from what looked like a dentists chair beside a worktable on which were implements that wouldn't have been out of place in an operating theatre. On the desk was also a computer screen on which turned a three D image of the device Khan had been working on in the garden shed.

Crawford slowly pulled his tracksuit top off. Holloway stood as if rooted to the spot, watching the big man, maybe surprised that what they'd discussed in the past now seemed to be turning into reality when all along he'd thought it was just another mad Frankie fantasy. He watched the big man for another beat, then carefully hoisted the attaché case up onto the table and opened it.

'Just pretend you're back in the butchers shop in Helmand, Nicky. I'm sure it will all come back to you man,' Crawford said as he lay back on the recliner chair and fixed Holloway with a spookily mad stare.

Holloway licked his lips, sweat starting to stand out on his forehead. 'Are you sure about this, big man? I know you talked an all, but—'

'Just do it, yeah.'

Holloway could see Crawford was beyond argument, his belief so ingrained and scarred into his psyche as to be immoveable, so he focused in on Crawford's right shoulder area, and said, 'okay, man.'

Holloway leaned forward and swabbed a moist cloth over an area below Crawford's collarbone on the right side. Then he drew some liquid from a vial into a hypodermic syringe, and said, 'I'm just going to shoot you up with a local,' as he slowly injected him.

Crawford stayed quiet, looking serene and calm.

Holloway selected a scalpel and tested the blade before turning back to Crawford and studying the shoulder area, waiting a spell for the anaesthetic to do its work. Then he leant forward again and made a short incision across the moistened area of skin. Crawford didn't flinch; instead he began to hum quietly under his breath – sounded like "Onward Christian Soldiers" – as Holloway busied himself around the incision area. The volume of Crawford's singing increased and then he began to laugh softly, his body starting to rock with movement until Nicky had to put a hand on to calm him, so he could complete the surgery. He gingerly used a pair of tweezers to gently lift away a flap of skin so he could survey the insertion area.

It took Holloway, calling on all his skills as an army trained medic, around half an hour to complete the insertion of the device built by Khan. When satisfied, he slowly stitched the flap of skin back into place, then leaned back to admire his handy work. Despite the ravages of heroin and alcohol abuse, Holloway still retained some facility as a medic and he was proud of his work.

He even forgot the heroin for a short while as he chatted with Crawford about how he needed to take it easy for a few days whilst the stitching healed, and how he must avoid extremes of temperature and stay calm. Holloway was to stay the night so he could monitor the patient. He handed Crawford a small mirror so the big man could admire his handy work. Crawford seemed pleased, expressed his admiration for Nicky's medical skills and then handed over a small chunk of heroin, saying he'd get the balance in the morning, if all was well.

Chapter Twenty Five

I waited, standing at the defence table, as the furore in the courtroom died down, and then I asked Khan, 'Okay. So you went back to the flat. Why?'

'To see Safia,' he said, simply.

'Tell us what happened.'

He drew a deep breath and then began to speak. 'It was after half seven when I got to the flat, probably around twenty to eight, as I remember Corry was on the TV, but Safia was in the kitchen washing up.'

He paused, eyes closed, as if re-running a movie in his head. I kept my mouth shut, guessing he wouldn't need any prompting from me.

'I, I went to her,' he stuttered. 'She turned from the sink and we kissed, just a simple friendly kind of hello kiss, like old times. But then I think maybe passion took over and it turned into something else.'

The court was silent, apart from the quiet hum of strip lighting and computer equipment. All eyes were on Khan. He stood, head bowed and eyes closed tight in concentration. There was just a thin patina of sweat on his forehead; otherwise he could have been sleeping.

'When we broke apart she smiled at me, and it..... It was like back before when we were happy. She had her hands in the sink, washing up the supper things. So I grabbed a tea towel and began to dry. Then, then.....' he said, stuttering again and pausing.

I turned slightly to look at Rose Tremayne, sitting next to me; she was watching Khan intently, a look of concern on her face. I made a kind of shrug and question mark kind of expression at her as if to say: what now? Should I go on?

She quickly nodded her head in the affirmative, but Khan was speaking again, 'I don't quite know what happened……she, she must have picked up the carving knife from the suds and she, she wiped it and held it up to the light, and, and………' he said, his voice becoming quieter, and then it was as if he had been hit by a bullet. He twisted violently, his upper trunk seizing as if he were having a minor fit. I made as if to move toward him but Rose grabbed my arm and stayed me, watching intently along with the rest of the court.

'I, I must have grabbed the knife; that's the cut on my hand,' he continued, voice calmer now. 'I can remember her screaming, and she was cut as well, as I could see the blood on her hands and over the front of her blouse.'

A single tear ran down Khan's face. 'Then, I……' he started, but his emotions were now too much, and he began to sob, slowly sinking down into his chair.

'My lord,' I started—'

'Yes, yes, Mr Calver, I quite agree,' Feldman said, for once acting like a real judge. 'Given the witness's need to compose himself,' he said, looking up at the clock, 'we will take a short ten minute break.'

I sighed with relief, but knew it was only temporary. In ten minutes time Khan's life would be on the line.

The little religious bookshop was in North London. Averill Lammy sat in one of the scattered chairs that were arranged in a semi circle around the small lecturn. She watched as Maqsood Qadir wound up his short lecture on Sharia law. His theme was that Sharia was entirely compatible with the English common law.

There were perhaps twelve people in the audience; young bearded men, a few Abaya clad women and a smattering of young student types, all very earnest. Qadir was a surprisingly good speaker, his speech dotted with modern parables which he interspersed with his flashy smile. And he clearly wasn't immune to feminine charms, his eyes frequently flicking over Lammy as he spoke, clearly wondering who she was.

As the lecture broke up Lammy made sure she was standing next to Qadir as he ordered a coffee at the little side bar counter. She smiled and said, 'interesting speech Mr. Qadir, but tell me, d'you really believe a woman's evidence is worth half that of a man's, under good old Sharia law?'

'I think you're trying to provoke me, miss..?' he said, smiling flirtatiously.

'Lammy. Averill Lammy,' she said extending her hand, which Qadir took and kissed. They got their coffees and went and sat in the corner.

'You seem, how can I put it? Somewhat out of place here? A young, glamorous American woman in an Islamic bookstore,' Qadir said, gesturing at their surroundings.

'Oh, just call me inquisitive,' she said.

They sat silent for a moment while Qadir openly examined her. Lammy sat, relaxed, despite the strong urge to wipe her hand where he had kissed it.

Qadir apparently finished with looking her over, pursed his lips and said, 'so if you're not a book buyer or a groupie, what are you? Let me guess: journalist, or perhaps British Intelligence?'

'Wow, that's quite a jump, and me with an American accent. How would that work, I wonder?' She said holding his gaze for a moment, a challenge, but also a hint of a come on. Then she sighed. 'But if I was from British Intelligence, maybe we would like to talk to you. You seem to be a man who knows what's going on around here. Perhaps we can help each other out, especially if, say,' she said, pausing as she focused on his eyes, projecting the challenge, 'you wanted to avoid being extradited to the States on Federal charges of being a foreign combatant in Iraq a few years ago?'

That got to him, although it only showed in the faintest of tremors in his eyes, the casual smile remaining. 'Wow, that's quite a jump as well, agent Lammy. But then I'm sure if there was a shred of truth in what you say, the Brits would have been all over me by now, and would no doubt be falling over themselves to offer me a non extradition deal if I spoke to them.'

'Touché,' Lammy said, then, 'but maybe we can still help each other. See, we've got this rogue agent running amok at the moment. Courtney Pascal used to be a rising star at MI5 until she got sent down, and now she's out spreading all sorts of rumours. We think she's just mischief making, but according to her, Mohsin Khan, famously on trial right now, as we speak, for the murder of his wife Safia, has been seen building bombs in a garden shed in Stoke Newington. Now, what d'you think of that, Maqsood?'

This time he couldn't hide the momentary widening of his eyes, his total surprise clear, before his almost instant, rigid self control was reasserted, smile just about still in place. Lammy watched him. She'd given a lot of thought about how she would play this. It was a definite risk showing her hand, but what was the alternative? They were out of time; the only way to blow the whole thing open and for her to get the career defining glory right now, was to chuck a grenade in the hole with Qadir, and then watch it play out. Throwing Courtney Pascal to the wolves was collateral damage and just part and parcel of the game.

Qadir watched her for a moment, his face blank, but his mind oscillating through probabilities. 'It's been most interesting, and entertaining, Miss Lammy, but I'm afraid I have no idea what you're talking about,' he said as he rose from the table and made a slight bow, before turning and making for the door. Lammy watched him go, a small hesitant smile playing on her lips – had she blown it? Time would tell. She got up and left.

As the door closed behind her, the man at the next table slowly unwound the keffiyeh scarf from around the lower part of his face, slipped his cell phone out of his sleeve, went to switch off the recorder, then froze when he realised he'd never switched it on. As he desperately tried to recall and make sense of the limited parts of the conversation he had heard, his finger hovered indecisively over the speed dial button for Commander John Condon.

'You said, before the break,' I said, looking down and checking my notes, "I must have grabbed the knife; that's the cut on my hand,"' I said, looking over at Khan, who stood impassively, watching me. 'Then, after saying you could see the blood, you started to tell us what happened. You said, "Then I," and stopped. Tell the jury what happened next,' I said.

This was it really. All the bullshit; all the build up; all the prep; this is what it was all about; the answer to this question. Khan's entire future rested on it, and did he care about it? It didn't seem like it to me. He stood there, relaxed, more like a man in a supermarket queue than a man on trial for murder.

For a long moment he was silent. I looked to my left at Rose Tremayne for a heads up, but she imperceptibly shook her head, indicating that I leave it be and wait. Khan's eyes were shut again, and as for the jury, well what can I say; riveted didn't really do it justice.

'I didn't kill her,' he finally said, softly. 'There was a light scuffle over the knife, I just don't remember it exactly. The knife did nick her on her neck and shoulder, but not deeply, just surface wounds, none of which I intended. It probably lasted less than fifteen seconds, almost like a fit, and when I came out of it, it felt like waking from a nightmare.

'Safia knew immediately what had happened, and she wasn't really hurt at all, the worst wound was to my hand. You know, for a while we just sat their hugging each other, and I cried. She held me like that until I had stopped shaking. Then she told me to take my blood stained clothing off and she put it straight in the washing machine.'

Khan's narration had been flowing freely but now he paused, opened his eyes and took a sip of water.

'What happened next,' I lightly pressed him.

'I said to Safia I needed to get some air, clear my head, but I also think I was very ashamed of myself, that I'd hurt her and didn't deserve to be in her presence, at least until I'd sorted myself out. I also remember saying that the knife was evil as it seemed to act as a trigger for my bad behaviour, and that I wanted to get rid of it for good. Safia agreed, so I left, taking the knife with me. Outside I thought what better place to get rid of it than down the drain – no one would find it there or be able to use it to hurt anyone else - so that's what I did; dropped it down there.'

I waited to see if Khan had anything to add but he seemed to have finished, so I asked, 'You say you went out for some air. What time did you leave and where did you go?'

'You know I've tried very hard to remember details, but it's hard, even with Dr. Tremayne's help,' he said nodding at Rose. 'I think I was only in the house for around maybe fifteen minutes, because I know Corry was still on when I left. I know I intended to just pop out and come straight back, but in the end I didn't go back and I don't know why. I probably just got waylaid in the pub and then went onto the Mosque. I know I was very upset about what had happened because I knew that I'd scared and hurt Safia, and I may have thought I would get some reassurance or support at the Mosque.'

'Are you positive you never went back to the flat that night?'

'Positive.'

'Was Safia alive when you left the flat that night?'

'Yes she was.'

'Did you kill Safia?'

'No I did not.'

This interchange had been delivered fairly quick fire, and now I paused to let Mohsin's answers sink in, before moving on to the next bit – we were nearly done.

'Now, we all saw earlier in the trial the recording of your police interview, and in that interview Detective inspector Stanton puts the question to you,' I said, looking down and checking my notes, '"You killed Safia, didn't you?" and in answer you said, "I must have…..I must have done it."'

Again I paused, watching Khan. His answer to the next question would probably seal his fate. He looked calm and untroubled and I didn't know whether that was good or bad; we were about to find out.

'Now, you've told the jury you didn't kill Safia. So why did you tell the police you, "must have done it?" You need to explain to the jury now, why you said those words?'

'I was confused and stressed,' he said quickly, then stopped as if realising that such an inadequate explanation for why he had effectively falsely confessed to murder, wasn't really going to cut it with the jury. He looked at me, as if hoping I could somehow dig him out the hole and answer the question for him, but I remained impassive, waiting, along with the jury.

'It's hard, sometimes….to explain,' he said.

'Have a go,' I said, sensing disaster unless he got a grip and started making sense.

He looked around the courtroom, clearly trying to get his thoughts in some kind of order. 'You have to remember,' he said, speaking slowly as if feeling his way along, 'that when they got me in that room, it was the start of a nightmare. Before we even got in there that Stanton was saying things; things about my daughters, saying they would be taken into care unless we sorted things out quick. That frightened me, but worse, of course, was trying to deal with what he said about Safia. I've seen death in the army, but not when its someone so very close, someone who you love; who is your life. I was completely destroyed by it; just numb. You just don't think straight when you're in that kind of state – logic just goes right out the window.'

He paused and sipped some more water. This was better, but he needed to take it somewhere. He continued, 'and Stanton was clever. He never said anything definitive, that he could be pulled up on. Then after the threats about my kids, he became my best mate, promising to help, get me out of there quick, but I needed to help them, sort of thing. When you're in that situation and the state I was in, you have no idea,' he said, looking over at the jury, 'what its like. Anybody who seems like a friend, you're going to grab hold of, and Stanton seemed like that.

'The other thing, and I guess you'll find it hard to believe, but its true, is that, because I literally had no idea where I had been that night – my memory at that time was completely gone – I was absolutely terrified, that maybe I *had* killed Safia. So in the end I just felt all the evidence was pointing that way, I was going to lose my kids anyway. It seemed like I didn't have much to live for, but what they were holding out to me, was the chance to see my kids that moment, if I cooperated. In that situation you don't think long term, your desperate, so the chance just to have it all go away and be reunited with the only thing left that you love seemed priceless, so in the end I gave them what they wanted so I could see my kids.'

It was the first time I'd heard any of this, but it did have the ring of truth about it – especially the bit about Stanton – and it was delivered in a calm and seemingly genuine way, and maybe it would convince some of the jurors. It was too late now, but if he had told me about Stanton's threats and blackmail, especially about his kids, all done away from the camera, we could have applied to chuck the confession out on the basis that it had been obtained by oppressive questioning from the police, but, that was history now. All in all, I was reasonably happy with what Khan had come up with by way of explanation.

We were just about done now, save for the repetition of an earlier question, but an essential one: 'Did you kill Safia, Mr Khan?' I asked

Give him his due, he turned full on to the jury and addressed them head on: 'No I did not kill her,' he said, forcefully. 'She was the light of my life, the mother of my children, and whatever problems I may have had with her, I would never, ever have killed her.'

I paused, allowing his final words to reverberate around the jury box, as he stood firm, facing them and holding their gaze. 'Thank you, Mr. Khan. I have no more questions. If you will wait there, my learned friend, Mr Patterson may wish to question you,' I said. Then I sat down.

Patterson stood before the jury, relaxed and authoritative. Now he was about to let loose his formidable forensic skills on my client. For all my dislike of Patterson, he clearly presented an attractive image to the jury; tall and commanding, his black gown immaculate, and all topped off with that magnificent horse hair wig. I could see him in my minds eye, twenty five years earlier, careening down the Olympic ski slopes in goggles and brightly coloured nylon, putting on a great performance, just as I guessed he was hoping to do again today.

'As a soldier, Corporal Khan, you were trained to kill, yes?' he asked, a subtly lethal question, disguised by the matter of fact tone in which it was delivered.

Straightaway Khan seemed on edge, sensing the cleverness of the question, with its inbuilt trap that whichever way it was answered, he would come out looking bad. He hesitated a moment – I hoped to God he'd nip that in the bud – and then he replied, 'I wouldn't say that, not specifically. We were trained to fight. That's all.'

'And fighting involved killing, yes?'

'I wouldn't put it quite like that, but I suppose you could say that.'

Then Patterson was moving on again. 'Now you've made great play over your feelings of trauma after you witnessed various incidents, for example private Franklyn being killed by the sniper, yes?'

'I was shocked and upset by what I witnessed, yes,' he answered.

'Did you attend any counselling sessions as a result of that trauma?' Patterson asked.

Khan was already starting to show signs of irritation, a sign that good advocacy is working. The witness is kept extremely tightly controlled by the use of strictly defined closed questions that allow no room for explanation in the answer. And we'd barely started.

'No I did not. I was a serving Corporal in the British army and it would have been......unseemly to do that,' he said.

'You could have taken sick leave, surely, if you were as badly affected as you say you were, and then sought counselling?'

'I'm afraid I just bottled it up, which of course made it worse, in the end,' Khan said, his first minor victory of the skirmish. I smiled behind my hand; Patterson wasn't getting it all his own way, but it was a minor victory, and that soon became clear as the afternoon wore on. Patterson used the same routine for each of the incidents we had led on earlier, essentially saying well if you were so traumatised why didn't you seek treatment.

I watched the jury as the questioning went on. I could see that there was a residual sympathy for Khan but as the relentless questions rained down on him I could also see certain jurors occasionally looking over at him, with questioning looks. What made it worse was that we had barely started, and Patterson was already scoring freely. I dared not start objecting yet, when there was so much more to come.

Chapter Twenty Six

Holloway pealed back the dressing and examined the stitching; it had sealed well and there was no more bleeding. He pulled it all the way off and dropped it in the waste bin. 'Looking good Frankie,' he said with a wink. 'We'll have you up and about in no time, mate.'

The front door bell rang. 'Must be our takeaway,' he said as he went out to the hall.

Crawford ran his fingers over the stitching. It felt firm, and he felt good, or as good as he ever felt these days, what with the pain and trying to walk round with chunks of metal in his back and shoulder. He rolled his legs off the couch and stood up, swaying slightly but then getting his equilibrium; he took a few paces and it felt even better. He moved to the table at the side and poured himself a large scotch. Holloway had warned him not to drink for a few days, but what did a fucking junkie know about anything? He drained the glass and poured another.

He listened to Holloway in the kitchen opening cupboards and clinking cutlery as he looked for plates; he sniffed the aroma of the Indian food and smiled. He felt like he was going to enjoy himself. He reached down to the drawer in the table and took out a huge hunting knife and smiled again as he tested the razor sharp blade with his finger.

As they sat eating, Crawford listened to Holloway as he prattled on about the good old days of the Afghan campaign. Crawford used the hunting knife to spear large chunks of beef in the thick brown curry sauce, and then chewed away, whilst a strange disconnected smile played on his lips.

'So you did take a memento?' Holloway said, eyeing the knife.

'This is a Holy knife, boy,' Crawford said, suddenly looking serious and scary again.

He seemed to be getting madder by the minute as far as Holloway could see. He said, 'boy we had some fun that night,' hoping to try and lighten Frankie's mood.

'I don't miss the killing,' Crawford said, cryptically, but his expression belied the words; his face seemed to reflect a kind of ecstasy, as if he were undergoing some religious rite of passage, but Holloway didn't seem to notice.

'Killing's nothing,' he added, leaning back and running his finger along the knife blade, his mind mired in nostalgia. Then, his face turning bitter, he said, 'If it wasn't for the brass, I'd be a fucking millionaire by now, but look at me. Riddled with pain twenty four seven; fuckers.'

Holloway's last small shot of heroin was fast expiring, pushing up his anxiety levels, and Crawford's mood seemed weird, even for him. There was not much more he could do for Frankie, the skin was firming up nicely and the stitches would dissolve soon, so maybe it would be best to get a chunk of Heroin and get the fuck out before the big man started getting really weird.

He wiped his mouth with his sleeve and stood up. 'Look, Frankie, I better be going, man. You'll be fine, just don't get too close to a heat source, yeah?' he said nervously, looking around. 'So how's about that big fix before I go? Say it myself, bro, I did a fucking good job.'

Crawford stood up smiling and moved towards Holloway. 'Yeah, you did a fine job, Nicky. Are you my brother or what?' he said embracing him. Holloway hesitated, then gingerly laid his hands on Frankie's shoulders, anxious not to jog the stitches. Crawford then leant back and studied Holloway closely, looking into his eyes. Then he shoved the blade of the hunting knife deep into Holloway' stomach, watching the surprise and shock freeze Holloway's eyes, and lock his grin into a macabre rictus. Then with immense power Frankie violently twisted the razor sharp blade, turned it back, then forced the blade upwards towards Holloway's breastbone, slowly eviscerating him whilst all the time minutely studying Holloway's face. And now he was humming onward Christian soldiers again. As the knife hit the breastbone,

Crawford smiled, and said, 'how d'you like them apples, Nickyboy?'

But Nicky couldn't hear him anymore because he was dead. Crawford slid the blade out and stepped away as Holloway dropped like a sack of potatoes. Crawford spat on the corpse and wiped the blade off on Holloway's jacket. Then he poured himself another scotch which he slowly sipped as he looked around the room, then Holloway's cheap disposable cell phone began to beep.

Crawford dug the phone out and pressed the connection button, and listened. He immediately recognised the voice of Qadir.

'Yeah, Nicky's in the toilet – you know what junkies are like,' Frankie said.

'Actually,' Qadir said, 'I'm glad I've caught you. I need you to clear up a loose end, before the wedding, or there might be no wedding.'

Crawford stiffened. 'What is it?' he said, keeping his voice calm, with some effort.

'An ex con named Courtney Pascal is causing problems, talking to people and meddling in things that don't concern her; she needs to be stopped,' Qadir said, before giving Crawford the details of where to find her.

Then Qadir was onto another topic. 'Lastly, I'm going to see our man tonight, after court, to get your insulin,' he said. 'Then we'll break our rule, and meet up – its too late for them to stop us now so I calculate the risk is acceptable – so go to the designated spot, and get rid of that phone.'

Pascal huddled in the doorway of an empty building and watched the front door of the house opposite. She'd been there for an hour after a brief visit to the dojo for a judo session, and now she felt cold as the sweat dried and chilled down her back. Then sheets of rain started to sweep across the street into the doorway making her shiver. As she checked her watch, the garage door slid up and out came the bike again; this time with only a single rider, and it wasn't Holloway. The bike stopped for a moment at the top of the driveway of the house. The driver leant down and adjusted something at the side of the engine plate.

As she watched, the rain started to dissolve the mud and crud that had been obscuring the registration plate of the bike. She managed to get a partial four digits before the rider sped off. No way of following and anyway she'd likely get more out of Holloway, who must still be inside, and he could identify the mysterious rider.

She waited a few moments more before moving out of the doorway towards the house, now in shadow, as the rain clouds moved away and the sun started to go down.

Next door, the old lady sat behind the net curtains and watched Pascal as she surreptitiously studied the house. She thought the girl looked strange, stick like; a waif. Pascal pressed the bell and waited; after a while, when no one answered, she turned and disappeared down the alleyway at the side of the house. The old lady, biting her lip, kept glancing over at the telephone on the side table.

Pascal looked in through the kitchen window at the back of the house. It looked empty, so maybe Holloway had left earlier. She tried the back door; locked. Then she looked at the side window, and it was open a crack. She pushed it wide open and levered herself up onto the windowsill, then edged her way in and down onto the floor. She remained motionless in the twilight silence as she acclimatised herself to the room and its rhythm and sounds.

Earlier, with the help of Christoff who was still working on the laptop when she had called, she'd checked out ownership of the house. It was owned by an Offshore company, which in turn was owned by unnamed nominees who could only be contacted via a Swiss law firm; dead end. However it was managed by a letting agency who she had also contacted. They told her it was already let under a long lease and the family were currently away for three months, so nothing doing, but they had plenty of other properties if she was interested.

She moved silently through the house using her phone flashlight, then in the utility room, which had no windows, she put on the powerful overhead light. The silver attaché case still lay open, but now empty, on the work table. She studied the array of surgical tools on the bench, and then she booted up the computer and began browsing, and immediately came to the 3d turning image. It was of a heart pacemaker. She leant back in the dentist's chair, thinking hard; what the fuck were they looking at pacemakers for? As she ruminated, filtering scenarios, her phone burst into life, Megadeth screaming loudly. She immediately muted the sound, and checked the caller; Calver! She diverted the call to voicemail and turned it off.

In the living room she found Holloway. She made damn sure the thick drapes were properly closed, then turned on the overhead strip lighting. He lay where he had fallen, on his back, his stomach and chest cavity gaping open and awash with dark, congealing blood. Pascal knelt down and carried out a minute examination of the body, noting the wodge of saliva on the forehead, evidently a last contemptuous gesture from the killer. To rip the guts open like that would have required a lot of power, and the guy on the bike was certainly big enough.

She moved over to the table to mix a drink, and there was a huge hunting knife lying on the silver drinks tray next to the half empty bottle of scotch. Pascal picked up the bottle and took a long drink; she coughed as the fiery fluid slid down her throat as she studied the knife without touching it. There were no discernible blood stains, so probably wiped clean.

She picked it up and ran her finger down the blade; it was razor sharp, not dulled by the killing. She had no doubt it was the murder weapon. She held it in one hand and raised the bottle to her lips with the other, and took another long gulp. Then the front door bell rang.

Pascal remained motionless for a millisecond, then she was moving fast, silently for the kitchen. She heaved herself back up onto the sill and edged her way out, just as a police constable hove into view with flashlight, grabbed her shoulder and said, 'you're nicked.' Then he shouted back over his shoulder, 'back here, I've got a live one.'

Mohsin Khan got to his feet and slowly began to make his way towards the exits along with the few other worshippers who were there for prayer that evening. Then suddenly there was Qadir again, standing with that maddening smile in place, watching and waiting.

Khan briefly considered just walking right through the guy, but then a fleeting image of his daughters floated through his mind, and he reluctantly stopped. He knew he had no choice but to go through with it. Qadir gestured for him to follow, back into the private area of the Mosque. In the book lined study room, Qadir turned to him, and said, 'D'you have it?' His tone was short and brusque; he was clearly in a hurry.

The guys arrogance was burning Khan making him want to lash out and clip the guy, but he knew he couldn't do that either. He said, 'lets get something straight, Qadir. I give this to you, I'm done. You leave my children alone and you never contact me again. You clear on that?' Khan said, his voice strong, with an edge of aggression.

Qadir smiled thinly. 'Of course,' he said. 'Provided that you continue to keep your mouth shut,' he added.

Khan watched Qadir for a moment, trying to gauge sincerity, but it was hopeless with a guy like Qadir. In the end he knew he'd just have to trust him. What other choice did he have. And as for what they wanted the device for, frankly, he didn't want to know. He just wanted to protect his family.

He lifted his robe up and delicately removed a belt which had a pouch attached to it. He moved to the table and carefully opened the pouch and removed a small metal box, like a tobacco tin. 'You need to understand that this stuff is pretty unstable,' he said as he slowly opened the tin. Qadir leant over his shoulder to watch. 'Excessive movements, light, heat, friction, any kind of stimulus, and you're gonna be fucked,' Khan added.

Inside the tin was a syringe, itself held in a kind of thick liquid jelly. 'This, my friend, is my special cocktail; meet modified Triacetone Triperoxide. You mix this baby up with what I made for you the other day, and you're gonna light up the world,' Khan said as he studied the syringe.

'It, it's safe for me to carry, yes?' Qadir said, the first hint of doubt and fear in his voice.

Khan smiled. 'Oh, it'll be fine, long as you don't drop it or set fire to it,' he said, enjoying Qadir's discomfort. 'You inject this into what I made for you the other day, at an ambient temperature, and you'll have just four minutes thirty seconds before it detonates, and then, to borrow a phrase: Kaboom!' he said throwing his arms up, and directing his smile at Qadir.

Khan carefully closed the tin, stood up and handed it to Qadir, and then turned and walked away towards the exit. Qadir watched him go; he licked his lips and his hands felt sweaty. He opened his attaché case and placed the tin securely inside, locked it up and left, hoping Crawford would be on time.

The met at Liverpool Street Station. If you wanted to hold a secret meeting someplace, you would be hard put to find a better location than one of the major train stations in London. They thronged with huge constantly shifting crowds of travellers, making surveillance and eavesdropping close to impossible.

Qadir, after engaging in some extraordinary counter surveillance techniques, was certain he had not picked up a tail. He was pleased to see as he arrived that Crawford was already there in the coffee bar, sitting at a crowded window counter sipping an espresso, and he had purloined the seat next to him with his jacket.

Qadir ignored Crawford and went to the counter and got a milky latte and then went over and took the seat beside Crawford, continuing to ignore him. He leaned down and placed the attaché case between them on the floor. Qadir was wearing an earpiece wired up to his mobile phone which he held open whilst he talked out loud, to what Crawford knew was an imaginary person, but it allowed Qadir to talk direct to Crawford, without any casual observer realising it.

'There's a problem,' Qadir said, watching the endless stream of travellers streaming by outside. 'The girl, Pascal, has been arrested at the house with a dead body, which I assume is Nicky Holloway,' he said, no hint of criticism or surprise in his voice. 'But I still need you to get to her, more than ever now, before she gets a chance to talk.'

Crawford merely nodded. He took his mobile out as if receiving a call and began to talk also. 'No problem,' he said. 'I'll find out where they've taken her from my contacts. Incidentally, you did say clear up all the rubbish when I finished in the house, and I just thought that Nicky came under that heading. Any objections?'

'None at all,' Qadir said.

Crawford swept his eyes over Qadir as if looking over at the counter, just to make sure the guy was still solid, then said, 'I'm assuming this girl's a little more than an ex-con if we're going to all this trouble, and how d'you find out so quick?'

'She's a loose end, is all, and you don't need to know. She apparently got wind of our little place in Stoke Newington and did some speculating and some talking, but they know nothing. The shed's gone now, and they're far too late to stop us, even if they did have the slightest idea what we are doing.'

'And the Mile End house is clean, no links to us?'

'Of course,' Qadir replied quickly. He finished his coffee, and said, 'if things go to plan, we won't meet again. The insulin syringe for your diabetes is in the case, and you know what to do. Good luck with the wedding on Friday,' he concluded with a short bark of a laugh as he finished his coffee. Then he stood up and moved away, still talking to his imaginary caller. A few minutes later, Crawford followed him out, only this time he was carrying the attaché case.

Condon sat in his office overlooking the Thames. Lammy had suddenly gone awol and wasn't answering his calls. He knew she was holed up in the US embassy with the ever expanding advance party preparing the ground for the US Presidents imminent visit.

Condon knew she was riven by divided loyalties, but he also knew she was intensely competitive and ambitious. That she was running some kind of solo operation was pretty clear from the somewhat garbled and ambiguous report he'd got from the mole he'd placed at Qadir's little lecture. He'd try her one last time and if she still wasn't answering, he'd pull Qadir in himself. As he picked up his cell phone to call her, his land line beeped.

He grabbed the phone; it was one of the grunts downstairs. 'Sir, an arrest in Mile End Road has been flagged up twice. It's a Miss Courtney Pascal, found at the house with the body of a Nicholas Holloway; looks like multiple stab wounds.'

It wasn't often that Condon was surprised by anything, but this did surprise him. Hard to believe that the Pascal of old would get caught cold with a dead body like that. 'Where is she?' Condon asked.

'Still at the scene, sir, and may be for some time. Looks like it's been assigned to,' the grunt said, pausing as he checked the record, 'a DI Richard Stanton.'

Condon terminated the call and told his secretary to call the team in immediately, and get hold of the investigating officer, DI Stanton.

As Crawford let himself in to the Boarding house in Stepney East London, he could hear the payphone on the landing, ringing. He ran for the stairs, as it could only be for him; he was the only one who used it. It was Qadir, on a public landline, sounding breathless, as if he had been running.

'She's still at the house,' he said, getting his breath back. 'I've got a spotter down there; looks like it may be sometime before they transport her. You're not far away. Take her out now, before they move her to the station, or we get blown. Nothing to lose now,' he said as he terminated the call.

As Crawford made his way along the landing to his room he wondered at the way Qadir had gone from calmness to open panic in such a short time. It seemed to reaffirm his long held view that when it came to it, the Arabs were just a bunch of sheep and camel shagging pussies. But he wasn't worried, dealing with the girl would be just another soldiering job, which he would carry out with his usual ruthless efficiency.

The room he entered was small with a chaotic mess of dirty clothing, empty wine and cider bottles and beer cans, all over the floor. The walls were covered with military type pictures of soldiers and combat, torn from magazines, newspapers and books. Crawford moved to the wooden chest at the end of the bed; he swept a load of dirty clothing off the top cover and then opened it. Inside was a mini arsenal, including an AK47 assault rifle, a number of handguns, anti personal mines and a couple of good old fashioned pineapples. Crawford hefted the two grenades, studied them briefly and then put them in his rucksack; then he left.

Chapter Twenty seven

Pascal sat on a chair in the kitchen amid the chatter of police radios as forensics and police officers moved around her. She'd been told someone would talk to her soon and then she would be transported to a police station. They'd taken her phone and she was dying for a drink; even coffee would be good right now.

She recognised Stanton as soon as he walked in; crumpled, red faced with beer gut hanging over his belt. Although she'd studied him carefully when he'd given evidence at the trial, she couldn't tell whether he recognised her or not.

He gestured for her to follow and led her into a small study room, little more than a large cupboard. He closed the door and turned to her. In the confined space his body odour was overpowering; stale sweat and cigarettes. He smiled a lazy smile, moving in on her whilst running his eyes over her. His manner didn't strike Pascal as lustful, worse in fact, he seemed kind of asexual more than anything.

'Talk now,' he said, voice low and matter of fact. 'Make it simple and don't complicate things by lying. I'm going to ask you one question. You give me a wrong answer; you give me backtalk, any lip, I'll hurt you, okay? So, why d'you gut the guy?' he said, eyes hard and dead as he watched her, waiting; unconcerned.

'Fuck you fat boy,' she said, deadpan. 'How about you caution me like you're supposed to, and then I get my phone call?'

The slap came out of nowhere, and the cliché seemed to be true; fat men really did seem to move awful fast. She rocked back against the wall banging her head, her cheek stinging like crazy, the bone radiating out aching pain.

Stanton moved in on her again, crowding her up against the wall, his beery breath making her want to gag. 'Maybe you didn't hear me right,' he said, languidly raising his arm. Pascal tensed, ready to block, feint and go for his balls, but he swung his other fist under and into her soft belly.

She bent over and retched, then sank down onto her knees, the room swimming, like she'd just had a skinful. Stanton stood over her, looking down, dispassionately. Just then there was a knock on the door, and it opened a crack, and she heard someone saying, 'Inspector, there's a call for you.'

Stanton looked back over his shoulder, and said, 'well tell 'em I'm busy, fuckhead, and shut the door.' He turned back to Pascal, who was now struggling back to her feet, but the guy outside hesitantly persisted. 'Sir, I think you might want to take this one; it's the head of counter Terrorism.'

Stanton paused, and turned back to the door, his eyes briefly showing disbelief, until the other guy gave him a confirmatory nod and handed him the phone. 'Get her ready to go to the station, will you,' he said as he put the phone to his ear and moved out of the room.

The police constable led Pascal into the living room and told her to wait there. She noticed her phone, wallet and car keys on a table in an evidence bag, along with the large hunting knife in another bag. She edged closer to the table which was adjacent to the large bay window. As she looked out on the arc lights and blue and white tape around the front parking space, it had the quality of a film in slow motion as the large bay window disintegrated and an object followed through, bouncing once on the floor in front of her, and then coming to rest. She had flinched as the window smashed, but she immediately identified the object as a grenade and she just had the presence of mind to grab the evidence bags with keys, phone, wallet and knife, and then she was diving and rolling as the blast came. She knew instantly, instinctively, that if she didn't get out, get away, right now, before they got her to a police station, she never would.

She was moving at speed as masonry, plaster, dust and fittings were still falling; the lights were all out and police personal were milling about in confusion, and someone was moaning loudly in the other room. She was covered in grey white dust, but so was everyone else, so she was able to pass unnoticed among them to the front door which was open, her ears still popping and ringing from the blast. She didn't have time to start thinking about why the explosion happened, or why SO15 had picked up on it so quickly, she just needed to get to her VW Golf around the corner.

She walked out, to the right, and then up the path to the front. A woman PC approached her at the gate, wide eyed but still alert. 'Get a fucking ambulance right now,' Pascal shouted at her, with as much authority as she could muster. The woman looked at her, perhaps in shock, until Pascal screamed, 'Now', which seemed to break the spell, as the woman tilted her head to her radio and started speaking. Pascal walked past her, and then began to run.

Within two minutes she was in her car and driving, but now she had to decide where to go. She knew she had a very small window of opportunity. After an explosion at a murder scene like that, something pretty much unprecedented, there would be a very short period of confusion, before anyone took control and focused in on her, so it was vital that she used that window of time to find somewhere to hide out whilst she figured out what to do. She guessed the police's first priority would not be her, but it soon would be. Once someone took control, and when SO15 turned up, with Condon no doubt close behind, the hunt would really be on.

Megadeth blared again, disturbing her thoughts. She ripped the phone out the evidence bag with one hand and clamped it to her ear; it was Christoff.

'Nothing doing on the laptop,' he said. 'It's clean, oh apart from a lot of pictures of Justin Beiber. I virtually scraped the hard drive, looking. My guess, if there's anything, it's on a flash drive somewhere.'

'Thanks Christoff. Look, I'm in a deep shit right now. No time to explain except to say I'm running. I figure I've got an hour or so before things really kick off. Sorry, but I'm on my way to you; eta about ten minutes. I won't stop, I'll just grab the laptop.

'Oh this is exciting,' he said as if commenting on a trip to the seaside.

As she arrived, she saw him standing in his doorway with the laptop and a small bag. He trotted down to the curb and passed the items into her through the window.

'What's in the bag, Christoff?' she asked.

He didn't comment on the white dust all over her, or the fact that she looked fit to drop. 'Oh, just some goodies from the past. I kept them, when you left. Don't know why. It's some fake ID's; passport, but also met and various warrant cards, press accreditation; you know the kind of thing.' He sighed and said, 'you know, Courtney, you never change. You look exactly the same now as when we first met, so the photo's are still spot on. I've also chucked in an old Nokia 8210 mobile – all the rage with drug dealers I'm told; police can't listen or triangulate them easily – and there's your old Beretta M9, for a bit of protection,' he said, slow smile spreading across his face.

'Christoff, I'm not 007 you know.'

'If you were, I'd have given you the Walther,' he said, and cracked a serene smile. Impeccable under fire, as always, she thought fondly; at least she had one true friend. 'Take care, Courtney,' he said, as he turned to go back in.

As she pulled away from the curb, she smiled for the first time. He was cute, as usual, not even asking where she was going or what she was going to do. And when they came, as they would, he'd tell them nothing. She gunned the engine, but then pulled to the curb. She needed to think, cold and hard, without emotion. First things first; she couldn't go home, not right now anyway. She opened the bag and took out the Nokia and then looked at her current mobile. All her important numbers were committed to memory, and it was a racing certainty they would track her phone and calls. She'd make one last call on it but better get well away from Christoff's before she did; even MI5 were capable of joining up the dots sometimes.

Twenty minutes later Pascal pulled into a lay-by and phoned Sarah, her mother's carer. Sarah was her usual unflappable self; like Christoff she asked no questions, just calmly confirmed she would happily move in for a week or so to watch over Pascal's mother. What was going to happen, she knew, would not take long now.

When she had finished her call, Pascal crossed the street to a row of refuse bins clearly put out for emptying by the residents. She lifted the lid of one, moved some rubbish out of the way and secreted her phone underneath. She hoped they wouldn't discover the ruse too quickly.

It was dark as Pascal settled back into her car seat and moved off. Now her mother was safe, her mind was clear and she was ready. She gunned the engine and accelerated away down the slip road and into the motorway, segueing into the traffic, adrenaline under control now, her mind buzzing away as she slowly analysed every twist and turn of the last few weeks, looking for answers.

We were into the second day of his cross examination. Patterson had been hammering away at our case for well over an hour of the morning session, and now he was intricately picking away at Khan's testimony about the death of the Afghan family, and Khan was starting to wilt. Patterson asked him to explain the discrepancies between his testimony and that of Nicky Holloway.

'I don't know,' Khan said, wearily.

'You "don't know,"' Patterson mimicked him. 'I think the jury are getting a trifle tired of hearing that, don't you, Mr. Khan?' Patterson said.

Khan had no answer to that one, so he just stood there, clearly desperately hoping Patterson's onslaught would soon be over, but I was guessing he was going to be disappointed.

'Now, we've heard a great deal about this stabbing in Afghanistan, and I'm sure the jury are as mystified as I am as to what relevance it has to anything, but, given that my friend, Mr. Calver,' he said, looking over at me with a thin smile, 'has seen fit to introduce it, lets have a look at the report prepared by Major Kendricks, shall we?'

Patterson was right that as I'd used the report, I'd have trouble if I now wanted to try and get it chucked out, but I knew Patterson wouldn't be foolish enough to risk a mistrial by trying to use any of the prejudicial stuff in there about drugs, so I felt reasonably safe with where he was going.

'The report was never published,' Khan said, suddenly seeming to come to life again. 'It's a lot of conjecture and hearsay, is what it is. None of its proven,' he added.

Patterson, ignoring him, was looking at his papers again, glasses perched on the end of his nose as he read. 'Oh it was a bit more than that, wasn't it Mr Khan. The report mentions alleged illicit use of ordnance, and fraternising with the Taliban troops, but that's not what I want to put to you here.'

'I was cleared of any wrongdoing. I didn't know the half of what was going on out there. Yeah, we had some problems, with some of the lads, but the brass got involved and it was sorted,' Khan said.

I was finding the exchange hard to follow as they appeared to be talking at cross purposes, but Patterson wasn't worrying, as every time Khan opened his mouth, he looked more and more defensive.

'Now, would you agree, Corporal Khan,' Patterson said, 'that this report, albeit unpublished, which was written some time after the Afghan knifing incident we've heard so much about, and was never made public, gives a fair indication of what went on out there?'

'I suppose,' Khan replied.

'So, let me read again from the report,' Patterson said. 'And this relaters to the investigators assessment of your various attributes. He says, and I quote: "Depending on what is decided about his future, we consider Corporal Khan to be an extremely able man who could be a considerable asset to the military."'

Patterson dropped the report on the table and took his pebble glasses off with a flourish. 'So on the one hand you present an image to the jury of a damaged, severely traumatised individual, subject to fits, nightmares, depression. Someone who the police can easily bamboozle into falsely confessing to a murder they didn't commit. And on the other hand,' he said, holding up the report again and reading from it, '"we consider Corporal Khan to be an extremely able man who could be a considerable asset to the military."'

I didn't even bother rising this time and said from my seat, 'is there a question in there somewhere?'

There was tittering from the jury box, but Patterson ignored me, continuing to press, saying, 'so which is it, Mr Khan? Which face do you want the jury to see today? The traumatised veteran with selective amnesia who apparently commits acts of which he has no knowledge, or the "extremely able man", who, "could be a considerable asset to the military"?

Khan looked from Patterson to me, probably hoping I could dig him out, but he was on his own this time. The silence stretched out, the jury watching and waiting, then he answered in the worst way possible: 'I don't know.'

'And there we have it again, in a nutshell, don't we, Mr Khan? You "don't know,"' Patterson said, pausing for effect, to allow the repetition to sink in.

Then he was off again. 'Now, I want to move on to the period after you left the army and came home to live with Safia, if I may. Were you ever violent to Safia?

Khan seemed affronted by the question even though we had discussed the fact that it would be asked because of the Sunday lunch tray throwing incident. I had explained to him that even though he might not think he had been violent then, others might disagree, so he should not try to deny it, but rather, try to explain it.

'I was never violent to her. I loved her,' he said. I felt like screaming, again. Maybe it was time for a little diversion, to try and ease the pressure on Khan, if I could. I edged some papers against my water glass, and then turning slightly, I let my elbow brush against it, causing the glass to topple onto the floor with a crash. I moved quickly with tissues, saying, 'I am so sorry, my Lord. Let me clear that up.' I looked up at Khan who was watching me, and I hope my expression got the message to him.

Patterson, seething, said, 'my lord, *really*, this is becoming ridiculous. My friend deliberately knocks the water carafe onto the floor to sabotage my cross examination of the witness.'

'My lord—' I started again to protest.

'Enough,' Feldman said, holding his hand up. 'I will deal with this when we have finished today, in the absence of the jury, and in the meantime we will take a fifteen minute adjournment – let everyone settle down,' he said, quickly rising.

I looked over at Patterson, and whispered, 'sorry old boy. Hand must have slipped,' and then I turned and walked away, leaving him staring after me, fuming.

I grabbed Khan as he came out of the toilet, and said, 'what the fuck are you doing in there, man? All the advice I gave you, weren't you listening? Are you *trying* to lose? I don't know, I don't know, I don't know,' I said, cruelly mimicking him, but I needed to get through to him or we'd be toast.

He looked at me startled, as if he didn't recognise me; eyes empty like he was in a dream. Then he pushed me off aggressively. 'Just do your job,' he said, and then over his shoulder, as he walked away, 'that's what my Daddy's paying you for.'

'Having fun old boy,' Patterson quipped, as he breezed past me. I stood and watched his retreating back, steaming, and then I tried Pascal's cell again, and once more got a continuous ringing tone. I was beginning to get very worried about her – even when she'd been very pissed with me in the past, she'd never gone AWOL for this long – but there was nothing I could do right now, not until I'd sorted Khan and got through the remaining court session.

As Pascal slowly dug her way out of a deep and troubling sleep, she couldn't seem to work out where she was. The sheets felt strange, luxurious and expensive, not like the scrappy old duvet she usually woke up in, and the suns rays streaming in through a gap in the curtains seemed wrong – too high. Must be late she thought idly, and then it all came rushing back; the flight from London through the night, the hasty discussion with Joan Franklyn; the woman's complete calmness in the face of her arrival, covered in white dust, almost sleepwalking from exhaustion.

She pushed herself up, plumped up the pillows, and lay back again as Joan entered the room with a coffee on a tray. 'Thought you were never going to wake up. I've been checking on you, and its gone two now,' she said as she placed the tray on a sideboard and brought the coffee over. 'You know it's strange,' she said, head cocked to one side quizzically; 'there's absolutely nothing on the news about any explosion in Mile end road.'

Pascal sipped the hot coffee as her mind began to wake up. She was surprised that she had confided so much in Joan which wasn't like her at all; maybe she was becoming human – better watch out for that. But back to the here and now: why the silence? By now SO15, or counter terrorism command at the Met, meaning Condon and his cronies, and almost certainly Lammy as well, would be controlling events. 'Sounds like a D notice to the media, although I can't think why,' she said.

'A D notice?'

'Its actually called a DA notice now I think, but its essentially a media blackout; a request from government to the media not to publicise certain things, usually bogusly justified under the catchall of national security.'

'So that means you're in the clear then,' Joan said, relief in her voice.

'Well no, not exactly. All it means is that the public won't be on the look out for me, but the police and security services certainly will, in spades, so I best not hang around,' she said, lifting the duvet and standing up. She moved to the mirror, the oversized male pyjamas she was wearing billowing loosely around her thin frame. She studied her reflection and noticed for the first time the white dust still all over her face and in her hair. Joan met her eyes in the mirror

'You have a shower, dear, right now, and I will have a breakfast – or should I say late lunch – waiting for you when you come out.'

Pascal hesitated, ready to argue, but then she saw Joan's face, and decided against it. So she went through to the en-suite bathroom and Joan went downstairs to prepare a fry up.

Condon, talking into his cell phone, watched Qadir through the two way mirror and marvelled at the man's calmness. They had brought him in about an hour ago in connection with the Holloway murder, as he was a known associate. He was not under arrest, just helping them with their enquiries, but even so, you might have expected to see some evidence of concern, but not a flicker, nothing.

'Okay, Jack,' Condon said into his phone, 'but I want you to get word to the prosecutor about Khan breaching his bail – we've got him on camera out on multiple occasions when he should have been tucked up in bed – so we want the judge to withdraw bail, and until he does, I want 24/7 surveillance, yes?'

Pause, whilst Condon continued to watch Qadir. 'I know the trials almost over and he's going to gaol, but just do it, yeah,' he finished, flicking his phone off as the door behind him opened and he heard Lammy's familiar anglicised Texan drawl.

'Hello, John,' she said. He couldn't quite stop himself from whirling around, a sarcastic quip ready, but dying on his lips when he saw the tall black man standing next to her.

She smiled and said, 'John, this is my boss, David Tolliver.'

The man regarded Condon with slow calculating eyes and a lazy grin, and the handshake was crushing but brief. 'Good to finally meet you, John. Heard a lot of great things about you,' he said, moving into the centre of the room, radiating authority.

'But now we've got ourselves a situation, right?' he said, the lazy grin gone now, along with any hint of friendliness. 'So I'll make this real simple as we don't have a lot of time. This Holloway, the vic, was seen a couple of days ago scoping out the US embassy. Now he's dead and the crime scene's obliterated. Was it a booby trap, or did the perp. Whass her name?' he asked clicking his fingers

'Courtney Pascal,' Lammy said.

'Yeah, her. Did she let it off, or what?'

'Sir—' Lammy started, but Tolliver ploughed on ignoring her and looking hard a Condon.

'See, John, with the president flying in, d'you think we're gonna fuck around here?' He let his words hang there a moment, definitely not looking for an answer. Then continued, softer, ' now we know there's a nexus between Holloway and the guy sitting in there,' he said nodding towards Qadir through the glass. 'You getting my drift, John?'

'How do you know—' Condon began, but Tolliver stilled him with a raised hand.

'We know quite a lot about Qadir, and I don't have time to go into it right now, suffice to say that your home secretary agrees with us that our presidents security takes precedence over any cockamamie murder case or operation your security services might be running right now,' he said.

Condon looked at Lammy reproachfully, but she kept her eyes firmly on Qadir in the interview cell.

'Two things, John: firstly, you need to arrest Qadir right now under the Terrorism Act; you can base the arrest on reasonable suspicion of preparation of terrorist acts, or conspiracy to commit murder, whatever you want. Then you can hold him for 14 days, without charge if necessary, by which time our president will have left.'

Again Condon attempted to break in and respond, but Tolliver stilled him with another casual and arrogant waive of his arm. 'Meantime, and secondly, following the arrest, we will be taking custody of Mr Qadir,' he said, his expression suggesting to Condon that to argue the point with him would be futile.

Condon wasn't totally surprised; there'd been rumours swirling around for weeks about the US advance guard and whispers about them having jurisdiction and investigative rights, as well as the right to carry side arms. Condon felt affronted by the American but knew he was powerless. Grin and bare it and say as little as possible was probably the order of the day.

'Oh, by the way,' Tolliver said, 'that was a smart move with the DA notice. We want to keep it in place whilst POTUS is here. Don't want to spook the natives – everything stays nice and easy until he's gone, right John?'

Tolliver cast a quick glance at Lammy to make sure he'd covered everything, to which she gave a quick nod. He concluded with, 'so, John, any questions?' lazy grin and slow eyes back on display.

Thankfully Condon's cell rang before he had to respond.

'You better get that, John,' Tolliver urged. 'It's probably your boss or the Home Secretary, to give you the heads up.'

Tolliver's complacency and arrogance irked Condon, but worse, it *was* his boss, who confirmed every word Tolliver had said in a short and brutal phone call. As Condon, ashen faced, flipped his cell off, Lammy put her hand on his shoulder, and said, 'I'm sorry about this, John.'

He shook her hand off as Tolliver looked up from checking his phone messages and said, 'and what's the deal on this witness, Courtney Pascal, John? A rogue ex-agent floating around out there could really fuck us. She needs to be hunted down and taken out, and if you can't do it, we can.'

Chapter Twenty Eight

They sat in Joan's large modern kitchen, beautiful green Aga range along one wall, immaculate work surfaces, cupboards, and every cooking utensil you could imagine along the other, with a large oak table in the middle at which they both now sat, sipping fresh made coffee.

A few minutes earlier Joan's niece had stopped by to collect her laptop; now they sat, Joan picking over the items in her son's old army box which Pascal had brought back with her, and Pascal, preoccupied and morose, fiddling with the antique Nokia phone that Christoff had given her.

'I'm all right, Joan,' Pascal muttered, having picked up on the concerned looks she was getting from across the table. 'I just needed a bolt hole to hunker down in for the night and think things through and now I'm ready to go again.'

Joan sat silent for a moment, watching her. 'After I lost Miles,' she said, looking away out through the back window into the garden, 'life just seemed to,' she shrugged, 'and being alone so much. Well, you know....' she said, her voice tailing off. Then she seemed to square her shoulders. 'Look, Courtney, Miles would have wanted me to help you, so I'm going to help you, and that's that,' she said.

Pascal was gradually warming, as much as she ever did to anyone, to this quiet, resolute woman. It occurred to her that she could do a lot worse, if she wanted someone to bounce ideas off, and Joan had a personal stake in all this; her son had been friends with and deeply connected to the main players.

Pascal said, 'this all started when Jonas Calver, Mohsin's defence lawyer asked me to help him. You know, running down witnesses, taking statements, getting background information, that kind of thing, and that's what got me involved with Nicky and what initially brought me here, to find out about Miles.'

Pascal flicked the Nokia off and continued, 'now I think that Nicky and Mohsin may have got caught up in something, something bad, against us all, and its possible they're linked in some way with a...' she paused, thinking quickly. 'A Muslim activist.'

Joan said, 'but Mohsin is more English than I am. I can't believe he would be involved in something like this.'

'Khan was – is – a master bomb maker and I believe he may have been pressured into doing something he didn't want to do, and because Nicky is weak and easy to manipulate, he was co-opted to help, but who was the other guy on the BMW bike? I think he's the main man and he killed Nicky and bombed the house to get rid of me and the evidence there.'

Joan said nothing as she tried to absorb what she was hearing; it sounded fantastical sitting in the genteel surroundings of her kitchen, sipping coffee. She said, tentatively, 'can't you. Can't you just tell the police?'

Pascal shook her head slowly, and said, 'I was arrested at the scene with the body, and I ran. For all I know, they may think I set the bomb off as well. If I go in, they'll bury me, whatever I say, so I have to stay out and find out what's going on, and clear myself.'

Partly to distract herself, Joan pulled out a belt from the box of Miles stuff and began examining it closely. 'What can you do?' she said, searching Pascal's face.

'Well I can start by trying to identify the biker; I've got a partial licence plate, and that's a good start,' she said, starting to perk up a bit.

Joan watched the waif like girl for a moment, wanting to hug her, but knowing she would not enjoy such a show of emotion. 'So you're going back, then?' she said, as she continued to idly examine the belt she had taken from the box.

Pascal nodded slowly, reluctantly.

Then there was a click as Joan continued to work the large rectangular brass belt buckle, and a light skittering sound as something dropped out of the buckle onto the floor. Joan leaned down and picked it up, saying 'what's this?'

Pascal only half listening, deep in thought, reached over and took the object, and then quickly sat up as she identified what it was. 'It's a flash drive,' she said. Joan instantly picked up on Pascal's excitement, delighted to see the first hint of a smile on the girls face. Pascal delicately placed the stick on the table and closely examined the belt buckle. It had an ingenious hidden compartment which had held the stick and which could only be opened by pulling and twisting the pin on the belt.

Joan watched fascinated as Pascal manipulated the buckle. 'Maybe we should have held onto the laptop,' she murmured. 'To see what's on it?'

'I'll check it when I get back, so I need to get going. Don't want you dragged any further into this.'

'You know, Courtney,' Joan said, 'this is the first time I've felt alive since I lost Miles. I *want* to help. Don't shut me out.'

Pascal watched her a moment. 'I won't. Now, I better get going before I change my mind,' she said, gruffly, pocketing the stick and moving to get her things together.

The cell now housing Qadir, situated in a building in a row of unobtrusive warehousing on the periphery of Heathrow airport, and owned by a CIA front company, was very different to the cell he had occupied at the police station.

This cell was large, bare and windowless and Qadir sat naked on the floor, shivering in a puddle of ice cold water, his left hand manacled to a ring in the wall. The area around his eyes was blue from bruising, his lip was split and his chest was red raw and speckled with flecks of dried blood.

As he moaned again through his broken teeth, the door opened and two large Hispanic men entered and walked briskly over towards him. As they approached he began to whimper and desperately try and shrink back into the wall, to make himself smaller.

'So much for Jihad,' Tolliver said with disgust as he watched the tableaux play out through the two way mirror. He hummed to himself for a moment and then turning to Condon, said, 'what d'you think, John?'

In line with his policy of saying as little as possible whilst going with the flow, Condon said, 'let's run him through the mill again, make sure we've got everything.'

'Before the break you said you had never been violent to Safia and—'

'I was cautioned for domestic violence three months before Safia's death,' Khan said, briskly breaking in on the prosecutor. 'I accepted the caution on legal advice and to avoid a prosecution, even though I wasn't guilty of anything more than having a shouting match with Safia. I assume that's what you're getting at,' Khan added, confidently holding Patterson's gaze.

Khan surprised me with the vehemence of his response. It was if he had been rejuvenated over the short break – maybe my ploy had worked – and now he was ready to carry the fight to Patterson, who was clearly also caught out by the changed tone. For a second he seemed unsure of how to pitch his next question.

'Well let me read an extract from Safia's witness statement, Mr Khan,' he said, turning to the jury with a hint of a smile, 'as we all know how forgetful you are.'

I decided not to object; let Khan have his head as nothing else seemed to be working.

Patterson began reading, '"....he had come home drunk again and he was chewing that disgusting brown muck he liked so much. All the family were there for Sunday lunch. During the meal he became more and more agitated. Then for no reason he picked up and threw the roasting tray and all its contents against the wall. I grappled with him to try and calm him down and sustained a scratch to my face from his nail. I was very frightened..."' Patterson put the papers down and removed his glasses. 'Is that a fair description of what happened, Mr Khan?'

'No it's not. As I've said, it didn't happen like that. We basically had a shouting match about nothing. I chucked the roasting tray, yeah, but the scratch, she got from Aisha when she scraped one of her plastic toys down her mothers face.'

'As you well know, Mr Khan, and I'm sure my friend Mr Calver will have reminded you, in order for the police to give you a caution, you must first admit that you committed the offence. Yes?'

'That may be so, Mr Patterson, but I didn't hit her, it was an accident and anyway, who's going to risk rolling the dice in a UK court nowadays. You'll likely get convicted there, even if you tell the truth – no offence,' Khan said looking over at the jury with a bob of his head. 'So anyone who's offered a caution – a glorified slap on the wrist from a copper – as an alternative to going to court, is going to grab it, yeah?'

'You think it's funny, do you Mr Khan? I see you're smiling at the jury, but do you think Safia thought it was funny? You come bursting in, drunk; a big, burly, frightening, ex soldier, attacking her in front of your children?'

'You're twisting things. It wasn't like that,' Khan said.

'So the police record is wrong. Safia is lying is she, Mr Khan?' Patterson said.

'She's not lying, but people see things differently, is all,' Khan replied.

'Let's turn to the day Safia died,' Patterson said. 'You say you returned to the flat at about twenty to eight and you can pin point the time by the fact that Coronation Street was on the TV, yes?'

'Yes.'

'Now, in your evidence, you present a very rosy picture of what you found when you arrived back at the flat, almost like something out of a Mills and Boon romance,' Patterson said, his mouth turned down as if he were sucking a particularly sour boiled sweet. He ran his finger along a line of the transcript of Khan's evidence in chief, and read extracts, 'you talk of, "kissing", it being "like old times", and "passion" taking hold. It was like before when you were "happy"?'

'Yes, it was,' Khan said.

'But we know, don't we, Mr Khan, from your own sister in law, Rana, that you had recently found out Safia was having an affair with Rashid Syed, and that she was due to tell you that very evening that she wanted a divorce. How does that square with your lovey-dovey, frankly, fantastical story of how Safia behaved that night when you arrived back?'

'I've already told you, we were reconciled. That was all behind us. We were making a *new* start, for Christ sake,' Khan said, the emotion breaking through as he looked imploringly at the jurors, willing them to believe him.

'So, Mr Khan, again, we come to it, don't we: Rana lying as well, yes? And you are telling the truth, again?'

'I'm not saying she's lying, I'm saying she's, she's mistaken,' Khan stuttered as he desperately sought an explanation that the jury might believe. 'Rana always hated me, right from the very start.'

'So yet again, Mr Khan, two witnesses tell us there was an affair, and she was about to leave you, and yet, they're lying. In fact, it's the exact opposite according to you – everything was rosy in the garden, she'd forgotten you're awful, drunken drug induced violent and frightening behaviour, your failure to get a job and your dossing around the house with your mates – now everything was fine and you were going to walk off into the sunset and live happily ever after, yes?'

'You're twisting things again,' Khan said.

'Who has a motive to lie, Mr Khan? Who is on trial for their life?'

Khan didn't answer, he just stood there alone in the witness box slumped over as if defeated. I desperately wanted Patterson's masterful cross examination to come to an end, but he wasn't finished yet.

'There was no reconciliation was there, Mr Khan?' Patterson ploughed on relentlessly. 'And you weren't going to let Safia and your two beautiful daughters leave you for a common cabby like Syed, were you? How could a man like you countenance that? No, Mr Khan, you decided that if you couldn't have Safia, then no one would, so you planned a murder, and you planned it like a military operation, but things went wrong, didn't they?'

'*No*,' Khan said, almost a shout. 'That's not true; I loved—'

'You sneaked back didn't you, hoping no one would know – the kids were on a sleep over, so it was perfect – and you killed her.'

'It's not true,' Khan tried again vainly.

'Lets face it, Mr Khan, you've only admitted to going back to the flat now, after all these months, because you know the evidence places you there. And all this stuff about PTSD and knives and trauma in Afghanistan, all just a convenient smoke screen, made up at the last moment to hoodwink the jury,' Patterson said.

'Let me tell you what I think happened, Mr Khan; you can correct me if I'm wrong,' Patterson said with a veiled grin at the jury. 'Time of death is stated as between 7 – 8 pm. You say you left the flat around 7.50 pm and I think you are telling the truth about that, because the evidence proves it and you can't avoid that. Police evidence – following extensive testing – is that the washing machine with the blood stained clothes inside, was switched on at 7.50 pm within the time of death window, and then you were seen outside the flat by Eddie Nelson at between 7.55 and 8.05 pm. You killed Safia between 7 – 8, switched the washing machine on at 7.50, left the flat about five minutes later, dropping the murder weapon down the drain, and that's when Eddie Nelson saw you, and then you made your getaway.

'I think you tweaked your evidence to fit your case, Mr Khan. Maybe Safia was washing up when you got back to the flat. Maybe she did hold the knife up and it set you off in some way, but the rest of what you told the jury about the knife accidentally catching Safia and cutting your hand was a pack of lies, wasn't it? You went there with a plan to kill her and you carried out that plan, didn't you?

'No, it's how I said. Safia was alive when I left the flat at—'

'And let's just take a second or two to demolish your other theory, shall we, Mr. Khan? That's right,' Patterson said, looking over at the jury and nodding his head at them as if they were all in agreement. 'Someone else, with a knife, just happened to come along, managed to get into the house, commit a brutal murder involving multiple stab wounds, make their escape, leaving not a trace of themselves behind, all within the space of ten minutes, whilst you, even on your own evidence, were in all likelihood still milling around the murder scene. Do you *really* expect the jury to swallow that?'

Khan was violently shaking his head. 'No, no, I—'

'All the evidence, Mr Khan, says you planned to murder Safia, and you did murder her. Look at the forensic evidence,' he said and then patiently counted off on his fingers, 'the knife with you and Safia's blood on it; Safia's blood on your clothing in the washing machine; the knife wounds; your presence at the crime scene at the time of death; and of course you had motive – she was leaving you and taking your children away – and last of all, what?' Patterson said, pausing with a kind of dramatic flourish. 'That's right, you admitted it – I'll just repeat that: you admitted it – to D I Stanton and DS Chandler, in the police interview that we all watched, when you said that you "did it".'

Khan just stood there shell shocked, seemingly unable to speak. I looked over at the jury and what can I say. Having it laid out like that in such a powerful way, with barely an answer from Khan, was hugely effective, and I could see from their eyes a subtle change. It looked like the little sympathy or goodwill we may have built up with them was gone. They now looked at him questioningly. They still wanted answers and he wasn't giving them any they liked.

In the end he just repeated, 'I did not kill Safia. I loved her.'

Eventually Patterson finished, but by then it was like watching a man pummel a dead horse. I took the opportunity to re-examine Khan and try and repair some of the damage but by then it seemed pretty hopeless. He reconfirmed his story that they were reconciled; when he left the flat at ten to eight she was still alive and he merely said those words "I did it" in interview because he had no memory at the time, and genuinely thought he might have killed her. I don't think the jury bought it.

I sat down feeling profoundly depressed. Then Feldman called a short recess. I felt a real urge to get out of court for a spell, maybe grab a couple of stiff drinks, but trouble is I needed to hang around as Rose Tremayne would be up next.

Chapter Twenty Nine

As I sat waiting for Rose Tremayne to show up, instead I got Dick Stanton. I guessed he was in to see the prosecution about something, and had decided to stop off and make my day. I ignored him, but then he came to a halt in front of me. I looked up from the paperwork I was pretending to read, and said, 'you want something, Stanton? Cause I'm kinda busy right now.'

'Yeah, right. Busy losing, I hear' he chuckled. 'We're looking for your weirdo friend, Pascal. Any ideas?' He watched me closely, alert for any telltale ticks.

I kept my face completely expressionless but behind the mask my mind was churning. What the fuck was she into now? Why would the police want her? I don't hear from her for days, just about to give her up for good; then this.

'What d'you want her for?

'Wrong answer. I ask the questions. I guess you don't know too much do you, Calver – story of your life really. She's wanted in connection with a murder, interfering with evidence and absconding. All hush hush though,' he said, delighting in my uncomprehending stare.

'You want something from me, Stanton, you better tell me what the fuck you're talking about,' I said, still trying to cover my shock; his words really did not compute – seemed fantastical.

He looked at me for a long moment, weighing up how much to give against what he could get from me. 'There's a DA notice on this, so you better keep your mouth shut,' he said. 'She was arrested at an address in Mile End Road yesterday, alongside the body of one of your witnesses, Holloway. He'd been carved up, just about gutted, and your little girl decided to run, taking the murder weapon with her.'

Stanton smiled because I couldn't help showing my shock as I tried to get my head around what he had told me. There was no way Pascal would have killed Holloway, but then I immediately thought about her dead step-father. Then reality broke back in. Right now there was absolutely nothing I could do for her. I had to concentrate all I had on getting Khan over the finishing line.

I looked up at Stanton's smug smiling face, and said, 'I can't help you, Stanton. I haven't spoken to her for days.'

He watched me, but this time I kept my face completely still.

'Maybe I should take you in,' he said.

I smiled. 'Go for it.'

I thought he might just bite, but then he shrugged, and said, 'I'll be back, so don't go anywhere.' Then he ambled off, and then Rose was approaching and I got up to meet her, thinking that whatever the hell Pascal had got herself into would have to wait; Khan came first right now.

Back at Thames House Condon, Lammy and Tolliver sat around the circular table in the conference room annexed to Condon's office. On a large screen on the wall they watched a recording of Qadir's final interview, although to call it an "interview" was perhaps the wrong word, as what they saw and heard was effectively the torture of a suspect.

They also held transcripts of everything Qadir had managed to say, less of course the screams and groans. Condon quickly re-read the final part covering a period of some 35 minutes, whilst Lammy and Tolliver watched the screen and listened; Lammy especially seemed mesmerised by the on screen action.

Tolliver's cell buzzed authoritatively; he listened intently and then said, 'clear it up,' and closed the call. 'Qadir didn't make it; cardiac arrest. Win some, lose some, eh, John,' he said and winked.

'So, what are we left with then, sir?' asked Lammy, almost simpering at Tolliver.

'We're left with the CIA and secret service having foiled a very dangerous plot against the president, that's what we're left with,' he said, watching Condon carefully. 'Right, John?'

Condon stared back, thinking. There seemed to be a shed load of loose ends. Apart from a few tortured grunts and screams, Qadir seemed to have answered none of the critical questions that had been put to him. But somehow that didn't seem to phase Tolliver who was already reporting to his bosses the smashing of a conspiracy between Qadir and Holloway to assassinate the US president, apparently by chucking a grenade at him as he entered the US embassy. There was some corroboration of this as Forensics had now established that the Mile End Road explosion had come from a British army type grenade thrown through the window.

Condon looked up at the screen to see the camera panning down Qadir's quite obviously dead body, the lens lingering on his bruised and bloody face.

'What's the problem, John?' Tolliver said. 'You don't look happy, old buddy.'

'I'm not,' he said looking up at the frozen image of Qadir's face. 'A guy gets beat to death, but, you ever see a man with a more serene and peaceful look on his face? That's not the face of a man who's just given up his life's work. That's the face of a man who's fought Jihad and got one over on us. The face of a man who's going to paradise to meet his seventy two virgins'

'You think he's sold us a dummy?' Lammy said.

'Maybe,' Condon said. 'Its interesting that he said the words "US Embassy", and "grenade", quite audibly and clearly, and essentially, nothing else, despite being put under enormous psychological and physical pressure.'

'And he didn't give up his trigger man either,' Tolliver said, smiling.

Maybe Tolliver wasn't quite as dumb as he looked, Condon thought as he reappraised the guy; he obviously hadn't completely swallowed Qadir's routine. But what about Lammy, Condon mused, looking over at her, surprised that she hadn't got more to say for herself. He was still convinced that she had picked up something from Pascal that she had yet to share with anyone else – even her own people, and that was a very dangerous game to play.

'What about the guy, Khan?' Condon said, just out of interest, to see what their analysis was.

'Believe me, John, if this was the States, we'd take the guy down now, but I'm told by your Home Secretary that whilst he's on trial, he's basically untouchable. But anyway, we've been all over him. Yeah he knows bombs from the army, but he's going to gaol, and, as I'm sure you know, his bail is just about to be withdrawn. He'll never make the street again, even with your loopy penal system.'

'You've got something else, haven't you?' Condon finally said, eyes back on Tolliver.

Tolliver nodded at Lammy. She said, 'actually, John we got it from you. We've been trawling way back over eavesdropped messages received from GCHQ. Qadir barely ever used that mobile other than for stupid or jokey kind of conversations that were almost always one way – he spoke and the other guy just listened. This just seemed to be another one of those calls until we had another look at the transcript. It took place way back in August, about the time of the Khan murder in fact. We don't know who the recipient was, although our guess is it was Holloway. It seemed to be about an April fools day prank or anniversary, but he also – almost seemed random - quoted the letters ASLPUS.'

'Why didn't you put it to him?' Condon asked.

'We were going to, but he died, remember,' Tolliver said, grinning and continuing to watch Condon, waiting.

Condon rubbed his face, mind running the angles, then the light bulb came on. 'April Fools day is this Friday, right?'

'Right,' Tolliver said.

'So what's POTUS scheduled for that day?'

'A visit to the American School London, in St. John's Wood.'

Condon leant back in his chair looking up at the ceiling. 'American School London President United States equals ASLPUS, yes?'

'Ten out of ten, John, but d'you know what my guess is?' Tolliver said. 'My guess is that the plot is dead, because Holloway was the trigger man, but we can't be too careful. POTUS, as you'd expect, has flatly refused to cancel the visit, so that place Friday will be locked down so tight that if you ain't on our list and you turn up, you'll be dead.'

Condon sat silent for a moment mulling it all. Then he said, 'so why was Holloway killed, and by whom?'

'Good question, old buddy. Maybe it was your ex-agent gone rogue,' Tolliver said.

Condon stole a glance at Lammy. She looked troubled as well.

'So what's your game plan, Tolliver?' Condon asked.

'My game plan, John, is that we carry on, low key, but behind the scenes, high pressure, digging, filtering, going to all our – and your – sources for Intel, trying to build up a picture; trying to identify if there's triggerman out there, someone we don't know about, a secret part of Qadir's cell. We need to trawl through all the known associates, army, Mosque, people Qadir, Khan or Holloway may have come into contact in prison or whilst serving, or anywhere.

'With POTUS dead set on the visit, we have a great opportunity to tease these guys out of the shadows and take them down, even if its in the School itself. Meantime we're on the highest state of alert. Obviously at the School and the embassy, as well as all other US installations in London. Even if they've built a bomb with PETN as agent Lammy suggests, its not going to help them none. We'll still take them down.'

'What d'you want from us?' Condon asked.

'Full cooperation, Old Buddy, which I know we'll get, because your Home Secretary says we will and I don't think she'd lie, do you John,' Tolliver said with sardonic smile as he rose to his feet and gathered up his papers.

'President's safe for now, but we need to keep on top of it.' He put his hand out and Condon rose and took it. 'Like to thank you, John from the US government for all your help so far, but we'll be running things hereon in. You take care now,' he said, gesturing for Lammy to follow, which she did after holding Condon's eyes for a long moment, but seeing no encouragement there, she got up and left. As they went through the outer door Condon could still hear Tolliver's booming voice insisting to Lammy that she was headed for great things after what she'd done on secondment, and that she was virtually guaranteed a promotion. Condon smiled to himself, guessing that Lammy was about to get some of her own medicine from Tolliver, whose main objective seemed to be to get into her pants.

After they had gone, Condon sat thinking for a long time, Qadir's silent, bloodied, frozen face staring down on him from the monitor. How the hell could they – he – just sit back and ignore murder and grenades on the streets of London? But as they'd said, their priority was POTUS, but with all due respect to the Yanks, his priority wasn't, it was the UK's national security, and that was what he was going to concentrate on. It didn't take him long to realise that if he really wanted to find out what the hell was going on, there was only one place left to go. Time to turbo charge Dick Stanton's Mickey Mouse search operation. He picked up the phone and gave priority orders for all branches of the security services to move in and cooperate fully with the Met in finding Courtney Pascal and bring her in, and they should pull no punches in the process. If anyone likely knew what was going on, it would be her.

Pascal sat in the lay-by checking the signal on the Nokia phone; it was clear and strong. She keyed in Christoff's number from memory whilst her mind wandered back to her parting from Joan around forty minutes earlier. It was such a long time since she'd felt an emotional attachment to anyone that it felt strange, but it also complicated things, crowding in on her and clouding her judgement when she most needed a clear head. Then Christoff's familiar voice was crackling through on the old handset.

All he said was, 'yes.'

All she said was, 'the block, one hour,' and clicked the phone off.

She was sure he would know where to go. He had taken her there once, early on, when she'd been a green trainee under his tutelage. It was a modern purpose built block of two flats that he owned in Southwark. One was a buy-to-let, but the other he kept, separate from his house in Highgate, as a secret bolt hole. He had dragged her there once very early on because of an emergency when the young man living there – whom she later found out was Christoff's lover - had attempted suicide. Christoff had rushed over there even though he had Pascal in tow, his mind in turmoil, and frantic with worry. Pascal had put her fingers down the boy's throat and got him to vomit up the pills before the ambulance arrived, thus saving his life, and that's where her bond with Christoff had first been made.

She put the little Golf in gear and pulled out back into the traffic, heading for Southwark.

As Dr Rose Tremayne walked across the courtroom, I was pleased to hear the rustle of papers and scraping of chairs; all positive sounds of a jury perking up, and as I looked over at them I could see some of the male members casting an admiring eye over her; always a good sign.

I took her through the usual foundational steps; qualifications, experience and what posts she currently held. It was all nice and gentle as I slowly worked her into a natural rhythm of question and answer, getting her comfortable and used to the court.

'Now, Doctor, on how many occasions did you see Mr Khan when assessing him?'

She checked her notes. 'I saw him eight times in all, spread over around five weeks.'

'And how did he present to you?'

'I have to say I found him something of an enigma,' she answered.

Not for the first time in this trial, I felt like screaming. Another of my witnesses completely unable to follow my advice to keep it simple and stick to the basics, or better still, the script. I frowned at her, my face hidden from the jury, but she didn't seem to notice, but Patterson did, quickly putting his hand up to cover a smirk.

Then she seemed to get it; she smiled tentatively, put her notes down and looked at the jury. 'What I found with Mohsin Khan was that he was – is – severely disturbed. He gave clear descriptions of vivid nightmares, dreams and visual flashbacks. During these episodes he sometimes spoke of being able to smell burning corpses and smoke from bomb damage. As a result he was often afraid to sleep. Like a lot of veterans he turned to stimulants, to drugs, both prescription and illegal as well as excessive consumption of alcohol, which of course simply exacerbated his problems.'

'Why was he like this, doctor?'

' Simply put, he was like this because of severe traumatic events, some of which you've heard about in his and Nicky Holloway's evidence, that occurred whilst he was engaged in combat missions in Afghanistan.'

'And what was the psychological effect on Corporal Khan, of these traumatic events?'

She turned to address the jury directly, and said, 'in my professional opinion, he now suffers from classic combat related Post Traumatic Stress Disorder and random amnesia, or what we now tend to call dissociative amnesia, which is a classic symptom of PTSD. We have a person who has experienced horrifically traumatic events, and in order to avoid reliving those events, his brain goes to great lengths to protect him by suppressing those frightening memories. Even now his recall of events is at best patchy. Again, this sudden, almost random recovery of memory which we have seen recently is also common in cases such as this one.'

I could feel Patterson fidgeting beside me and guessed he was getting antsy. I moved on to the next question.

'Doctor, you've heard evidence from the defendant and his sister in law, about an incident where he became distressed and threw a roasting tray against the wall?'

'Yes.'

'In your professional opinion, again, doctor, how would you characterize for the jury what happened there, given that your diagnosis is that he suffers from PTSD?'

'Well it's interesting that, until recently, he had no recollection of this incident. But again it could just be him suppressing something that was unpleasant. We must however be cautious about jumping to conclusions; Safia was allegedly carving meat with a knife; Corporal Khan suffered a recent traumatic event where he was knifed in the neck. Can we link the two events?'

She was flying now, completely unaware of me, and far more important, she wasn't attempting to insult the jury's intelligence – which could be fatal – by asking them to jump to conclusions which were too simplistic or obviously contrived to fit in with our case; she was making them work for her.

'The connection is of course superficially attractive, but I cannot sit here and tell you definitively that the two events are linked. I would however say there is a high probability that they are.'

'So the carving knife used by Safia acted as a trigger for Khan's behaviour that led to the caution?'

'I believe so, yes.'

'Now, doctor, you've heard the defendant's testimony that he returned to the flat the night of the murder, and that whilst Safia was washing up, she held up the carving knife to the light, causing him to have what, in my ignorance, I'll call a turn, or a fit. Can you, in your expert opinion, explain to the jury what you think happened there?

'I believe it's the same as the previous incident. The inadvertent brandishing of the knife by Safia during washing up produced a similar reaction in Khan to that which occurred on that previous Sunday lunch incident. The knife acted as a trigger for his behaviour, causing the incident that took place.'

'Why is it, Dr Tremayne, that Mr. Khan did not simply explain what happened to the police when he was questioned by them immediately after the murder. His first statement to the police was that he couldn't remember anything from when he initially left the flat at 5.50 pm to when he was picked up by the police at the Mosque at 9.15 pm. Subsequently, with your help and treatment, he then testified that he did go back and the incident with the knife occurred.

'In my professional opinion, his initial statement that he couldn't remember anything was perfectly true. A classic case of an incident occurring that he found extremely frightening and unsettling, is instantly repressed; random amnesia. His brain, to protect him, suppresses an unpleasant event – and don't forget he seemed to have an incredibly strong emotional bond to Safia and if he felt he had hurt her with the knife incident this would put immense pressure on his subconscious to protect him by such suppression.'

'Is it not equally possible, Dr., that he *did* kill her during this incident, and has say, manufactured this scenario – his testimony – to escape responsibility?' I asked. I knew that this was an extremely risky question – bordering on the insane – but for my money, since we were already dead and buried, why not roll the dice. I heard a rustle from the jury as they perked their ears up.

Tremayne paused at this curve ball, casting a veiled, puzzled glance at me, but staying cool. She said, 'no, I don't believe Mohsin Khan's testimony was manufactured.'

Why not?

'Logic, really, and my personal knowledge of the man. Remember, at the outset, he didn't deny anything; he said: I can't remember. The defendant, and this seems a view endorsed by the prosecution, is a very able and intelligent man. If he wanted to manufacture evidence to avoid responsibility, my opinion is he would have denied the murder outright, and provided an alibi; he did none of those things, which leads me to believe he spoke the truth.'

A sliver of hope; I noticed from the corner of my eye the attractive lady juror with the glossy auburn hair imperceptibly nodding her head in agreement, but no time to think about what that might mean right now. I said, 'finally Doctor, have you any explanation as to why Mohsin Khan should have, as the prosecution would have it anyway, admit to the murder?'

'I think the clue is in the words he uses. He says I "must have" done it. He doesn't say, yes, I *did* kill her, and there is a fundamental difference. In a situation where he has no knowledge, because his mind has blanked it out, and he is repeatedly being told during sustained and expert questioning by experienced police officers – and don't forget he's a man used to deferring to authority – that all the evidence conclusively points to the fact that he did kill her, I would suggest it is reasonable for such a man to accept what he is being told.

'I think, at the end of the day, you have an intelligent truthful man who genuinely cannot remember what happened, being told by people in authority, that the only conclusion from all the evidence, is that he carried out the murder, and he has accepted it, hence the use of the words, I *must* have done it. Add to that the extreme stress he was under and his vulnerability; his wife has been stabbed to death; he's promised access to his children if he "helps" the police; he's suffering from severe PTSD, and withdrawal from alcohol and drugs; a perfect storm, and the only real way out for him is just to give the police what they want and it will all go away. That's what I think happened.

'As an aside, there have been significant studies in recent years going back to Gudjonsson about the psychology of interrogations, the vulnerability of suspects and how seemingly perfectly well adjusted individuals will confess to crimes they have not committed. And of course there are myriad reasons for this,' she said, pausing and casting a respectful glance at Feldman, before saying, 'and I can certainly address the jury on these issues if the court requires.'

I think I'd got about as far as I could with Rose, and I think she had acquitted herself well, but the real test was about to arrive with Patterson's cross examination, and I could tell he couldn't wait to get at her. I smiled reassuringly at her and said, 'thank you, doctor Tremayne, I have no further questions for you.'

Feldman then adjourned for lunch.

Chapter Thirty

Pascal sheltered in a covered bus stop across the street as squally spring rain swept in from the east, dampening the waning afternoon sun. She had been watching Christoff's block for five minutes or so and had seen nothing untoward; then out of the corner of her eye she spotted an approaching figure walking fast down her side of the street, baseball cap pulled down tight.

She moved out onto the pavement and as the figure came abreast of her, he muttered, 'the back; ten minutes,' and then he was past her, walking away.

Ten minutes later he opened the door and quickly ushered her in. 'You must have seriously perturbed someone, Courtney my dear, because the world and his dog are out there looking for you.'

They moved into a large windowless room that looked like a computer laboratory, dominated by a central console with monitors and a number of keyboards.

'Jesus, Christoff? Where d'you get this stuff?'

'Oh, its just some bits and bobs I've picked up over the years,' he said modestly.

'Well, I've got something for you,' she said, holding out the flash drive.

He took it without comment. Then he said, 'let's get you a drink, and then we can get down to business. Scotch do you?'

'That'd by fine, my man,' she said as she sank back into a deep leather chair.

Feldman looked over at the prosecutor, and said, 'any questions Mr Patterson?'

'Yes indeed, my lord,' he said as he rose to his feet.

'How long have you been practicing psychiatry, Mrs Tremayne,' he asked.

'My lord,' I interrupted, 'whilst I can appreciate my learned friend might want to belittle our experts professional standing, the correct form of address for this witness is *doctor* Tremayne, not Mrs. Tremayne.'

'I'm *so* sorry, *doctor* Tremayne,' Patterson corrected himself, gracelessly. 'Would you like me to repeat the question?'

'Seven years,' Rose replied, calm and unruffled.

'Seven years, eh,' Patterson said. 'Bit of a novice then?'

'Not at all,' she replied. 'The Royal College of Psychiatrists consider me to be an expert in the field. I've also regularly lectured, and run workshops, for them. Indeed this year at the International Conference in Birmingham, I'm running a lecture entitled: PTSD the modern soldiers burden. You're welcome to come along, Mr Patterson. You might learn something,' she said. Beautifully done, but I hoped she wouldn't get too cocky.

Patterson ignored the jibe. 'The army don't agree with you, do they, doctor Tremayne?' he asked.

'I'm sorry?'

'The army don't agree with your diagnosis of PTSD, do they?' he said, leafing through a report.

'They are on record as saying they disagree with the diagnosis of PTSD, but then they always say—'

'Just a yes or no will suffice, thank you, doctor,' Patterson said, cutting her off mid-sentence, not wanting the jury to hear the full answer, but I'd get it in, in re-examination later.

'No, they don't agree.'

'In fact, doctor, isn't it true that the army also disagree with the characterisation of these combat events we've heard so much about as being traumatic?'

'That's true, but again—'

'Yes or no, doctor?'

'Yes.'

'In fact,' Patterson said, again reading from the report, 'the army deny Khan witnessed the shooting of a colleague, or indeed that he witnessed anything particularly fierce, over and above what you would expect during normal, robust, combat missions. That's true, yes, doctor Tremayne?'

'Yes, but—'

'Indeed I have here a—'

'My lord,' I interrupted, 'might it not be helpful to the jury if the witness was allowed to answer the questions put to her?'

I could see some of the jurors nodding out of the corner of my eye, but Feldman was having none of it. 'I see nothing wrong in Mr Patterson's questioning of this witness, Mr Calver, and you of course can revisit these issues if you wish, in re-examination. Now, if we can move along,' he concluded.

'Were you aware of the glowing reference given by Major Scott on behalf of the defendant when he left the service, doctor Tremayne?' Patterson continued.

'I believe I did read it during my preparatory work for the assessment.'

'And how do you square that with you diagnosis? I quote from Major Scott's reference: "Corporal Khan is one of the most courageous, stable and reliable soldiers I have come across in my long army career, and he has proved himself to be an outstanding leader of men." Hardly the description of the gibbering cowardly wreck you portray in your evidence doctor?'

'I don't believe Major Scott has psychiatric training, and there is always a pressure to say nice things in references.'

'So Major Scott is lying, doctor?'

'Of course not.'

'Now, doctor, we've heard evidence, and I don't believe it is disputed, that the defendant did and does imbibe significant levels of drugs, prescription and non prescription, as well as alcohol, yes.'

'Yes.'

'Surely, doctor, that complicates diagnosis? I mean,' Patterson said, turning to the jury,' how can you tell whether its just self induced drunken, drugged up behaviour, or PTSD?'

'It can be difficult, but I stand by my diagnosis.'

'In fact, isn't it the case that we see a constant stream of veterans raising PTSD to excuse all manner of criminal behaviour when very often it's actually the result of drink or drugs, and PTSD is a convenient excuse, as we have here?'

'I don't agree.'

'Now, you're aware we have a report from Consultant Psychiatrist Dr James Kemble, and we shall be calling him as a rebuttal witness.'

'Yes.'

'You're also aware, that both he and the army vehemently disagree with your diagnosis. The army say that "at no stage has there ever been any suspicion or suggestion that he might be suffering from PTSD as a result of his experiences in Afghanistan", whilst Dr Kemble seems to suggest that the most Khan suffers from is what he refers to as an adjustment disorder.'

'Is there a question in there somewhere?' I asked, without rising from my seat.

Patterson unperturbed, 'how do you square your diagnosis, with that of doctor Kemble's?'

Tremayne paused whilst she formulated a response. 'With respect, Mr Patterson, I don't have to square my diagnosis with that of Dr Kemble's, because I disagree with his diagnosis. He seems to be saying in terms that there is a tendency to pathologize normal emotional reactions to stressful events or to overdiagnose what are essentially ordinary depressive disorders and come up with PTSD, when in many cases we should be diagnosing a milder form which he calls adjustment disorder.'

'Well we'll be hearing from doctor Kemble soon enough,' Patterson said, 'but let's talk about amnesia for a moment, shall we. It's very easy to feign, yes? I mean all I have to do, really is say, sorry, I can't remember – I've got amnesia, yes?'

'That's true as far as it goes, but of course, in many such cases the primary use of psychiatry is to analyse whether such claims of amnesia are genuine or simply manufactured to avoid criminal responsibility. In this case I am satisfied that the defendant genuinely does and has suffered from amnesia.'

'Again, as we will hear, and as you know, doctor Kemble fundamentally disagrees with you.'

'I am aware of that, but I stand by my diagnosis,' Rose answered calmly.

'Can you explain, doctor Tremayne, why it is that the defendant seemed to have no trouble at all in remembering the so called Sunday lunch carving knife incident – he was questioned at the time by the police, and gave an account of what happened – and yet apparently couldn't initially remember the incident on the day of the murder when he alleges that the washing up knife incident occurred,' Patterson asked, then looking over meaningfully at the jury, added, 'that is of course until all the evidence placed him there and then he conveniently remembered it?'

This was a discrepancy that I had worried about as well, so I was concerned to see how she would deal with it.

'I don't know, is the simple answer. There are many reasons why—'

'Thank you, doctor,' Patterson said, again brutally chopping off her testimony. He paused to look at some papers, and then he was off again. 'Now, doctor Tremayne, you testified at length about all the terrible pressures and stresses apparently brought to bear on the defendant by the police, and how all this and his vulnerability conspired somehow to force him to admit to the murder, which he now says he didn't commit?'

'I don't believe the words he used carry the meaning you attribute to them, but, yes, I believe he made that statement, in order to get relief from that stress and pressure, and so he could see his children.'

'And how does that square with Major Scott's glowing testimonial that the defendant is courageous, stable, reliable; an outstanding leader of men. Does that sound like the kind of man who rolls over in the face of a bit of turbulence and some determined questioning by the police?'

'There are different types of stress and pressure, and they all affect people in different ways,' she answered, clearly starting to wilt under Patterson's onslaught.

'Very profound, I'm sure, doctor, but not particularly helpful as expert evidence,' he said, before steamrollering on without a pause. 'Now, you testified, in terms, that because we all accept the defendant is an intelligent man, if he was fabricating his evidence, he would flat out deny the murder and provide an alibi, rather than coming up with this, I can't remember, then I can remember, vague kind of explanation?'

Yes,' she said, warily.

'But isn't that just the point, doctor Tremayne?' Patterson asked, looking over at the jury, again. 'He is a highly intelligent, sophisticated, and I would say, manipulative man, and his explanation for what happened is entirely at one with that. It's a version of events that is impossible to pin down or delve into. It's masterful really, like smoke, so vague, but so clever as well. A straight denial with specifics would allow him to be pinned down, and his story shown as false, and he's far to clever to allow that to happen.'

'Again, my lord,' I queried, mock wearily from my seat, 'is there a question in there somewhere?'

But Patterson didn't need an answer, and anyway, Rose had none to give. I think Patterson was just about done by now but he hammered away for another tortuous half hour during which Rose just about managed to hang on in there. Then I re-examined her briefly and allowed her to explain what Patterson had prevented her from saying, which was that essentially the army's default position was to deny PTSD in every case, because to admit it would have cost implications in respect of increased pension entitlement as well as compensation claims in litigation and all such publicity was damaging to the army.

Then finally I hoped we were done for the day as I sat down with relief, but no, Patterson was back up on his feet again. 'My lord, I know its late in the day but I have been passed some information relating to the issue of bail and I have instructions from the CPS to make an application,' he said, looking around at me.

Shit, I thought. Now what the hell was he up to.

'Where on *earth* did you get that?' Christoff asked, flicking a glance at the fearsome knife Pascal had just removed from her bag.

'Mile End,' she said, running her finger down the blade.

Christoff was working on a laptop into which he had plugged the flash drive provided by Pascal. 'What possessed you?' he asked absently, concentrating on his screen.

Pascal smiled one of her rare smiles. 'Heat of the moment stuff I guess. You know—'

]'Ruddy hell. It's encrypted,' Christoff said, squinting at his screen, fingers running across the keyboard. 'I'm going to have spend some time on this.'

Pascal sipped her scotch. 'Okay, but first I need you to track down a partial plate number I've got for a BMW F800,' she said, handing Christoff a scrap of paper with the letter and three numbers on it. 'Can you give me anything, before you get to work on the drive?'

He looked over at her, about to say something, then changing his mind, said, 'I'll have a go. Let's see what we've got.' He leaned into his screen, fingers flying over the keys again. After twenty minutes or so during which Pascal consumed a couple of bottles of Bud, he leaned back and said, 'There's only one BMW bike in London of that make that has a plate with those four digits and its registered to a Mr Roger Sanford. And here's the address,' he said handing back the slip of paper with it written on it. 'It looks like a block of flats over in Stepney.'

Pascal took the details, then took the little Nokia phone out of her pocket and toyed with it whilst she sat gazing into space.

'What's troubling you, Courtney?' Christoff asked.

'Oh, that prick, Calver, the lawyer. We had a falling out and now I can't seem to get hold of him. I'll try him again on the way.' She stood up and bagged the knife. 'I'm gonna check out this address now, Christoff. See if you can crack that stick open while I'm gone.'

'Be careful.'

'Always.'

Stanton hated fucking spooks. Nerdy kids who thought they were in some kind of Hollywood movie, and then looked down their expensively educated noses at the good and righteous cops on the beat. He leaned against the wall and sipped his coffee and listened to the big chief, Condon, yapping away to a group of brownnosers whilst at the same time sporadically speaking into his cell phone, as they tried to draw a bead on Pascal. If he ever got hold of her again, she wouldn't get another chance to run. No siree. Maybe it would be another death in custody, if he could set it up right, and him knowing the ropes so well now, they'd never touch him.

He dug a crumpled pack of cigarettes out of his pocket and unthinkingly stuck one in his mouth, thinking all the while of how best he could hurt the girl without leaving bruising or marks.

'Excuse me, excuse me.'

Stanton, broken out of his reverie, looked at the little dickshit wet behind the ears college boy in front of him.

'There's no smoking in here, sergeant.'

Stanton studied him a moment and then pushed himself away from the wall, the young man immediately shrinking back as he took in the bulk and intimidating menace radiating out from Stanton.

'What did you say to me, boy?'

'Hey, Stanton, its no smoking in here,' Condon shouted over the heads of the group around him. 'And get over here; we're starting to get some information in now and you need to hear this.'

Stanton scowled and then reluctantly ambled over as Condon continued. 'After tracking Courtney Pascal's mobile phone all the way to a refuse dump in South London, our bright boys finally realised they'd been had,' he said, to laughter. Then added, 'but seriously folks, tech boys say the explosion was caused by a grenade; modern military ordnance still in use by the British army. Good news though, we've also got some CCTV of Pascal's car coming into Southwark, South London, about an hour ago. So get on it, people.'

Yeah? Fuck you, Stanton thought. I've got a better idea, I'll just mosey on down the Bailey and have another crack at that shyster lawyer, court should just about be finishing up for the day right now. Whenever he'd crossed paths with Calver in the past, that freaky little bitch was always somewhere in the background, so the way to run her down was through the lawyer. Stanton ambled out of the office ignoring the shouts querying where he was going. He was on a mission, so fuck'em.

I rubbed my eyes, trying to keep awake as Patterson droned on. I cast an eye at the jury box and one of the women smiled at me and tapped her mouth as if yawning. I smiled back acknowledging her. Then I tuned in again to hear Patterson say, 'my lord, its been a long day and my application need not concern the jury if you wish to release them.'

So Feldman did, and as the jury made their way out Patterson slid some police statements across to me and I flicked through them. It seemed pretty clear that for some of the time during the trial Khan had been under surveillance. There were a number of statements and apparently some photographs showing he had been out when he shouldn't have been – ergo, multiple breaches of his bail conditions. I knew he had been out when he shouldn't have, but I didn't realise it was so extensive – and why the hell was he under surveillance when he had been charged months ago? I walked quickly over to Khan and handed him the statements.

'Looks like you've been moonlighting, Mohsin. Care to explain?' I said casually.

He wouldn't meet my eye when he looked up from scanning the documents. 'Look, Jonas, I don't want to argue about this, or oppose their application. Let them withdraw bail. Trials nearly over, isn't it. Might as well get used to it, right?'

I was too tired to argue with him, and the thought of not having to joust with Patterson and Feldman for another hour or so was too tempting to refuse. But one question stuck in my mind and wouldn't go away. I looked him full in the eye, and said, 'you're the boss, Mohsin, but tell me, why the fuck are you still under surveillance?'

'I have no idea,' he said. I didn't believe him, but then I thought, what the hell does it matter now, our goose was cooked with all the evidence in, so why get heated about it.

So when Paterson finally stood up to address Feldman, I shocked them both by casually interrupting with, 'I think I can significantly shorten things here, my lord, by saying that, although no admissions are made by the defendant to these alleged breaches of bail conditions, he has instructed me not to oppose the application.'

Feldman and Patterson looked at each other, and then Feldman said to me, 'a very sensible decision, if I may say so, Mr Calver. Now—'

'But,' I said, interrupting him, as I wasn't quite finished yet, 'we do have some serious concerns about the papers on which my learned friend is basing his application. The statements suggest the defendant is still under surveillance by the prosecuting authority, months after he was charged. Why is that? Not only that, some of the statements are heavily redacted, suggesting the involvement of the security services, and we demand to know why?'

'You *demand*, do you?' Feldman said, eyebrow raised enquiringly, warning lights starting to flash. 'Do you really think it is appropriate, Mr Calver, to *demand*, anything, of a High Court Judge?'

It had been a very long and trying day and I had really had enough of this pompous dick and his double act with the prosecutor, but still I had to try and stay calm. 'My lord. No disrespect was intended to the court, but we would like to know why this defendant—'

'I'm sorry, Mr Calver,' he said. 'You see, it's not an explanation I require of you. What I require is that you withdraw your rude and disrespectful, *demand*, yes?'

'No.'

'What?'

'I said, no, my lord. I'm not going to withdraw it. It's valid and expresses my clients anger at what is clearly an unwarranted intrusion into his private affairs by the prosecutorial authority, and as I've already said, no disrespect was intended to this court by my use of those words.'

Sometimes I was my own worst enemy, and this was an example. I just couldn't let it go and back down.

Feldman sat and watched me for a moment. Finally Patterson stirred beside me and started to rise, but Feldman held out a hand staying him, so he slowly settled back into his chair.

'I need no assistance from the crown, thank you, Mr Patterson,' he said, nodding. 'What we have here is rudeness and contempt for my position and authority in this court, and a refusal by Mr Calver to abide by a clear judicial direction that he withdraw his demand. I will give him one further chance to abide by that request, or I will find him in contempt,' he said. He looked at me; this was no joke.

Finally he'd got me exactly were he wanted me by skilfully using my tiredness, animus against him, and simple provocation, and I had risen to it like a salmon, without thought. But now I'd gone way too far to yield.

'I can't do that, my lord. I have—'

'That's all, thank you, Mr Calver. I find you in contempt of this court, and this includes the earlier incident where you wilfully knocked over of a glass of water in a flagrant attempt to disrupt Mr Patterson's cross examination of the defendant. You will now spend a night in the cells, to purge that contempt. When you are brought up in the morning, I will expect you to withdraw your demand and provide me with an apology. If you don't, I will consider that you are maintaining your contempt and I shall act accordingly.'

Feldman looked around the courtroom for an usher or bailiff but then smiled as I heard the courtroom door open behind me. I turned to catch DI Dick Stanton entering.

'Excellent timing D I Stanton. I wonder, as the court bailiffs seem to have disappeared, if you wouldn't mind escorting Mr Calver down to the cells,' Feldman said.

'No problem,' Stanton replied, reaching out to take my shoulder and push me down to the cells, but I wasn't finished yet. I batted his hand away – I knew he wouldn't play up in front of a judge.

I remained standing at my desk, ignoring Stanton. 'My lord, this isn't over,' I said. 'You can muzzle me in here, but not outside, and putting me in a cell overnight so I can't prepare for court tomorrow? I don't think so.'

'Your arrogance, Mr Calver, is perhaps only outweighed by your impudence. The trial is almost over and if you can't do your prep in a cell – I'll allow you to take your trial papers with you – then you shouldn't be practicing. Now, again, take him down,' he said and this time he rose and left the bench.

Stanton turned and gestured with his head for me to move. As I picked up my papers he grinned, and it reminded me of the scene in the movie From Here to Eternity when Judson, the guy running the stockade, realises he's got Maggio coming to stay.

When we got down to the holding cells, there was a whispered confab between Stanton and the custody guys about what to do with me. Khan and the other prisoners had already left for Belmarsh, so consensus was I would have to stay there for the night. While they were arguing my cell buzzed with an incoming text. I dug the phone out and read it; it was from an unknown number: *calver im on run, things breaking fast, call me. pascal*

What the hell did that mean? And then Stanton was in my face again, grabbing the phone, and crowding me. 'I'll take that, Calver,' he said and winked at the security guy. Then he looked over at me after reading the text message, and said, 'must be my lucky day. You put behind bars where you belong, and here,' he said holding up my phone triumphantly, 'the icing on the cake – your little friends location.'

By now I had a prison officer each side, holding me so I knew it would be pointless to try and reason with him. They moved me away as Stanton ambled off humming to himself as he scrolled through my private text messages.

Chapter Thirty One

I soon realised it was a waste of time lying down and trying to sleep, so I sat back up and looked at the pile of court papers lying in the corner of my cell, but I couldn't face them either. My mind strayed and drifted, flitting like a butterfly from Pascal, to Carman, to Khan and back again, but that only seemed to remind me how impotent I was, locked away beneath the Old Bailey.

I thought about Pascal's text and tried to remember the exact words, but I couldn't as I'd only caught a glimpse of it before Stanton had grabbed it. And when had it come in; maybe it was already stale. I knew it said she was on the run which seemed to fit in with what Stanton had said to me earlier. One good thing though; she was talking to me again and for some reason I found that immensely comforting.

But just what the fuck was going on in Pascal's world? I tried to fit the pieces of what she had told me together in some kind of order but got nowhere, so eventually gave up. Then the anger at Feldman resurfaced, which was good as it stopped me from wallowing in self-pity. One thing was sure; when I'd done with Khan I was going to make it my life's work to nail Feldman, whether through the appeal courts or more direct action.

I stood up and looked through my cell bars at the screw who sat at a desk staring at some type of tablet. He had seemed unexpectedly reasonable when I'd spoken to him earlier. I guessed he was probably pissed at having to stay and babysit me overnight, especially as there were no facilities for it. The court merely accommodated prisoners during the day. Feldman had apparently been contacted by the staff and told they had no transport to take me to a prison or hold me over night, but he hadn't given a toss, making it clear they were to hold me anyway, and he would take responsibility.

I watched the guy some more through the bars for a while until I could tell he was aware of my gaze. He finally looked up and said, 'you okay in there?'

'Oh, so so. Nothing that a few beers wouldn't cure, right?' I said.

'You and me both,' he said, smiling as he tapped something in on his screen.

If I'd had to guess, looking at the guy – early thirties, toned and fit – I'd say he was probably swopping words, and possibly more, with online girls or boys on his tablet. 'Listen,' I said, 'you know I'm a lawyer, and in order to practice I have to comply with the judges orders.'

'Yeah, well I heard you didn't, and that's why you're in here.'

'No, man, that's just a game. The point I'm making is that if I were to break out of here, go on the run, anything like that, my legal career's over, and I've got a trial to finish tomorrow.'

'So what are you telling me,' he said, smiling, without looking up, as he saw an image come up on his screen.

'What I'm saying, is that I'm not going anywhere, and you can bank on that even if you were to open my cell and give me the door keys.'

'You're crazy. Why would I do that?'

'Because I've got a hundred here says you will, and I'm sure you've got better things to do than sit around here and watch me. Lets do a deal, buddy? You go and get me some drink, and then you can leave if you like. Up to you, long as your back by, what should we say, four thirty, five a clock. Who's gonna know? I'm sure as hell not going to tell anyone.'

He sat watching me for a moment, trying to discern a catch or a wind up. 'And the hundred?' he said.

'Half now out of which all I want is a cheap bottle of corner shop scotch, and you get the other half when you get back in the morning.'

Again he watched me for a moment. Then all he said was, 'cool,' before he got up and came and opened my cell door. Then as he was about to go out and get my booze he stopped and said, 'oh, that fat cop. The psycho one. He left your mobile phone. Said not to give it back to you until the morning, but, fuck'im, right?'

'Right,' I said as he opened a drawer and took out the phone and handed it to me.

I sat on my bunk and sipped cheap scotch out of a paper cup; Barry, my minder, had long since disappeared into the night. I didn't want to get drunk but what else did I have to do; even the thought of nailing Feldman on appeal for his latest piece of judicial malpractice failed to raise my spirits; any result on that would be months away.

I started to rehearse my closing speech in my head, then realised I had never checked my phone after Barry had handed it back to me. In fact the phone had been switched off, so I jacked it up, then realised the battery was virtually flat. There were a load of the usual miscalls from Emma, the bank, SRA and the few assorted clients who had my cell number, and also a new text message. Hoping the battery would last long enough for me to read it, I tapped it up.

For a time, long after the screen had gone dark, I just sat and stared at it, unseeing, the words of the text message chiselled into my psyche:

"*carmen did not betray u. long story. right now need talk urgent. nicki dead but news blackout. something big going down & im in middle. pascal*"

The first five words of the message spiralled around inside my whiskey addled brain, and I couldn't get past them. The rest of the words and her earlier cryptic text message were completely obscured by the magnitude of what those first five words meant to me. Pascal may have had lots of faults but I knew she'd never lie about something like that – she knew what it meant to me, especially after Corvino's.

In the end it was just too much to contemplate, and eventually I succumbed to the scotch and the bone cracking weariness brought on by months of stressful, nerve shredding trial work. I gratefully slipped into the welcome embrace of sleep, but even there I couldn't escape dreams of Carmen, where I called out, but she wouldn't come, and in the shadows I sensed another presence hiding there. I strained to see if it was me, but then it turned to nightmare as Patterson revealed himself, surging from the darkness.

Frankie Crawford carefully unzipped and removed his uniform from the suit carrier and hung it on the outside of the wardrobe. He leaned forward, blew on and then lightly rubbed one of the medals on the breast pocket, then turned and looked around the luxurious Kensington hotel room, his eyes lingering over his half unpacked bag on the bed with the little syringe box lying alongside it.

He moved to the minibar and took out a couple of miniature whiskey bottles, cracked the lids and drank them in quick succession as his mind briefly revisited the scene at Mile End road. He was sure, but not certain, he'd got the girl with the grenade, but he simply couldn't have risked hanging around to find out, but it was worrying that so far there had been nothing on the news. Not much longer he thought as he lay back on the bed. Maybe he should go out and enjoy his last night on earth.

Stanton sat in the unmarked car in a quiet south London street. The thirteen year old rent boy he'd just picked up and frightened the shit out of was now bent over, head busy working away in Stanton's lap, the wet slippery sucking sounds, music to his ears. He shouted into his phone trying to get it through to the tech boys at the Met how urgent it was that they get a triangulation on the phone coordinates he'd given them.

Stanton groaned loudly as he ground the child's small head into his lap.

'Are you okay, Inspector? Only it sounded like you were dying,' the caller enquired on speakerphone.

'Just get me a fucking location, yeah? And not a fucking word to the spooks or Condon,' he said, snapping off the connection.

He lifted the child's head from his lap and looked with disgust at his face. 'Clean yourself up. You want your mother to see you like this,' he said, leaning across the boy, opening the car door and shoving him out.

Pascal stood across the street and studied the dingy block of flats. It was a sixties purpose built with no discernible architectural merit, but probably worth a fortune, being in London, even if it was only Stepney. She figured it was possibly council or housing association owned, given the state of the buildings.

She pressed the doorbell and waited, heard some barking and then the door was being opened, but only a crack. 'Yeah, what is it?' a gruff female voice asked from within.

'I'm looking for Roger Sanford,' Pascal said.

'He's not here,' she said, starting to push the door shut.

Pascal made a quick decision and thrust out her fake met warrant card. 'Look, madam, we don't want to announce to the whole street that the police are here, but we urgently need to speak to Mr Sanford in an ongoing investigation, and I'd stress here, he's not a suspect, just a witness.'

The door held firm for a beat, and then opened wide to reveal a small shrew like woman with a hard bitten look on her face. She studied Pascal for a moment, suspicion radiating out of her, clearly slightly taken aback that the waif like girl could be a police officer.

Pascal felt it required something more. 'We're working under cover, so please forgive the dress. Look, can I come in for a brief word please?'

The woman still looked suspicious, but then nodded reluctantly and stepped aside ushering Pascal into the hallway and onwards towards a lighted room at the end. She said, 'your too late. Mr Sanford moved out today.'

She led Pascal into a large kitchen where they both came to a halt. 'Sorry to see him go actually. He was no trouble, virtually never here, and even when he was he would be up on the roof with those bloody pigeons. Dirty bloody things. Rats with wings I say,' she said with a mirthless laugh.

It was slowly dawning on Pascal that the block was in fact some type of boarding house, something she thought had gone out of fashion in the fifties. Looking round the kitchen she could see now that it had a kind of communal look to it.

'Look Mrs?...'

'Piper.'

'Mrs Piper, I can't tell you much other than he is a witness to a serious crime and we urgently need to speak to him. Can you tell me anything about him, and could I see his rooms?'

As Mrs Piper lead her upstairs, Pascal noticed on the landing an old fashioned payphone. In the room, it was clear it had been meticulously cleaned; there was nothing, no hint of a human presence. Mrs Piper said he had never had anything there save for a change of clothing. She believed he might have had another place somewhere as he would disappear for months on end, and then would just show up out of the blue, but the rent was always paid in advance, the perfect tenant. She had no idea what he did for a living as he was particularly private and uncommunicative, but each to his own.

As they went back down stairs, Pascal stopped at the payphone. It was attached to the wall and there was a shelf sticking out with a kind of blotter on it, on which had been written numbers and half written notes as well as a load of doodles and swirls, some faded, some recent.

'Funny you should stop and look at that. He's the only one who used it, my other two boys have smart phones and wouldn't be seen dead with it,' Mrs Piper said.

'Would you mind, Mrs Piper if I stopped here for a bit and had a look. See if I can get a lead on him?'

Mrs Piper looked reluctant, as if she was now anxious to get rid of Pascal. Pascal put on the most social friendly face she could manage. Even after years of practice it still wasn't up to much and she knew it, but it seemed to do the trick.

'Ten minutes,' Mrs Piper said over her shoulder as she made her way down the stairs.

Pascal hit pay-dirt on the fourth call. It was the Excelsior Hotel in Kensington and Mr Sanford was booked in for the night. Did she wish to speak to him? Pascal hung up and was moving fast down the stairs before the hotel receptionist realised there was no one on the other end of the line. Pascal didn't have time to waste, she needed to get a bead on the guy who'd tried to kill her.

Barry shook me awake, handing me a paper cup of coffee, whilst demanding the rest of his money. My head felt like someone was using it as a kettledrum. I looked around and there was bustle everywhere; prisoners being brought in and logged, phones ringing, doors clanging, cons horsing around and shouting. I checked my watch and couldn't believe it was already quarter to ten. I looked up at Barry standing over me, waiting. I dug out my wallet and saw I only had a solitary five pound note left.

'Barry, soon as I get to a cash point today you'll have your money,' I said, looking into his eyes and trying to generate sincerity whilst trying to ignore the banging in my head. 'Hey, I'm a lawyer, you can trust me,' I added, but I don't think it helped.

'Okay, Calver,' he said grudgingly, 'but I want it today.'

'You got it,' I said, getting up and starting to gather up my papers.

Barry turned to go, then turned back and said, 'Oh, Judge Feldman called down and said to release you and he'll deal with you later this morning or after court.'

'That's white of him,' I said, digging out my cell. 'Say, Barry, you got a phone charger down here?'

'Hey, Calver, I'm not your house boy. Look in the bottom drawer of the desk.'

Just twenty five minutes later I stood at the defence table. In a way it was good, not having any more time left to fret about all the crap swirling around inside my head. Now I just had to get on with it. I had scrubbed up as well as I could, given the woeful state of the Old Bailey's toilet facilities, and my rumpled, slept in suit was just about presentable, if you didn't look too close and see all the creases and scotch stains.

Feldman had ignored me since he had come into court, and that suited me just fine; the less I thought about him, whilst trying to give the speech of my life, the better. Now he looked down at me from the bench and nodded with a gruff, 'proceed.'

I took a last look around the courtroom as I steadied myself to begin, my eyes sweeping over the jury, all sitting attentive, then onto the bench and Feldman with his monstrous sideburns – even they seemed somewhat subdued today – and then on to Patterson with his gang of CPS flunkeys arrayed out behind him, then on over the visitors gallery and on, but then I stopped dead, snatching for reverse. I tracked back to check that my mind wasn't playing tricks on me – it wasn't, because there was Carmen, in the gallery, sitting, coolly returning my gaze.

It was such a shock after having her centre stage in my dreams overnight, suddenly, without warning, to have her appearing like that, staring right back at me. It floored me, rendering me speechless for a second. I tried to recover my poise and bearings, the taste of stale whiskey and bile flooding the back of my throat, my prepared speech completely gone from my mind as I flailed around. Then as I slowly tried to regain control, and as I heard Feldman prompt me again with, 'Mr Calver, you may proceed,' in the background, a terrible suspicion arose in me: Patterson had brought Carmen along simply to do what she had so effectively just done; destabilise and unsettle me enough to screw up my closing speech.

I struggled to get a grip, but then as I looked up towards the jury to start speaking I caught sight of Patterson's triumphant expression. He knew he'd hit me where it hurt, in my heart. Now I could see the lady juror who'd earlier feigned a yawn, watching me with mounting confusion, and then Feldman was jumping on my back again, berating me waspishly with, 'Mr Calver, I don't know if you're hoping to communicate with the jury by telepathy, but if you don't start your address this instant, I will move straight to my summing up and you can sit down.'

'Forgive me, my lord,' I said, swallowing quickly and then, again, I was hit with a kind of thunderbolt of revelation. I may be some slick, clever lawyer, but I wasn't good at the emotional stuff, but now it was beginning to filter through; if Carmen hadn't betrayed me, then I could get her back – however long it took. Finally, there might be hope, and that was Pascal's gift to me, wherever she was right now. And then I smiled, and Patterson saw it, and I thought make of that whatever you will you sorry son of a bitch, because I'm coming after you, and he saw it, and he turned away.

'Ladies and gentlemen of the jury,' I said, in the time honoured way, and I could feel the lightening crackling off me as I began to weave my magic. You had to believe something like that, to be any good, so I did, in spades.

Chapter Thirty Two

Pascal sat in the small hotel bar sipping a Gin and Tonic whilst she took stock and checked her phone. Nothing from Calver. Maybe when he got round to reading her text messages he'd wake up and call her, or maybe he had read them and was just being a grade A asshole.

She phoned Christoff. While she waited she looked through the ID documents he'd given her and selected a passport, making sure it had a Met warrant card with it, and then he picked up. 'Courtney, you're going to want to see this,' he said, absently as if he were working on something complicated whilst speaking. 'Exploding—'

'Listen, Christoff,' she broke in, 'I think I've got a line on our mystery Mr Sanford. I'm at the Excelsior hotel Kensington. They've confirmed he's booked in for the night. Can you phone up now and book me a double room in the name of Elizabeth Rafferty, that's one of the passports you gave me. Tell 'em I'll pay in cash at the desk and check in within the hour. Then get over here, like now, because the answers we need are going to be here, and bring the laptop and anything else you need to crack the rest of the stuff on the flash drive,' she said.

She signalled the waitress for another G & T, and then sat mulling things over and watching the girl on reception through the glass door of the bar. She watched the girl answer what she assumed was Christoff's call, and then two minutes later the text came in from Christoff confirming the room was booked and he would make his way over as soon as he could.

I tended to start most of my closing speeches in the same way, by restating the obvious; that is, that in order to convict, the prosecution must prove guilt beyond reasonable doubt. Now, we all know that, but do we all know what it means? Do we hell.

So I explained to the jury that essentially, beyond reasonable doubt meant, they had to be sure – that was it. They had to be sure of guilt. Not almost sure, and even if they thought he'd *probably* done it – that still wasn't enough. If the prosecution weren't able to satisfy the jury so they were sure of guilt, then Khan was entitled to an acquittal. Trouble was, I'd bet my last bottle of scotch, they were sure he'd done it – damn sure.

Then I moved on and asked the jury: 'so what is the prosecutions case? I know, you're probably just as confused as I am,' I said, allowing myself a quick smile, directed at Patterson and his CPS cohorts sitting stony faced at the prosecution table. 'But let me try and tease it out for you. Essentially they say that when Mr Khan came back to the flat that night, Safia told him she wanted a divorce, so he killed her. Nice and simple. So lets look at it. So Mr Khan was at the crime scene? Well of course he was, he lived there and he doesn't deny he was there that evening, but his clear evidence was that he left the flat at ten *to* eight – Coronation street was still on the TV – and when he left Safia was still alive.'

'Now we all heard DCI Stanton's witness, Eddie Nelson. Yeah, that's right,' I said, hoping I had got just the right amount of mocking contempt in my voice. 'That's the guy who's testimony's been chucked out by the court of appeal. We all heard him say that he saw Mr Khan outside the flat at the latest, five *past* eight, fifteen minutes later, but Mr Khan says he was long gone by then. Does it really matter? Yes it does; it's a small point maybe, but it does matter, because time of death is accepted by both sides as being between 7 and 8 pm that night and we say someone else went into that flat after Mr Khan had left. So, who are you going to believe, a decorated veteran, or a professional informant? I leave it to you, but think about it.'

The point I had just made about the timings was not really important evidentially, but I had reason for raising it; it was another opportunity to rubbish their witness and, by association, their whole case, and every little bit helped in my dogged pursuit of reasonable doubt.

I moved on. 'Now, if things went down the way the crown would have it, why on earth would Mohsin Khan put the blood stained clothing in the washing machine afterwards? This is a man with a degree in chemistry whom you would expect to be extremely forensically aware, and who would know that putting clothing through a wash would be unlikely to eradicate all traces of blood,' I said, addressing the juror who'd feigned yawning – a pretty redhead with sultry green eyes – and now she was slowly and imperceptibly nodding her head.

'But as you know, members of the jury, we do not accept the crowns contentions anyway. Mr Khan testified that he and Safia were reconciled, they were starting again and were both excited about the prospects. Rana disagreed, but she grieves for her sister and wants someone to blame, and who better than Mr Khan, a man she has disliked since day one and whom she was hoping Safia would leave. Again, think about it.'

I paused to take a sip of water. The last part of my speech had been poor. I could feel it, like I was losing my rhythm and direction, and the force of the points I had was being lost because I was making too many small weak ones instead of a few very strong ones. I needed to up my game and stay focused.

Condon had been surprised when he got the call from Lammy. He thought she would have been long gone, brownnosing away like crazy with the rest of the gang around POTUS, but he couldn't disguise the little rush of pleasure he got at hearing her voice.

Now they sat at a table outside a wine bar in Covent Garden watching the early midmorning crowds. Things had been a bit awkward to start with, and she hadn't seemed quite as full of herself as usual, and then it had all started to come out. She'd been frozen out. Even accepting that she was pretty junior she had still thought she would be involved in the high level security protection work going on around POTUS, but she had been disabused of this very quickly, and then totally sidelined. Tolliver had become distant, taking all the credit, and her promised promotion turned out to be a desk job stateside in some field office out in the boondocks, and she didn't want it; she wanted to stay in London.

They sat, awkwardly, sipping their white wine, Condon itching to say I told you so, but just about keeping a lid on it. Instead he commiserated somewhat as he too had been pulled out of the loop regarding security for POTUS; it now being dealt with by more senior officers.

Lammy smiled. 'No one, but no one is going to get though the ring of steel they've now got around our guy; impregnable don't even get close,' she said.

Condon agreed and then for something to say, to fill in the awkward silence that was developing, he mentioned the problems they were having, reeling Pascal in.

'You still think she's got the answers, John?'

'She's found alongside Holloway's dead body. The guy's been eviscerated, and I've no doubt the knife she took, when she escaped custody, was the murder weapon. In escaping there was an explosion, although it does now look as if that was from a grenade chucked through the window. Now I don't know how many criminal offences that might amount to in the States, but over here that's a pretty impressive list. But more than that, just prior to all this, he's surveilled scoping out your embassy. He was clearly deeply involved in whatever was going down, and he's solidly connected to all the main players. At the very least she's got some very serious questions to answer. Don't you think?'

'You don't think she killed Holloway, do you?' Lammy asked.

Condon returned her look, a slight smile starting to play on his lips. Then he said, 'No, I don't. Not unless she was threatened in some way. Holloway was basically a weasel. A not very strong ex-soldier, junkie, physically gone to seed and, I'd say, completely incapable of frightening someone like Pascal. I know she might not look like much physically, but don't forget she's a black belt at judo and it would take one pretty tough hombre to take her down.'

They both looked around at the crowds, and Condon signalled the waiter to top up their wine. He said, 'So, Averill, don't you think maybe its time you told me what you got from her, now? I'm guessing its not much, and you're ambivalent about what value it has, and whether you can parlay it into something with Tolliver, or whether holding on will get your ass straight into a federal gaol? There's no more time; Friday April first is tomorrow – its shit or bust?'

'You know what, John,' she said. 'You know all I know, seriously. Okay, I did maybe tell Qadir that Pascal was a rogue agent and was saying bomb factory about the shed in Stoke Newington, but that's it really. And I'd rather my guys don't hear about any of this, and there's no reason they should, as none of it's now relevant – overtaken by events.'

She expected Condon to remonstrate with her, but he was looking thoughtfully into the distance. He said, 'so the grenade was clearly to silence her. Why? And how did they know she was there so quickly? Part of the cell has gotta still be out there, hasn't it?

'With Qadir gone, and POTUS locked up tighter than a rats ass, I'm not sure it matters now does it. They've got blanket security all over London; it's over John.'

'Yeah, maybe. But wouldn't you just love to have a crack at Courtney; get her in the interrogation room and find out just what the hell she knows about all this stuff. Cause you can bet it's a hell of a lot more than we do.'

'Have you tried the simple stuff, like just phoning her?' Lammy asked.

'We tried that, but she didn't answer and then she stuck her cell phone in a refuse truck. Oldest trick in the book, but my boys fell for it and ended up chasing their tails across London. We tried her flat as well, of course, and obviously no trace there; dead end.'

Lammy laughed and said, 'what about Christoff?'

Condon looked up at her, and she could see something move in his eyes, a hint of excitement; something he hadn't thought of. He said, cautiously, 'what about Christoff?'

'Oh come on, John, they're close as hell, still. Even I knew she'd been talking to him recently, and he's been helping her. You don't think she's been doing all this on her lonesome, do you?'

'Jesus,' he said, as he pulled out his cell phone.

The girl had said her name was Farida and she looked Pakistani British, but she reminded Frankie of Mai, the love of his life and the girl Mullah Abdullah had had killed out in the badlands of Afghanistan. The Paki girl, obviously a high end escort, working the lunchtime crowd, had come onto him in the hotel bar and Frankie hadn't minded a bit, especially as this was to be his last night on earth. He was determined to go out in style and she was just unlucky – wrong place, wrong time – but that was life.

They were kissing, having come into the hotel room, but now the girl pulled away, the come on look still there, but now she pouted and waived her finger back and forth across his face. 'Money first lover boy,' she said, running her tongue around her lips, 'then we can party.'

'How much?' Frankie asked, but his voice sounded odd, dull, disconnected.

The girl was high on cocaine and wasn't bothering to read the signs or watch Frankie's face; he was just another dumb punter to be played. If he was loaded with cash, she'd put some drops in his drink, skin him, and skip. If not, she'd play, and maybe get his credit cards – she knew a guy who could fence them. She said, 'five hundred,' and then when she got no reaction, she added, 'baby, that's nothing for what I'm going to do to you.'

'Or I to you,' Frankie said, and then he hit her, almost breaking her jaw.

Pascal finished her drink, took out her warrant card and went out to the reception desk. Within ten minutes she had established her cover story with the manager and his assistant. She was following up routine enquiries about Mr Sanford. The receptionist confirmed he was booked in for one night in room 36. She thought she had seen him go up to his room with a lady friend earlier and didn't think anyone had left since.

Pascal emphasised the investigation was secret and under cover and so even if a police officer came or asked questions they should disclose nothing without referring it back to her first. Pascal then confirmed her booking which they fast tracked before handing her the key for Room 26 which was directly below Sanford's room.

I watched the jury as I weighed my next move. I needed to get into the tricky area of the lover, Rashid Syed, where Feldman had already ruled that his evidence was to be disregarded by the jury. So if I alluded to it full on, Patterson and Feldman would jump down my throat, so caution was the word.

'Now you heard from both DI Stanton and Rana Chaudhry about this affair that Safia was allegedly having – its been floating around out there all through this trial – so lets deal with it head on. It is Mr Khan's case that there may have been some ups and downs in the marriage but they'd weathered the storm and were reconciled, and he was very clear about that.

'Of course if you accept that Safia and Mr. Khan were reconciled and starting again, Mohsin Khan has absolutely no motive for this murder – but someone else surely did....' I said and then left it hanging there, hoping again it would make the jury latch onto the point and start thinking about it.

Time to cut to the chase, or more likely, long past it. I said to the jury, 'so let's talk about that tiny piece of metal found lodged in Safia's rib. Where did it come from?' I asked, holding my gaze on the jurors, willing them to think about it. 'It's the one critical piece of evidence that the crown have found it impossible to explain away. We know from their expert, Dr Kohler, that it did not come from the knife found in the drain, so where did it come from? When asked, Dr Kohler could not exclude the possibility that it came from the tip of another knife or implement, broken off in the wound. Perhaps a knife with a wider blade than that found, which might explain the measured width of some of the stab wounds – which didn't fit the drain knife – suggesting another knife being used in the attack.'

I paused again to sip water even though I was sick of the taste of it by now. But these pauses were important to the delivery and flow of the speech, and also represented natural places to stop where I wanted the jury to pause and allow what had just been said to settle and start percolating, before I moved on.

'Remember what Mr Khan told you in his evidence. He said there was a struggle with Safia because when she was washing up, she happened to hold up the carving knife, and this had triggered a reaction in him, a reaction we can trace right back to his stabbing in Afghanistan. And the superficial cuts on Safia's body bare this out. So it fits. Essentially it's a rerun of the Sunday lunch incident; a knife flashes before Khan, it sets him off and there's a tussle, but its far short of a savage and murderous knife attack.

'Ladies and gentlemen of the jury, lets be clear, Mr Khan says someone else came into that flat, someone who may even have been watching, waiting for him to leave,' I said, pausing again and listening to the jury fidget around as they absorbed this latest highly speculative point.

'Mr Khan's case is that someone else entered the flat as soon as he left, certainly before eight o clock, with a large knife, and that person murdered Safia. The washing machine had already been turned on by Safia at around ten to eight just as Mr Khan left with his knife to drop it down the drain. The attack that followed was so vicious and frenzied that the tip of this knife broke off. It was over very quickly and we believe the killer was in and out of the flat all within ten minutes, tops.'

I paused again for another sip of water, wishing it was vodka. Then I switched my angle to bring in Rashid Syed again, the lover, by the back door. 'Now you will remember I put a number of questions to the investigating officer in this case, DI Stanton. He confirmed that the police had carried out an extensive search both in and outside the flat, but no other knife has ever been found, certainly none to match the piece of metal found lodged in Safia's ribcage. But remember also that I asked DI Stanton about whether he had questioned Mr Syed about the murder.'

I looked up at Feldman who just watched me. Although he'd chucked out Rashid's evidence he couldn't stop me accessing it in this way. 'Remember his answer? They only questioned Syed as a witness, never as a suspect, and what else?' I asked, and then waited before answering as dramatically as I could, 'they *never* searched Syed's house. That's right. They never searched his house.'

This time the jury did more than fidget, there was some quiet murmuring, until Feldman put a stop to it, but I'd got my patsy out there again.

But I still had another couple of points to tie up before I sat down. 'Now you heard a lot about Mr Khans traumatic experiences in Afghanistan as well as a lot of quite complicated expert evidence from Dr Rose Tremayne, and in a way I should perhaps apologise for putting you through that, as the sum total of all that evidence is really just to assist you in dealing with a couple of small points.

'Firstly the Crowns rather weak assertion that Mr Khan's words in police interview that I "must have done it", amount to an admission to murder. We say that during this interview Mr Khan was in a vulnerable state suffering PTSD, and the evidence from Dr Tremayne clearly points to amnesia and memory loss. Khan repeatedly made it clear to the interviewing officers DI Stanton and DS Chandler that he couldn't remember what had happened, and yet they continued to browbeat him. They then essentially traded an offer that the interview would end and he could see his kids if he would just admit to killing his wife even though he could not remember having done so. I will leave it to you, members of the jury, whether you believe that in such circumstances it would be right or fair to treat Mohsin Khan's words in that context as being an admission of anything, let alone guilt of murder. Subsequently, with the help of Doctor Tremayne and as you've heard from his own lips, he was able to piece together what had happened that evening.

'Secondly we would ask you to accept that Mohsin Khan is a rather disturbed individual. You've heard lots about what happened to him in combat missions and also that he suffers from PTSD and has to stay medicated most of the time. He overindulges in alcohol and drugs on occasion as well, but we are not asking you to approve of his lifestyle choices, we are asking you to understand him and his behaviour. For example when he threw his plate against the wall that Sunday lunchtime, or when we say he returned to the flat that fateful evening and suffered a similar relapse with the knife and Safia, before leaving the flat.

'They are not things you or I would necessarily do, but they are things that a man in Mohsin Khan's particular frame of mind might very well do. It also of course should be said that because of his state of mind, where you do not accept his evidence, it does not mean you have to believe he is lying about it; it is more likely he is confused or cannot remember.'

I leaned back against the hard ridge of my chair for a long moment as I reviewed what I'd said, and then I looked down for a final check over my notes. The jury watched me silently, waiting. Finally, I looked up and said, 'remember what I told you about reasonable doubt when I started. You must be *sure* of guilt before you convict. And remember that tiny piece of metal lodged in Safia's rib. That may be the only thing now standing between Mr Khan and a life sentence in prison. That, and your sense of justice,' I said, and I remained standing for a long moment ranging my eyes along the jury box, and then I murmured, 'stand firm,' to them, something I'd read that one of the great advocates of yesteryear had said to a jury at the end of a long speech which ultimately saved his client from the hangman's noose. And then I sat down.

Chapter Thirty Three

Stanton sat in his car trying to process what the tech guy was telling him. The guy kept talking about Bluetooth, Wi-Fi, NFC, GPS and the fact that the phone was a Nokia. So fucking what? He wished to Christ they'd speak English – he guessed the guy was a jungle bunny – the country seemed to be full of niggers these days. As he listened to the guys gibberish, he thought back to one of the few books he'd ever read; more of a picture book really, with its wonderfully graphic photographs of lynching's in places like Alabama. He wished to God he was putting the rope around this guys neck right now, but then he was buffeted back to partial reality by the coons voice, with its barely restrained sarcasm, saying, 'you've heard of Google maps surely, sergeant?'

He bit back the racial epithet that sprang to his lips, and instead said, 'I understand you can't get an exact location on the phone, only a general one. Just give me the area size and the name of the streets, and I'll get an A to Z.'

'I thought they went out with the Ark, sergeant. If—'

'Hey, fuckhead, just give me what I asked for. Don't make me come down there. You really wouldn't like it.'

There was silence for about five seconds and then the tech guy gave him what he wanted. Stanton scribbled down the street names surrounding the area, and then he told the guy he hoped he would die of cancer, before terminating the call. He checked miscalls – Condon and the station chasing him – and smiled; fuck'em. There was a local nick a few streets away where he was sure they'd have an A to Z and a computer he could use. He put the car in gear and slowly pulled away from the curb.

There was silence in the court for a moment as the jury digested the last words of my speech. I looked over at Khan and he nodded, unsmiling. Then as the jury began to move around and Feldman organised the papers on the bench, I looked up and there was Carmen, watching me. There was no smile or acknowledgement, then she looked away.

As Feldman began his summing up to the jury, I tried to dispassionately review my closing speech, but I think I already knew it wouldn't be enough to save us. Khan had been there with a blood stained knife at some point during the hour that Safia died, and I doubted whether the jury would be able to get past that simple fundamental point, whatever I said to them. And who knew what the hell they would make of all the weird stuff about amnesiac PTSD behaviour, even if they understood it. I wasn't optimistic, but I was relieved it was over.

As Feldman's summing up progressed it was predictably biased in favour of the prosecution although probably not enough to trouble the court of appeal with. I began to make detailed notes anyway, just in case.

Ludmila from reception called up to say Christoff had arrived, so Pascal told her to send him up, together with a couple of super burgers and a bottle of Smirnoff and ice.

They didn't speak as Christoff unpacked his tennis bag, digging out pieces of high tech equipment and setting up on the desk in the corner. Pascal tipped Ludmila a tenner when she brought the food and drink in, reminding her to call up immediately if Sanford left his room.

Christoff ran a cable off his laptop into the wide screen TV up on the wall, and then hit a key on the laptop and immediately images began appearing on the TV screen. Initially it appeared to be just a convoy of army trucks running down a mud road in blazing sunshine.

'There's a lot of this, what I call combat busman's holiday snaps, just the guys on patrol out in the desert, and a bit of horsing around. When they engage the enemy, which is pretty rare, there's not much to see, just lots of noise, shouting, shooting and the sound of running feet. I'm still working on opening some of the other encrypted areas, but have a look at this,' Christoff said, moving his cursor up onto a screen icon and clicking, causing the picture to change again, this time forming into a shot of what looked like a large sandpit surrounded by cheering tribesmen with guns. Pascal could pick out amongst them, Khan and Holloway. As the camera panned down she saw to her amazement that the crowd were focusing on a couple of very large rats that were moving sluggishly around the sand pit.

'You working for National Geographic now, Christoff.?' Pascal asked, munching through a burger, lettuce and ketchup dropping all over her lap.

'Don't talk with your mouth full, Courtney. Just watch this,' Christoff said as one of the rats exploded.

Pascal stopped munching for a second as she tried to process what she had just seen. As the smoke and pieces of bloody rat rained down on the wildly cheering tribesmen, she asked, 'what was that? I mean, I know what it was; it was an exploding rat, but how did they do that? Was it a round, a grenade, I couldn't see.'

'That was the 3.30 at Haydock Park, transposed to the badlands of Afghanistan, with rats instead of thoroughbred race horses. Oh, and the bets were not on who wins, but on who blows up first.'

'Okay?' Pascal said, drawing the word out.

'yeah, okay, but there's a bit more to it than that. I've watched it a few times and basically what you've got here is a bomb laboratory.'

'Explain.'

'Mohsin Khan was – is – clearly some kind of explosives magician; I mean he's gifted. This is how it worked; they, that's essentially Holloway and Khan got a rat, implanted some explosives in it, sewed it back up, and then when it was healed, a few days later, organised a desert meet for the heavy betting Taliban Mujahadeen boys.'

Christoff paused and took a sip from the water bottle he'd brought along. 'But that's the easy bit. The key of course is the detonator. How'd they do it?'

Pascal looked blank, waiting. Christoff noticed her eyes straying to the other uneaten burger. 'Go on then, Courtney,' he said, 'wouldn't want you to starve now, would we.'

As she grabbed the other burger, he continued, 'what I didn't show you, was earlier, where we see Khan injecting the rat with what must be the detonator.'

'Let me guess,' she said, munching away. 'Mother of Satan, yeah?'

He was reminded again of why she had stuck out so much when she had first come to him as an awkward, socially dysfunctional trainee. And she still had that capacity to surprise him, this strange waif like girl with the ketchup dripping off her chin.

'How do you—'

'It's probably Triacetone Triperoxide, TATP, or the variant Hexamethylene, but I'd like to know how he managed to stabilise it enough not to blow his hands off,' she said.

'Yes it would be good to know wouldn't it,' Christoff said, looking glum. He sighed, and said, 'Courtney, you better tell me everything you know.'

Pascal poured herself another shot and then told Christoff about Khan and the bomb factory in Stoke Newington; then the house in Mile End Road. She told him what she'd seen, what she'd found and what she suspected.

When she'd finished Christoff sat for a moment, pensive. He said, 'you see, its not just that they seem to have stabilised the detonator – we know TATP is highly unstable, extremely sensitive to impact, temperature change and friction – its that they seem to have worked out a way to time when the detonation will take place.'

'How do you make that out,' Pascal asked.

'Just before that rat explodes, the camera zooms in and focuses on that particular one.'

'The cameraman knew it was coming?'

'Precisely.'

'So, let me sum up,' Pascal said, looking Christoff in the eye, 'Mohsin Khan and his crew have managed to stabilize one of the most volatile explosives in the world for use as a detonator, as well as developing a system, albeit a little rough and ready right now but workable, for calculating when the detonation will take place when the TATP mixes in with the primary explosive charge.'

'Again, precisely, my dear,' Christoff said, and then added, 'this is what every crazy fundamentalist Jihadi crackpot from Bradford to Teheran has been waiting for. You know,' he said as the horrifying potential of the discovery started to sink in, 'the problem was never really getting explosives onto a plane – any chump can do that – it was always getting the detonator on board, but with this, they've solved it. I don't think there's currently an airport in the world, and that includes Ben Gurion, that'll spot this stuff.'

'Shit,' Pascal said.

Christoff got up and stretched and went to the window to pull the blinds down; as he turned back to Pascal he said, 'so from what you're saying, this Sanford upstairs, is quite possibly, literally, a walking time bomb.'

'Yeah,' Pascal said, slowly draining her glass of vodka, 'but you don't know the half of it.'

And then, finally, Feldman was finished and the case was passed over to the jury. As they filed out of court to start their deliberations I looked up at the gallery, but Carmen was gone.

Nothing more I could do for Khan now, so I ambled out of the court room into the corridor, digging out my phone; I'd take one last shot at getting hold of Pascal on the new number she'd used to text me. As I held the phone to my ear listening to the ringing tone, I could see Patterson through the bustling crowd, talking furiously to Carmen. As my phone kept on ringing Patterson turned abruptly from her and stormed away. As he brushed past me, his black gown billowing away behind him, I looked up to see Carmen watching his retreating back with a look of anguish. Then her gaze shifted slightly and locked onto my eyes, just as Pascal picked up.

'Christ sake, Calver. Where you been, in a fucking Trappist Monastery?' Pascal said, but I could sense the relief in her voice.

But now I was all but mesmerised, as Carmen tentatively approached me. 'Jesus. Talk about bad timing,' I murmured.

'What's that?'

'Look, I just finished in court – jury's out. Looks like Carmen and Patterson just had words and she's here…..,' I said, just as she reached me and my voice tailed off.

'I'm at the Excelsior Hotel in Kensington and things are kicking off. Suggest you get over here – fast,' she said, but I wasn't really listening.

'Calver, you still there?'

'Look, I'll have to talk to you later,' I said, cutting the connection.

Then Carmen was standing right in front of me looking up at me with those big luminous eyes.

'Let's get out of here,' I said.

She watched me for a moment and then nodded.

Pascal held her phone up and just looked at it. 'God *damn* you Calver,' she said, chucking the phone on the bed. She went to the mini bar and dug out a miniature Martel Brandy and cracked the lid, raising it to her lips. As she sipped she noticed Christoff had gone quiet, sitting hunched over his laptop, face inscrutable.

'What you got?'

'When you were giving me the rundown, just now, you mentioned Kendricks report and the Afghan knifing. Well I've just decrypted the last piece on here and you need to see this, but you'll need a strong stomach,' he said.

Pascal dropped into a chair, eyes fastened on the screen, and said, 'hit it,' and Christoff pressed play.

Stanton sipped coffee and lolled back in a spring-back chair. He was enjoying a bit of banter with Southwark Nick's old style custody sergeant. They were reminiscing about the good old days before the Police and Criminal Evidence Act came in. A golden time before everything got recorded and filmed, when you could kick the shit out of a suspect and not have to put up with a lot of bleating do-gooders. As the sergeant ferreted around in a wall cabinet looking for an old A – Z London street map, Stanton waxed lyrical about policing in the USA where he said you could shoot an unarmed nigger in the back and get clean away with it. That, he said with envy, was about as close to being the perfect work environment as he could possibly imagine.

'Here you go, Dick,' the sergeant said, flourishing the dog-eared blue, red and white street map. Stanton immediately began plotting the co-ordinates he had been given, pencilling in a small complex of roads and alleys in Kensington. As he plotted and absently chatted, a black Police Constable poked his head around the door and said, 'Sarge, there's a call in from SO15 looking for DI Stanton.'

'He's not here,' Stanton said, winking at the sergeant.

'Well, will you take the call, Sarge?' the PC said uncertainly.

'What's the matter, boy?' Stanton said, without looking up. 'Deaf as well as dumb? What d'you think, Mike?'

Sergeant Mike grinned, showing a row of crooked yellowing teeth. 'You see what they're sending me now, Dick? Straight off the banana boat.' He turned to the young constable, and said, 'just tell them we haven't seen him. I'll take responsibility.'

'Yes sir,' the PC said, then remembering something else, he passed the sergeant a large photograph, adding, 'and this just came off the flyer about the Holloway case.'

Stanton studied the blow up carefully. It was a picture of a Christoff

Wisliceny wanted in connection with the search for Courtney Pascal.

Five minutes later Stanton was back on the street clutching the flyer and the A – Z street map.

For a few moments after the film finished and the screen had gone dark Pascal just sat motionless, looking into space and thinking hard. Then she said, 'did you recognise the knife, Christoff?'

She walked over to the table and picked it up.

'You jest, surely,' he said, grinning grimly. 'How could I miss it.'

Pascal began to pace. 'Calver needs to see what's on the flash drive, and this,' she said, holding up the knife again and then chucking it onto the bed. 'He said the jury are already out, but that doesn't matter; he needs to see it, and fast.'

'You want me to go?' Christoff asked.

'Would you, Christoff? I have to stay and see this through with Sanford, find out what the hell is going on, or I'll never get free.'

He knew she was right but he hated leaving her to go it alone; she noticed his look. 'Hey, Christoff, I can look after myself,' she said, full of bluster.

'I know that, Courtney, but would you please wait for me to get back before you do anything rash? I'll only be gone an hour, tops.'

'Don't worry,' she said, unconvincingly.

He held her eyes for a moment, and then got up and grabbed his things ready to go. As he was about to leave, she said, 'wait. Let's swop phones. You take mine and I'll take yours until you get back. If they're monitoring Calver they may have picked the number up, so this might confuse or throw them off temporarily, and if Calver phones back he can fucking well wait for me this time. Anyway everything he needs from me is now on that flash drive, so guard it with your life.'

'I've got a reserve phone here as well, just in case,' Christoff said, holding up a Samsung. 'I'll use this one, but I'll take yours with me as well and keep it on. It may throw them for a while if they've hooked into it.'

Then he looked at her for a long moment and even though he knew she deplored shows of affection, he couldn't help it; he threw his arms around her and gave her spindly frame a good hug.

'Get going, Christoff,' she said gruffly.

He smiled as went through the door. He knew she had a soul somewhere deep down inside, it was just finding it that was sometimes the problem.

Five minutes later, as Pascal was re-watching the copied Afghan tape, the desk phone rang. It was Ludmila – Sanford had left the building. Pascal asked about the girl; no he had gone alone, so she was probably still in the room. After a bit of prompting, Ludmila admitted she thought the girl was probably a prostitute.

She needed to get into Sanford's room while he was out. She couldn't wait; she'd get Ludmila to watch out for Sanford and she'd take a chance on winging it with the prosy. She told Ludmila to meet her outside room 36 with the key.

Chapter Thirty Four

We sat, for the most part silent, in a little pub not far from the Old Bailey. A sprinkling of after work drinkers having a last jar before the commute home, came and went and mingled around us, unseen. For the first time in years I felt tongue tied and nervous as I watched her; I sensed a weariness there that I hadn't seen before and it made me sad.

'Your speech was good,' she said as she fiddled with some pork scratchings I'd bought at the bar with our Gin and Tonics.

'No it wasn't,' I said. 'But thanks anyway.'

'Well James thought it was good, but he said it wouldn't be enough.'

'He's right.'

It felt good just to sit with her, after the rattle and hum of the trial had died away; to slowly chill, watching her, drinking in that indefinable something that had mesmerised me since the first time I'd seen her. I felt a need to talk, but didn't know what to say; maybe it would come, but then her phone was buzzing, crashing the moment. I watched her check the screen, frown and tap the reject call button. Then she looked up at me and smiled.

Even as Christoff came down in the lift he was starting to have second thoughts about leaving Courtney on her own. For a start he knew she wouldn't wait for him to get back if anything kicked off. She could handle herself he knew, but dealing with a guy like that, after what he'd apparently done to Holloway, and who was literally a walking time bomb, that was something else.

He was acutely conflicted about what to do as he exited the hotel and began walking, looking for a taxi, but after thirty metres or so he came to a halt. He stood for a moment, mulling, then turned and retraced his steps back to the hotel. He wasn't going to leave her to face Sanford on her own and if it was as urgent as she seemed to think it was, they could just courier the stuff over to Calver.

Stanton ambled down Kensington High Street, map and photo in hand as he zeroed in on his search zone. Although he looked disinterested he was in fact acutely aware of everything going on around him and was examining the faces of passers by and scoping out the coffee bars, shops and other premises fronting the street.

It was just by chance that he saw the man. The guy was walking too fast and he had a baseball cap, which looked too young for him, pulled down tight as if he were trying to avoid being recognised, but Stanton had got a good look at the guys face as he'd stopped and looked up. Looked like the guy might have forgotten something and had decided to go back for it, as now he was walking back the other way. There was no doubt about it; it was Christoff Wisliceny alright.

Stanton casually began to track the guy and almost immediately he turned into the Excelsior Hotel. Stanton followed cautiously. As Christoff waited for the lift, Stanton flipped his warrant card, and said, 'I need to talk to you. It won't take a moment if you'd just like to step into the bar,' he added, gesturing to the adjoining glass doors.

Christoff studied Stanton for beat. There was something very disturbing about the guys eyes, so Christoff decided not to make a fuss and see what the cop had to say. They moved into the bar and took seats at an empty table. As the waiter came over, Stanton flipped his warrant card and muttered, 'scram'.

Pascal stood just inside the door of room 36. Ludmila had just let her in, after knocking and getting no answer. Now she had gone back down stairs to watch for Sanford.

Pascal breathed slowly as her eyes began to make out the contours of the empty room, identical to hers one floor below. She flicked the light switch on and looked about. The room was neat and tidy, could have been uninhabited apart from the dress uniform hanging on the front of the wardrobe.

Pascal moved through the room towards the bathroom, entered and then came to a halt as she surveyed the contents of the bath. At first glance she thought the girl, whose hands and feet were tightly bound with masking tape, was dead but then she noticed the slight rise and fall of her chest. There was unpleasant purple bruising around the eyes and mouth. She pulled open an eye; it looked clear. The girl was obviously heavily sedated, but was breathing freely, albeit slowly and was probably safe for now.

Pascal went back into the bedroom and started a minute search of the room. She soon came upon a drugs stash in the bedside table; looked like Ketamine, Crystal meth and also some other tablets she guessed were Rohypnol, the date rape drug he'd almost certainly used on the girl.

Christoff studied Stanton carefully, having just realised he was obviously the fat cop Pascal had mentioned. How did he track them to the hotel? Did he know Pascal was here? Probably not, or he would be handcuffing her right now.

Stanton in turn sat and watched Christoff as well, trying to unnerve him, but it wasn't working, the guy seemed cool, unruffled.

'Where's Pascal, Christoff?' Stanton asked mildly.

'Who?'

'Word of advice, you fucking fairy,' Stanton said, voice still mild. 'You mess me around, we go up on the roof and I chuck you off. Tragic accident –

suspect fleeing arrest. Happens all the time, and who's going to worry about one less shirt lifter.'

Christoff smiled, relaxed, and said, 'you know, Inspector, most homophobic guys are secretly scared they're gay; that's where all the hate comes from, sexual insecurity. Ring any bells?' Then he turned his Samsung cellphone over and flicked the replay switch. Stanton's voice came out loud and clear, '…we go up on the roof and I chuck you off.'

Christoff watched Stanton. He guessed MI5 and SO15 must have linked him and Pascal and that's how Stanton knew who he was. They must have somehow tracked Pascal to this hotel, although it was clear Stanton hadn't yet worked out she might be here too, but that would come. And lastly why was this fat, none too bright DI here on his own in a case that clearly warranted a heavy duty security service involvement? The only viable explanation was that Stanton was out on a limb, glory hunting maybe, and hadn't yet called it in. Christoff needed to divert attention and draw the guy away, if he could.

Smart spook, but you're retired, so it don't cut no ice with me,' Stanton said. 'Fact is we got a fix on her and she was hereabouts recently and you have been linked to her. This is a murder enquiry, and so you're welcome to join your little friend in the dock and face a conspiracy charge— '

'She was here but she's not now,' Christoff said quickly, and then Stanton's phone went off. He studied the screen, irritated, but then connected, turning away and putting his hand over his mouth as he listened.

Christoff listened in as Stanton said, 'you sure we're still looking at Southwark?' Then he grunted a few times as he listened.

As Stanton terminated the call, Christoff said, 'look, I don't want any conspiracy charges and I'm prepared to help, so long as you help me.'

Stanton watched him a moment then said, 'go on.'

'We met here earlier, but she's gone now. She asked if she could drop by my flat in Southwark so I lent her a key, but she'll be long gone by now. However,' he said, pausing to give the impression he was struggling whether to give her up or not. 'We are due to meet back there later today, don't know when, yet.'

'Why you here now then?' Stanton asked, still suspicious.

'I'm only back because I happened to meet a very nice young waiter here earlier,' Christoph said, wondering whether he should flutter his eyes and tap into Stanton's homophobia, but deciding against it. 'And he promised to meet me here in, oh,' he said, looking at his watch, 'about forty five minutes. I just couldn't wait, you see.'

Stanton's lifeless piggy eyes regarded him; impossible to tell whether or not he was buying it, even though the Southwark reference fitted in with what he'd just been told over the phone. It might be enough.

Then Stanton's cell rang again, and he did the same routine of looking at the screen and scowling, probably calculating he wouldn't get away with not taking it, so tapping it through; must be the boss, probably Condon, Christoff calculated.

Stanton turned away to listen again, but Christoff managed to piece together some of it, the gist seeming to be that Stanton was saying that he hadn't found anything yet but was following up enquiries, and after a few muttered 'Yes sirs,' the call was finished.

Stanton continued to study Christoff, then he abruptly stood up and said, 'lets go, but first I'll check your story with the desk staff.'

Christoff, rose to his feet and said, 'no problem, officer. My waiter friend will doubtless be disappointed, but so be it. Where are we going?'

'Southwark.'

At the reception desk Christoff stood back behind Stanton and imperceptibly shook his head in the negative at Ludmila, instantly stilling the question she was about to blurt out. She seemed a sharp cookie as she picked up on it immediately, simply stating she could not recall having seen Pascal.

Whilst this interchange took place, behind them, Roger Sanford entered the hotel, unseen and shielded amongst a group of three other guests returning to their rooms.

'Hey, Calver, what's happened to all your records?' Carmen said as she hovered over my much reduced music library. I'd had to get rid of a lot of stuff when we'd split up and I had moved into the flat. 'And still fixated on Alice in Wonderland, eh,' she said, looking around at some of my Tenniel drawings on the wall. 'And CD's as well,' she said, laughing. 'What's *happened* to you?'

I smiled sheepishly, but God it felt good to see her so happy and relaxed, *and* in my flat. When we'd finished our drink in the pub earlier, I really didn't know what to do, so I'd chickened out and said I had better be going, maybe thinking I better get hold of Pascal after all, but Carmen had surprised me by asking if I minded if she tagged along. I knew enough about her to know she was seriously pissed with Patterson about something and didn't want to see him right now. I guessed it would all come out soon enough.

'umm, Johnny Guitar Watson, that's more like it,' she said as she dug out one of my albums and carefully placed it on the turntable and put the needle down. As the strains of "A real mother for ya" started to drift out of the speakers, Carmen began to move to the music.

I popped the cork on a cheap bottle Aldi red wine I'd had floating around the flat for weeks, splashed most of it into two very large tulip style wine glasses, and passed her one, which she took and sipped from as she carried on moving to the music.

'Dance with me, Calver.' she said, but she looked sad when she said it. 'Remember, like old times.' She put her glass down and held her arms out to me.

I didn't want to get drawn in again; didn't want to get hurt; I'd always been an emotional coward. I watched her, and saw the disappointment start to bleed into her eyes when I made no move towards her. And then I thought, fuck it, when it comes down to it, what do any of us ever really have in life that matters, and then another random phrase blew into my mind from somewhere – to be vulnerable is to be a warrior – and then I went to her.

We gently embraced to start with and then I could feel her arms begin to tighten around me and then the dam broke and she was sobbing, holding me tightly and shaking. I put my hands gently on her back and held her as she wept; I put my face in her hair and whispered that it was okay.

Stanton had made Christoff drive the car whilst he had made phone calls. On entering the Southwark flat Stanton had carried out a cursory search, but he hadn't looked in Christoff's rucksack, so as they entered the flat, Christoff surreptitiously dropped it behind the settee.

Stanton finished looking around and came over and said, 'sit,' pushing Christoff back into a chair. Then he took a shortened old fashioned police truncheon out of his pocket and began slapping it against his hand. 'Now,' he said, 'we're going to talk.'

Christoff swallowed hard, trying to keep his fear at bay. It was a long time since he'd been out in the field or had to do anything more strenuous than debug a computer.

Chapter Thirty Five

Pascal heard the stifled moans from the bathroom; sounded like the girl was beginning to come round. She went back in and had another look. Maybe the tape was cutting off her circulation. Pascal bent down and began to pull away at the bindings and as she did so the girl moaned and attempted to thrash her legs out.

The click behind Pascal was loud and unmistakeable. She stopped moving and slowly turned her head. A large man stood leaning against the doorjamb, a gun, looked like a Glock 9mm, was held loosely in his hand, vaguely pointing at her, and the guy was smiling.

'My, my, look what the sweet lord Jesus has brought me today,' he said.

For field craft the guy got a straight A starred. To move like that, virtually without sound, took great skill and determination. Pascal hadn't heard a damn thing. Lesson: do not underestimate this guy, and, question: why the fuck hadn't Ludmila called up and warned her?

'I'm from housekeeping,' she said, tentatively. 'I just came in to clean…..'

'I don't think so,' he said. 'No, you're the girl I should of taken care of down Mile End Road, but never mind, I can fix that now.' He eyed her up. 'You don't look much but I know you're ex MI5, so don't get cute. Get up.'

Pascal rose slowly to her feet watching him all the time, just looking for the slightest chance, but he watched her the same way, very cautious and alert. 'Move,' he said.

'What about the gir—'

She never got to finish the sentence as the mans hand with the gun pistoned out like a pile driver, connecting with her temple in an explosion of pain, causing her to drop to her knees.

He watched her dispassionately. 'Good. You're learning. Now, again, move,' he said, gesturing with the gun.

She got to her feet, hamming it up as much as she could – maybe it would give her an edge later on.

They moved into the bedroom. She was pretty sure now who he was. She had discovered it knocking around in Kendricks file when she was digging through it; an old photograph taken from a distance, but she could see the likeness now, and all the other evidence confirmed it. She took a good look, assessing, and evaluating. She'd already warned herself not to underestimate the guy and that wasn't going to happen again. He looked cool, calm, calculating and highly proficient.

'So you're Frankie Crawford, the fourth man,' she finally said.

He gave a little clap and then theatrically bowed to her. Looked like a hint of a sizeable ego hovering there in the background; maybe a guy who liked to be praised and admired for his cleverness a little too much, and maybe she could use that.

'What's the plan then, Frankie?' She asked.

He smiled. 'You really have no idea, do you?' he said, and now she could see he was juggling a small metal cylinder in his hand, tossing it up and down in his palm. She watched him.

'Tell you what. I'll give you a little test. See how clever you are,' he said, flicking the little cylinder over at her.

She snatched it out of the air, her hand moving like lightening.

'I can see I'm going to have to watch you, Pascal. Nice moves,' he said, playful, then serious again, 'okay, hotshot, take a look and impress me. If you're good, maybe I wont have to kill you.'

She opened the cylinder, took out the tightly rolled piece of paper, opened it up and read the message. She sat down on the couch, her mind starting to boot up, to run the variables, adding in what she guessed. She leant her head back on the arm of the couch, eyes closed.

After a few moments she opened her eyes and sat up straight, her eyes moving around the room, finally coming to rest on Crawford's uniform, hanging pristine, on the outside of the wardrobe.

She looked again at the code E11IGO.

'You've been awarded the Victoria Cross, I know. When's the Investiture, Frankie?' she asked, stomach starting to churn.

'Hey, April Fools day, tomorrow, right, Pascal?'

'Tomorrow,' she repeated slowly, mind whirring, fear rising exponentially. 'Elizabeth Second Investiture. Go, yes?' she said, in little more than a whisper. Her face was frozen, trying not to show any shock, but inside she was reeling and astonished. Just how the fuck could the whole of the UK security establishment, with all their resources, miss this. 'I don't understand,' she said.' I thought the Investiture was months away.'

'I think you're not the only one,' he said, and laughed softly. 'Last year, they found out the original date clashed with something more important coming up in the Royal calendar, so it was brought forward, but it seems not too many people picked up on it, and what with the US president being over here right now as well, it kind of overshadowed things. Oh, and I also changed my name by deed poll to Sanford which probably helped,' he added with a satisfied smile before saying in the way of a newscaster, 'heads will roll, or fly, or maybe even bounce.'

He got up and went over to the table and picked up a roll of masking tape and told Pascal to hold her hands out together, and then he wound the tape around her wrists, tightly, about ten times, and then pushed her back into an armchair.

'What are you going to do at the Investiture, Frankie?' she asked, a terrible premonition rising in her that she already knew the answer.

Frankie pulled a bottle of Grant's whiskey out of a Sainsbury's bag and poured himself a large one. He noticed Pascal licking her lips, so he walked over and held the glass to her mouth. She sucked up a long draft, some of which went up her nose leaving her coughing and spluttering, but thankful for the shot.

Then he went over and sat in the other chair and watched her as he sipped his drink. Pascal waited.

Christoff wiped away the blood that was dripping off his broken nose, holding both his hands up to do so, as they were now handcuffed together. He guessed Stanton was probably going to kill him. The man had the look of a psychopath, someone who had probably kept it well hidden for years, his job giving him plenty of opportunities to indulge himself without being detected, but now it was raging completely out of control.

He could hear him banging around, searching in the bedroom. He hoped to God Stanton wouldn't switch on the desktop in there and see the homemade adult movies – he doubted if the fat detective would approve.

Christoff tried to martial his thoughts. The one thing he had going for him was that it looked like Stanton had swallowed the line that Pascal was on her way over, arriving in maybe two hours time. To convince Stanton of his veracity Christoff had had to endure a significant level of punishment from the cosh, around his kidneys and stomach, before giving up the details of Pascal's phony itinerary. Stanton had bought it for now, but Christoff was going to have to think of a way of getting out of this before the two hours was up.

He tried to think coolly, to remember all those years out in the field and come up with something, but he was getting old and he was rusty. Looking down at his cuffed hands, he felt utterly hopeless, and as his hope ran out so did his spirits.

Stanton came back in from the bedroom, patting his pockets. 'I'm out for ten to get some fags, so I need to make sure you stay calm while I'm gone,' he said, looking at his watch. 'Stand up,' he added, and as Christoff rose to his feet, Stanton slammed the tip of the cosh into his solar plexus. There was a whoosh of air from Christoff's lungs as he bent over, starting to retch as Stanton viciously swung the cosh down on the back of his neck; Christoff slumped down on the floor out cold.

Stanton grunted with satisfaction, grabbed the door keys, checked his watch, and then made for the door. There was a newsagent just down the street, and the girl wasn't due for a while; he had no doubt she was coming; the pansy was so broken now, he wouldn't dream of holding out, not on good old Dick Stanton; no siree.'

Pascal watched as Frankie sipped his drink and quietly hummed under his breath – it sounded like a hymn.

After a while he said, 'it's beautiful,' enthusiasm starting to suffuse his voice. 'But the key is the detonator and that's where good old corporal Khan comes in. Mind you he wasn't too happy about it. Had to be persuaded, like, if you know what I mean,' Frankie said with a chuckle. 'Running those monster fucking rats was like a big laboratory for him – allowed him to stabilise the liquid TATP and then get pretty definitive detonation timings – lucky the Taliban punters never found out about that.

'So tomorrow morning I bowl up with all my medical papers covering my pacemaker, shrapnel injuries, and best of all my diabetes which allows me to bring in the syringe full of TATP, instead of Insulin, and I breeze through security. Four and a half minutes before I am due to go and get my medal I will inject the detonator into the pacemaker.'

'But how will you do the injection. You cant just take a syringe out in front of the crowd and security services and inject yourself?' Pascal asked, still doggedly trying to get all the detail even if it was too late.

'So, welcome to my special invention,' Frankie said, getting up and going over to his uniform. He unbuttoned the tunic and held the flaps open. 'See this little cloth rig here,' he said pulling the small tassels out. 'I just hang the syringe in here and when the time comes I just reach up inside the jacket, direct the needle point to the injection site, and press the plunger. Four and a half minutes later, as her Majesty leans forward to pin the VC to my chest, the injected TATP will detonate the PETN explosives packed into my pacemaker and it will be, Hasta La Vista your majesty.'

Pascal tried to keep her voice calm as she imagined the carnage and horror that would follow such an explosion. 'How the hell can you be sure that you will get your medal exactly four and a half minutes after you inject?'

'It'll be as near as dammit,' he said. 'Buck house run these things like clockwork and I watched loads of film of Investitures. They're almost military with their timing and precision, and I've no reason to think they're going to change that any time soon. I'll be first up, and anyway, I have alternative plans to "dawdle" or "scamper", depending on running times. Don't worry, I'll get her.'

From her secondment in the early years, Pascal knew Crawford was right about the royal timetable for such Investitures, they were run with precision and there was barely ever any time slippage.

'And of course they'll never suspect a white British veteran would ever be a cowardly suicide bomber,' Pascal said, hoping to goad him.

'Fuck you, Pascal. What would you know of courage. Kicked out the service for popping your own step-dad, was how I heard it. What was it, same old song. He abused you as a kid and you got to like it so much that when he tells you he's too tired to give you another one, you kill him.'

Pascal jerked upwards at her bonds, making Crawford smile, but as she did so, she felt the first small tear in the tape from her thumbnail.

'Why the Queen, Frankie? Hardly a red hot military target, is she?' she said, anxious to keep him talking, keep him revealing.

'She's still head of the armed forces, so she can pay, and boy will this make a splash. No one is ever going to forget me in a hurry, that's for damn sure.'

The dull empty feeling in Pascal's stomach was slowly turning to anger. How was it that no one saw this coming – connected the dots – because it was so obvious. And just what the fuck were Condon, Lammy and Co doing about it; they were the ones being paid the big bucks to protect everyone. Forget it, she admonished herself; no time for that now; concentrate on finding out what was going on and then try and work out if there was anyway of getting out of this alive.

'You wont make it, Frankie. Never. They'll nail you way before you get anywhere near the Queen,' she said.

'Think so?' Frankie said, casually. 'You know, same time that coded message was sent to me, a similar message was communicated by mobile phone, and we all know what happens to mobile phone communications, right?'

'What did the message say, Frankie?' Pascal asked, dread starting to creep into her gut again.

'Well it may have mentioned something about the US president visiting the American School London, tomorrow morning, at the same time I'll be picking up my VC,' he said, watching her for a reaction.

She had none. She was numb. GCHQ would have hoovered up the message, and when they put it together with Holloway's visit to the embassy, even with Holloway dead and Qadir likely in custody, the result would be inevitable. Tomorrow morning the security services would be looking the other way, focused exclusively on POTUS and his itinerary.

Pascal, defeated, stared blankly down between her knees at the floor, her mind in turmoil. Fact is unless she could think of something, in less than twelve hours, death and destruction would rain down on a bunch of innocent people, including the Queen.

As Christoff came round, he was lying on the bed, hands now cuffed behind his back. Stanton stood to the side of the room watching, as if transfixed, one of Christoff's home movies on the wide screen TV. It depicted Christoff on his knees avidly blowing a tall athletic looking young black man.

In his hand Stanton loosely held the knife from the rucksack, and a long strand of spittle hung from his lips as he continued to watch the screen, mesmerised. Christoff checked the bedside LED clock; he'd promised Pascal would be here ten minutes ago. If he didn't do something now, he would never get out alive.

He swallowed hard, shut his eyes tight, mentally shook himself, and then said, slowly, teasingly, 'd'you like what you see, Inspector?' trying all the time not to break Stanton out of his trance like state.

'Oh yeah,' Stanton sighed.

After a moment, Pascal, said, softly, 'why?'

'Why?' Frankie repeated, as if surprised. 'Because the British government took away my life. Everything. That's why.'

He walked over and held his refilled glass to Pascal's lips and she took another swig. He seemed to be in a dream now, talking animatedly and enthusiastically. He said, 'you know before it all went pear shaped, life was real sweet. We were getting a ton of heroin in dealing, and the bets on the side, and I was shipping it out on transports to the UK. Mohsin may have been some kind of fucking genius with explosives, but he had no idea what we were doing, not the half of it – he thought it was just a bit of cash on the side. It was all me and Nicky, and we used Milesy as well, under protest, until he bought it.'

'So what went wrong?'

'What went wrong? Everything went wrong. It was to be my big score; the one to set me up for life, but the army found out, seized everything and closed down the operation, then hushed it up, and started splitting us up, me out the unit first. I would have made nearly a million five on that transport, but worse, I was carrying product for the Taliban commander, and when he found out he wanted his revenge, so he killed my girl, Mai, love of my life. She was pregnant with my child. He had her raped multiple times, eyes gouged out, then he personally beheaded her, and sent me the clip.'

Crawford now looked completely gone, eyes closed, head lolling back. Pascal slowly inverted her hand to try again to bring her thumb nail up and into contact with the tape around her wrists. It was painful now and cut off the circulation but she had to try. At the same time she began to move her wrists;

to jiggle them to try and loosen the tape.

'Then in the action I got the VC for – and it wasn't bravery, I'll tell you. I just didn't care anymore by then – I got filleted with small pieces of shrapnel, so now I'm in pain twenty four seven. Who wants a life like that?'

Pascal switched tack. 'So what was the deal with Qadir? How does he fit into all this?'

'Qadir thought I was doing all this for some Jihadist bullshit reasons, but I just needed him for his organisation, infrastructure and back up. What a dick. All the Muslim conversion stuff, apart from poor old Nicky, was just a crock of shit, but he believed it. But it doesn't matter what my motives are, he still gets a massive publicity coup for his terrorist cause.'

Pascal could discern most of it now, having viewed the stuff on the hard drive which Frankie still didn't know she had seen. She subtly massaged his ego some more. 'And because you split from the group, the other three, way back – it even seemed like you'd fallen out with them – the security services never connected you with them. And your still stationed out there aren't you, as a mentoring instructor at the Afghan National Army Officer Academy. So I guess you've been flitting back on leave and staying at the boarding house, yeah? Gotta say, Frankie, using a carrier pigeon instead of modern comms – awesome,' Pascal said, no longer trying to hide her grudging admiration for his planning skills, but also still trying to build the rapport.

Frankie took a shot of scotch. 'Some plan, eh,' he said.

Pascal looked down at her taped hands. She was getting tired now, trying to work on the tapes without him seeing. 'So what you gonna do now?' she asked, trying to keep her tone bright and confident

He eyed her up, sipping his drink. 'I'm going to have a last night of lust and passion, that's what I'm going to do. You know, Pascal, it's lucky you're not my type – never liked skinny dykes – otherwise you'd be looking forward to a threesome with my friend in the bath, ' he said as he went over to his drugs stash, and took out some Rohypnol tablets, and then crushed a couple into a glass of scotch and brought it over.

He took a sheaf knife from under the bedcovers and then held the tip of the blade against the side of Pascal's head and said, 'so I don't want to be disturbed when I'm having my fun,' as he held the glass of drugged scotch to her mouth. She started to struggle but then the knife tip drew blood, and she realised she really had no choice, so she swallowed the scotch, trying to keep some in her mouth without Crawford seeing it.

He watched her for a moment, then he pulled her up and lead her into the bathroom and sat her on the toilet seat. The girl in the bath was moving now and her eyelids were fluttering as if she were about to come around. Frankie lifted her up and led her into the bedroom. Pascal quickly spat out the little liquid she had retained in her mouth and then Frankie was back moving her into the bath. He taped her ankles together, and her mouth, then he stood at the door and said, 'sweet dreams,' as he pulled the light cord, blanketing the room in darkness as the door closed.

As the darkness descended Pascal began to work on the tapes around her wrist as she pondered her predicament. Where the fuck was Ludmila? Something must have gone seriously wrong, but if Christoff had got the flash drive to Calver they might just make some connections from what was on the drive, but it was a stretch, a very big stretch. If she was honest, she knew it was far too late for that; if anyone was going to stop Crawford it would have to be her. But now she could feel her eyelids drooping and her head began to drop; she tried very hard to fight it, but in the end it was too much.

It was gone 4 am and Stanton seemed to have forgotten all about Courtney Pascal. Christoff had the scarf around his neck, constricting his airflow, which Stanton was pulling inexorably tighter and tighter as he raped him. Christoff bit down hard with what teeth he had left on his bunched up underwear that Stanton had shoved into his mouth to stop him from screaming. He was bent over the side of the settee and there was blood dripping down the backs of his thighs, and Stanton was still not finished, some two hours after it had all started.

He guessed it wouldn't be long now; ever since Stanton had discovered the Crystal Meth stash in the bedside table he had become wilder and wilder. He had also discovered Christoff's stash of women's clothing and now Stanton was dressed in just 9 inch stiletto's and red fishnet stockings, his face powdered, and lips thickly rouged.

Tears blurred Christoff's vision; he tried to fix on something good, so he thought about his mother, and then he thought about Pascal, and he hoped she would forgive him for letting her down and understand that he could not have got back. He began to weep, choking into the bunched up underwear lodged in his throat, as Stanton tore away at his insides, grunting and calling him unspeakable names.

Then just at the corner of Christoff's blurred vision, through the streaming tears, he saw the distinctive green serpent on the handle of the hunting knife, just showing from under the couch cover in front of him. It was out of reach and his hands were still cuffed, now out in front of him, and he was just never going to be able to reach it, and even if he could, how was he going to use it. Even with the meth and whiskey Stanton was still immensely strong. Christoff dropped his head onto his forearms in despair.

Then Stanton shoved into him particularly hard, groaned, and then stopped and stepped away, the scarf around Christoff's neck immediately loosening. He watched out of the corner of his eye as Stanton staggered, tottering on the high heels, over to the side table, picked up the half empty bottle of scotch and took a swig.

Christoff, still collapsed, bent over the arm of the couch, looked back at Stanton and as their eyes met he instantly knew it was a mistake. Stanton looked wild and mad, the red lingerie draped over his fat frame, and the heavily rouged face, all combining to create a grotesque apparition, but when their eyes met, a sliver of reality seemed to pierce the madness, bringing Stanton briefly back to earth. He said, 'where's that knife, girl, cause I'm gonna cut you as we go.'

Stanton moved towards Christoff, taking another swig from the bottle, his eyes searching over the floor and onto the couch as he came.

Christoff knew he'd only get one chance as Stanton came alongside him. He'd been slowly, tantalisingly edging forward, his fingers now almost at the knife handle. Now he shoved forward, clasping the handle with both hands, and turning and moving up off the bed in one lunge upwards, but the knife had caught in the thick couch cover, and it was snagging it and dragging it back, but Stanton hadn't seen the knife and thought Christoff was making a break for it so he kept on coming. The razor sharp blade went straight through the cover and into Stanton's stomach, his forward momentum embedding the blade, and running it right through the gut and deep into the spinal column, where it stuck.

Stanton uttered a bellow of rage, and with the last vestiges of his strength he swung the bottle over and down with all his might onto Christoff's skull, the bottle shattering, showering blood, bone, glass and scotch into the surrounding air, as Stanton collapsed onto Christoff's prone body.

Chapter Thirty Six

Frankie woke with a jolt, beeping from his watch alarm shearing straight through his black dreams, the LED showing 8.30 am. He turned his head slightly and immediately drew back as his eyes met those of the dead girl, staring back at him from the pillow alongside.

She had been good value for a while, until she'd realised he was going to kill her and then her responses had tailed off dramatically, so he'd strangled her slowly, enjoying that last look in her eyes just as her life was extinguished. And at least there was no blood to clear up.

Frankie looked over at his uniform hanging there pristine, medals glinting; he smiled; the uniform looked immaculate, fit for a Queen's parade. Then he remembered the dyke spook in the bathroom. She had managed to track him down, so maybe others could too; better to be a little bit cautious. Instead of killing her he'd take her along as insurance, a hostage in case anyone tried to fuck with him.

He slowly rolled off the bed and onto his feet. He took a black woollen hat out of his bag and went to the bathroom. The girl was snoring through her nose. He put the woollen cap on her head and pulled it right down over her eyes so she could not see. Wouldn't want to unsettle her too much seeing the dead girl.

He manhandled Pascal out of the bath and back into the bedroom where he pushed her down into the armchair. She mumbled in her sleep and grunted and sounded as if she were beginning to wake up.

Frankie picked up the dead girl, pleased that rigor had not yet set in, and carried her through into the bathroom and dumped her in the bath. Then he called down to the desk and confirmed he would be staying for another night. He made it clear that he was not to be disturbed at all that morning, even for room cleaning as he would be resting, and also, most importantly, no calls or visitors whatsoever were to be put through or entertained, however urgent they might say it was – no exceptions. Anyone who mattered was aware of the situation and already had his mobile number if there was a problem.

Pascal was completely disoriented when Frankie finally pulled the woollen hat off her head. She blinked her eyes and looked quickly around the bedroom as the dizziness in her head began to recede. Frankie then ripped the tape off her mouth, making her wince at the pain. He smiled, watching her, gauging her general state.

He walked to the door, opened it, stooped down and picked up a breakfast tray and brought it back to the table. Scrambled eggs, bacon, tomatoes and toast, and Pascal couldn't believe it but she was famished. Frankie smiled, watching her, then he pushed the plate across the table to her. Pascal manhandled a fork into her hand and managed to start shovelling food into her mouth, lifting both hands, bound together, up to her mouth.

As my 8:30 a.m. watch alarm beeped I rolled over and reached out my hand but all I found was bare bed space. Carmen had gone, but I still felt elated until I remembered the trial and Pascal, and it came like a splash of ice cold water on my face.

I got up and checked my mobile. There was a text from Emma from late yesterday afternoon, saying I needed to be at court by 9.30 am. The jury had asked some questions and the judge wanted everyone in for it. What the hell was that all about I wondered.

I ran for the bathroom, my mind starting to buzz. The problems of the trial and whatever the hell Pascal had got herself into had effectively been blown away by Carmen zapping me and obliterating everything else in my head. I hadn't been able to think straight about anything else, but now the real world was starting to push back in and a slow realisation was beginning to spread through me that Pascal was in deep shit and needed my help. But I couldn't help her yet; I had to get to court first and sort that out, and then I'd see what I could do. I tried her cell anyway on the off chance – straight to voicemail.

At first he thought he was dead; it was pitch dark and silent, but then the terrible pain in his head and the weight on his chest convinced him otherwise. Christoff slowly started to delicately move around, then after a few moments of summoning up all his energy, he heaved the dead weight of Stanton off his chest and onto the floor. His watch beeped; it was 8:30 a.m.

He sat on the couch with his head in his hands for a while as he tried to unravel what had happened. His head swam with dizziness and he felt like he was going to throw up. Then he felt the wet hot stickiness of blood running down his face onto his neck so he staggered to his feet and weaved and stumbled into the bathroom.

As he examined the bloody scarecrow staring back at him from the mirror, he delicately pressed the area of fractured, bloodied bone around the wound on his forehead where the bottle had smashed. It seemed solid, but he knew head wounds could be dangerous, but it would have to wait. He had to get the stuff to the Old Bailey, then he could start worrying about himself.

He dug out some antiseptic cream, cleaned the wound, applied it and then wound some bandage around his head. With a woolly hat pulled down he figured he should be able to pass without arousing too much comment. He went through and retrieved the rucksack and the knife. Then he stood over Stanton's corpse and tried Pascal's phone; no answer, which he'd expected. He looked down at Stanton, now looking strangely shrivelled and small, the gaping wound in his fat gut now turning purple with congealed blood. He'd call it in after. He took a last look around and then went for the door.

Later as I approached the Old Bailey, almost at the door, a small figure emerged from one of the alcoves at the front. At first I thought he was a street drinker or a crazy as I could see white bandaging, stained with red, sticking out from under his bobble hat, but then I registered the clothing, which was expensive.

The man put his hand out to stop me. 'Mr. Calver,' he said, and I could see he was struggling to speak, 'I have something from Courtney here that.....that you must see,' he gasped. He held out a beat up old rucksack, then he stumbled against me and fell. The guys at the door had been watching and I shouted for them to call an ambulance as I knelt down and checked him out. He was breathing with difficulty but was out for the count. I gingerly lifted the bobble hat and could see the bandage was soaked with blood.

'Where's that fucking ambulance,' I shouted.

They assured me it was on it's way. I put my jacket under his head and grasped his hand and gently squeezed it, letting him know I was there. I put my other hand inside his jacket and checked his wallet for ID. Although Pascal was incredibly closemouthed about her past, this was the one name I did recall her mentioning as a kind of mentoring figure from her early years. I seemed to remember we'd even considered calling him as a character witness for her sentencing hearing, but in the end she'd said no, typically never being able to reach out to anyone else for help.

'It's okay, Christoff, buddy, you're safe now,' I said. The one thing that stuck in my mind as I knelt there was that he hadn't said anything suggesting Pascal was in mortal danger. He just said I needed to see whatever was in the rucksack, and I held onto that fact for comfort – that maybe Pascal was fine – as I watched the ambulance turn in at the top of the road and approach us. I stood up and watched as they got him onto a stretcher and lifted him in. I gave them my details and told them to let me know what was happening. Then I saw the police car enter the road at the top and knew it was time to go, so I grabbed the rucksack and walked quickly into the building. I guessed it would take them some time to get around to me.

Condon and Lammy stood to the right of the entrance, just underneath where the name of the American School London was etched into the concrete wall above their heads. They were stood behind barriers amongst a phalanx of secret service guys with coaxial cables hanging around their ears, and the worlds accredited press, awaiting the arrival of POTUS.

Neither was very happy, Lammy because she was stuck out here, acres away from where all the real action was taking place inside, and Condon, because he had a funny feeling they were still missing something, and they still couldn't get a line on Pascal.

When Condon's cell went, as the presidents motorcade swept into view, he grabbed for it, desperate for something, anything, on the location of the elusive girl. He listened, eyes widening, Lammy watching. He grunted a few times, asked a few questions and tapped the phone off, watching, but not seeing, the circus unfolding in front of them.

'What?' Lammy said, eaten up with curiosity, maddened at Condon's silence.

'Christoff Wisliceny just turned up at the Old Bailey and handed Jonas Calver a rucksack. He apparently had a serious head injury and collapsed; he's now in St Mary's Hospital intensive care unit undergoing emergency surgery; skinny is, they don't think he'll make it.'

They stood looking at each other. 'You thinking what I'm thinking, boss?' Lammy said. Condon didn't answer, just started moving away, cell to his ear, ordering them a car for the Old Bailey.

I pressed the stop play button and sat staring into space, thinking. I was alone in one of the interview rooms with a borrowed laptop and the flash drive stuck into the side port. I got up to stretch and try and think it through. I knew I had something here, but the question was: how the hell could I use it, with the jury already out, deliberating.

I picked up the large knife and studied it closely, running my finger down its razor sharp blade. Then I dug out my phone and called Emma and told her to get hold of the Home Office Pathologist Dr. Kohler, and get him to court right now, urgent. If necessary lie; tell him it was a request from the judge, but get him here; I'd take responsibility.

Then the usher had her head round the door; judge wanted us all in court.

As I approached the courtroom door two people, a tall distinguished looking guy and an ice cool blonde, stepped away from a group and into my path. I smelt cop. The guy flashed ID and said something about counter intelligence and they needed to speak to me, but I didn't like their arrogant air of superiority. Fuck'em, I thought as I elbowed my way through. I said, over my shoulder, 'you want to speak to me, get in line. I've got a trial to run.'

A few minutes later as I settled down at the defence table I looked up in the gallery and there they were, looking down at me daggers, but that wasn't the only surprise. As Feldman entered court he was accompanied by two other judicial looking figures, a man and a woman, who took seats either side of him.

He introduced his two new friends as senior judges and explained that they were there as part of a Judicial Studies review and that we should take no notice of them. That made me smile, as Feldman was clearly going to have to take notice of them. He already looked decidedly uncomfortable, no doubt because it meant oversight. He would have to be a little bit more careful if he wanted to continue to favour Patterson with his rulings.

Then he turned to the jury and said, 'I've called everyone in this morning because I understand you have some questions you would like to raise,' he said looking down at his papers.

'My lord,' I said, rising to my feet. 'Before you deal with that I have to advise the court of a startling development. This morning vital new evidence has come into my possession that goes to the central issue in this case, and I would like the leave of the court to adduce that new evidence.'

'My lord,' Patterson said, rising swiftly to his feet, 'this is most irregular.'

'On the contrary, my lord,' I continued, 'cases such as the crown against Hallam in 2007 and, funnily enough, the crown against, Khan, in 2008, all say that additional evidence may still be called *even* after a jury has started its deliberations, *if* justice requires it.'

I checked the bench and was pleased to see I had certainly piqued the interest of Feldman's two new colleagues, although he looked less happy. I remained standing, and continued. 'My lord, I do appreciate it is highly unusual to have a jury interrupted in their deliberations in this way, but as the cases make clear, it is not unheard of. I also appreciate that my learned friend and yourself will wish to know what this new evidence is before ruling, so can I suggest – the jury can stay in there seats, as it will only take ten minutes or so – we adjourn to your chambers where I will sketch out this evidence and you can decide?'

I could tell Feldman had no intention of agreeing to my request, and then Patterson was on his feet as well, to put his objections, making it unanimous, but then a funny thing happened. The rather eminent looking judge to Feldman's right leaned over and whispered in his ear. Feldman looked deeply uncomfortable for a moment as he listened, then he nodded unhappily and said, 'we'll go to my chambers.'

Relieved, I grabbed the rucksack containing the laptop, flash drive and knife, and followed them next door.

As Pascal finished up breakfast, Frankie, looking immaculate in full dress uniform, said, 'maybe I'll take you along this morning?'

'You kidding me? I'm dead anyway. I'm guessing you already killed the girl. Where is she?'

'Hey, you're gonna be my insurance, case your friends turn up,' he said.

'If you're taking me along, you better tell me how you're gonna play it?'

'In five minutes, we are going to go down to the basement car park. The lift goes down direct so we wont need to trouble the reception desk. So you get yourself ready,' he said as he moved to an attaché case and began taking various items from it, including papers and a small diabetics syringe box which he then secreted in his uniform pockets.

All Pascal had on her was her wallet and in her other pocket the old ID's Christoff had given her. Frankie knelt down and removed the ankle tape and covered her bound hands with a coat, and then he was peeping out the door, and beckoning to her when it was all clear, and then they were hustling out the room.

They were silent as the lift powered them downwards, then Frankie was leading her over to what looked like an old model silver BMW series 5 car. She noticed it was conveniently parked in an area shrouded away from the scope of the few CCTV cameras monitoring the car park. Frankie told her to get in the boot, saying it would only be until they got out on the road, and as she had no choice she clambered in and rolled onto her back. Frankie re-taped her ankles, and before she could move into a comfortable position for travel he quickly reached down and stretched some more masking tape over her mouth, and checking that her nostrils were clear, he stepped away and slammed the boot shut, sealing her into pitch black darkness again.

As I pressed the stop play button on the laptop – it was only half way through the clip, but they didn't know that – I leaned back in my chair, silent, watching them. It was their call now. Patterson was studying the knife carefully. The other two judges sat away from us, in the corner, keeping out of our discussions.

'Doesn't look good for your client, Calver,' Patterson finally said as he put the knife back on the table, clearly and unsurprisingly trying to work out what my angle was. Why would I seek to call evidence that was potentially damaging to my client?

'Well we're happy to take the risk. After all, we all want the truth here, don't we?' I asked, immediately thinking how ludicrous that sounded in a room full of lawyers.

Patterson was about to reply, but Feldman, no doubt picking up on the troubled glances he was getting from my two guardian angels sitting in the corner, beat him to it, with a curt, 'I'll allow it. Please set it up for viewing by the jury, Mr Calver.'

We moved back into court and with the usher I set up a screen for viewing. As Feldman briefly explained to the jury what was happening I looked up in the gallery and was pleased to see Dr. Kohler, with a rather puzzled look on his face, taking his seat. I nodded to him, hoping I would soon be able to clear up his confusion as to why he had been called back to court. There was a hush as the lights went down and the darkened screen burst into life, transporting us thousands of miles back to a mud hut in Afghanistan.

The car was moving and Pascal was scrabbling around, trying to move as well, but it was hopeless; unless she could get her hands free, she wasn't going anywhere. She tried the wrist tape again and now there was no give there at all. Then she raised her hands up to her mouth but then remembered it was taped closed too, and then she banged her head on the inside boot locking device, and would have screamed but for the tape over her mouth. It felt hopeless, like it wasn't worth even trying and she could feel the hot tears of anger and frustration dripping down her cheeks and then, because of the angle she was lying at, running into her ears.

Then suddenly she thought of her father; he just seemed to flit into her mind out of nowhere, the coolest guy she ever knew. He'd once worked for months under cover against the IRA in Belfast in the 70's and she knew, although he'd never talked about it, that his cell had been betrayed, and he was the only one who'd walked away from it. What was it that he'd always said to her – she knew it was a silly old cliché – but when he'd said it with that quiet deadly self assurance of his, it had always hit the mark: don't get angry, get even.

She began to relax her muscles and lower her breathing, and most of all, she started to think and analyse her situation, calming herself. Then she reached out to the boot locking device and felt all over it. There was something there; a slight hard edge of metal, and if she could just manoeuvre the tape around her wrists somehow onto that edge, she might be able to get somewhere.

She felt the car slow again as she painstakingly and laboriously began to work the tape against the metal edge. It was central London traffic and very slow, but if he was driving to the Palace it would not take long, and then what? There was no way he would be able to take her in to the ceremony, so what the hell was he going to do with her? He was clearly worried that maybe someone, somewhere might have got a handle on the plot so she was insurance for the time being. If they came for him, he would use her, but they were fast getting to the stage where he wouldn't need her anymore, and then what? would he just kill her? Probably. Or just leave her bound in the boot to die, or get discovered after the bomb had done its deadly work?

She knew from her time at SO14, the Royal protection squad, that the award ceremony would start bang on the nail at 11 am, and Crawford, as the recipient of the highest honour would be first up. She tried to calculate back to the last time she had seen a clock, and then how long she had been in the car travelling. She reckoned, on a conservative basis, that there couldn't be much time left, so Frankie needed to get a move on.

Then the vehicle stopped and she could hear voices, then they were moving again, but much slower, and after about a minute she felt the vehicle take a steep turn, and then reverse backwards, and then they came to a stop and she heard the handbrake being applied.

She felt the car tilt as Frankie got out and then she could hear him talking, sounded friendly, to someone, then silence. Then without warning the boot lid opened, but not fully and Frankie was leaning in through the gap studying her.

'Your lucky day,' he whispered down to her. 'You'll be okay,' he said, testing the tape around her wrist. He was obviously in a hurry and didn't notice the tiny inroads she'd made into the tape. He looked down again for a moment as if thinking about something, and then he said, 'tell them why, okay. Tell them if they'd left me alone, none of this would have happened. And tell them this has got nothing to do with Islamic fundamentalist shit. Have a good life, Courtney. It's been nice knowing you; in another life, who knows…' he said with a final piecing look, a smile and then he slammed the boot shut.

At first it was hard to make anything out; the screen was dark with just a sort of shimmering or flickering intermittent flash in the background, but then the picture began to lighten and then audio kicked in, and the sound of heavy footsteps and loud and laboured breathing could be heard.

I'd seen the clip at least four times so I knew what was coming, but the jury didn't, and they were totally absorbed with what was on the screen. The picture lightened up some more and you could make out the dim surroundings of the inside of some type of hut and then you could just about divine some shapes of people standing around in there. Then the camera, obviously housed in the helmet of one of the soldiers, panned around and as the focus got better, there was Corporal Khan materialising through a screen of beads with a huge knife held to his throat.

There was a gasp from the jury when this happened and I paused the clip there so they could see the knife, and in particular the distinctive green serpent design on the handle, as well as the long unblemished silver blade. I pressed play again, and immediately we heard the sound of a gunshot, shockingly loud in the silent courtroom.

Then we watched Khan fall awkwardly, blood flowing from his neck, and the young Afghan man behind him also falling backwards, and then there was shouting and screaming and the camera shook violently and there was fast movement and a blurring of the picture, which then went dark and silent.

Here I pressed stop again, and nodded to the usher to pull the lights up. I lifted the knife off the table and held it up to the jury, and again there was a gasp as they recognised it and the green serpent design.

'My lord, earlier today I took the liberty of asking Dr Kohler to return to court,' I said, gesturing at the door of the court as he came through it. 'So he can deal with identification of the knife, and I wonder if I might call him back to the stand?'

The way things were going, with the jury completely engrossed and the two judicial point-men watching his every move, Feldman didn't really have any choice but to agree. He nodded and Dr Kohler moved into the witness box where he settled himself.

'Doctor, you've now had a chance to examine this knife,' I said, holding it up again for the jury, 'and compare it with exhibit MK12, being the small piece of metal found lodged in Safia Khan's rib, yes?' I said holding up the bagged exhibit in my other hand.

Kohler nodded, 'yes.'

'And what are your professional conclusions from that comparison?' I asked as I handed the knife and exhibit over to him.

He was silent for a long moment, and then he said, 'subject to carrying out some confirmatory scientific testing I am convinced that exhibit MK12 is the broken tip of this knife. You see,' he said, holding the small piece of metal to the end of the knife, 'it is a perfect match.'

Chapter Thirty Seven

Frankie stood stiffly to attention as security at the Palace checked him over. They were, as he had anticipated, extremely respectful and almost apologetic as they patted him down and examined his papers.

They checked over the letters from his GP and his medical card listing his heart problems and type of pacemaker; his diabetes and insulin requirements, and also some detail about the metal fragments embedded in his shoulder and back, papers he had regularly had to produce when travelling through various airports around the world.

There were various beeps as Frankie passed through the screening, but the examiner just nodded him through. As he handed back Frankie's papers and syringe box, the Royal Protection officer saluted him, and said, 'it's an honour to meet you sir. Have a great day.'

Pascal banged her wrists against the inside of the boot and screamed through the tape over her mouth. She was drenched in sweat and just could not seem to make the slightest tear in the heavy duty masking tape. She smashed her wrists against the boot locking mechanism again, about to give up and maybe try something else, when suddenly she felt a slight tear and give in the tape.

She pulled her wrists apart as hard as she could and it was definitely there. Then she began a mad scrabbling, ripping and pushing the taped area repeatedly across the metal edge in a frenzy, and then she could feel it start to seriously rip, and then it gave, and her hands were free.

Pascal just lay there in relief, breath coming in huge heaving sobs as she slowly got herself together again. She ripped the remaining tape off her wrists, then from across her mouth, ignoring the pain, and then from around her ankles. Then she felt around underneath her and at her sides.

She felt some large hard shapes under her. They felt like tools; a hammer and some large screw drivers. Pascal stopped and listened carefully, but could hear nothing. She called out help a couple of times, then screamed at the top of her voice, but there was complete silence. She grabbed the largest screwdriver, and attacked the boot locking device, sliding the tip in and madly levering out. There was a loud crack, but still, the lock would not budge. Pascal grabbed the hammer and began smashing at it, but it was immoveable. She thought of trying to cut or break her way into the back seat, but didn't think that would be any easier.

Then she swung the hammer again, smashing with all her might. There was a distinct clicking sound, a pause, and then the boot lid sprang open, and she was temporarily blinded by the sunlight streaming in.

'Thank you, doctor Kohler,' I said. 'You can sit down now.'

I'd expected mayhem and noise but instead there was an eerie silence, the jury watching me, wondering what other rabbits I was going to pull out of the hat. We were nearly there but I had to stay focused and finish the job. 'My lord, with your leave, I'll now play the rest of the tape,' I said.

As Feldman, under the watchful eye of his two judicial neighbours, muttered, 'proceed', I pressed play.

Pascal hauled herself out of the boot and looked around at her surroundings. It took her about five seconds to realise where she was. It was Wellington Barracks on Birdcage Walk, a stones throw from the Palace, and home to various regiments of foot guards. Frankie had parked the car in what looked like an official space. Pascal looked around, but could not see a single person. She tried the car door and was surprised when it opened, but there were no keys. She sat in the drivers seat and checked her face in the mirror. Not too bad. Then she looked through the ID's Christoff had given her, praying it would be there. It was, but of course it was way out of date, although that wasn't obvious unless you were looking for it. It was her old SO14 Royal Protection Branch warrant card from when she had been seconded at the start of her career.

She got out the car and started walking fast. Why not just grab a policeman or get a phone and call it in? Because she was wanted which meant they would be very unlikely to believe anything she said, and by the time she could get through to them, it would be too late. No, she was on her own, and the only way would be to try and stop Frankie herself, if she could get in.

The courtroom screen flickered and a soldiers face suddenly appeared out of nowhere, in high definition technicolour. He was saying, 'if you're not with us Milesy, you're against us. And you know what that means. Some clumsy trooper lets off a stray round and it goes clean through your head, know what I mean?'

The camera panned down again and there were two women whimpering and cowering, kneeling in the corner beside the dead body of an older Afghan man, with Nicky Holloway standing over them with his rifle trained on them.

Then there was the sound of walking, then the camera lifted up fast and came down into a fixed position, lens trained on the middle of the room. I had worked out that Franklyn had obviously removed his helmet here and left it on top of something like a shoulder high cabinet with the cam still running whilst he had left the room.

In the corner of the shot Khan could be seen lying on the floor, bandaged and seemingly unconscious on a stretcher. I was ostensibly showing this footage to show that what Khan had told the jury – that he had been unconscious after the stabbing incident – was true. And we had now reached the spot where I had stopped the clip when earlier showing it to Feldman and Patterson in chambers, but now I let the tape run on. I figured and hoped it would be a few moments before Patterson twigged what I was doing, and tried to stop me.

Then the screaming began, coming through clear on the audio, awful keening wailing, and the sound of flesh on flesh, blows and swearing, and right at the edge of the screen just discernible, the soldier could be seen, on top of the elder Afghan woman, moving up and down as he violently raped her.

As Patterson stood up screaming for me to stop the tape, I ramped up the volume, drowning him out, as we watched transfixed as the soldier stood up laughing from the Afghan woman, and began to stab her five or six times in the face, neck and chest as her screams became progressively weaker, the green serpent on the handle of the knife flashing in the light.

There was one final short sharp scream which came to an abrupt halt, then silence as the tape finished.

Frankie stood to attention and then leaned forward to shake hands as the Queens equerry-in-waiting introduced himself and then led Frankie down various long corridors to the ballroom which was now filling up with friends and family of those who were to be honoured.

Frankie was directed into a side room where someone was to brief him on what was to follow. As soon as the door closed Frankie removed the tin box and then carefully placed the syringe into the cloth rig just under the breast pocket of his uniform tunic. He buttoned up and smoothed down the jacket so that nothing showed.

Then the door opened and a man dressed like a butler came in and began to explain the procedure that was to follow.

At the gates to the grounds of Buckingham Palace, Pascal breezed through with the guards barely looking at her ID, and then she was approaching the familiar entranceway, which she knew would be a hell of a lot tougher.

The adrenaline was running full on now, but she still needed to dig deep for inspiration. In all these types of situation it was the appearance of confidence that usually won the day; if you could project it, even though you didn't feel it, you might edge it, so she called on what acting skills she had, pumped her chest out and strode up to the two men on the entrance doors.

'We got a situation here,' she said flipping her warrant card at them. 'We're liasing with SO15 and I've come down direct from Commander John Condon, just to mingle with the crowd. This is not, I repeat not, a heightened threat situation, but we are looking out for a couple of people who've been tagged recently and might show up. And guys,' she said with an inclusive smile, 'can we keep things low key, yeah?'

There were two of them, the senior guy, a bit of a pin up boy with body to match, was all smiles and cooperation, but the other guy, younger and weasely with a bookish look, who she guessed was probably a rookie, learning the ropes, was not. He looked immediately suspicious, but kept his lip buttoned, deferring to his boss.

'Hey, no problem, ma'am, but I'll have to call it through,' pin up boy said, picking up his phone and gesturing for the rookie to let her through.

Pascal nodded and began moving away from them down the corridor.

As she walked away the rookie watched her, his face troubled. The name on the card had looked familiar and he knew he'd seen her somewhere before but he couldn't place it. As his dumbass boss prattled away on the phone, he went into their side office to look through the flyers he'd seen.

Frankie checked his watch and right on queue as the hand swept eleven, the band struck up the National Anthem as he stood in the wings. Not long now Frankie thought as he offered up a silent prayer and whispered goodbye to his mother. He slipped his hand up inside his tunic and grasped the syringe. He manoeuvred the needle around until he could feel the tip at the injection zone, checked his watch again, and then he very carefully and slowly pushed the needle into his flesh and then depressed the plunger.

He felt nothing apart from the initial prick, which made sense as the needle had gone into the fake pacemaker and not his vital organs.

As the lights came up in the courtroom, for a moment nothing happened, then there was an explosion of noise as everyone in the room began shouting, jumping up and speaking all at the same time.

I needed to get my last piece in quick before Feldman pulled the plug, so I stood up as order was called.

'My lord, this knife,' I said, holding it up again, 'has never been in Mohsin Khan's possession. We can link it directly to the man you have just seen wielding it and, and we can show chain of custody.'

'And just who is the man wielding the knife, Mr Calver?' Feldman asked.

For a moment I was stumped, but Khan wasn't. He said, from the dock, a tone of wonder in his voice, 'that, my lord, is Mr Frank Crawford.'

'And where is Mr Crawford today?' Feldman asked.

'I think you'll find, my lord,' Khan said, looking confused, 'he's at Buckingham Palace right about now, receiving the Victoria Cross for conspicuous bravery.'

I heard a commotion up in the gallery and turned to look as the two cops, or whatever they were, jumped up and began to race for the exits, shouting into their cell phones as they manhandled people out of their way.

Then I sat down. I felt.......I don't know how I felt. Shattered, elated and confused. Starting to savour what was, I guess: victory. I looked around the courtroom, feeling strangely detached, a silly smile on my face, whilst pandemonium reigned everywhere else.

The Rookie could see her now, Courtney Pascal, as she moved among the guests making her way towards the front as the National Anthem wound down. The rookie quickened his pace until he was a few paces behind her, and then he reached out and grabbed her arm.

'Excuse me,' he said quietly, wanting to remove her into custody without causing a scene or disrupting the ceremony. 'You're under arrest for—'

Pascal tried to shake his arm off but he held on firmly, grip tightening. Pascal could see the Queen now a few metres away, standing, shimmering in a cream coloured outfit, jewels flickering around her ears and head. Then the master of ceremonies said, 'Private Frank Crawford, 16 Air Assault Brigade. For his actions on………..

Pascal turned back, and shook his arm off, and whispered in a hiss, 'get the fuck off me, or I'll have you busted back to traffic.'

But the rookie had the bit between his teeth now and could see his name in lights. He persisted, voice still low but firmer now, 'you're Courtney Pascal wanted for the Nicky Holloway murder and bombing and I'm taking you in,' he said.

As the master of ceremonies finished the citation saying ….'when injured and under sustained enemy attack. The Victoria Cross,' Frankie stepped forward and bowed, and then straightened up as the Queen leant forward to pin the medal upon his chest.

The courtroom was still full of noise, but the uproar was starting to subside, and now the senior Crown Prosecutor for the South Eastern region had arrived and was talking animatedly with Patterson, who was violently shaking his head. I guessed they'd come to talk about dropping the charges against Khan, and Patterson was none to pleased about it. Then I remembered Khan, the man it had all been about, and I glanced over at the dock. Looked like a love in, son and father hugging and talking over each other. Then suddenly, in the midst of it all, it hit me: where the fuck was Pascal? I ran for the door, grabbing for my cell, just like the cops had a few moments earlier.

At the back of the Ballroom there was a commotion of some kind and as the rookie turned back to see what was happening, Pascal shook his arm off. Then she was running towards the dais as Frankie straightened up, his head cocked to one side as he answered a question from the Queen.

Pascal didn't quite know what she was going to do but as she closed the gap on Crawford all the things her father had taught her in the dojo from age 3 to 15 kicked in and her reflexes took over. There were shocked shouts and she sensed movement on the periphery as the Queens protection officers registered the threat and sluggishly began to move towards their primary, but then Pascal was there and Frankie was turning to face her. She grabbed both of Frankie's hands as if she were taking up the offer of a dance, but her body carried on moving, pulling Frankie as she moved into a roll down onto her side and then back, still pulling Frankie and swinging her legs up against him, but now using his body weight as she continued rolling into a back somersault and heaving with all her might and pushing out with her legs. It seemed like slow motion, as if it might go on for ever, as if Frankie's body was rooted to the spot and would never move, but then it was inching up into the air at the end of Pascal's arms, then faster and as it reached the parabola of its arc, Pascal let go, leaving Frankie's body flying into space towards the wall. Pascal's last thought was that, finally, maybe, she had done something her father would have been proud of, and then there was a deafening explosion.

Epilogue

I had been coming everyday for a week now and was beginning to lose hope. Pascal just lay there wired up to a load of machines, not moving or saying a word. There had been mutterings about turning off her life support, but they couldn't find any next of kin, as her mother wasn't competent, and I wasn't about to agree to it.

Shrapnel from the bomb had hit her skull, causing a fracture and a brain bleed and put her into a deep coma. The surgeon said she could wake up normal tomorrow, or never wake up. Take your pick.

When the bomb had exploded, Frankie had been obliterated, apart from his breast bone, which was found embedded in the ballroom ceiling. In the end Pascal had been the only serious casualty; the Lord Chamberlain had a broken finger and some in the audience had suffered cuts and bruises.

The fallout from the bombing had been huge. There was to be a Public Enquiry covering the whole security apparatus, and heads had already rolled, including Condon, and Lammy had been quietly shipped back to the States.

One other big plus was that Christoff Wisliceny was going to be alright and there would be no charges against him over the death of Stanton. Personally I reckon he should have got a medal for that. As to Safia's murder, it turned out that Frankie had been asked by Qadir just to scare her, but had gone too far. Khan's murder charge was quietly dropped and there were to be no charges against him for the bomb-making either, after I'd successfully argued duress – which the CPS accepted.

As I idly toyed with Pascal's mobile phone, recently handed back to us by MI5, my mind wandered. We were finally doing okay; Feldman had slunk away, as had the SRA and the complaint. And now I was a something of "name" criminal defence attorney and had already picked up some big private payer cases which augured well for the future, so Emma was happy.

As I looked over at Pascal again, the phone in my hand began vibrating, and then it burst into life at full volume, the terrible cacophony of Megadeth, and I couldn't find the button to switch it off. Then I sensed movement on the bed, a flickering of the eyes, and then they were opening as the thrash metal song played out, and then the tears were running down my face as the waif like girl smiled and held her hand out.

'Give me the phone, Calver, you big girls blouse,' she said.

Then we both turned to the door as Carmen poked her head in and told me it was time to go, but then she saw Pascal, and her face broke into a smile of pure joy.

THE END

About the Author

Mark Young practiced as a lawyer and ran his own law firm for 10 years. Now he can be found banging away at a keyboard deep in the heart of Suffolk. This is his first novel.

www.mark-young.com

Lightning Source UK Ltd.
Milton Keynes UK
UKOW02f2131131216

289915UK00001B/115/P